# DEATH SCENE

# DEATH SCENE
## *Thirteen Songs for Guy*

**Jeremy Beadle**

First published in September 1988 by GMP Publishers Ltd
P O Box 247, London N17 9QR, England
Second Impression June 1991

**British Library Cataloguing in Publication Data**

Beadle, Jeremy
Death Scene
I.Title
823'.914 [F]

ISBN 0-85449-088-4

Distributed in North America by Alyson Publications Inc.
40 Plympton Street, Boston, MA 02118, USA

Distributed in Australia by Bulldog Books
P O Box 155, Broadway, NSW 2007, Australia

Printed and bound in the EC on environmentally-friendly paper
by Nørhaven A/S, Viborg, Denmark

*For Pascal, because it was his idea.*

# Part One
# NO MORE MISTER NICE GUY

# 1: At the Club

If Marcus Grey hadn't encountered Michael Hamilton until considerably later that night, a lot would have been very different. After all, it is highly improbable that he would have become involved, either directly or remotely, with the events surrounding the murder.

In years to come Marcus would recall this fact and wonder, sometimes whimsically and sometimes with a degree of irritation. But it was, at best, a speculative line of inquiry. The facts stood: at not much past 11.30 on the night of August 15th (a Friday), he had spotted Michael Hamilton leaning against the bar at the club. He could be fairly sure of the time because he had just looked at his watch, wondering if he could stand any more of this – 'this' being the general hanging around, eyeing-up and waiting, all of which he found extremely distasteful but, alas, equally extremely necessary on occasions. He looked straight from his watch into Michael's gaze. Threading his way expertly through a gang of clones, Marcus made towards his ex-lover, whose first reaction was an ironic bow.

'I wondered,' Michael half yelled over the insistent thumping music, another feature of 'this' intensely disliked by Marcus, 'how much longer it was going to take before you noticed this gorgeously handsome man staring at you.'

'As modest as ever,' Marcus returned, smiling as if to acknowledge that Michael's self-description was not unjustified.

'How unusual to see you here,' Michael bawled on. 'I thought you hated "these places" as you used to call them. We used to argue about them.'

'I do. We did.' Marcus's educated Scots accent clipped and toughened even these monosyllables. 'But needs must, et cetera. And anyway – ' and he shrugged.

'Ah.' Michael laughed. 'So the great quest for the impossible dream goes on? I thought, dare I even say hoped, that you might just have grown out of that by now. But even you can't seriously

9

delude yourself that Mr Right is bopping around in here somewhere waiting for Heaven with a Jean Brodie accent to descend upon him... Actually, you probably can.'

'It's not entirely unprecedented,' Marcus rejoined as pleasantly as he could. 'Anyway, it's just as unusual to see you on your own. We used to argue about that too.'

The two young men exchanged a smile, not at all malicious. Michael nodded his approval of Marcus's riposte.

'Technically I'm not,' he said. 'Unfortunately. But I'm working on that.' He raised his glass and looked into it mischievously. 'Perhaps you could solve my problem. Take him off my hands as it were.'

'I'm sorry,' Marcus replied, 'but you know I never approve of your taste.'

'No. Guy's not really your type. Pity. Actually, he's been gone so long that I'm beginning to hope he might have run off with someone.' Michael surveyed Marcus again, a little more than idly. 'I take it you're on your own?'

'Yes – and looking around I rather hope to remain so.'

'Present company excepted, I hope.' Michael still stared intently. 'I don't suppose – for auld lang syne or whatever, Marco?'

'It's hardly Hogmanay,' he returned uneasily, attempting to defuse the plunge into intimacy. So as to avoid Michael's steady blue eyes he looked around. His glance halted at a rather lugubrious, brown-haired figure leaning against a wall and looking as though he felt, in equal parts, terrified, confused, miserable and contemptuous. He was obviously a little older than Marcus or Michael – probably in his early thirties, Marcus guessed – and hardly conventionally handsome, in fact a little on the fleshy side. But there was something about him – his eyes and mouth particularly – that caused Marcus's eyes to rest for long enough to merit the term stare. The man became aware of the stare and began to return it somewhat uncertainly. Marcus smiled, very positively.

'Excuse me, Michael,' he said without turning back; but Michael caught him by the arm.

'Hang on,' Michael said, but then stopped. He laughed. The man, having moved forward to meet Marcus halfway across the bar space, had halted, apparently deterred by Michael's act of possession. Michael let go of Marcus's arm.

'Him,' he laughed again. 'Actually, I met him earlier. An old admirer of Guy's. They were very close once, before me. He's rather intense – might quite suit you, thinking about it. I suspect he's probably quite interesting in a way that Guy's far too superficial and stupid to appreciate. Bring him back, please, I'd like to meet him properly. Apart from anything else, it might be amusing to find out what he did with Guido when they went off together earlier.'

Marcus gave Michael a look betokening slight exasperation and began to move across the bar. 'By the way,' Michael called after him, 'he's called Dominic.'

Marcus pushed his way to where the reputed Dominic still stood. 'Hello,' he said in his best breezy Scots manner, 'I hear you're called Dominic.' The sad brown eyes looked at him and a slight nod of the head suggested agreement. 'I'm Marcus.' Suddenly, almost rudely, Dominic stuck out a hand. Marcus shook it firmly.

'I hate these places,' Dominic shouted. 'Do you know Guy Latimer's boyfriend then?' he went on immediately.

'We used to be an affair years ago. At university – and for a year or so after.'

'Was that a Scottish university?' Marcus named it. Dominic smiled. 'Ah. I nearly went there. I nearly went there twice, actually, once to learn and once to teach.' He paused, looking uncertain. 'He's – er – very handsome, isn't he?'

'What, Michael? He'd make a fine chocolate box, I suppose.'

'Oh, he's very gorgeous, in a cinematic sort of way,' Dominic said. 'Too good-looking by half. He and Guy make a pretty pair, don't they?'

'Well – I've never actually met this Guy person. Were you and he once – ' Marcus allowed a gesture to finish his sentence for him.

'Not exactly. Not really. We were – well, how could I put it? – very close.' Dominic made a rueful little laughing noise and muttered something under his breath, of which Marcus caught enough to suspect it of being 'the little shit.'

'Would you like a drink?'

Dominic nodded. 'I'd kill for one.'

'Follow me.' Marcus took Dominic's hand and dragged him to the bar. Michael had been keeping a careful eye on them, and made sure that he was waiting in exactly the right spot to greet them. He appraised Marcus's act of physical appropriation, giving his ex-lover a knowing glance.

'Making your intentions clear, hmm?' He surveyed Dominic critically. 'Tell me, have you done away with Guy?'

Dominic gave him a strange look. 'Unfortunately, no.' Marcus enquired what he wanted to drink. 'Whisky and Coke. If that's OK.'

'And for me a gin and tonic,' Michael added, 'even if it isn't OK.'

'Bloody parasite, Hamilton.' Marcus attempted to negotiate with a moustachioed tee-shirted barman. Dominic stared, almost defiantly, at Michael.

'You'd not seen or talked to Guy for a while before tonight, had you,' Michael said, more a statement than a question.

'Can we not talk about Guy, please?'

'Guy told me you adore gossip.'

'But I don't like talking about Guy.'

'No. So it seems. And you don't like clubs, to the point of paranoia, I've been told. Yet here you are. What else has Guy told me about you?' For the first time, Dominic looked Michael directly in the eye – and, surprisingly, smiled. The effect, in Michael's view, was not at all bad. Guy had been less than complimentary about Dominic's appearance, but that now seemed a little unfair.

'I can guess, in fact.' At this point Marcus turned round and proffered drinks. 'That I'm hopelessly and sordidly promiscuous.'

'Are you?' Marcus laughed. 'That's a relief.'

'Actually, no. Not as much as Guy thinks, anyway.'

'Oh God, are we still talking about this Guy creature?'

'Michael is.' Dominic seemed to be growing in self-confidence. The bar was filling up, becoming hotter and hotter, and the three of them seemed to be confined in an ever-decreasing space. 'By the way, you seem to have mislaid him.'

'Yes – so it would seem. I might call it a night soon, in fact. But tell me – did you and he have a fight or something? Have you strangled him and hidden the body somewhere? I suppose in here you could stand it against the wall and no-one would notice.'

'You could stand it on the dance floor and no-one would notice,' Dominic glossed.

'I hate these places too,' Marcus chipped in. 'Why don't we go?'

'What, back to your place?' Michael asked mischievously. 'Actually,' he went on, 'I shall accompany you to the bus stop or whatever.'

'What about Guy?' Dominic asked.

'He has a key. If he hasn't fled back to Mummy. Actually, I don't think Mummy would have him back at present. Daddy certainly wouldn't. In fact, Daddy threw him out.' Michael announced this almost with pleasure, as if he were looking forward to its effect.

Dominic stared at him. 'Seriously?' Michael nodded.

Marcus watched this exchange, beginning to feel that the situation was running beyond his control. Something about Dominic had made an instinctual appeal to him, something not merely physical: but Michael's insistent intrusion was beginning to amount to something inauspicious. He wondered whether his best bet might not be to make some future arrangement to meet

Dominic, but even as this thought was building up to action, Dominic turned and gave him an open, inviting smile – the best yet.

'This must all be very boring, Marcus. I'm sorry. I'm trying hard not to be interested in Guy Latimer's doings – actually, I'm not very interested, but I am a bit of a gossip.' He paused to drink. 'I think your idea was the best.'

'Which idea?'

'Going. Actually, would you like a coffee?'

'What, here?' Marcus looked at him quizzically.

'No – there's a late-night coffee bar just across the street. It's gloriously scrofulous. I used to eat there a lot.'

'Will it still be open?' Marcus queried. 'It's midnight.'

'Certainly it will. Let's go over there and talk properly. I'm beginning to go hoarse.'

'Am I included?' Michael asked demurely. Marcus looked at him with distaste and disbelief. 'Well, I'd like to talk as well, Marco. To you as well as to Dominic. And I'm very bored here.' He yawned to underline this point.

'Och – since when were you ever bored in a club, Michael?' Marcus thrust his hands in his pockets.

Dominic engaged him with a look of distinct amusement.'Since he started going out with Guy, perhaps?'

'Well,' Michael said, 'if I'm beginning to provoke Dominic to unkind remarks, I can't possibly lose you yet.' He smiled sweetly and twinkled his blue eyes flirtatiously at them both. 'Please let me have a coffee with you.'

'Oh, for God's sake. Come on then.' Marcus started forward, hoping to clear a path through the now thick crowd of check-shirted, short-haired men. 'Do you have a coat or anything?' he asked. Dominic shook his head, but Michael shouted back that he had. 'Well, we'll see you outside,' Marcus retorted pointedly.

They threaded their way around a corridor designed to resemble an underground tunnel, halfway along which Michael stopped to join the queue for coat-reclamation. Marcus and Dominic climbed a staircase down which they could feel the cooler night air gently blowing. It was a relatively mild night in what had been, taken all in all, a poor summer: but anything fresher than the sweat, dried ice and amyl nitrate-permeated atmosphere they had left would have seemed cool and sweet, even the summer breeze of mid-London. Marcus breathed a huge sigh and Dominic made an audible gulp. They reached the exit point, a security man to each side, one vetting newcomers – there was still a sizeable queue for entrance, as it was in club terms still early – and the other watching departures. A dinner-jacketed figure also wandered around. 'Good night gentlemen,' he said with complete insincerity.

Marcus looked at him and then at Dominic. 'What a nice man,' he commented drily. 'God, you look hot.'

Dominic smiled, but it seemed to be a slight strain. Now they were outside, in a covered arcade very dimly lit: to their left as they came out was the narrow street, the lights of pubs and restaurants still flickering where cleaning or late-night eating was going on. People were flowing down towards the Embankment. A steady stream turned off into the arcade, obviously heading for the club.

'Right,' Marcus said decisively, 'we'll give him five minutes.'

'Why is he so determined to stay with us?' Dominic asked. 'Are you and he getting back – I mean, are you sure you – ?'

'Look,' Marcus put his hand on Dominic's arm, 'Michael's a born stirrer. He's determined to get you to say something.'

'Oh, I know that much. He wants something to tell Guy. I'm not playing that game.' He gave a little laughing sigh. 'In a way I'm very tempted, but – '

'That kind of thing is always very tempting.' There was a pause. 'So. Marcus. Marcus What, or don't you want to say?'

'Grey. By name and pretty much by nature.' He laughed. 'That's one of Michael's wee funnies.'

'Doesn't strike me as madly apposite. Did you say you hated clubs?'

'Absolutely.'

'So why here, now?'

'I could ask you the same question.' Marcus looked at him and grinned. 'I would expect the same answer I'd give.'

'Oh – I did have a reason over and above the obvious. What do you do?'

'For a job or in bed? For a job, I serve the bastard Government, however reluctantly, in the Department of Overseas Funding. In bed – well, we'll discuss that later. What do you do for a job, if any?'

'Like you, I serve civilly. Except my job's a self-parody. I administer administration. I make hugely important decisions about reference books, stationery and statistical information. My one regret is that the Russians wouldn't pay a brass rouble for such information as I might possess.' He sighed.

'What was that you said about teaching?'

'Oh – a previous incarnation. I was an academic. I chucked it. It chucked me too, I suppose.'

'Any regrets?' Marcus thought he could detect wistfulness in this brief, monosyllabic explanation. 'Well, you must have.'

14

'Not particularly,' Dominic said almost too casually. 'I'd probably have done myself in if I'd stayed there.' There seemed to Marcus no attempt in this remark to elicit sympathy or even further inquiry. And, as if to confirm this impression, Dominic continued, in a fairly matter-of-fact manner, 'It's every bit as restricting as it's made out to be. I don't miss it. I mean, a lot of rotten things happen here that couldn't have happened there, but that's not to say I'd rather have been protected. Oh look, here's Michael.'

Sure enough, here was Michael. He had retrieved a rather stylish jacket which he was coolly carrying over one shoulder. Marcus surveyed his ex in the outer world: he saw no great change, except an even greater emphasis than he remembered on the niceties of style – a certain degree of fadedness to the jeans, which were leg and crotch enhancing without being at all vulgar; a certain cleanness to the designer sports shirt, without it seeming to be pure affectation. Michael still looked very good indeed: but something singularly failed to move Marcus even to nostalgia. He knew, from sporadic contacts between them and from general gossip, that Michael was proving very successful as 'something in the City', and there was a certain air of glossiness, even opulence, about him now. Gossip had never mentioned Guy by name, but then gossip of that particular kind was something Marcus tended, wherever possible, to avoid.

He turned to look at Dominic: there was no contrived style about Dominic – indeed, if anything he verged on the scruffy – but he did at least look as though he were capable of moving, acting and responding without calculation or consideration of his own appearance. He seemed to be on the verge of several conditions, none very desirable – scruffiness, tears, fatness – but his very condition of not actually quite being in any of these states enhanced, in Marcus's eyes, his appeal. His age was difficult to guess: Marcus assumed that he was at least five years his senior (which would have made him thirty), but he could have been five years at least beyond that. And underneath all this was a boyish charm, notable most in the eyes and the smile – and the sudden, surprisingly swift gestures and movements.

'So,' Marcus said, 'shall we go and visit this coffee bar?'

'Let's,' Michael said. 'I adore slumming. Will it be full of Embankment residents, Domenico?' If he had been hoping to provoke a reaction with this little pet name, he failed. As far as Marcus could tell, it didn't register.

'One or two,' Dominic said. 'You know,' he went on, 'I'd love to get one or two of them in there' – he gestured at the club – 'and see what happens. Maybe this one,' he mused, pointing at a pair of legs sticking out from between an enormous commercial garbage can and several impromptu bags of rubbish which created a sinister black plastic silhouette. The rubbish was just a little way in front of them, not quite in the light of the street. They moved along, and were just short of level with the legs. 'Shall I buy him entry to paradise?' Dominic asked.

'Oh, don't be silly,' Michael remarked. 'You're rather hard on the scene, aren't you?'

But Dominic moved nearer the prone body and squatted down by him. For a moment he was lost in the shadows. Marcus heard him address the figure gently, as if trying to wake him. Then he let out a cry.

'Jesus wept oh God,' he said in a single breath. He leapt up and ran to the opposite wall of the passage, where it looked as though he was going to be sick. But he wasn't quite. Michael stared at him, and then at the body lying on the ground. Marcus approached the recumbent form with trepidation.

The first thing he noticed, of course, was the legs. But he now realised that they were encased in what looked like fairly pricey, carefully faded 501s just like Michael's. This suggested that the figure was hardly an ordinary wino. But in the midst of all the rubbish and the shadows it cast, Marcus made out what had provoked Dominic's reaction. The figure was clearly not a tramp at all, but a fair-haired, well-dressed young man. The fairness of the hair was unmistakeable, even though it was smeared with a dried brown mess which could have been shit, had the face not been so appallingly mutilated. Only the eyes and the mouth remained intact, the eyes an icy shade of blue discernible even in the shade, the mouth twisted, but only slightly. This was as much as Marcus could notice in the moment he could bear to contemplate the sight.

'Marcus?' Michael said, almost with concern. 'What's got into the pair of you?'

Marcus went over to where Dominic was standing trembling and put an arm around him. Michael wandered, cautiously, to view the sight. He let out a long whistle. 'Thank Christ I'm not as squeamish as you two,' he said. 'But it is fucking disgusting. I'd better call the cops.'

'Michael!' screamed Dominic. 'Can't you see who it is?' Tears rolled down his face.

'Well, like that I don't see how anyone could — '

Dominic ran over to him, grabbed him by the neck and twisted his head. 'Look, for fuck's sake, look. It's Guy.' He let go of Michael immediately, and Michael stared down at the figure again.

'Christ Almighty.' Marcus had now moved across to join them. He looked down at the thin, expensively-clad legs, at the surprisingly muscular torso and at the mess that topped it all off. So at last he had met Guy Latimer. He felt numb, sick, confused: he also felt some concern for Dominic. Michael still seemed the least affected of the three of them, but that would be only in character. Indeed, he now seemed already to be regaining a certain necessary efficiency.

'Look, I'll go and call the police. You two wait here. I'll be back as quickly as I can. Marcus — look after him, he's obviously pretty shaken. OK?'

He dashed off down the alleyway towards the street and in the direction of Trafalgar Square. In a dim perplexity Marcus wondered why he'd gone that way. In the meantime he put his hand gently on Dominic's shoulder.

'Oh God,' Dominic said suddenly, 'I feel terrible.'

'That's fairly understandable,' Marcus replied, attempting levity. 'I mean, I think it's horrible and I never met him, so how you must feel, well... You were close, you said, once?'

'Quite recently, in fact. We only stopped seeing each other about three or four months ago. I hadn't seen him until tonight, though, since then. I didn't want to. It was horrid seeing him tonight. I remember wishing — well, I —' and at this, Dominic broke down into total incoherence. Marcus kept his hand on Dominic's shoulder: suddenly, violently, Dominic threw himself into Marcus's arms and began to weep strenuously.

As Marcus patted and soothed him, a fair-sized group emerged from the club, trendy-haired London boys, some wearing makeup. 'Ooh, look at the brazen tarts,' one of them called. 'Watch out, Lily's about,' another yelled not unsympathetically. Marcus felt an irrational surge of anger, which he tried to control. How could they know what had happened? How could they be blamed for misconstruing the scene? They passed by, giving whistles and smiles. Dominic didn't emerge from his hiding place.

Running feet could be heard, heralding Michael's return. Breathless, he approached them. 'The police are on their way. And an ambulance.'

Sirens were already audible. Dominic looked up from Marcus's chest. The blaring sound grew louder and louder, cutting a swathe through the Friday night hubbub. Dominic stood up straight: and all three braced themselves to meet with authority.

# 2: Digging Your Scene

Detective-Sergeant Morgan found the going as tough as he had feared. The club owner and manager did not take at all kindly to the prospect of losing one and a half of the two most profitable nights' takings, and the word 'harrassment' was flung around fairly liberally. The possibility of getting helpful witnesses to come forward from the club itself seemed remote, amd Morgan could sense the sullenness rising up from the vast dance floor when he interrupted the night's entertainment to announce its premature closure and to request assistance. It annoyed Morgan that the Chief himself wasn't there to do all this; he'd have enjoyed watching his boss cope with the silent resentment of a self-styled persecuted minority. But this was Friday night, so the Chief had pushed off, and hurried efforts, which would certainly prove fruitless, were being made to get him back. After all, this was likely to be a tricky business.

Most probably, in Morgan's initial view, it was some kind of mugging by a kid or kids who saw queers as an easy and soft target. Of course, and most to be feared, it could be a maniac, the start of a sequence. Finally, and at first thought least likely, it could be a premeditated attack by someone known to the victim. One of the uniformed boys jokingly suggested a lover's tiff, and made a few remarks about the viciousness of 'these boys'; but Morgan was trying hard, in his own mind, to avoid such prejudicially-based reasoning.

Mind you, this was difficult when the potential witnesses behaved so recalcitrantly: and Morgan did not look forward to questioning the three who'd found the body. That little farce with the ambulance men hadn't helped either: Morgan would have thought that the blood was a bit dried to be a serious potential hazard to health, AIDS virus or no AIDS virus. Still, the ambulance men had been as docile as children compared with the uniformed boys and the pathologist's assistants. When they'd got over complaining about the risk and demanding rubber gloves and rubber everything else, they'd complained about the position of the body and the impossibility of doing anything useful impeded by garbage in a poor light.

Eventually the Chief radioed in: 'Absolute confidence in you, Stuart, I'll take over in the morning', the usual story recently. It was a fairly open secret that he'd shelved any real intention of taking work more seriously than a bare minimum since his second failure to get promotion to Superintendent – which was all very well, but Morgan failed to see why he had to carry an idle, mostly clapped-out, usually drunk DCI whose legendary bluff Northern charm was beginning to wear well beyond thin.

Anyway, by that time the body had gone for post-mortem, the area had been carefully searched, the contents of the dustbins were being examined: all a waste of time, he was sure, as the knife that had been used to cut the poor bugger up was most likely to have been chucked in the river if it had been chucked anywhere. Morgan, surveying the scene again to fix it in his memory, considered the pathologist's initial reaction.

'Vicious business by the look of it, Sergeant,' he had said, without looking round from where he knelt over the corpse. 'Fair bit of blood lost; wounds inflicted both before and after death. Clear sign of bruising around the throat, as well. I'd guess he was actually killed by strangulation. Nasty. We may be dealing with a maniac.'

'Oh Christ. Field day for the Press,' Morgan sighed. Press attention was arguably the worst hindrance facing the police these days. 'Do we have a rough estimate of the time of death? Or will that have to wait?'

'I'd say as a guesstimate – not less than two hours, not more than four. How long since we were called? I mean, since it was discovered?'

Morgan consulted a note he had made, thinking how swiftly a young man had become an 'it.' He shuddered, as he tended to at such moments. Suppose it had been himself. Or his own son. This kid must have been a young teenager once, probably not long ago. 'About an hour and a half. It's taken us quite a while to get rid of the onlookers.'

'Can't have been easy; not if you just turfed 'em out of that place prematurely,' the pathologist joked grimly. 'They'd want some entertainment out of their evening.'

Morgan nodded: the pathologist's gleeful contemplation of a maniac at large still daunted him. He hoped that it was a simple mugging: and initial brief exploration suggested it might have been. There was no money in the pockets, not even loose change, no keys, no travel pass; only a handkerchief and what looked like a cloakroom ticket. That was odd, though: it meant that the boy had gone out of the club leaving behind whatever he'd gone in with. That complicated the mugging idea. One of the first things to do would be to cash in the ticket.

But then he had to see the three who'd found the boy. He'd kept them behind, in the club, commandeering the manager's office – under much protest, of course. Uniformed boys were looking after them, and he hoped they'd managed some courtesy and tact. The last thing they needed on top of it all was complaints and resentment, particularly from articulate witnesses. He knew they were articulate from their identification of the body as that of Guy Latimer. The oldest of the three had seemed badly shaken, but that could have been for any number of reasons.

Morgan turned away from the place where the body had been found and entered, for the second time, this famous gay club. It was all so alien to him. He'd never really come into contact with homosexuals before; he thought he had no real feelings on the subject. He knew he didn't like the way a lot of them carried on, the way they seemed to jump from bed to bed, particularly now there was this AIDS about. He wouldn't, he knew, be at all happy if his son turned out to be that way inclined. But he wasn't prejudiced; at least, he didn't think he was. Anyway, he supposed, homosexuals are people and murder is murder. He looked around dubiously. He found the glitter of the club rather tawdry – he'd never been much of a one for that kind of stuff, had Stuart Morgan – and the suggestive drawings on the walls annoyed him.

He yawned and made his way up to the manager's office. The first thing to confront him was a console of a dozen TV monitors, all showing the empty, but still lit, club. In three elaborately comfortable armchairs sat the three men, Palmer, Grey and Hamilton, while two uniformed policemen sat around the desk where they had commenced paperwork. But so far no questions had been asked. Morgan wanted to have first crack himself, as he felt that stories were easier to break down before they'd been built up by repeated telling.

He summoned the two uniformed men over to the doorway and gave his orders in a low voice. 'Right. I'm going to see them one at a time – Palmer, then Grey, then Hamilton. You've got all the details of addresses, 'phones, or not?'

'Oh – you said no questions.'

Morgan marvelled at the constables' literal turn of mind.

'OK, so I did. Right, after I've seen each one they'll be free to go, unless they want to wait for each other or something.' One of the constables sniggered. 'I suggest we drop that sort of attitude as well. This is murder: and murder is murder. Now these are three intelligent people, as far as I could tell, and the first sign of prejudice will get them screaming from the rooftops. And we don't need complications like that. Right?'

The two policemen did not seem noticeably chastened, but nodded. 'OK, take Grey and Hamilton off – get them coffee or something and then bring them back outside here. Out of earshot, right? And send DC Bowen up to me when he's finished scouring garbage.'

Ken Bowen was more insurance on Morgan's part, an initial impulse to have a witness to ensure that all was done correctly. He re-entered the office and addressed the three waiting figures.

'Now. I want to talk to each of you individually: it's only a talk at this stage, nothing formal. That will all be done at another time, in more officially correct proceedings. But first, I would like to know which of you actually knew the deceased? I know Mr Palmer and Mr Hamilton did – what about you, Mr Grey?' Grey shook his head. 'Fine. Now I'd like Mr Grey and Mr Hamilton to go off with the two constables for the time being: and perhaps – Mr Hamilton – you could give them details of Mr – er – the deceased's – next of kin and so forth.'

There was all that merriment to look forward to, the tearful family. In these circumstances, all that might well be more difficult than usual.

Grey and Hamilton stood up: some form of look passed between Grey and Palmer. No doubt about it, Palmer was easily the most upset of the three. Morgan sat on the front of the desk and watched the two younger men file out. The door was shut behind them. Morgan essayed a smile of condolence.

'Right, Mr Palmer. You actually discovered the body?' Palmer nodded. 'Would you like to tell me what happened? Take as long as you like, now – anything you can remember may be useful.'

Palmer sniffed and gulped.'Marcus and I – Marcus Grey, that is – came out of the club and waited for Michael.'

'Mr Hamilton?' Palmer nodded. 'Marcus Grey: Michael Hamilton and – what's your first name?'

'Dominic.'

Yes, Morgan thought, that made perfect sense. He smiled, to encourage Palmer to continue.

'After a few minutes – three or four, I suppose – Michael came out with his jacket – that's why we were waiting for him, he was getting his jacket from the cloakroom – and we were going to go for coffee across the street.' He named the coffee bar. Morgan was aware of it: occasionally the uniformed boys had to evict tramps from it. 'I was making a joke about paying for a tramp to get in here, and I saw these legs and I thought it must be a tramp, so I went over to have a look, really just to annoy Michael and it turned out to be

Guy.' He shuddered.

'You knew straight away that it was Guy – ' Morgan paused to think – 'Latimer? Despite the state of the face?'

'Yes. The eyes, the hair, the shape of the body, the legs, the clothes. Everything.'

'I see.' Morgan switched his voice into neutral tone. 'And when did you last see Guy Latimer alive?'

'Well – earlier this evening, but before that I hadn't seen him for months.'

'I'm afraid,' Morgan said carefully, 'that in a case such as this it will be necessary to ask questions of a personal and – shall we say – indelicate nature. So, I must ask, and will have to ask again, about your relationship with the deceased. I would also like to know what happened the last time you saw him alive.'

Palmer looked up. 'I appreciate what you say, Sergeant – was it Morgan, I can't quite remember?' Morgan nodded. 'Well, Guy and I had been very close friends. No more than that. A lot of people thought we were lovers and I liked people to think that. I dare say I encouraged one or two people to think that. But we weren't. Earlier this year, late April, early May, we went to Italy together. A friend had loaned me a flat. Ten days after we got back, Guy manufactured a quarrel between us and dropped me. There was a hysterical exchange of borrowed possessions by post, but I didn't see him or speak to him again until this evening. I didn't want anything to do with him. I didn't this evening, actually. But he absolutely insisted.'

Palmer shifted in his seat and sat up a little straighter. He seemed, as far as Morgan could tell, to be trying to force himself, almost physically, into a state of concentration and coherence.

'I'd been there about half an hour. I don't know what time it was exactly – maybe ten thirty, maybe – well, it can't have been much earlier. Anyway, it felt as though I'd been there about half an hour from the number of songs I'd heard. I went to the upstairs bar to buy myself another drink and watch a few videos – pop videos, that is – and just as I got to the bar, I spotted Guy and this other chap who turned out to be Michael Hamilton.'

'Was that the first time you'd ever met or seen Michael Hamilton?' Morgan interrupted.

'Yes. Absolutely. Anyway, I pretended I hadn't seen them, but then, suddenly, Guy came over and accosted me. Michael came with him. I tried hard to be pleasant enough but uninterested, and hoped they'd go away. Guy asked me where I'd been, why I'd dropped him. I said that wasn't exactly accurate, but we were obviously both better off now. He asked me what I was doing at the

22

club. I didn't give him any real answer. Then he said he really wanted to talk to me, alone. I said I didn't really want to talk to him, alone or otherwise. He said I was being selfish. I gave in, like I always did.'

'Why? Why did you give in, I mean?'

'Because I didn't want him to start attacking me in front of his – Michael. I felt incredibly stupid and small, and I thought Guy was having a good gloat – you know, "Look at this gorgeous man I've got. So much better than you." '

Morgan reached in his pocket and took out a packet of cigarettes. He offered it in Palmer's direction, but the offer was refused: Morgan slowly lit one for himself. He was rather surprised at the level of honesty and directness he seemed to be confronting.

'Would that have been in character?' he asked, 'gloating?' There was an old saying among senior murder squad detectives: 'Know the victim and you'll know the murderer.' Morgan had never known this maxim to work: how could you hope to know a dead man or woman you had never met?

'Oh yes,' Palmer replied. 'Totally. Well, in my experience, anyway.'

'Would you say your experience was – extensive? You implied a moment ago that you were close. Was that over a long period of time?'

'We were very close for just over a year. I would say that each of us knew more about the other than anyone else alive. Except possibly our families. And then, only his mother really knew him. I mean, his father and brother and sister didn't know he was gay, even. I mean, he could hardly tell his father, could he? Oh – '

Morgan got the impression that Palmer felt he'd committed a faux-pas, but quite an amusing one, for he covered his mouth guiltily, blushed, then laughed a little.

'His father's a policeman, you see. Down in Surrey. Would you believe a dog-handler?'

Morgan tried to laugh a little too, although inside he felt a certain exasperation. This would give the tabloid boys a lovely angle: 'PC's SON IN GAY CLUB DEATH HORROR RIDDLE' or some such savoury analysis.

'I see what you mean,' he said. 'They are, by and large, a bunch of bastards. So, Guy Latimer waltzes over to you with his new – with Michael Hamilton – and says he wants to talk to you. You agree reluctantly and – then what?'

But at this point the door opened and Ken Bowen, young, keen, aggressive and dim, literally marched in.

Morgan immediately regretted his earlier decision to bring Bowen in; he felt Palmer would hardly respond well to Bowen's manner, although he hadn't missed the flicker of interest in the eyes when Bowen had appeared. Bowen, perhaps, would do better for dealing with Hamilton, who gave a first impression of being a right clever smooth sod.

But then Morgan thought of a way of getting rid of Bowen usefully. 'Oh, Ken,' he said, fishing in his pocket, 'go down to the cloakroom and see if you can get anything for this. See if the people in the cloakroom remember giving it out at all, or if they can work out when they would have given it out.'

Bowen glowered at Palmer, then at Morgan, and left with hardly an audible sound. Obviously, Morgan deduced, the dustbin had not proved fruitful.

'Was that – on Guy's body?'

Morgan nodded. 'So. You were about to tell me.'

'Yes...I suggested going down to the coffee bar – the one in the club, that is, but Guy said that Michael had all their cash on him.'

'May I interrupt? He said he had no money on him?'

'He implied that. So I offered to buy him one. He accepted reluctantly. He always did. We went downstairs. I asked him what he wanted to talk about, and he started prattling on about Michael. I wasn't really listening. I just told him I didn't think it was in very good taste to discuss his boyfriend with me. He accused me of being selfish. Again. I asked him if there was anything specific he'd wanted to say. He started talking about sex again, which I thought was calculatedly unpleasant.'

'What sort of thing – just general boys' talk?' Morgan tried to check his tone for facetiousness at this.

'Well – more to do with the dangers of AIDS, as far as I could make out. It was awfully noisy down there, and Guy was ever prone to jabber. No, you see, he used to – when we were friends – go on about how dangerously promiscuous I was. Anyway, he said did I really know every way it could be caught? Was I sure? I asked him if he wanted me to snuggle up at night with a few pamphlets, and anyway what business was it of his? He told me I was being selfish. Again. So I told him I'd had enough of all this, and if he wasn't going to fuck off then I would. And then' – he gave one of those brittle, humourless, melodramatic laughs – 'I said something really vile. And incriminating.'

'Actually so?' Morgan saw limits to the detective's role as general priest-confessor figure.

'I said' – and now Palmer adopted the most neutral and

expressionless tone imaginable – 'I said "I wish you were dead and I wish that for one second you could see yourself or know yourself to be hideous, deformed and without those pretty looks of yours." ' Palmer smiled. 'I've never had a wish come true before.'

Morgan looked at him sharply. 'Did you kill him, then?'

'No.' A rueful shake of the head. 'The awful thing is that I wish I had.' Dominic looked up. 'Do you think he was murdered? By someone he knew, I mean?'

'Well,' Morgan pondered, 'your guess is as good as mine at this stage. Medical Science hasn't made its views known yet. What would you say if you were me?'

'To be honest,' Dominic said, 'if I didn't kill him, I can't think who did. I mean, he didn't have a lot of friends – at least when I knew him. Maybe if his father had found out he was gay – something Michael said suggested he might have – '

'What was that exactly?'

'Michael said that "Daddy had thrown Guy out." And that his mother wouldn't have had him back either. Mind you, his mother may be a nutter, but she's far too scatty and disorganized to murder a half-dead fly. Anyway, of his friends – well, Derek Wilkinson is as spiteful as Guy, Phil Roxby wouldn't do anything that might ruin his hair or his clothes and I can't see why his boring wimpy cousin Terry would want to. The brother and sister – sorry, I'm doing your job for you.'

Morgan stubbed out his cigarette, and waved his hand as if to pardon this transference of duty. 'Now,' he said. 'Marcus Grey. Where does he fit in?'

Dominic blushed. 'We – well – we picked each other up this evening. The first time he saw Guy was out there, as a corpse. Odd though – odd coincidence. He's an ex of Michael's. University days apparently, in Scotland. He told me he hasn't seen Michael in ages: he'd only just run into him when he and I sort of, well – ' An odd mixture of pride and embarrassment overcame him.

'An unfortunate and curious coincidence, then,' Morgan said.

'You could say that.'

'Do you believe him?'

'Yes, actually. I honestly think, Sergeant Morgan, that, outside his family, I'm the only person in the world who ever felt strongly enough about Guy Latimer to make the effort to kill him.'

Morgan looked at Palmer. 'That's an odd, and somewhat dangerous thing to say, Mr Palmer. And presumptuous. What about Hamilton?'

'Ha, ha,' Dominic said. 'I got the impression that Michael was half hoping to ditch Guy. He wasn't interested in the least in finding him when we left – didn't seem to care at all.'

Morgan looked at him appraisingly. Then he asked Dominic for a few personal details which were provided. 'We'll need to see you formally in the next couple of days. I'm afraid that I can't be any more exact at this stage until things become slightly clearer. But for tonight you're free to go – we'll take you home of course – unless you want to wait for – '

'I think I should wait for Marcus, even if only to say a proper goodnight,' Dominic said, rising slowly to his feet. 'God, I'm cramped.'

He passed Morgan, staring steadily at him.

'Did you kill Guy Latimer?' Morgan asked with an abruptness that surprised himself.

'No,' Dominic replied. 'Unfortunately I didn't.'

Morgan winced at this: but was it merely an unfortunate tendency or a cunning double bluff? He paced the room, waiting for Marcus Grey to be ushered in; but first Ken Bowen appeared.

The ticket had yielded a rucksack, which Bowen had brought directly up without examination. He placed it on the table where Morgan had sat during his conversation – interview would have been too strong a word – with Palmer.

Morgan looked at his junior assistant. 'No luck with the rubbish, Ken?'

'No, nothing, sir.' Bowen didn't always call him 'sir,' but tended to at moments of high seriousness and drama. 'Did that one tell us anything?'

Morgan detected from his tone of voice that Bowen too was unsympathetic to the setting and protagonists of this crime. Had he noticed Palmer eyeing him up? Morgan hoped not.

'One or two things of interest.' He reached for another cigarette. Bowen didn't smoke, so the offer wasn't made. 'I'll try and fill you in when I've seen the other two. Anything done yet about getting in touch with the family or whatever?'

'I doubt it sir. It's Friday night.'

'Bloody typical. The family home is in a small village – '

'Yes, sir, we've got that much. Mother, father, brother, sister.'

'Right. Well done. Now Mummy's a bit iffy, so Palmer told me, in the upstairs department. And the cream of the jest, Ken, is Daddy.'

Morgan looked at Bowen with amusement, of a grim nature admittedly, but amusement nonetheless. Bowen returned an almost disapproving look to his senior.

'Police Constable Latimer, dog-handler in the Surrey Constabulary.' Bowen raised his eyebrows and dropped the near disapproval. 'He seems to have thrown his darling son out recently, I was told.'

'Because he was queer?'

'That was Palmer's guess. Anyway, we'd better get people – including a WPC – round to the Latimers. Maybe get in touch with Daddy's station. After all, he may be on duty now.'

'He may be in town, sir.' Bowen said this neutrally, but his implication was only too clear.

'What, dripping in gore?' Morgan almost laughed. More tabloid headlines loomed in his imagination: 'SHAME OF MY GAY SON – KILLER PC TELLS ALL.' Just what everyone needed. At this point Marcus Grey was shown in.

Morgan scanned the young man. He wouldn't have sussed him as bent was his immediate instinct: tallish (five eleven, probably), strong physique, obviously some kind of athletic background; short, wiry, fair-red hair, grey eyes – a distinctive, strong face, if not a classically handsome one: but none of that fussy dress or haircut sense that Morgan dimly associated with the homosexual world. Funnily enough, he thought, although less smart and less physically in good shape than Grey, Palmer had definitely had that fussiness about him – you could tell with him that the clothes, the style generally, were an effort. Latimer had obviously had it, judging from the corpse's clothes; Hamilton, on first sight, had it in its highest form, almost elevated to the status of art.

Morgan proffered a greeting. 'Mr Grey. Do sit down.'

Grey, hands thrust deep into the pockets of his light brown canvas trousers, strolled over to the row of armchairs and threw himself into one. Morgan turned to Bowen and prepared to take a risk.

'If you could arrange someone for the Latimers, Ken, then come back?'

'Of course, sir.' Bowen, naturally, never called him anything other than 'sir' in front of members of the public. For one dreadful moment Morgan feared he was going to get a salute. But the DC managed to leave without it. Morgan, relieved, offered Grey a cigarette: a brief hesitation was followed by a refusal.

'Just a brief chat, Mr Grey, to be followed by more formal discussions later today or Sunday.' Grey nodded. He seemed relatively alert. 'So, tell me in your own words, as slowly and with as much detail as you can manage, what you can recall about the discovery of the body.'

'Right.' Even in one word, the accent stood out. 'Dominic and I left the club together and waited for Michael to get his jacket. We were going for coffee at some place Dominic knows – across the road from here, I think – and Michael had latched onto us.'

'So you weren't keen on having Mr Hamilton there? He'd more or less invited himself?'

'Very much so, yes. I was not at all keen.' Grey's accent had an interesting way of underlining and emphasising these clipped words. 'I hadn't seen Michael for a while before tonight, and I find him rather difficult to get on with now. Anyway, after a bit Michael emerged. We set off. Dominic saw what he thought was a wino having a kip, and pretended he was going to give him some money to get into the club. He went up to the – well, you know – and then he ran away and almost threw up. I went to have a look and I almost threw up. Then Michael went to have a look, but of course Michael didn't come anywhere near throwing up.'

'Cool customer, is he?' Morgan asked reflectively. Grey nodded. 'Did you recognise the body?'

'Oh no – I never actually met Guy Latimer. I'd never heard of him before tonight. I don't know whether I would have recognised him anyway – Michael didn't seem to. Dominic did, though. But – I'd never met him.'

'And Mr Palmer? How long have you known him?'

'Oh God – ' Grey giggled, which seemed slightly incongruous. 'At that time maybe about half an hour, perhaps slightly longer.' He rubbed his face, as if embarrassed. Morgan tried to preserve neutrality of expression.

'Would it be indelicate to ask you a little about Mr Hamilton?'

'Not at all, from my point of view. Mr Hamilton doubtless wouldn't agree. We were contemporaries at University. We had a – well – ' he shrugged, 'from about the middle of the second year up to a few months after we both moved down to London. It didn't work out, so we called it a day. We didn't have much in common by then. That was about three years ago. We haven't actually met for about eighteen months.'

Grey seemed to deliver all this without any great emotional involvement of himself, which encouraged Morgan to probe a little deeper.

'So did it upset you that he was – with' – Morgan was conscious of overstressing the preposition for its euphemistic value – 'someone else?'

'What, tonight, you mean?' Marcus laughed. 'No, not at all. I don't really give a fu – damn about what Michael does. Anyway, when I met him in the club he was alone.'

'Waiting for Latimer?'

'In theory. He didn't seem at all interested in where he was or if he was up to anything. He didn't seem worried about going without him.'

'I see.' Morgan pondered. 'One point. When Mr Palmer found the body, did he touch it at all?'

'I don't think so. But it was lying in the shadow of the rubbish, so it was a bit difficult to see. But I don't think so.'

At this point, Ken Bowen came back. Morgan wondered if he could usefully ask Grey anything else, but decided this wasn't really necessary at that moment. He got off the table again.

'Right, Mr Grey, thank you. You've given some personal details to one of the officers outside?' Marcus nodded. Morgan repeated the offer of transport.

'Well, I think Dominic's waiting, so – '

Morgan smiled. 'Don't worry about it, Mr Grey,' he said with a stretch and a yawn. He could sense, without looking, that Ken Bowen was glowering with disapproval. Grey got up, jumped up almost, and set off purposefully out of the room; but as he reached the door Morgan shot a question at him.

'From your – brief acquaintance, would you say that Dominic Palmer could have killed Guy Latimer?'

Marcus wheeled round. 'Not so far as I can tell.'

'And Michael Hamilton?'

Marcus grinned. 'Too great a risk to his career, murder.' He turned away, then turned back. 'Is that it?'

Morgan waved him on, and turned his attention to the rucksack. Opening it, he took out cautiously a thin blue cardigan, bought, according to the label, from a fashionable designer-wear chain. Then an expensive Walkman, which he tentatively turned on, only to be informed (to the accompaniment of violent electric guitars) that there was panic in the streets of Carlisle. A set of keys; and a wallet containing no money but a cheque card, an automated bank machine card and a credit card. A building society book which Morgan set aside without opening, preferring instead to examine a fairly new travelcard wallet, which contained a pass valid for a month, due to expire in a fortnight, and an identification card. Morgan stared it. It was his first sight of Guy Latimer's face.

There was no doubt that the photo was Latimer; underneath it in the space provided someone, presumably the boy himself, had written G. M. LATIMER in large block letters. Of course, it was difficult to tell how anyone really looked from a black and white photo from an automated booth: but the immediate qualities which struck Morgan were youth (he looked about eighteen); insecurity (the attempt at a posed smile was belied by a glancing look in the eyes); and – for want of a better word – beauty. Anyone who looked this good in one of these photos must have had a lot in the way of looks.

The final item in the bag was a diary. Morgan opened this to the page devoted to personal information just as the cool, well-dressed, dark-haired young man entered the room.

'Sit down, Mr Hamilton,' he said. Hamilton nodded courteously, pulled carefully at each cuff, then walked slowly over to an armchair and sat down.

Morgan looked again at the diary: Guy M. Latimer – whose blood group was A, who possessed a driving licence, a passport, bank and building society accounts, a credit card, but no TV licence – had recently crossed out his Surrey address and telephone number, and replaced them with a London number and an address in Hackney. In the same amending pen (black as opposed to blue) a work telephone number had been added. Morgan read the Hackney address aloud. 'Is that right?' he asked.

'Yes,' Hamilton nodded.

'Would it happen to be your own address, Mr Hamilton?' Morgan fixed the handsome young man with what he hoped was a steely glare. Something told him that Michael Hamilton was going to be somewhat less forthcoming than the other two, and he wondered why. Hamilton, however, returned the stare without any discernible embarrassment.

'In fact, it is. Guy was staying with me for the time being.'

'I gather he was kicked out of home,' Morgan said, 'or so Mr Palmer says you told him.'

'Yes. Daddy threw him out. I take it you know that Daddy's one of you.' This was offered with a definite hint of insolence. Morgan thought it might be tactful to ignore this.

'Why?'

'Why do you think?' He shrugged. Morgan waited for elaboration, but nothing emerged.

'About how long ago did this happen?'

'Five or six weeks ago, I think.'

'And how long had you known Guy Latimer when he moved into your – flat?'

'House.' So Hamilton was as well-heeled as he seemed. 'I would say about three weeks.' Again, no further elaboration.

'How did you meet?' For a fraction of a second, Morgan thought that Hamilton was not going to condescend to answer. He seemed to be staring somewhere else.

'We were in a pub in North London,' he said suddenly. 'Near King's Cross. It was a Wednesday night. I noticed this boy – Guy as it turned out – sitting on his own, looking depressed. I decided to try and – well – cheer him up.' He laughed. 'With limited success. That look turned out to be his natural expression.'

'I hope you don't mind my asking an indelicate question, Mr Hamilton, but I'm afraid where murder is concerned – '

'Yes, we did sleep together, if that's what your "indelicate question" was, Sergeant,' Hamilton interrupted truculently. 'I can't see how it's relevant, though. I can't see that my sexual arrangements are of any importance in tracking down either a maniac or a mugger.' He smiled insincerely in Morgan's direction.

'So you think Guy Latimer was killed by a maniac or a mugger?'

'A maniac for choice. Well no-one in their right mind could have done that. And not even poor old Dominic was sufficiently crazed with passion to carve Guy up like that.' The young man laughed lightly. Morgan stared at him again, this time with puzzlement.

'Did you know Mr Palmer, then? He claimed you'd never met before this evening.'

'Oh, no, we hadn't. But Guy had told me so much about him. That's why I was so fascinated to meet him. He didn't seem anything like Guy's descriptions of him at all.' Morgan was struck by Hamilton's willingness to elaborate on points which were, for immediate purposes, tangential.

'So what happened this evening?' he asked with pointed simplicity.

'Guy and I arrived here about quarter past ten. We'd been to a film earlier, in Portobello Road.'

'What film?'

'I thought this was informal,' Hamilton replied, but quite calmly. 'Do you follow the cinema, Sergeant? It was a film about lesbians called *Desert Hearts*, not recommended viewing in the Met, I imagine. We went to the 7.10 showing. It finished around nine. Then we had a cheap meal in Soho. Would you like the exact name and the menu?'

Morgan paused as he lit himself another cigarette. 'I think we can let that degree of detail wait, sir.' If Hamilton wanted facetious formality, he could have it. He noticed that Bowen, who had been sitting unobtrusively behind the table, was beginning to look extremely sour indeed. 'So,' Morgan went on, 'you arrived here about 10.15. And then?'

'Well,' Hamilton said, thinking, 'Guy spotted Dominic almost straight away. It was all I could do to stop him rushing up and accosting the poor bloke.'

'He was keen to see Palmer?'

'He was keen for Palmer to meet me. However, I persuaded him that we should go for a drink upstairs first. Unfortunately, poor Dominic accidentally – at least I assume it was accidentally – more or less followed us up there, and, before I could stop him, Guy had dragged me over for a chat.'

'Why do you assume that Palmer's following behind you wasn't deliberate?'

'Oh, when Guy started talking to him, he was so totally thrown by the whole thing, anyone could see that. He tried very hard to get away. I've never seen Guy quite so persistent and tenacious in a conversation, actually. If I hadn't known better, I would have thought that perhaps he'd overcome his cowardice.' Hamilton smiled knowingly; Morgan gave him a questioning glance. 'With men, Sergeant. Guy was by nature and inclination extremely promiscuous, but physically a coward. Deep, deep yellow.'

Morgan reacted to this with surprise. Hamilton seemed to have a knack of being as explicit and direct about others as he was discreet about himself.

'Anyway, I knew he didn't fancy Dominic. In fact, I was pleasantly surprised by Dominic's looks, because Guy had led me to expect an obese elderly derelict. But then Guy's taste is essentially superficial.'

'What did Guy and Dominic talk about?' Morgan asked, trying to push Hamilton away from tangents again.

'I couldn't really hear. I wasn't listening, to be honest. My attention was – well – elsewhere.' Hamilton fluttered his eyes to make it quite plain what he meant. 'All of a sudden, I gathered that Guy was dragging Dominic off for a chat.'

'Were you concerned?'

'Why should I have been? I'm sure if Dominic ever did want to murder Guy, he'd have done it ages ago. No, I simply told Guy that either we'd find each other later here or I'd see him at home some time.'

'And then?'

'I just wandered around; danced for a bit; bought a drink. Then I saw Marcus – in the downstairs bar, this was – which was a pleasant surprise. Then Marcus saw Dominic. It became clear that they had a fairly strong mutual interest. It also became clear to me that I was knackered and wanted a good night's sleep, so I decided to leave with them.'

'I gather the idea was to have coffee.'

'Oh – I wasn't seriously going to interrupt them. Well, I might have joined them for a quick cup, for two reasons. One, to annoy Marcus. Two, to get a chance to talk to Dominic.'

'So you decided to leave. And what,' Morgan asked with more than a trace of acerbity, 'about Guy?'

'What about Guy? Look, Sergeant, Guy was getting to be a bore. I'm not monogamous by nature – who is if they tell the truth? – and Guy's been far too used to people dancing attendance on him. I rather assumed that Guy would either turn up, or he'd find another bloke. I didn't really give a damn which. So we left. And then we found the body.'

'You all left together?'

'To be absolutely pedantic, which I suppose is what you want, no. I got my jacket from the cloakroom. I met them outside. Dominic made a few acid remarks about clubs in general.' Hamilton paused, as if pondering. 'That, I suppose, was the oddest thing about the evening, really.'

'What, Mr Palmer's acid remarks?' Morgan found Hamilton's talent for non-specific obliqueness somewhat maddening.

'No – well.' Hamilton played with a floppy bit of hair at the front of his hairstyle, obviously designed to be toyed with coquettishly. 'Marcus hates clubs with a passion. It was one of the major differences between us. So it was odd to see him here. From everything Guy had said, Dominic has an even stronger loathing for them than Marcus. So. How strange that two violent haters of the gay scene should venture to the same club on the same night at more or less the same time. Must be something in the stars, don't you think?'

Morgan stared at the now blank TV monitors. Then he turned back to the young man. 'You say you got your jacket from the cloakroom. I don't suppose you can remember the number of your ticket?'

Hamilton laughed. 'I've never been a great one for Trivial Pursuits,' he said. 'I'm afraid that useless pieces of information don't stay with me. They used to mark initials on the back of the cloakroom thing, actually, but they seem to have given that up recently. What a pity this didn't happen earlier.'

Morgan clenched his fist to control his irritation. 'I gather you didn't recognise the body immediately?'

'No. I mean, I had an appalling sense of familiarity, but I didn't recognise him in the same way that Dominic seemed to.' He stroked his eyebrow. 'But then, Dominic knows Guy so well. Better than I do, certainly. Dominic loved him madly, you see.'

Morgan ignored this, although he absorbed the implications. 'How old was Guy Latimer?' he asked.

'Twenty' – Hamilton paused – 'three, I think. No, twenty-four.'

'I assumed he was younger from this photograph,' Morgan said, waving the travelcard wallet.

'Everybody always did. He had a very young manner, too. You'd never have guessed he'd been to one of England's premier universities. He used to pretend to be ashamed of the fact as well. Affectation. Like his politics.'

'Was he politically active?'

'There was no sense of the word "active" that could be applied to Guy. Oh, on occasions he'd throw some money at a charity. Like all socialists who have any money at all, he was a complete charlatan.'

'What do you do for a living, Mr Hamilton?'

'I work for an American bank.' He named it: the name was familiar to Morgan, for a reason he couldn't quite remember.

'And Guy?' Morgan referred to the front of the diary again. 'What was his job?'

Hamilton shifted: Morgan thought he could sense unease. 'Actually – well – he refused to try to get any kind of proper job, and when I met him he was just mucking about temping. So, anyway, I knew there was a vacancy on our switchboard, so I – ' The defensive air which had descended on Michael Hamilton amazed and rather cheered Morgan. 'I got him the job,' he concluded simply.

'So he worked at your bank?' Morgan decided to push the point.

'Yes. Just on the switchboard, though.' Hamilton seemed chastened.

'One thing,' Morgan went on, 'Mr Palmer said that Latimer told him that he had entrusted whatever money he had with him to you for the evening. Is that correct?'

Michael laughed. 'Yes. All fifty pence of it.'

Morgan thought for a moment, then looked at his watch: it was well past three. Time enough to continue this later in the day. And he really shouldn't do too much without the Chief; tact and procedure both demanded that.

'Well, Mr Hamilton,' he said, 'we shall be in touch over the next two days or so to arrange a formal session, so I suggest you let us drive you home now and tuck you up.' Hamilton smirked. 'Of course, it would be nice if we could just have a look at Latimer's belongings...'

Michael gave an audible sigh. 'He really didn't have much at my

34

place. He hadn't really had a chance to go back and get much of his stuff from home. He wasn't allowed back in the family home, you see.'

'Nevertheless,' Morgan smiled sympathetically. 'It would be pleasant, sir. And it needn't take long.' Michael opened his hands in a gesture of resignation. 'Thank you. That's all for now.'

Michael Hamilton stood up, an almost accusingly hurt look on his face, brushed himself down and began to stroll out. Morgan played his trick again.

'Did you do it?' he shot out. Michael turned and faced him, fixing on him a stare that was meant, Morgan supposed, to be crushing.

'You've got to be joking,' he said. 'Incidentally, it might occur to you that I'm not covered in dried blood.' He walked out without allowing Morgan a reply.

Morgan walked over to the armchairs where his interviewees had faced him and sat down carefully: the chairs were so low that they seemed designed to create an inferiority complex. He looked across the room at Bowen, who had a sneer a mile wide on his face.

'Well, Ken, what did you make of all that?'

Bowen snorted. 'Stuck up bastard, Stu.' Genuine prejudice over-rode Bowen's sense of formality. 'A bit fond of himself. Just what you'd expect, I suppose.'

Morgan looked across at him, through half-closed eyes. 'How do you mean, exactly?'

'Well – ' Bowen made a throwaway gesture ' – you know. Homos.'

'What about Grey?'

'Hardly got to see him, sir.' The sense of a put-down from his superior had restored propriety. 'He seemed a slightly different kettle of fish altogether. Not at all typical.'

Morgan yawned and rubbed his eyes. Then he began speculating. If Latimer had had no money on him, could he have been killed by irate muggers? Why had he been outside, though, without his bag? They'd have to check with the cloakroom, the doormen and the security guards to see what, if anything, any of them remembered.

He looked at Bowen again. 'I think this is going to be tricky, Ken. Things don't quite add up. Chuck that diary over. No, hang on, I'll come over there.'

He rose to his feet wearily and went back to the desk. He flicked through the diary, looking at the address section at the back and a few typical weeks in Guy Latimer's life. Either he hadn't done a great deal or else he never noted down most appointments.

Occasional scrawls stood out. 'Drink with Phil.' 'Dominic's birthday.' 'Italy.' 'France.' 'Michael.' The most recent entry, for the day before his death, read simply 'JP 1 p.m.' An entry two weeks earlier, Morgan noted, said the same thing. He turned to the address section again; but P yielded only Dominic Palmer and there was no way that the J in either entry could have been a malformed D.

Morgan sighed. Looking down at the effects in front of him again, the discreet blue and gold of the building society book caught his attention. Idly he opened it – and was rewarded with a jolt. Credited to Guy Latimer's account was the sum of £21,723.47.

# 3: We Are Family

Breakfast in the Latimer household was traditionally a sporadic, get-your-own affair. This was particularly the case at weekends as, left to themselves, no member of the household had a regime remotely in common with any other member. Malcolm Latimer's appearances and hours depended largely on his shifts of duty; Phyllis, his wife, tried to fit her hours around his, so as to avoid him wherever possible. Gillian had, until recently, often been away at a boyfriend's, and before that had had a brief marriage: but restored at twenty-one to the family home, she tended to be up earlier rather than later on Saturdays in the hope of getting up to town for shopping, and later rather than earlier on Sundays. Eighteen year old Colin had what might be termed an unambitious schedule: up late, then television for the morning and, depending on the time of year and the temperature, a round of golf, a game of tennis or a trip to Stamford Bridge in the afternoon. Over recent weeks, the golf and tennis had gone by the board a bit: since Guy had left suddenly there was no-one to drive him to golf (unless his mother was in a good mood) and no-one to play tennis with, unless he rang up his friend Rob and organized something, which was often too much trouble because Rob wasn't all that good. Not that Guy was all that good either, but he didn't take any organizing. Or he hadn't until he'd left.

But now tennis with Guy was irrevocably a thing of the past.

Woken in the early hours of the morning, all the Latimers had made a further attempt on sleep after the news had been broken to them by the earnest young policewoman, but for all of them it seemed to have proved pointless. However, they felt individually and collectively that it would be wrong, almost morally, to display too much grief and to console one another too openly. None of them was really, to be truthful, sure about what the others felt. And then, cousin Terry was staying the night. Not that that made things exactly difficult: after all, Terry's branch of the family were close enough. But any extra person under a roof always means extra artificiality of some kind amongst the residents.

Terry was, in fact, the first to move around the house next morning. Phyllis Latimer came down in her dressing gown to the kitchen at eight o'clock or so, to find him sitting staring at a cup of coffee. She felt an immediate surge of resentment: why had it all been so much easier for her sister Carol's children and marriage? Carol's husband had always been successful and relatively civilized; her sons had both gone to university, both shown interest in girls, were both capable of behaving properly at social events. Phyllis had had a terrible life: she was always in a fragile condition, and who was there to give her support and comfort? Guy had been precious little use anyway, and Colin was, in his own way, quite as useless. She just hoped he didn't go the same way as his brother, that was all. When was he going to produce a girlfriend at last? Malcolm wouldn't rest now until he did. And surely, now that this had happened to Guy – well, it was a kind of lesson, wasn't it? If he hadn't been – well, that way inclined (how he'd always forced her to use that dreadful word 'gay'), he wouldn't have been at that place, so he would still be alive.

Phyllis's resentment floundered around in search of a substantial mooring station. It seemed so unfair that such a thing should happen to her. She dithered in the kitchen doorway until Terry asked her, in his neutral but perceptibly 'educated' tones, if she'd like some coffee. She nodded, rather frantically. Terry rose to his feet and addressed the business of coffee-making, slyly surveying his aunt as he did so. She was a frail-looking woman in any event, but today she looked as though she was about to fall completely apart. Her customary pallor was intensified to ghostliness; the grey roots to her light brown hair were even more visible than usual; and her eyes, always restless, were darting about almost manically. Of course, that was all hardly surprising. Terry wondered if he looked haggard as well: he had taken care not to look too messy, but from time to time he affected an air of nineteenth-century Romantic sickliness. The Romantics were the only English writers he condescended to read. He placed a fresh cup of coffee on the table. Phyllis sat down and stared at it, then looked up and stared at him and said, simply, 'Why?'

'I really don't know,' he said, wondering if it would be too intimate to put a consoling hand on her shoulder and deciding that it would far exceed the bounds of propriety. 'There are so many nutters around these days – '

'But why, Terry? Why did he have to be like that in the first place? That's what I don't understand.' She put her arms along the table top.

'What, gay, you mean? He didn't seem unduly worried about it.' Terry shrugged.

'No – he was always thoughtless and selfish. He just couldn't be bothered to make any effort with girls, that was his trouble.'

'Look – isn't this a bit academic now? I mean, if he'd been the biggest womanizer going, he'd still be dead – '

'But he wouldn't! That's obvious, isn't it?'

'You can't possibly say.'

'I blame that Dominic for all this. He led Guy on. Made him think it was clever.' Her eyes had stopped fluttering now and had fixed, obsessively, on a point in vacancy. Terry looked at her, amazed. It was only recently that he had come to have any idea of his aunt's true feelings on the subject of Guy.

'From what Guy told me, Dominic never led him anywhere. And they hadn't seen each other for months.'

'So how come he was there last night?'

'Coincidence. It's a very well-known and popular club. A lot of straight people go there.' A thought struck him. 'Unless you're trying to suggest that Dominic – ' He couldn't think of a useful way of completing the sentence.

'They're a spiteful lot,' Phyllis hissed, clenching her fist.

Terry decided that debate was probably not the best way forward here, and was about to change to a practical and procedural tack when his cousin Gillian appeared in the doorway. She looked red-eyed; and immediately she tried to say 'Good morning', she yawned and gave up the whole attempt. The Latimers were not by nature very sociable, least of all with each other. Terry waved a mug at her and she nodded glumly and sat down next to her mother, but without any form of physical contact taking place. As far as Terry knew, mother and daughter did not get on terribly well: Phyllis had been appalled at Gillian's youthful outrages, of which the failed marriage was the most respectable by far; Gillian, it was said, despised Phyllis's passive acceptance of her situation, her marriage, and her – as Gillian saw it – retreat into the world of mental illness.

So Terry had heard: of his Latimer cousins he knew Guy best and Colin quite well, but Gillian hardly at all. He would never have gone away on holiday alone with either Colin or Gillian: he knew Colin well enough to know that they had little or nothing in common, but he didn't know Gillian well enough to know even that. Terry was really rather in awe of her: not so much because she was slightly older than himself, but because of the publicness of her past hell-raising history.

Latimer family relations were an endless topic of conversation and amusement for the Diffords, Terry's family: but now that Guy was gone, an avenue of communication was permanently shut down. Guy had been popular with Terry's mother, but she had warned Terry himself about getting 'too close'. After all, she had said, he didn't want Guy getting over-dependent, if he knew what she meant.

In those days Guy still hadn't told Terry he was gay: that official announcement had been made only relatively recently – five months previously, to be exact – in a cafe in Paris. It had been of more surprise value to Guy himself, to find he was able to tell another member of his family apart from his mother, than it was to Terry. Of course, everyone had heard about Dominic and Dominic's preferences: it was quite a topic of conversation with the Diffords, what Guy and his older, clever queer friend might have got up to. In fact, after the great announcement, Terry had quite incurred Guy's petulance by asking whether he and Dominic did actually – well, you know. Then he compounded the felony by asking the same question about Derek Wilkinson. Terry's mind ran on a little: he wondered if Phyllis's suggestion had really been serious, that Dominic could have – well, it was fruitless speculating. Terry had never even met Dominic. He placed a cup of coffee in front of Gillian.

'Well, I'm glad someone round here is capable of doing things,' she said with only the merest hint of malice. She ran her hand over her forehead. 'I just can't – well, it's ridiculous.' She suddenly seemed likely to cry.

'Oh, shut up!' Phyllis hissed. 'That's just hypocrisy. You were always jealous of him.' Her voice was small, harsh and dry.

'No I wasn't. And I didn't throw him out. If you hadn't done that – ' Gillian's voice increased in volume.

'That wasn't me. That was your father. What was I – ?'

'You could have stood up to him for once in your life. Colin and I wanted to. And if you hadn't thrown him out – ' Gillian's voice cracked as she started to cry. Phyllis grabbed her by the arm.

'Can you really say you approved of his – well, can you? And let me tell you something,' she went on almost in triumph, 'it would still have happened. He'd already met that boy he was living with. He was practically living there anyway, you know that as well as I do.' Gillian didn't answer. Terry watched, fascinated by this performance.

'Did you ever meet Michael?' he asked, almost out of provocation. Both women shook their heads. Gillian looked up, sniffing a little, inquiringly.

'Did you then?' she asked. 'Guy showed me a photo when I met him for lunch last week. He was very good-looking, I thought, but I never actually met him.'

Terry sat down at the table again. 'I did. I stayed the night there a couple of weeks ago after I went to a film with them. Michael seemed – well – very pleasant. Very self-confident. Guy was very fond of him, you could see that.' A thought struck him. 'Gill, where were you last night?'

She looked at him with suspicion. 'Round at Suzy's,' she said, but was obviously not certain about this. 'Why?'

He ignored her question for a moment. 'We were in town together,' he said to his aunt, 'at the theatre, weren't we?'

'Yes. Yes, you know that as well as I do.'

'Terry, what are you going on about?'

'It's just – you didn't get back until quarter to one. Uncle Malcolm got back at half twelve in the car. We were back just after twelve fifteen. I was just thinking – could we all appear to have had the time to do it? I mean, to kill Guy?'

Gillian gave a half shriek. 'Oh, Terry, that's disgusting.'

'Hey, listen,' Terry said soothingly, 'I'm just trying to be practical. Someone killed Guy. Chances are it was a nutter or a mugger or something or someone like that. But it might still be useful for us all if we can prove where we were when it happened. Don't you think?'

They looked at him in amazement. 'Are you seriously suggesting – ?' Gillian began with quiet, miserable fury.

'Well,' Terry said defensively, 'just before you came down, your mother was seriously suggesting that Dominic Palmer did it. Weren't you?' he concluded bluntly.

A sound made the three of them turn and Colin, tall, dark-haired and as good-looking as ever, appeared in the doorway, looking as rough as any teenager with his physical attributes could. 'Couldn't sleep,' he said, which was for him a revolutionary statement. 'Any coffee going?' he asked, staring imploringly at his mother. Terry rose to his feet again.

'I seem to be coffee boy this morning,' he said pleasantly. 'Anyone else for more?' There seemed to be a general demand, so he refilled the kettle.

'Did I hear shouting?' Colin asked. His mother and sister exchanged guilty looks. 'Christ, what do you want to waste time shouting at each other for? We should get out and get the bastards who did it.' One of his hands involuntarily clenched itself to a fist. Terry looked across at his cousin.

'So you didn't do it?' he asked.

'For Christ's sake!'

'You were here all night, like you said you were, then?' Terry asked. 'You see, when you came in just now we were discussing alibis. I don't think any of us had a really convincing one. Except Gillian, possibly.' Colin glowered moodily at him. 'Your mother seems to think that Guy's old friend Dominic was responsible.'

'Terence, I don't think we should really be talking like this,' Phyllis said, in a voice which bravely failed at self-control.

'Why not?' Terry clutched the handle of the kettle in a kind of excitement. 'Don't you realise that everyone else will talk just like this? The police certainly will. I mean,' his voice rose to a gleeful level and an almost messianic fervour seized him, 'you can't keep it to yourselves. This is real tabloid paper stuff, whether it was maniacs, Dominic, Michael, Colin – whoever. And,' he went on, addressing the three sullen hostile glares from across the table, 'unless we all know what we're going to say before we actually get round to saying it publicly, officially, then the possible ramifications of publicity, of everything, are – well – enormous.'

'Oh God,' Phyllis said, placing her hands over her face. 'Why did he have to be like that?'

'Don't be stupid, mum,' Colin growled, 'that's got fuck all to do with it.' He covered his mouth with his hand, as usually the expletive would have drawn a reproof. Circumstances were hardly usual though. 'Are you suggesting we all lie then, or what?' he asked Terry directly.

'Not lie exactly,' Terry said. 'I mean, it's no skin off my nose at all from that point of view.'

'Christ, don't you care?' Gillian asked.

'Of course I care,' Terry replied. 'After all, Gill, I was as close to Guy as you were. And he never actually told you or Colin he was gay, did he?' Silence greeted this. 'Of course I care. But I mean that the publicity isn't going to affect me. My name isn't Latimer. Everyone I know knows about my gay cousin. It doesn't worry me, but it obviously worries you lot. I mean, Colin, how are the lads down the Shed End going to take it? And what are the coppers down the station going to say?'

As if on cue, a heavy tread in the doorway signalled the arrival of the patriarch. Theoretically he was on duty later in the morning, but this was obviously going by the board now. Unlike his wife and daughter but like his son, he had made some token gesture toward dressing and washing, so that a haphazard shaving had taken place, leaving little patches of dark, slightly greying bristle on his heavy, jowled face. It was the face of a man who had been good-looking in a masculine, forthright, impressive way: and Terry, as an outsider, was always struck by the actual resemblance all three of his children bore to Malcolm Latimer.

Guy, of course, never used to acknowledge this. 'Colin and I take after mum and your mum,' he always said: but good looks were not really the stock in trade of the Anderson blood. Terry and his elder brother were pure Anderson: the pale complexions, the long nose, the longish chin, the watery brown eyes, the light brown hair. But Guy, Gillian and Colin all had a firmness, a definition of appearance, which worked out as extreme good looks in the males and aggression in appearance in Gillian; this could have come only from the Latimer strain. Guy had, it was true, inherited a deceptively fragile colouring from the Andersons: but for a blue-eyed blond brought up in England he was surprisingly ruddy. His spindly legs had been his most genuinely Andersonian trait.

But there was nothing spindly about Malcolm Latimer; he had always been muscular. True, he was going to seed now, muscle turning to flab; but he was still an imposing figure. Terry knew, as much from experience as hearsay, that his uncle still dominated his children by threats of force and more; and it had been said that Guy had nursed a bruise or two at least about his body when he had been forcibly ejected. Now, Malcolm Latimer fixed Terry with a dour look.

'Am I to understand that you think we find the news embarrassing, Terry?' he asked in the kind of tone policemen normally reserve for heavy irony and satire.

'I assume you do,' Terry said, his blazing certainty rather dimmed by his uncle's physical presence. 'Particularly in view of where the body was found.'

'And who found him!' interjected Phyllis bitterly.

'Yes,' Malcolm Latimer said, 'it's all bloody awkward. Guy's as thoughtless in his – well, he always was a selfish little bugger.' It struck Terry that here, uncharacteristically, husband and wife agreed. 'Let's hope they get whoever did it as soon as possible. We don't want all this dragging on. Terry's quite right.'

'I don't believe you two,' Gillian exclaimed, rounding on her parents. 'Just because Guy wasn't everything you wanted him to be, you seem almost glad as he's dead. Supposing this had happened while he was still at university – oh, it'd have been tears of grief for the beloved son then, wouldn't it? But just because he wasn't earning a fortune and preferred men to women – God, it makes me sick.'

'That's quite enough of that,' her father said heavily. 'I don't think you can blame me for the way you three have turned out. But your cousin is right, anyway. We've all got to stick up for one another and keep nosey parkers out of this.'

'I'm not sticking up for you!' Gillian spat out. 'I'm not telling any lies to save your neck. I mean, for all we know you went up to town last night and – '

'Take care, madam,' Malcolm thundered, raising his hand to her. 'And if you won't listen to me, listen to Terry.'

'Are you seriously suggesting we should all cover up for each other?' Colin asked Terry.

'I never suggested that,' Terry said. 'I simply said that it would be useful if we thought out together exactly what we were going to tell the police. About where we were last night and about Guy. I never said anyone ought to lie. I mean, as far as I know, no-one has any need to, do they?' Irony was not a quality the Latimers traded in, so if Terry had any ironic intent here, it was completely lost.

'Anyway, they'll be here soon,' Colin said, his eyes staring at the kitchen wall clock.

'Another thing,' the head of the family said, 'we've got quite enough in the way of practical worries to occupy ourselves with over the next few days. So I don't think we need to argue – what with the inquest and the funeral.'

'Oh, you are going to have one,' Gillian said bitterly. 'You're not just going to dump him on the council rubbish tip.'

'I've warned you, young lady – '

'Oh, fuck off, dad,' she said wearily, rising to her feet, only to be forced down again by a swingeing blow to her face. Terry gawped, astonished. He had never actually seen Malcolm Latimer strike anyone before: he had only heard about such incidents from Guy. Gillian let out a little cry. For a moment she sat motionless. Then she stood up.

'Has anyone taken the dogs out yet?' she asked, a catch in her voice.

No-one replied immediately. Eventually Colin looked up and said, 'Doubt it.'

'Well, I might as well,' Gillian said. She looked out of the window. 'Oh, it's raining.'

'Don't forget to put a jacket on or something,' her mother said. Malcolm Latimer stared at his wife.

'She can probably work that out for herself,' he said scornfully.

'Oh, for God's sake,' Gillian said, brushing past her father as she left the kitchen. He took the seat she had vacated. 'Any tea or coffee going?' he asked.

The kettle had boiled and turned itself off; Terry, who was still standing by it, turned it on again. Malcolm Latimer shook his head and stared down at the table. 'God, what a business,' he said to himself. Colin and Phyllis, on either side, glared at him with expressions of pure unadulterated dislike. This seemed to go on for ever: he grew visibly uneasy and eventually rose to his feet. 'I'll be back for coffee,' he said to Terry, and walked across the kitchen towards the garden door, through which he disappeared. As soon as he had done so, the doorbell rang.

'Shall I get it?' Terry volunteered, but Phyllis shook her head, pulled her dressing gown firmly around her and rose to her feet. Terry was struck by how much Guy would have enjoyed that moment: it was purest melodrama, a genuinely cinematic gesture which needed Bette Davis at least to do it justice. Guy had always revelled in such moments. His aunt left to open the door. Terry looked at Colin. 'How are you feeling?' he asked.

'How do you think? You seem cheerful enough, anyway.'

'That's not fair.'

'No, it isn't really, is it? You were right, anyway. You knew him as well as we did.' Colin scratched his head and then stretched his arms. His tee-shirt came adrift from his jeans, revealing flexed stomach muscles. Terry felt a sudden pang of nausea at this sight. 'Did you ever meet the famous Dominic?' Colin asked suddenly.

'Never quite,' Terry replied. 'I was almost going to once.'

'Yeah, me too.' Colin propped his chin on his hands. 'Do you think Dominic did it then?'

'Well – I think it was probably a gang of some sort. That's most likely.'

'Maybe,' Colin replied a trifle uneasily. 'Could Dominic have, though? I mean, he was a bit nutty, wasn't he?'

'From what Guy said,' Terry said carefully, 'he could get quite worked up and possessive. The problem is,' he went on, 'that from what I know, I'd have thought Dominic could quite easily have done it. And your ma definitely thinks he did.'

At this Phyllis walked back into the kitchen and looked at her nephew curiously. 'It is the police,' she confirmed quietly. 'Colin, could you get your father, please?'

Colin rose slowly, laboriously, and ambled out of the kitchen door. Phyllis paused and regarded Terry again. Terry smiled at her reassuringly.

'Are we going to tell them?' she asked.

'What – about Dominic?'

'Well – that too, I suppose.'

'Oh,' Terry said, 'I imagine the police know about Dominic already. And there's no point, really, telling them what they already know, if you see what I mean.' He smiled.

'Yes,' Phyllis said distantly, 'I think I do.'

'What are the policemen like?'

'Oh – like policemen.' Phyllis Latimer had turned quite pale, even more so than before. She began to clench and unclench her fists slowly.

'Like Uncle Malcolm?' Terry teased.

'No – they're not like that sort of policeman. Well, one of them probably isn't.'

She looked away from Terry to the window. Before Terry could make any comment on her observation, Gillian reappeared in the kitchen doorway. She was holding a dog-leash and wearing a light blue kagoule Terry recognised as Colin's.

'I see the police have arrived,' she remarked nervously. 'Look – ' she stopped. 'I don't know whether I ought to mention this, but, well – you know Colin said he was here all the time yesterday?' She put her right hand in the kagoule pocket. 'Well, there's this.' She pulled out a railway ticket. 'Return to London. Dated yesterday.'

# 4: Body Talk

Chief Inspector Oldcastle surveyed the gentlemen of the Press with a weary and definitely jaundiced eye.

'I think I've said all that can usefully be said at this stage,' he asserted in his gruff Northern tones, affecting not to see hands still excitedly raised. 'Bloody Sunday sex-sheets,' he murmured to himself as the *News of the World*'s representative tried to push his way through his peers so as to impress himself more effectively on the proceedings. The two were old sparring partners and Oldcastle had even sometimes quite enjoyed their little contests: but in this particular case he wasn't in the mood for dealings of any kind with the Press.

It was the sort of case where they wanted lurid details and sensational developments. Unfortunately there wasn't enough substance in the details, whatever their implicit luridness: and without any substance to go on, swift developments were out of the question, sensational or otherwise. And in that kind of situation, in Oldcastle's experience, the Fourth Estate seemed to feel it had a free hand to speculate in the most unhelpful manner.

If he'd had his way, mark you, there wouldn't have been any of this Press Conference stuff: his motto was to only tell them what they needed to know when they needed to know it. Oldcastle's compromise between his own beliefs and those of his superiors, for whom he had scant respect – 'Old School Tie Southerners, the lot of them' – was to tell the Press what, in his view, it needed to know at the times he was ordered to. So, in this case, he had explained quite simply that a body had been found after midnight outside a well-known London club near the Embankment, a club notably popular with London's homosexual community. The body had been positively identified as that of Guy Malcolm Latimer, aged twenty-four, currently living in Hackney. Cause of death was asphyxiation caused by manual strangulation, although the victim had been severely wounded about the face. The body had been found by friends of the victim. The boy's family had been informed and were unavailable for comment; and it was too early to offer any views concerning the perpetrator or perpetrators of the deed.

Oldcastle failed to see why he should then have to stand through a whole load of damn fool nonsense about the boy's father being a policeman, whether he had really thrown his son out, the time of death, was Latimer homosexual himself, had he been found by his lover or lovers, had anyone been detained, had the victim had AIDS...All this was just none of their bloody business. Even the so-called quality papers seemed to be taking a garish interest. And then there was the laddie from the Poofs' Own Paper, as they called it on the Force. Would the Inspector care to comment on the inadequate police concern for and protection of members of London's gay community, and did he see this crime as part of the rising tide of violence against gays? No, he wouldn't, and no, he didn't.

One thing was clear to Oldcastle: this was not a piece of random violence. It was, it should be said, clear to Oldcastle primarily because it was clear to Morgan: Stuart Morgan was far too ambitious a lad to make a definite assertion that something was clear when it wasn't. Yes, an ambitious boy, Morgan – needed to be, young family and all that. Much good would it do him, Oldcastle thought, if he wasn't part of the right mob. Bloody Masons.

Having fought his way back from the Press Conference Room to his office, Oldcastle found Morgan waiting for him with that brawny monstrosity Bowen.

'Well, Stuart,' he said, ignoring Bowen, whose IQ he reckoned as being in single figures, 'I've seen to the jackals. I think we can expect them to play this one up. Unless a member of the Royal Family does something sexually titillating between now and this evening.'

Oldcastle went over to his cupboard, unlocked it and took out a bottle of Scotch and a tumbler. He waved the bottle politely at Morgan and his sidekick in the full confidence of a refusal. 'So,' he went on, pouring himself a liberal measure, 'what did we get from the family?'

'Not a great deal, sir,' Morgan said, digging his hands into his pockets. Nice suits that boy always wears, Oldcastle thought. 'There was almost what you might call a conspiracy of silence,' Morgan went on. 'For what it's worth, I got an impression of as much embarrassment as grief. Particularly with the parents.'

'And did they all have cast-iron alibis?' Oldcastle asked cynically. Morgan laughed.

'Not a single one of them. Except the girl and she could be lying.'

'Bloody marvellous.' He swigged his Scotch. 'Don't you long for that marvellous detective story world where they've all got perfect alibis and all you've got to do is prove who's lying? Real people never have the faintest bloody idea where they are now, let alone where they were then.' He looked across at Morgan. 'Well, let's hear it.'

Morgan took his hands out of his pockets again and gestured at a chair. Oldcastle waved permission, so Morgan sat, and at the edge of the room Bowen followed suit. Morgan pushed a strand of his dark hair back from his forehead and began in that mildly irritating intense way he had.

'To start with. It wasn't just the Latimers there – a cousin of the dead boy's, one Terry Difford, is staying with them. He got on OK with all the family – and he and the deceased went on holiday together earlier this year. Difford and the mother were in town together last night, at the theatre they say. They drove up to town and back. The play finished around 10. I've checked that with the theatre. They say they didn't hang around afterwards, drove straight home, arriving about quarter past midnight. Traffic was quite heavy. At home the younger son – Colin – was waiting. He says he was in all night watching telly. Alone. PC Malcolm Latimer drove back from looking after his rabbits and other wildstock at half past midnight. He keeps them near some allotments about a half mile from his home. No-one else was there, of course. The girl – Gillian – says she was round at a friend's, but I'm inclined to believe she was with some bloke she doesn't want the family to find out about. That would be about par for the course. She's got a track record in that area, I gather. She's also got a criminal record – the only person involved who has.'

Oldcastle gave a derisive snort. 'Seems like Constable Latimer was a model father. What did she do? Prostitution?'

'No, sir,' Morgan said with a polite grin, 'breaking and entering. With her then boyfriend, later husband, now ex-husband.'

'And just how old,' Oldcastle asked in his weariest tones, 'is this wicked lady?'

'Twenty-two, sir.'

'Impressive. And,' Oldcastle went on, as though struck by a late thought, 'how – why – was the good Constable himself with his rabbits until the small hours? Are we supposed to swallow that one?'

'Not necessarily, sir. It may be there's a woman involved – preliminary enquiries suggest that the marriage has been firmly on the rocks for quite a while now. But neither parent seemed unduly upset at the news. The sister seemed the most cut up of them, actually.'

'What about the cousin?'

'Well, sir, he seemed fairly self-possessed. I suspect he rather fancies himself – you know, just done a year at university, so knows it all. He's a fairly cool customer from what I could tell. Almost as much as the boy's – er – friend, Hamilton.'

'So.' Oldcastle decided to summarise. 'No-one has so far adequately accounted for themselves at the time of death. Right, Sergeant. What are the facts? Somebody gets the lad in the alleyway, slashes his face, strangles him, legs it – maybe even into the club. This all happens around when?'

'11.10 to 11.30, the autopsy and the evidence narrow it down to. Latimer was alive at 10.30 plus and dead by 12.15 or so. Palmer, Grey and Hamilton are consistent about the state of the body when they found it.'

'Right. Now why wasn't it a gang or a nutter, Sergeant? You seemed fairly certain, but you haven't graced me with your explanation yet.'

'Well.' Morgan smoothed his hair down and scratched his nose. 'I think a gang would have attracted attention that close to a fairly busy street. And there's no sign of any struggle. If it had been a gang, I imagine more garbage would have got upset; and they'd probably have kicked him a fair bit. And there are no serious bruises anywhere on his body apart from the neck and slight marks on the arms. It just doesn't add up to a gang.'

'And an unknown maniac?'

'Well – no sexual interference for one thing. You usually expect that with nutters, even ones who claim divine inspiration. And again, the lack of any sign of a struggle. And anyway, there's Latimer himself.' Morgan stopped and mused.

'Well, what does that enigmatic utterance amount to, Stuart?'

'My first instinct,' Morgan said, fixing Oldcastle carefully with an intense look which drew nothing more than a weary blurred stare, 'was what I imagine yours probably is. Some nutter lures the boy outside for a bit of nookie and then stitches him up. But there's two things wrong with that. Why go outside, when it's more risky outside than in, because everyone's up to it inside? They've even got a room specially set aside for it. And then – everyone tells me that Latimer just didn't go in for that kind of thing. Hamilton says he was a physical coward. Everyone suggests it would be highly out of character for him to go into a clinch anywhere with someone he hardly knew at all, least of all in a public place. Which suggests that his assailant was known to him. So you can see. If he went out there with – or to meet – someone he knew, he would be so taken aback by the assault that he probably didn't have a chance to struggle, yell or anything.'

Oldcastle pondered. Morgan's reasoning seemed fair. 'Is this information about Latimer accurate? I mean, what's its source?'

'Michael Hamilton, his family and a couple of friends of his – Derek Wilkinson and Phil Roxby.'

'Are they fairies, too?'

'Roxby is gay, yes, sir.' Oldcastle caught the implicit criticism of his vocabulary. 'Wilkinson may be. But they're very different types. As are the three lads who found the body. It's been quite an education for me so far.'

'Well, I'm pleased to hear that, Stuart,' Oldcastle said without a trace of sincerity. 'But are any of these witnesses reliable? What details do you have about any of them? How many could be just covering up for their own benefit? Let's have a run down and then maybe we can work out some kind of strategy. What about these two other boys you've dredged up? Are they likely candidates for the sweepstake?'

'Wilkinson possibly, Roxby definitely not. Roxby was at home all night with his boyfriend. Home is a flat quite close to Hamilton's house in Hackney. Roxby and Latimer worked in a bookshop together a couple of years ago. Roxby still works there. Latimer was sacked, by the way, under suspicion of nicking stock.'

'Family trait, it would appear.'

'Roxby, on the other hand, is not at all suspicious. Limp-wristed, trendy, Northern, very direct. Quite pleasant, in fact. A complete contrast to Wilkinson, who's shifty and furtive, but mainly on his own account. He's known Latimer for years – old school friends, in fact. Works as a sound engineer for the World Service at Bush House. Conveniently was working late alone last night – hardly a million miles from the Embankment, though, Bush House. Tried very hard to imply that he has a girlfriend and that he had some more than intimate relationship with Latimer. He seems convinced that Palmer is our man.'

'Oh?' Oldcastle turned round from his close scrutiny of the bottle. 'Is this a widely held opinion?'

'If Guy Latimer's murderer was being elected,' Morgan replied, 'Dominic Palmer would be in on a landslide. So far, of those I've talked to, only Grey and Gillian Latimer have neglected to suggest him at least as a candidate. And Grey claims not to have known either Palmer or Latimer before last Friday. In fact he only made Latimer's posthumous acquaintance, he says. Hamilton managed to dismiss the possibility of Palmer's being the killer on the grounds that Latimer wasn't interesting enough to murder. A fairly typical pronouncement from Hamilton, that, I should add, sir. He loves talking about everyone else's private life but his own, and he never seems to have a good word to say for anyone. Least of all, Latimer.'

'You make our Mr Hamilton sound immensely charming,' the Chief Inspector said without a smile. He heard a grunt of 'Bastard' from Bowen and assumed that label was meant to apply to Hamilton rather than present company.

'Oh, he has a kind of charm, sir. He just doesn't choose to exercise it on the Police. He's very good at his job, we've found out – very smart, very trendy, generally very cool. Typical, you might say, of the new City breed. Lots of cash made very quickly. I don't know how relevant it is, sir, but I gather that his firm's under a fairly intense scrutiny by the Fraud Squad at present. In fact, Hamilton's name is not unknown to them. But they don't actually have anything on him, only suspicions. As I say, he's an ultra-cool customer. He's being particularly cool about his relationship with Latimer, I might add, but I'm not entirely disposed to believe him. Latimer had already moved quite a lot of stuff into his house. Including these.'

Morgan reached inside his jacket and produced two sheets of white folded paper from his breast pocket. He reached forward and placed them on Oldcastle's desk. Oldcastle went over to his desk and unfolded them.

'I hope you've issued a receipt for these, Stuart.'

'Hamilton was only too glad to part with them and get rid of us,' Bowen said from the margins.

'Well,' Oldcastle said, 'how extraordinary. Wills.'

'Perhaps not so odd,' Morgan said, 'looking at his building society book.'

'That was in the rucksack, was it? Well, how much?'

'Over twenty thousand.'

Oldcastle's face froze. Eventually he managed a response he felt to be sufficiently in character. 'Not bad for a young lad.'

'Not bad for a young lad who'd never had a steady or well-paid job,' Morgan emphasised. 'Not bad for a young lad who only had a tenth of that three weeks ago.' He produced the building society book and handed it to his Chief. Oldcastle looked at it while Morgan talked him through the recent entries. 'On the 19th of July he had just over two thousand. On the 20th of July he takes out all but a couple of hundred. On the 25th he puts twenty thousand in.'

'Well what the hell's going on?'

'I can't be sure sir, but – '

'And look at these wills,' Oldcastle went on. 'They're both made within the last month.' He looked again at one of them. 'This one's dated August 14th,' he said, genuinely surprised for the first time that day.

'Yes,' Morgan grinned. 'It supersedes the other one. All perfectly legally correct.'

'Hang about,' Oldcastle muttered, taking one document in each hand. 'This lad made one will on July 31st, leaving everything to his brother Colin. Then, exactly two weeks later, he makes another one, changes his mind, and' – he looked carefully at the paper in his right hand – 'well, that's rum, Sergeant.'

'Yes, we thought so, didn't we, Ken?' Morgan said rising to his feet and taking the document out of Oldcastle's right hand. 'He leaves everything he possesses to Dominic Jonathan Palmer.' He placed the document on the desk.

'I thought you said to me this morning that Palmer said – '

'He did, sir, he said all that: how much he hated Latimer; he hadn't done it but he wished he had; he hadn't seen him for at least three months.' Morgan walked around the desk to the window at the back of the office and stared out at the bleak, unimpressive rows of building backs outside. 'It begins to make less and less sense. Given the method, the style of the murder, Palmer fits perfectly as long as the motive is spite, revenge or whatever you like to call it. If there'd been some kind of reconciliation, that motive falls down – '

'Leaving, Sergeant, a far more common and obvious one. Is Palmer well off?'

'Apparently not, sir – he's usually in bad odour at his bank.' Oldcastle nodded at this, but Morgan turned to face him square. 'But it doesn't match my impression of the man, sir. And he didn't seem to know about the will or the money from what he said last night.'

'Maybe. Are you trying to tell me that you don't think Palmer would be capable of murder if it wasn't for emotional reasons?'

Morgan nodded. 'If the motive were money, Hamilton would be a more likely candidate. But he had nothing to gain. And then there's the brother. After all, twenty-four hours earlier he'd have been the beneficiary. But I wouldn't have figured the brother as spiteful enough for the wounding.'

'So you see the wounding as spite-based, Sergeant?'

'Don't you, sir?'

'Not necessarily,' Oldcastle said, shaking his head, letting the earlier will flutter from his left hand to his desk. 'It could simply be designed to look that way, to distract our attention.' He sighed. 'Tell me about the brother.'

'Typical eighteen year old boy. Works in an office, doing accounts. Supports Chelsea.'

'Chelsea supporters are usually handy with knives.'

'He's never been in any trouble.'

'He's never been caught. Most soccer hooligans get away with it. The clubs let them – they need the gate money.'

Morgan stared almost rudely at his Chief, wondering if the cynicism were real or affected. 'Anyway,' he went on slowly, 'he hasn't got any form. No-one has – apart from the sister. Palmer's witnessed an accident involving a police car and been in an accident himself. But that's it otherwise. As you appreciate, sir, facts are a bit difficult to come by. There's no trace of the knife, and I doubt there ever will be. No prints on the body, of course, or on anything else that might give us a lead.'

'Yes.' Oldcastle gave the distinct impression of feeling that it was not enough, and that Morgan was somehow personally to blame. 'So let's have a quick run-down of names, ages and so on of our principal characters, shall we?'

Morgan obliged, wondering again, principally about how much the Chief was actually taking in. He'd hit the Scotch pretty hard in the short time they'd been talking. Personally, he found it sad that the block on promotion could have such an effect on a man: after all, Oldcastle was, in his way, a good cop. His bluntness had had its results. It might cut two ways in this case, Morgan felt: it would probably be a useful tool for breaking down Hamilton, Wilkinson and maybe even the Latimer family. But he didn't see much productive coming out of its effect on Palmer or Grey or Roxby. Morgan wound up his routine factual recitation. He himself was already so familiar with these facts that he found them boring.

'Right,' Oldcastle said, 'have you seen any of the staff at the club yet? I hope to God somebody has.'

'They were all questioned this morning, sir,' Morgan replied. 'One interesting item. Only one, but it's better than nothing. They all started off by insisting that no-one could go out and come back in again without having to pay twice, and then eventually they all admitted that practically anyone could get away with it, providing they're charming enough, handsome enough, or bribe the right amount. None of them seems to remember Latimer leaving at all, either alone or in company. So that's no use. A couple of them, who weren't on the door at the relevant time, knew him by sight. But some more of them were friendly with Michael Hamilton: and one of them eventually admitted to letting him nip in and out on the quiet last night.'

'Hamilton?' Again Morgan detected a genuine note of interest, and wished that he knew some way of keeping it going. 'So,' Oldcastle went on reflectively, 'Mr Hamilton probably went out, then. Interesting. I never trust a cool bastard in a case like this, Stuart. Yes,' he rubbed his hands gleefully, 'I think I shall enjoy meeting Mr Hamilton.'

'He doesn't seem to have any very clear motive,' Morgan said cautiously. He never dared address Oldcastle as 'Peter', even when the use of his own Christian name seemed to offer an implicit invitation.

'Been at the Agatha Christies again, have we, Stuart?' Oldcastle laughed. 'Motive is a bit overrated as a concept, I think. You know as well as I do, lad, that if you find the right person, the motive comes wandering behind them wagging its tail. In any case,' he said thoughtfully, 'haven't you given me to understand that he was getting a bit fed up with Latimer?'

'Getting a bit fed up is a pretty poor mo – reason.'

'Aye. Of course,' Oldcastle took up again, returning to the bottle of Scotch, 'if everyone thinks it's Mr Palmer, then...But it would be much more entertaining if it weren't. More of a challenge.' He poured a further measure. 'Are you sure you won't, Stuart? You make me feel like an old soak.'

Morgan decided to do the polite thing. 'I could use a small drop, actually, sir.'

Oldcastle produced a second tumbler, and poured a distinctly large drop into it. 'Bowen?' he said, clearly expecting the answer 'No.'

'Well, that's very kind of you, sir,' Bowen began, but Morgan shot him a quick headshake, 'but perhaps I'd better not.'

'Right, Stuart, there you are.' Morgan took his glass of warm whisky and nursed it delicately. It wasn't stuff he drank at the best of times. The sensation at the back of his throat when he summoned up the nerve to drink was strange, electric, and the immediate effect on his head was not helpful. Oldcastle must, he thought, be a seasoned expert to remain as in touch as he seemed to be after as many as he'd had already. It appeared to have quite a beneficial effect on the Chief, suddenly, when allied with the challenge of problems and difficulties.

'Well,' the Chief Inspector went on, at last taking his seat behind his desk, 'I think, to start with, I want to see everyone myself...The whole bloody lot. Palmer, Grey, Hamilton – and what about this Grey character, Stuart? Is he genuinely out of the running? He probably had the opportunity. And I want to see all the Latimers and the cousin and all those friends, the doorstaff who knew the two of them, the ones who were there when it happened. Everybody. And what about these personal effects you promised me, from the famous rucksack? And who drew up these wills? Who witnessed them?'

'A Miss Katy Goldsmith,' Morgan replied. 'A university friend. She drew them up and had them witnessed at her flat.'

'Well, we'll have a word with her, then.'

'As for the personal effects – ' Morgan reached into his jacket pocket and pulled out Guy Latimer's diary. 'This, in my view, is the most interesting.' He gave it to the Chief Inspector, who began turning the pages slowly and carefully.

'Well, either Mr Latimer led a very boring life, or else he kept his secrets even from himself,' he said. 'Oh, a sudden rush of films. Old films,' he said, raising his eyebrows.

'I deduce he was a Bette Davis fan,' Morgan said. 'I gather that's not uncommon in the – er – gay world.'

Oldcastle looked at him quizzically. 'I'm a bit of an admirer myself,' he said. He resumed his perusal. ' "France",' he read aloud. 'That would be with this – what did you say the cousin was called?'

'Difford. Terry Difford.'

'Yes.' He turned again. ' "Italy". Quite the little globe-trotter, our Mr Latimer. Was that with Difford too?'

'No, sir. That was with Dominic Palmer.'

'Was it, by God?' Oldcastle sat back in his chair.

'Interestingly, I gather Palmer arranged it all. The only thing Latimer had to do was pay his own fare out there.'

'So Latimer used to sponge off Palmer?'

'It's not quite that simple, sir,' Morgan said, waiting to be asked for further explanation, but he wasn't. Oldcastle turned the diary's pages backwards and forwards.

'What's JP? Or rather, I suppose, who's JP?'

'The only P in the addresses is Palmer. Can't be him, though.'

'So we don't know. As he saw this JP the day before he was killed, we bloody well ought to know.'

'That's rather what I feel. Roxby couldn't throw any light on that – and he's the only one I've mentioned it to, so far.' Morgan, still standing at the window, turned and looked out at the scenery again. 'That diary is quite fascinating in its own elliptical way,' he said.

'Elliptical,' Oldcastle said, not without irony. 'I suppose that's one word for it, Stuart.'

He closed the diary and placed it carefully on the desk. 'So,' he said, finishing off his Scotch, 'what's the timetable? Inquest opens when? Monday?'

Morgan nodded. 'But we've let the body go, sir. It's told us all it can, and I think the family want to go for an early funeral. Probably on Tuesday.'

'Let's hope their haste doesn't mean they're trying to hide something. And is there any chance that the analytical geniuses in forensics might have looked at the blood samples and so on by Monday?'

'Probably Tuesday at the earliest, sir. It being the weekend.'

'That's their bloody excuse, is it? I don't see why I have to slog when no other bugger's going to. It would be quite helpful – and I'm sure you'd agree – if those traces of blood inside one of the club loos could be counted in or out. It might clear up our picture of what actually happened.' He sighed. 'Beggars can't be choosers, I suppose, Stuart.' He twisted his head round to look at Morgan. 'So. How shall we do this? Who shall we chat to first? When?'

'I'd say Grey first, later today. Then the family, tomorrow morning. Then everyone else.'

'And Mr Palmer?'

'Oh, I'd leave him till the end.'

'Right. And then we'll know exactly what everyone thinks we ought to be asking him and why he's the people's choice.' Oldcastle rubbed his hands. 'Actually, I'm almost looking forward to it all. Particularly to meeting Mr Hamilton.'

On hearing this, Morgan almost audibly breathed a sigh of relief. It meant the Chief was going to put in some effort, if only to start with.

# Part Two
# SWEET TALKING GUY

# 5: How Will I Know?

On Saturday, Marcus and Dominic spent an evening ignoring the television together.

They had now been in each other's company for the best part of twenty-four hours, and so far the novelty value seemed to have been quite comfortably sustained. Oddly enough, up until then they hadn't really discussed the murder or anything very much connected with it; yet the very fact of it had thrown them into a kind of intimacy which they probably wouldn't, in Marcus's view, have got anywhere near otherwise.

In that sense it could almost have been called a blessing in disguise – a pretty effective disguise, admittedly – because they had quite quickly discovered that they had a deal in common. Films, books, theatre: both enjoyed hopping around from subject to subject, dissecting, praising, annihilating at will and at random. They didn't agree at every point, but they rather enjoyed their disagreements. Marcus, for example, didn't share Dominic's breathless reverence for weepy American melodrama, although he did rather enjoy sitting and listening to Dominic's solo performance of *Now, Voyager*. And, aside from any topic that they might enjoy throwing around verbally, there was always sex.

Marcus had been quite prepared for Dominic to be too shaken, too upset by events for any kind of sexual performance after the Police had escorted them home. Thus he had been taken completely unawares by the sudden passionate attack launched upon him the moment he closed the front door of his flat. Was it partly relief? Pure sexual drive? It even crossed his mind that the passion might have been born of triumph. Dominic was under suspicion of murder, after all, on his own admission. But whatever caused the physical intensity, it was very far from unwelcome.

A 'phone call in the early afternoon had woken them: the Police announced a sudden wish to see Marcus as soon as possible, 'to eliminate him from their enquiries.' Marcus had offered them

Dominic as well, but this offer, although politely received, had been equally politely declined. Dominic, they said, would be interviewed in due course, most probably on the Monday; but as seeing Marcus should be a relatively straightforward matter, could they come and see him now? Marcus asked for an hour's grace. Dominic, hearing all this, looked a little perturbed.

'I suppose they want to put me through the shredder,' he said, partly in gloom, partly in whimsy. 'In which case I shall go home.' He was sitting up in bed, inadequately covered by half the duvet. Marcus, in his dressing gown, came round the bed and sat down next to him. He rested his hand on top of Dominic's.

'And what are you going to do after going home?'

'Oh, God knows. I hate Saturday nights. Watch telly, I suppose.'

'You could always come back here. If you'd like to.'

'Would you like me to?'

Marcus raised his eyebrows in mock exasperation. 'Why do you think I made the suggestion?'

Dominic looked back at him, giving an almost childish stare. Then quite suddenly, and with surprising strength, he took hold, hard, of Marcus's hand and pulled; and, as Marcus lurched forward, grabbed his neck with his free other arm. Marcus found himself effectively gripped, his face a few inches from Dominic's. Dominic smiled and ran a hand over Marcus's cheek.

'Nice butch stubble,' he said, and began to nibble it with his teeth.

'I prefer using a razor as a general rule,' Marcus said with some difficulty, 'but this has its – Dominic, what are you – ?'

'You know perfectly well,' came the muffled reply from inside Marcus's dressing gown as Dominic's fingers and tongue worked down his body. Marcus gave a taut sigh of pleasure.

'Are you going to come back, then?' An indistinct sound floated up his body. He tugged on Dominic's hair. 'Are you?'

Dominic's face popped up. 'Don't you know it's rude to talk with your mouth full?'

Marcus laughed and rested his arms on the other's shoulders, clasping them behind his neck. 'Are you going to?'

'Yes. If I can work out how to get there and back, I'll be back here by six. I'll bring some food. Talking of which – ' he ducked down again and Marcus surrendered to the experience again.

Afterwards they lay together, holding each other a little fretfully, aware that the Police might be there any moment, yet loath to let go. Eventually, Marcus moved; and Dominic, with a surge of energy, disappeared from the flat within ten minutes.

But, as promised, he returned promptly on the stroke of six. And again he subjected Marcus to physical assault. Marcus was beginning to wonder where all the energy came from. They lay on the sitting room floor, naked, in front of the television, which was drivelling away contentedly to itself. Dominic rested his hand on Marcus's chest; reciprocally Marcus stroked his hair. Again the thought crossed his mind: was Dominic a murderer? It had clearly seemed a distinct possibility to the Police, particularly in view of one piece of information they had 'let slip' – far from accidentally, he suspected.

'So,' Dominic murmured lazily, 'how were the Sergeant and the hunky Constable?'

'The hunky Constable was not in attendance.' Marcus looked down his body at the top of Dominic's head. 'You didn't fancy that appalling gorilla, did you?'

'Oh, I've got lousy taste,' Dominic remarked cheerfully.

'Instead I had that guy Morgan and some Inspector – or was he a Chief Inspector? – who I assume is his boss and an old soak by the appearance and smell of him. Bluff Northerner.'

'Great stuff. Just the kind of figure to have a deep and instantaneous rapport with the gay community.' Dominic raised himself, and sat up, swinging his legs round so that they were over Marcus's. 'And do they think I killed Guy?'

Marcus was stunned by this question's directness. 'Ah – er – they asked about you. They asked about Michael. That's all. They didn't really ask me very much more than last night. But they – ah – told me quite a lot.' Marcus hesitated.

'Well? Or shall I wait and read it in the Sunday papers?' Dominic seemed flippant enough about the whole thing.

'Well – they definitely think that he was murdered. I mean, by someone he knew.'

'Yes. That was obvious, really.'

'Was it?'

'To anyone who knew Guy. He was paranoid about physical proximity. Even if he fancied people in the street, in bars, on buses and tubes, he'd run a mile before he'd let anyone touch him. So it must have been done by someone he allowed to go near him.' Dominic paused. 'How was it done, anyway?'

'He was strangled.'

'That makes it even more likely it was me,' Dominic said. 'I've got a morbid strangulation fetish. Before or after he was cut up?'

'They didn't say. Do you think it's particularly wise to make remarks like that?'

'Just what the nice policeman said. Actually, I don't think it matters. I'll get nailed for it. So who cares?'

Marcus sat up and gripped Dominic by the shoulders to shake him, but Dominic leaned forward suddenly and kissed him. Marcus broke free of the kiss.

'Look, Dominic,' he said in a low, urgent voice, 'you've got to start taking this seriously, for Christ's sake, or you're going to end up on a murder charge.'

' "A mudder charge",' echoed Dominic, mimicking Marcus's accent, and continuing in his best Jean Brodie: 'Well, for those who care about that sort of thing, that is the sort of thing they care about.' He reverted to his normal tone. 'How do you know I didn't do it? If you didn't do it, that is?'

'Do you think I did it?'

'Of course not.' Dominic laughed. 'You've only got one motive, which doesn't seem to realise its remote and feeble potential, i.e., viz., that you were jealous of Guy and Michael and wanted Michael back – and anyway, you don't fit the necessary job description as knowing Guy well enough to be allowed to go near him.'

'And who does fit that description?' Exasperation was beginning to seize hold of Marcus.

'Me. Michael. Phil Roxby. Derek Wilkinson. His family and his cousin Terry.' He pondered. Then he laughed. 'Oh yes – Katy Goldsmith.' He laughed again. 'Anyway, they'll get me for it. I know that. I'm not sure how much of a flying fuck I give.'

'Did you do it?' Marcus asked directly. 'I'd rather assumed you didn't. I still think you didn't.'

'So do I. But what does that matter?' Dominic leaned across so that their noses were touching. 'Anyway, this could all be a brilliant performance. I could be a jealous psychopath, a mad, blood-lustful creature.' He placed his hands around Marcus's neck and squeezed, quite hard. Marcus felt a pang of terror, as Dominic did not stop this immediately: instead, he shifted his position so that he and Marcus were intertwined. Just as fear began to set in, Dominic stopped.

'You see,' he said, smiling, 'you're not quite sure, are you?' He looked down his body and laughed, a little ruefully, and Marcus saw that this performance had given him a hard-on. Marcus made a grab at it and held on. Dominic gasped, not entirely in pain.

'Right. Now I've got you where it counts. So let's have a bit of seriousness. Tell me truthfully why you think everyone will say you killed Guy.'

'You've got the oddest chat-up lines I've ever heard, you know. Are they all like you North of the – ow! All right.' He laughed again. 'If you keep doing that, you won't have anything to hold onto – it'll get all moody and go away.' Marcus relaxed his grip a little. 'Ooh, that's nice. Look, do you really want to talk about this? I mean, why does it interest you that they're going to get me for something I didn't actually do?'

'Oh Christ, Dom – why do you need to ask that? We've spent a day together, very enjoyably. I was perhaps thinking,' Marcus went on, allowing a note of sarcasm to enter his voice, 'that we might spend time together in the future. Which might prove difficult if they put you in jail.'

'Are you serious?' For the first time in the conversation Dominic's voice lost all trace of irony. 'I mean, about seeing each other again?'

'You seem surprised. Look, Dominic, usually I'm a fairly wary person when it comes to relationships – '

'That's odd. Usually I'm not. But then I don't get much opportunity to try. But listen, Marcus. You can never be sure I'm not guilty. And they will pin it on me. You know what the Police are like. They hate us all, they hate gay people.'

'There are gay policemen, you know.'

'Usually married with kids. No, listen. They'll want a quick result, and the papers will be pushing them all the way. Guy's family will close ranks and protect each other, even though they hate each other. Michael can't have done it. Everyone thinks I did it. And the problem is that I sort of wish I had. I'm not sorry. I'm actually quite happy that Guy's dead. Can you imagine how free I feel, now that there's no Guy Latimer in the world? I hated him so much, Marcus, so much that I very nearly went mad with it once. Perhaps I did go mad, though. Perhaps I killed him. It happens.' He stopped. 'I'm sorry. This doesn't make me seem a very attractive proposition.'

Marcus put an arm round Dominic's shoulders. 'Did he hurt you very badly?'

'Yes. Yes he did. But it was partly my fault. I allowed him to.'

'You hadn't seen him for ages, had you?' This question Marcus tried to ask casually, but his intent was far from casual – and that shone through. He had been amazed by what the Police had 'let slip': and he was still perplexed by something he had 'forgotten' to tell the Police.

'Is this your impression of that eminently reasonable, oh so sympathetic copper?'

Marcus cursed himself. He was insulting Dominic's intelligence if he tried to be subtle. 'All right, I'm sorry. Sorry, sorry, sorry. Look, Dominic, last night before we found Guy, you said something which you didn't explain. I mean,' he waffled on, 'I'm sure there's a perfectly good explanation – ' He stopped suddenly. 'Then there's something the Police told me. Guy made a will. Actually he made two in the space of two weeks, the second two days ago.'

'Fascinating. But how does that concern – ?' Dominic stopped suddenly and his jaw literally dropped. 'No. Please don't tell me what I think you're going to. Tell me he left it all to Michael. Or his thuggy brother. Or his drippy cousin. Please.'

'Ah – no,' Marcus replied in clipped tones. 'He left the lot to you.' Dominic covered his face with his hands. 'You replaced his brother as sole beneficiary to the estate of Guy Latimer just over twenty-four hours before he was killed.'

'Oh God. Well. That's it, isn't it?' Dominic was now completely subdued and deadened. 'No way out. Do you know, I could almost believe that Guy had done it himself to get at me. I really could.' He shrugged. 'So what was he worth? Couple of thousand?'

'Twenty.'

'Twenty thousand?' Dominic collapsed physically.

'Well it's hardly a fortune you could retire on – '

'With my financial track record it's a fucking fortune beyond my wildest dreams. So there's two counts now. I hated him more than anyone I've ever known and I stood to gain substantially from his death. Oh fuck, fuck, fuck!'

Marcus took hold of Dominic's flesh, which had gone cold, dead to the touch almost. 'Hey,' he said, 'come on. A minute or two ago you didn't seem to care. Why the change?'

Dominic looked at him miserably. 'Just something a Scottish boy said to me, that's all. It made some difference.' He looked down again, but not quickly enough for Marcus to miss the moisture in the corner of the eyes. 'Some difference,' he mumbled again. Marcus put his hand under Dominic's chin and lifted his head gently.

'Last night,' he said softly, 'you told me that you had another reason for being at the club. Well, a positive reason. I didn't tell that to the Police.'

'Marcus – supposing – ' Dominic's voice was cracking, and it was difficult to believe that this was the same person who had recently seemed so cynically self-possessed and uninterested, 'supposing I had killed him. I mean, I wanted to. I really really wanted to. He did me so much harm. So much. I never realised how much until – well, recently. I hated his looks, his taste – everything. And supposing I had – well, what would you do? And even if they can't prove it's me, if they can't prove it's someone else, how will you

64

know?' He was becoming incoherent. 'Do you think that was the reason I was there?'

'No.' Marcus shook his head. 'It may have had something to do with Guy, but I don't think it was that.'

'Honestly, it didn't. Nothing at all to do with Guy. I didn't want to see Guy ever. Ever.' He started crying. Marcus wrapped him in a warm hug and let his head fall on his shoulder.

'You must have loved him very much,' he said simply. 'Do you want to talk about it? You don't have to, you know.'

'Oh, I don't mind talking to you,' Dominic sniffed. 'But how can I tell them? The Police.'

'You don't need to tell them more than you already have.'

'But they'll ask. And how can I explain the money?'

'Do you have to?' Marcus didn't see the relevance of this.

'Well, I can't explain it to myself. I mean – ' Dominic looked up, suddenly angry – 'why the fuck was Guy making wills, anyway?' He wiped his cheeks with the back of his right hand. 'God, I'm being a bit melodramatic here, aren't I?' he gulped.

'Well – ' Marcus grinned affectionately, 'maybe a little. But it's good value.'

'As a performance, you mean?' Dominic gave him a look which was almost dangerous – a flash of something unknown behind the brown eyes. 'Don't you see, Marcus, that's exactly what it might be. I used to do a lot of acting, you know. I'm reliably informed that the little boy lost act is one of the best in my repertoire. So my landlord says, anyway.' He shivered a little, and rose slowly to his feet. 'I'm going to put some clothes on. For the time being, anyway. Also, I'd quite like a drink.'

Their clothes lay strewn around the sitting room. Dominic pulled on a pair of rather camply-patterned boxer shorts and a tee-shirt and left the room. Marcus jumped up, pulled on his blue linen trousers and rather grubby sports shirt and followed. Dominic was in the kitchen, fiddling with bottles.

'You're not ruining whisky with Coca Cola again, are you?'

'No. Just a couple of harmless, orthodox gin and tonics. And don't knock Scotch and Coke. It holds dear sentimental memories for me.'

'Is that what Guy used to drink?'

'God, no.' Marcus sensed that Dominic was making a great effort of pulling himself together. 'I'm not sentimental about him at all, you know. In a way that's a shame. I mean,' he went on, handing Marcus a large drink, 'I can't look back at the good times we had together and feel that twinge of nostalgia. That's the trouble with hating someone you used to love. Someone you used to adore. You begrudge every minute you ever gave him. You resent every penny you ever spent on him, with him. And you know that you're being ridiculous. Guy and I had some great times together. We practically had our own private language, a whole code system no-one else understood. And yet it was all based on a fallacy, an illusion. My fallacy, my illusion. My incapacity to see what Guy was really like, how he really felt, what he really thought.'

'What he really thought about you?'

'About me. About anything. Sorry.' Dominic leaned back against the stainless steel sink; Marcus accordingly rested himself against the fridge. 'This is all madly abstract. Concrete facts: Guy Latimer and I were introduced by a mutual friend at university, when I was a post-grad student. The guilty party was a very good, straight friend of mine called Simon. We had another mutual friend called Katy Goldsmith, whom you may rightly suspect of being a woman. She is now a phenomenally successful lawyer, in fact I bet she drew up Guy's wills. When I first met him, he was having all kinds of problems over coming out. I mean, he was in many ways madly socially insecure. He never lost that. He was young for his age. I suppose that's why Katy did her damnedest to protect him from me. Joke. She thought I'd terrify and bully him into being something he wasn't i.e., viz., gay.'

Marcus squinted over his drink. 'But Guy was gay, wasn't he? I mean – '

'Oh yes, a real little fruit. But Katy didn't like the idea. She even dragged Guy into bed to try and prove the point.' Dominic laughed. 'Hopeless, apparently. Well, largely so.' He gestured with his drink-free arm. 'Some initial success, which I suppose is more than I ever managed to get out of him. So much for my terrifying, bullying, overpowering personality.'

'Did you ever actually try, though?' Marcus asked a shade drily.

'Well now, there's an interesting question. I suppose you think I must have done.'

'I would have assumed you did. But I can see that you might not have.'

'I almost did. Once. Literally, on one occasion. But it wasn't particularly serious. I was far too much in awe of him to risk losing what little there actually was between us.' Dominic stared into his gin. Marcus gave another puzzled look.

'Forgive me for saying this, but the impression I'd got so far was hardly of an awesome, imposing personality. I mean, to judge from what Michael said, Guy was a timorous creature. Obviously this girl Katy didn't think much of his powers of self-determination. You yourself have said he was socially inept. I mean, the bit I find hard to understand is how you came to get so wound up about him. Was it his looks, or what?'

'I didn't used to think so. But maybe it was.' Dominic looked up, a little guiltily. 'Marcus, I wish I could explain. But I can't. I fell. I fell hopelessly. And I let him see how hopelessly I'd fallen. More or less from the word go.'

Marcus drew a sharp intake of breath between clenched teeth. 'Fatal,' he added, in case Dominic had missed the import of the hiss.

'Absolutely. Guy humiliated me in front of a whole group of people, in the simplest way possible. He just didn't show up. A simple ploy, and one he was rather good at. He used to vary it – sometimes he'd be excessively late, you know, hours rather than minutes – and he would always offer some kind of apology. But never an excuse. It would always be a winsome smile and "I just didn't feel like it" or "I completely lost track of the time." There was one train from Surrey he consistently missed on ten consecutive occasions. But he always knew I'd let him get away with it. He once put the 'phone down on me for a soap opera. But he knew I wouldn't kick up a fuss. He once failed to show up on my birthday because, quote, "I don't like seeing other people." What he meant was that he didn't like being seen with me by other people. Particularly other gay people.

'You know I've never actually met his friend Phil Roxby? I'm not trendy enough. I was allowed to meet Derek Wilkinson once, but only once. Apart from that I was too shameful an accoutrement. I wasn't even allowed to meet his fucking family. He never invited me to his home or took me out to dinner or anything. Because it was supposed to be honour enough for me that he would condescend to be seen at all with me, or spend a moment in my company. After all, I'm so unattractive, so hideous, so old. He used to enjoy pointing out massive numbers of people he'd rather be with than me. He even used to get me to tell him what sex with them would be like. I mean, as far as I know, Michael was his only sexual experience apart from Katy. He got all his sexual kicks through fantasy. But he made me do even that for him. He got into a fabulous habit of ringing me up to tell me how fed up he was of being celibate and how he'd be prepared to do it with anyone; but the one exception was always understood, always there, even sometimes explicitly stated, just so as I wouldn't forget – whoever else, not me. Never me.

'Does this explain things to you more clearly?' Dominic was now very carried away on a tide of unpleasant emotional reminiscence. 'I mean, can you see how things were between Guy and me?'

Marcus said nothing. He looked at Dominic carefully, and realised that he was trembling slightly: the drink shook in his hand as he raised it to his lips. Marcus still found the situation difficult to conceive: Dominic was clearly articulate and not, in his eyes anyway, unattractive. Could he have killed Guy Latimer? Doubtless release from a subjugation of the kind he had just described might induce a feeling of freedom bordering on anarchy, but freedom to murder..? If Dominic could lose sight of his own good points when overestimating Guy in one way, he could possibly be equally capable of losing sight of moral standards when exaggerating Guy's importance in a completely negative manner. Marcus didn't see how Dominic could really have committed the murder, but he tried putting himself in the other's place to see if he would have felt any compunction in harming Guy. He felt he probably wouldn't have had the slightest bit of remorse. And then, of course, there was the money. Marcus didn't dare look at Dominic to ask him what he felt he must.

'Look,' he said, 'do you mind if I ask you about money? I mean, are you financially OK, or are you like me, i.e. in a bloody mess?'

'Probably worse,' Dominic said, gently now, 'in that my bank have written me off, keep me on a tight lead, and nobody else will take my business.' He laughed ironically. 'So yes, the financial kite would fly. That's why I could almost believe Guy planned it himself.'

'But if he hadn't seen you for months, how could he know your financial position?'

'He fucking caused it. For a year he ponced off me, in the subtlest way, always insisting he didn't want to. Then he pushed me into a holiday I couldn't afford, because without me he wouldn't get rent-free accommodation. He gave me countless depressions which forced me into countless shopping sprees and booze binges. And when he faked a row and ditched me, the bank foreclosed. For the last two months I was seeing him, I was living in daily dread of that particular axe. He knew that. He even managed to lend me some money, just enough so that when I repaid it to him – grand queeny farewell gesture – it put the finishing touches to everything. I had to grovel to get the bank to honour that last cheque to him. Thank Christ they did. The humiliation of sending Guy a rubber cheque would have finished me. It was bad enough having to post-date it. So the fact it was post-dated told him all he needed to know about my finances.'

'But' – Marcus felt he could look Dominic in the face again now – 'you surely couldn't have known that Guy had named you in his will, could you? After all, he only did it the day before he – was killed.'

Dominic laughed ruefully. 'Marcus, when you told me about that just now, didn't it occur to you? I mean, weren't you expecting a little more surprise? Well – I was a bit surprised. You see, I thought he was joking spitefully. I thought it was a spur of the moment lie meant as a jibe. I didn't believe him for a moment. And I certainly haven't mentioned it to the Police yet. But he did actually tell me last night. In anger. Well, in spite – Guy was never sufficiently emotionally involved with anyone to feel anger. And, for all I know, somebody heard him tell me. He wasn't exactly muttering. Well, you can't in that place, can you?' He sighed. 'What happened was that I got fed up with listening to him and pointed out that I couldn't afford to buy him any more coffee, but that was largely his fault for bleeding me dry in the good old days. He told me for the four hundredth time how selfish I was, and if it made me feel any better then he'd left me all his money in his will. That was more or less the parting shot. He didn't tell me how much he was worth, though.'

He sighed again. 'Hey ho,' he uttered aloud, then he put down his glass on the draining board and stepped forward so that he could take hold of Marcus's arms. 'Don't you see?' he said, staring into Marcus's eyes, 'I'm really rather sunk.'

Marcus put his glass down, and returned the physical contact. 'Do you want to go on talking about this?' he asked. 'Or shall we change the subject? After all, it's not fair of me to put you through all this, when the Police will again soon.'

'I'd rather talk to you about it,' Dominic replied. 'I think it's probably more important to me that you should believe me than that the Police should.'

'Frankly, I'd rather it was the other way round,' Marcus said. 'You've told me enough for me to know that you're worth ten Guy Latimers, so who gives a fuck if you did cut him to shreds? I mean, I don't think you did – ' He stopped. 'Well – '

'Look, can I chop up an onion or something useful? You know, make a start on dinner.' Dominic broke away and started opening drawers. He had volunteered to make them a pasta dish. Marcus directed him to the right cupboards, and Dominic began chopping vegetables. Marcus meanwhile replenished the glasses.

Dominic watched him with what seemed to be affection. Marcus returned the look. He felt sure now within himself that his destiny was somehow linked with Dominic's, and he was determined to do what he could to prevent him from being suspected any further of Guy Latimer's murder. In short, Marcus Grey felt sure he'd fallen in love. Of course, being a Scot he was pragmatic and wary: and he realised that Dominic would probably be wary, too, and somewhat scarred as a result of his experience with Guy. Marcus put down the gin bottle and reached for the tonic. 'How do you know,' Dominic asked with a grin, 'that I don't want a Scotch and Coke?'

'Bloody heathen!' growled Marcus. 'What is this bloody Scotch and Coke thing, anyway?' He reached for the whisky bottle, but Dominic indicated that he hadn't really intended his question to be taken seriously.

'Ah. It's a rather personal thing.'

'Oh, all right, if you don't want to tell me – ' Marcus felt that his attempt at friendly indifference was pretty poor and more akin to tetchiness. He suddenly was offended: after all, they'd been talking about 'rather personal things' fairly deeply, so it seemed unfair to clam up all at once.

'That's not exactly what I mean. I do want to tell you. I mean, actually it's all very tied together with all this.' He resumed chopping. 'You know I was the last of the three of us – you, me and Michael – to see Guy alive? Well, you never did, of course.'

Marcus said nothing, merely nodded. But he instantly thought that this was true so long as Michael hadn't killed Guy.

'That was some time round quarter to eleven, eleven. The club was still pretty empty. I suppose Guy must have been killed fairly soon after our little discussion ended. Look, Marcus, I can actually say fairly definitely where I was and what I was doing then and who I was with. I mean, I know. But I can't tell the Police.'

Marcus swallowed hard, feeling the unfamiliar pang of jealousy. 'You mean you were with someone,' he said levelly. He thought for a moment. 'You mean, having sex, don't you?'

Dominic nodded. 'Actually, we did have sex, yes. I hadn't really intended to, nor had he, but that was the thing about Dennis and me, we could never keep our hands off each other.'

Marcus swallowed again. Dennis. 'So you'd met this man before?' he asked, excessively casually.

'Yes. Oh yes. I'm in love with him. Well – I was last night anyway.' He turned to look at Marcus again. ' Please don't be angry with me. But I don't think so little of you that I can lie to you.'

'I have no rights over you,' Marcus replied coolly. Suddenly he was feeling a little sick, winded. He had gone too far too fast.

'Oh, Marcus, don't be ridiculous,' Dominic said, with a slight wail to his voice. 'You already have very definite rights over me, if only for your kindness. And let me explain about Dennis. I love him. He loves me. But it is over, finished, past and done with. It has to be. Because he also loves his wife and his ten year old daughter. He loves his home. He loves comfort and security. He loves me enough, perhaps, to give up his wife. But he doesn't love me enough to give up everything. Not unless I had some financial stability to offer. So it is over. I knew it was, anyway, even though he agreed to meet me last night. He'd been refusing to see me for weeks.'

Marcus began to relax a little. He tried a smile. It seemed, judging from Dominic's reaction, to work. It wasn't quite how he felt yet, but he was beginning to move towards it.

'So,' he said, moving over to Dominic and putting a reassuring arm around his podgy waist, 'what happened last night?'

The reassurance worked both ways as Dominic carefully nestled into his arm whilst continuing to mingle onion, garlic, pepper, mushroom and tomatoes. Dominic explained how Guy had accosted him in the upper bar, giving Marcus more or less word for word the same account he had given Detective Sergeant Morgan.

'So he was prattling on about AIDS and danger and to be honest I wasn't listening. Well not very carefully. You see, I'd arranged to meet Dennis by the cloakroom at eleven. I just wanted to get rid of Guy. He was the last person in the world I wanted to see right then. You see, since the whole thing with Dennis happened, particularly since it became obvious that he was going to chuck me, I started resenting Guy like crazy – you know, I kept thinking that if it hadn't been for him, I might have been financially stable, or I might have had the self-confidence to fight harder for Dennis, or I might have met him earlier. Crazy and stupid things. And he was just prattling on about AIDS.

'Well, we're all worried, but Guy – really, I mean, Michael seemed pretty sensible from the brief glimpse I got. I asked him what he was getting at. He accused me of being selfish again. We had our little exchange about money and he told me about the will. Oh yes, he said that would show – how did he put it? – show me and my friends just who the real mercenary little shit was. A phrase a friend of mine used of Guy to his face once. After Guy had spent an evening with us ignoring me every time I tried to talk to him. Anyway, after we'd said all this, it was just past eleven, so I just went off to meet Dennis. After all, that was why I was there.'

He laughed. 'Dennis and I went behind the stage to have a private chat, which ended up with me giving him a blow job. Then he told me – just like that, as brutal as you like – that that was just for goodbye. That it would have been different if I'd had any money at all saved up, even two or three thousand, but he couldn't afford maintenance and another flat and the kind of upbringing his daughter deserved and the kind of life he wanted us both to have. He put his cock away and walked off and out. Leaving me there with – well, not exactly egg on my face, and tears in my eyes. So I wandered off and decided to get pissed. The next thing I knew, you were looking at me. Thank God.' And Dominic stopped chopping vegetables and turned and kissed Marcus gently on the mouth.

'Thank you. So-o,' Marcus continued, elongating his vowel, 'you actually have an alibi. Well, that's good.'

Marcus was, in fact, still a little perturbed. He didn't want to get involved with someone he genuinely wanted simply because he happened to be on the rebound. He supposed that he preferred this explanation to Dominic's being the murderer, but not by as great a margin as he should have done. However, Dominic seemed to have other ideas. He gasped and laughed, almost in mockery.

'Yes, but Marcus – ' Marcus knitted his brows in puzzlement. 'Look, I can't possibly use it.'

'What, because you were having sex? I know it's not strictly legal in a public place, but – '

'Oh, don't be silly, not that. First of all, there's Dennis's family. His wife knows that he's gay, but obviously his daughter doesn't and mustn't. Neither do the people at his office. And his job is very important and very security-conscious. He'd be sacked if they found out.'

'Och, I'm surprised you're quite so prepared to protect him – after all, he seems to have used you pretty badly – '

'No.' Dominic shook his head vehemently. 'I promised once not to give him any hassle or problems. And I can't. I mustn't. But anyway,' he laughed ironically, 'even if he could back me up, it wouldn't help – '

'Of course it would. It covers you for the time of death.'

'Only possibly. Not definitely. I could still have nipped outside before meeting you. The timing can't be certain. In fact, if the Police heard all this, they might decide I definitely must have done it.'

'Well, I don't see – ' Marcus began, but Dominic laid a finger over his mouth.

'Of course, you don't want to. Think. What did Dennis say to me?' Marcus thought. Realisation dawned. 'Right. Two birds with one stone. To get the man I was in love with using the money of the man who'd damaged me so terribly. Neat. And what a great alibi, too – drops me completely in the shit, in fact. And really, Marcus, it leaves you just where you were. As far as knowing whether I'm innocent or not goes.'

Dominic picked up the vegetable knife again. Then just for a second he feigned a stab at Marcus with it. Marcus, naturally, flinched. Dominic put the knife down again and promptly burst into tears.

# 6: Uptown Girl

The early evening sun bathed the carefully restored facade of the Kensington Georgian terrace, making it look strangely, arctically chilly. The pure white shone like snow. Oldcastle muttered something inaudible under his breath; Morgan, who delighted in sotto voce comments and had quite an ear for them, strained to decipher his Chief's utterance, but failed. From previous experience, he knew that the Chief Inspector was no great fan of this part of town: it most strongly epitomized the London he despised, the London he'd learnt to despise in his Yorkshire youth, the London of 'flash buggers,' from the Hooray Henries to Chelsea Football Club. In many ways, Morgan knew, Oldcastle felt more at home in Brixton than he did amidst the upwardly mobile social splendours of some newly-restored Georgian des. res.

Over the telephone, Katy Goldsmith had sounded to be every bit a part of this world. It was clear that she had her social pecking order neatly worked out: and equally clear that the Police came fairly low down on it. Her 'agreeing' to see Morgan and Oldcastle at all seemed to have depended on her willingness to sacrifice some pre-dinner social event, and she regarded their visit, to judge from her tone, as part nuisance and part favour to 'poor Guy'. Interestingly, Morgan got the further impression that 'poor Guy' hadn't really featured too high on her list of social priorities, either: it was a purely tonal impression and could very well have been wrong, but still it was there.

She certainly, at any rate, sounded as though she was born to all this lot: at a guess, her parents would have a country cottage with a few horses at its disposal, as would she when she decided to get married. Morgan, who for all his Welsh name was London born and bred – though he had taken his degree at UEA – always felt that he should have aspired to this kind of lifestyle (a word he vehemently detested, in any case) more than he actually did. But then, when you called it a lifestyle, you said everything about it: it was neatly, carefully designed and planned, fashionable, and above all lacking in any real individuality. A lifestyle showed that if you had taste in anything it was only in designer labels; and principally, a lifestyle showed that you had one thing in abundance. Money. Disposable income.

The car pulled up outside one of the indistinguishable houses: Morgan peered out and saw that the number on the porch pillar was actually the one they were looking for. He jumped out of the car and ran around the other side to open Oldcastle's door. The Chief Inspector frowned at him as he struggled out onto the pavement. 'God Almighty, you're not a flunkey,' he said with a bluff disdain.

But Morgan knew that his boss was equally capable of sitting in the car waiting for the door to be opened. The fact that he hadn't suggested that he was still interested in the case, despite a somewhat disappointing afternoon revisiting all the bar staff and door staff, who had merely solidified their evidence of the previous day. This had followed on from an infinitely more frustrating morning conducting the Latimer family to view their loved one's body. Of that lot, only the cousin had seemed at all straightforward. It struck Morgan that the other Latimer boy, Colin, would probably be quite forthcoming in his own taciturn way if handled correctly: but Oldcastle hadn't really helped with his almost explicitly stated assumption that Colin spent his weekends beating up old ladies, smashing windows and carving up Arsenal, Tottenham and West Ham supporters.

Yet despite the day's slow progress, Oldcastle still seemed enthusiastic enough as they made their way up the steps into the porch and to the front door. Morgan scanned the six bells and pressed the one next to a card marked 'GOLDSMITH'. A crackly deep female voice asked who was there and, on being told, a buzz came from the door to indicate that it was prepared to give way.

Inside, the hall was neat, tidy and extremely blue. Morgan heard a clatter coming down the stairs; he looked up and saw on the first landing a girl of medium height and dark colouring. Not exactly pretty, but extremely distinguished. A long, but not big, nose; eyes he could see even from the length of a flight of stairs: and altogether more individuality than he had expected. It struck him that she was suddenly embarrassed; she was pulling down slightly on her short skirt. However successful she was, she was also, Morgan appreci-ated, still very young; and he had never before been more conscious of his own natural heaviness, something almost antedeluvian about himself.

'Are you the policemen?' she asked in a deep, fruity voice. 'Well, stupid question, really,' she added before they could reply. 'Do come up. I'm afraid there isn't a lift.'

Still encumbered by a sense of his own heaviness, Morgan climbed the stairs, slightly ahead of his Chief. He heard another Oldcastle mutter – this one sounded distinctly like 'Steady there, boy.' Like an ever elusive phantom, Katy Goldsmith remained a landing ahead of the two detectives until they reached the second floor. There she leaned against the lintel of an open door, looking, despite her colouring and size, like a portrait of Marlene Dietrich. She waited and allowed Morgan and Oldcastle to reach her.

Without moving her body, she gestured with her arm into the flat: 'Sitting room straight ahead.' At the end of a longish dark hallway another door stood open: all other doors were firmly (and, to Morgan's mind, purposefully) closed. They made their way into a white, spacious room, furnished with a beige suite, scatter cushions, an expensive stereo system in an expensive cabinet, with what seemed like hundreds of records and tapes strewn around it. On the glass table the day's copy of *The Observer*, in its various chunks, was ineptly folded up. On top of the flimsiest section of the paper lay a paperback Morgan recognised as a novel which had, to everyone's surprise, failed to win several major literary prizes in 1984. He picked it up. Funny how he'd lost his appetite for reading these days. He often wondered if it would return, or whether the job had devoured it. He heard the sitting room door close and, almost guiltily, he put the book down again. Katy Goldsmith stood, back against the door, surveying him.

'Have you read it?' she asked. Morgan shook his head. 'It's rather overrated in my opinion. I'm not sure I'll ever actually finish it,' she explained. 'I should have listened to Dominic.'

Oldcastle looked at her quizzically. 'So our Mr Palmer dispenses literary advice, does he?'

'None better.' Katy walked across the room and very authoritatively sat down in an armchair, thus preventing the two policemen from forcing her into the settee. Morgan was thus relegated to perching on one end of that voluminous couch, evidently designed to make people look slothful and untidy.

'I suppose,' she went on, in a tone of voice which strongly implied that other people's habits are very tiresome, 'that if I offer you any kind of drink whatsoever you'll remind me that you're on duty.' Oldcastle looked as though he was about to deny this, but Katy headed him off. 'So,' she said simply, 'I shan't offer. Now – what can I tell you about poor Guy? Or do you want to talk about poor Dominic instead?'

Morgan registered that despite his literary advice Dominic Palmer didn't hold a higher position in the pecking order than Guy Latimer.

'Well,' Oldcastle said in his best paternal manner, obviously not too put out about the unoffered drink, 'I think we'll want to talk to you about both of them at some juncture. But first of all, Miss Goldsmith, I'd like you to tell me what you were doing last Friday evening.'

'I was at my boyfriend's. Look, do you mind if I smoke?'

Without waiting for a reply, she pulled out a packet of cigarettes and a lighter from a shelf under the table. Morgan eyed these hungrily as she lit herself one. She affected to ignore this.

'My boyfriend's name is Stephen Bishop. He lives in Clapham.' She gave them the exact address. 'I'm afraid that there was no-one with us, so no-one can corroborate my story.'

'You didn't leave the Clapham house at all?'

'No. The first I knew of all this was when you rang me yesterday afternoon.'

'And when did you last see Guy Latimer?' Oldcastle asked.

'Thursday afternoon. He rang me at the office just after lunch and said that he wanted to make a new will. I arranged to meet him here at four o'clock. He seemed not to be at work that day. I can get time off pretty easily at the moment,' she added, but refrained from elaborating any further. 'Guy was late, of course.' She laughed. 'He had the most appalling sense of time. I know he used to drive Dominic round the twist. Poor Dominic's always so madly punctual. If he's on his own.'

'So he arrived some time after four.'

'Some time after four thirty, in fact.'

'Did he say where he'd been at all?' Morgan interpolated, hoping that Katy Goldsmith might have some light to shed on JP. 'At any time during that day?'

'No. Not a word. I don't think I asked, anyway, and Guy didn't tend to volunteer information of his own free will.' Katy frowned. 'You must realise, Guy and I hadn't been very close recently – not for a year or more. By a pure freak I saw him twice in a fortnight. Well, that was business.'

'Aye,' Oldcastle cut in, decidedly Yorkshire, 'now tell us about that. Why does a healthy young man of his age, who isn't a millionaire by any manner of means, start making wills and then changing them every other minute like somebody in a soap opera?'

Katy laughed at this. Morgan was struck by how little grief there seemed to be for Guy. This wasn't, though, as much of a novelty as he would have liked it to be. Particularly amongst the sophisticated, death reminded the living that simply being alive is a good thing, and they couldn't help feeling smug. And now there seemed to be a reaction against the piety of never vilifying the dead, to the extent that it seemed to be getting harder and harder to find anyone prepared to be nice about a deceased person. Katy stopped laughing and began to answer the question.

'Guy adored soap operas. He longed to be Joan Collins or someone, you know. I can just imagine that he would have changed his will every fortnight for fifty years, simply for the drama of it.' She paused, as if to emphasise that she was intending to be serious now. 'Guy led a very boring life for the most part,' she explained. 'He was so cripplingly shy and socially incapable. Not much by way of personality, you see. And it took him so long and so much agony to decide that he was gay, too. Then he went back to living at home after university. A mistake, I thought. I almost offered him a room here, but – well, Guy wasn't, as I'd found out when we were students, the easiest person to live with. Half the time he wanted to confide in you, the other half he didn't want you near him. It's so sad that this had to happen just when he'd managed to escape his awful family and find a new boyfriend. But it was typical of Guy that it took a row to get him to move out. I mean, he and Dominic could easily have got somewhere together when they were going out, but Guy just wouldn't.'

'Hang on,' Morgan said. 'Palmer and Latimer were "going out", you say?' This didn't tally with what had been said so far.

'Oh yes,' she said, 'on-off-on-off. A kind of gay Burton and Taylor. Of course, it was all Dominic, the impetus for it. I mean, he was crazy about Guy. Guy liked being adored. And he liked being organized. Dominic ran his social life for him. Dominic was really very good for Guy. I doubt whether he'd have got hold of this Michael, or had the courage even to row with his family and walk out that way, if Dominic hadn't helped him find himself a bit. Well – a lot, actually.'

'Now then,' Oldcastle said in his best bluff manner, 'you make it sound like this lad Guy was a bit – well, to put it bluntly – unscrupulous.' He let his accent savour the vowels of this last word.

'Oh' – Katy leaned forward and gestured with her cigarette, as if taking part in a television debate – 'No, no. No. Not at all. Well – not the way you mean. You see, Dominic always puts himself in the way of being used. I've seen him do it before. That's the sad thing – his personal relationships always seem to end up in extreme situations. He gets far too involved with people who can't get involved to an equal extent. It happened before Guy. But until all this happened, I thought they must have made it up in some way.' She stubbed out her cigarette. 'Because of the will.'

'Ah yes,' Oldcastle said drily, 'the will. Which brings us back to where we were. So perhaps you'd care to tell us about Guy Latimer's two wills. Both of them. What happened when he came to see you, exactly what he said, did, gave you to understand.'

Katy leaned back again and nodded. It was not a particularly agreeable nod, and she suddenly more or less contradicted it. 'Well, I can't reasonably be expected to remember everything exactly.'

'As far as is reasonably possible,' Oldcastle said patiently. 'In your own time.' And he too sat back, a movement Morgan recognised as being a sign of taking root.

Katy thought for a moment. 'I hadn't seen Guy for several months. I'd had a change of address note in early July and I kept meaning to ring him, but I've been far too busy. And I was away for a week.' Morgan was highly amused by the self-justification that emanated from all this. Clearly 'poor Guy' had been more or less on his way out of the Katy Goldsmith social calendar. 'Then he rang me up one Monday evening, and said he wanted to see me fairly urgently. He said it was "sort of business" as long as I wasn't intending to charge him. He wasn't any more forthcoming than that. So we arranged to meet for a drink after work on the Thursday. I suggested a pub, but he more or less insisted on our meeting here. I gave way quite easily, because Guy doesn't usually – didn't usually have strong views about things like that – about much, in fact. Besides which, it made life easier for me. So – ' she paused and gathered her thoughts again. 'Guy arrived about five.'

'He was alone?' Morgan threw in.

'Yes. Well – yes and no. He came in here alone, but apparently his friend Michael was somewhere in the vicinity.'

'Just on the first occasion?'

'No. Both times he told me Michael was around shopping. That was – well – a bit odd. But fairly typical Guy, in many ways. He was fairly bad at groups of more than two.'

'Hang on,' Oldcastle said, 'you're telling us that both times he came up to see you to talk wills, Hamilton came to the door with him more or less, but just hung around outside. That sounds a mite implausible, Miss Goldsmith, begging your pardon.'

'I'm sorry, but that's how it was. It'll probably seem even more "implausible" ' – Morgan could almost hear the inverted commas being put around Oldcastle's chosen adjective – 'when I tell you that Guy said it was Michael's idea that he should make a will in the first place. Particularly as Michael could perfectly legitimately have witnessed both or either of them. I mean, I assumed the second time that Guy was just going to put Michael in his brother's place, but then – '

'Fine.' Oldcastle interrupted decisively. 'I don't mean to appear rude, but if we could confine ourselves to strict chronological sequence, it would be of the greatest assistance. I'm sure it'll help you in recalling events too. You see, I'm afraid I don't have quite your agility of mind. The Sergeant here is more of your man for a tangled narrative structure. Never puts anything in the right bloody order, do you Stuart?'

Morgan smiled weakly; he never relished the role of butt to relieve the tension. It wasn't clear in this case, either, whether the tactic had worked. 'Now,' Oldcastle went on, less jovially, 'Latimer arrived, accompanied by Hamilton, who didn't come in.'

'As I said, Guy said he went shopping or something. I didn't actually see him. Not a glimpse.'

'Did you try to?' Morgan asked, getting a rude glare for his pains. He realised that the implication behind his question was, in its way, quite rude.

'Not particularly,' Katy said with more than a drop of acid. 'Guy arrived. I let him in. He came upstairs. He entered my flat. We both came in here. No – I made some coffee, then I joined him in here. We sat down.' The policemen looked at each other. They recognised parody when they heard it. 'I asked him if he was in a hurry, as he seemed to want to get on with things, and he said that Michael was hanging around nearby, maybe shopping. So you see, it might have been a convenient fiction, to prevent things going on too long.'

Oldcastle nodded. 'Right,' Katy resumed efficiently, 'I made a few social pleasantries, like asking him about his new address, about Michael, but he really didn't give me much by way of reply. He told me quite a bit, though, about the row with his father.'

'Really?' Oldcastle sat up. 'Please elaborate.'

'Guy said that he'd got home from work one evening in late June to find that his bedroom had been ransacked and various books and magazines and pictures taken from his drawers and shelves.'

'What – porn?' Oldcastle's distaste made itself plain.

'No. That's not Guy's style at all. Mainly novels and gay

newspapers, I think. Well, he said he had a choice then – either to pretend that it hadn't happened, or to have a row about it.'

'And he chose the latter?' Morgan deduced.

'Well, he said that when he went downstairs again, he found his mother and father in the garden. And they were burning all these things of his. Quite openly. So he didn't have a choice any more. Actually, he said it was the first thing he'd seen his parents do together since he was about five. Anyway, they shouted at one another. Guy's father asked him how he dared pollute the house with this filth and told him either to get a woman or to get out and it was no good running to hide behind Mummy's apron any more, while his mother just told him what a disappointment he was, how loathsome she found him. That really shook him, actually, because she'd known he was gay for a couple of years. He'd never had any idea she felt so strongly.

'Anyway, his father went on shouting about perverts, his mother went on telling him he was evil, and that Dominic and Michael were evil too, not to mention me, although that seems a bit odd as I'm a woman. With all that going on I'm not so surprised that Guy behaved as stupidly as he did.'

The two detectives waited, but Katy obviously decided that her narrative called for a bit of suspense at this point.

'And how exactly was he stupid?' Oldcastle asked impatiently.

'Well, if he said what he said he said.' She stopped, as if to admire the inelegance of her sentence structure. 'He said that he called his mother a loony old bag – which has some truth in it, by the way – and then suggested to his father that he'd joined the Police because he really fancied men in uniform and he'd noticed how he eyed blokes up on the street.'

Morgan winced visibly and Oldcastle let out a whistle. PC Latimer was a physically crude and effective specimen, they had found, and probably not the sort of man to take that kind of remark lightly. Of course, Malcolm Latimer himself hadn't come up with any of this detail – nor had any of Guy Latimer's other friends. The Constable's description had been of a 'scene' in which a few words were spoken, he shouted, his wife wept, and Guy, overcome by remorse, left immediately after packing 'a few things.' No book-burning, no abuse from Guy: and definitely not what seemed likely to emerge now.

'I think you can guess what happened,' Katy went on. 'Crunch. Wallop. Blood and bruises. So Guy said. And the promise of more if he turned up at home again.' She paused. 'I assumed he was telling the truth. It's not the kind of lie Guy told.'

What was the kind of lie Guy told? Morgan wondered. And did Katy Goldsmith realise the inference that could be drawn from this almost casual phrase? 'I mean,' she went on, 'I don't know what his family have told you. I don't think his brother and sister were there. I don't know if he told them what happened. He told his cousin – the one he went to France with.'

She stopped and reached for her cigarettes once more. Again Morgan's hungry eyes were ignored. 'Anyway, Guy told me all about this. Then he said that Michael had suggested that he should make a will, because if anything happened to him, his mother and father would get his savings. And he had no intention of letting them near his money.'

'Well, now,' Oldcastle said slowly, 'did he say whether he thought anything was likely to happen to him?'

'No, not really.'

'Not really? Did you get the impression he was being threatened, then?'

'No, not at all. I just thought he was being paranoid. I don't know whether he thought his father was going to murder him, or whether he thought Dominic was plotting some hideous revenge – '

'Do you think either of those is likely,' Morgan jumped in.

'Well, either of them's possible,' Katy replied, mulling the ideas over as she spoke. 'His father's a brute, like most – ' She prevented the generalisation actually being uttered in the nick of time. 'And Dominic's certainly extreme enough, although he tends to threaten suicide rather than murder, but – '

Oldcastle held his hands out in front of him slightly, like a conductor. 'Can we just go back to the story line for a moment?' He made a levelling off gesture. 'So Guy Latimer made a will on Michael Hamilton's advice so as to prevent his parents getting their hands on his money. Right. Now. In the first instance he named his brother as heir. Did he give any reason for that?'

'Well' – she looked into the air for inspiration – 'not quite as such. All he said was, and I quote, "Colin's safe enough for now." I didn't probe. But I did get the impression that it was a temporary measure. As it was. So, I drew up a document and my flatmate and her boyfriend, who happened to be in, signed it as witnesses. Guy finished his coffee. I offered him some alcohol. He refused and left. We didn't arrange to meet or anything, just promised to get in touch sometime.'

'Did you discuss anything else on that occasion?' Morgan asked.

'Not especially. I asked if he and Dominic were speaking again yet. He got a bit embarrassed, so I made a joke and changed the subject. It seemed the kindest thing to do at the time. I wish I'd pushed it a bit now.'

'Now, yes,' Oldcastle said, implying all kinds of negligence on Katy's part. 'I take it that no other motivation behind this passion for will-making emerged.'

'Not particularly.' She headed off another question about to be provoked by her choice of negative phrase. 'Look, Guy had a distinctly morbid streak. He wouldn't sleep with anyone for ages because he was terrified of catching AIDS. He even worried when – well, that doesn't matter.'

She blushed a little and looked around behind the armchair at the wall. Both Morgan and Oldcastle jumped to the same conclusion. They looked at each other and Katy caught them doing so. She laughed lightly and unconvincingly.

'It was only once and a total fiasco. A very long time ago. He's not even my type. I prefer – well, men, I suppose, rather than boys.' She smiled at Morgan, to make it quite clear that he was everything, in her eyes, that Guy Latimer wasn't.

Interesting, Morgan considered, what a bit of self-provoked embarrassment can bring on. Until then he'd thought her quite attractive and admirable. It was strange how his brief immersion into this odd world had shaken his attitudes: after all, he'd have agreed with her instinctively not so very long ago. The Guy Latimers, Michael Hamiltons, Dominic Palmers of this world – well, they weren't quite part of it, were they? But then you met them properly. Then you had to stop generalising if you were going to do your job properly. Just as you had to stop generalising about football supporters or policemen. What surprised Morgan was how little Oldcastle was generalising. Either that or he was saving it all for Michael Hamilton or Dominic Palmer, or for when he got bored with it all. At least, so far only Colin Latimer had been subjected to the Chief Inspector's worst side. That had been truly dreadful.

'Well, son, what kind of knife do you use? 'Course you use a knife, all you Chelsea boys – what do you call yourselves? Some fancy name or other – you've all got knives.'

'I haven't got a knife,' Colin had replied belligerently, his handsome face a picture of depressed truculence. 'I don't belong to no Firm. I just watch the football. And I wouldn't stitch up my own brother.'

'Yes, but he was a disgrace, wasn't he, son? A nasty little queer. I bet they'd take the mick something dreadful, the other boys in your mob. And anyway, you thought you'd get his money, didn't you?

You didn't know he'd cut you out, did you? A waste of time cutting him up, really, wasn't it?' Morgan had wondered through all this whether Oldcastle seriously entertained this theory in any way whatsoever. 'You hated him really, didn't you?'

Colin had sat, morose, stiff. 'He was my brother. Like any brother he was a bastard sometimes. But I wouldn't kill him. You must be sick or something. I was here all night watching telly.'

In fact, he had not delivered himself of all these views and explanations at one and the same time, but in response to various reruns by Oldcastle of his central line of questioning. Morgan still could not fathom what the purpose of this attack had been; this approach to Colin Latimer wouldn't bring anything to light. It was by treating people as individuals that you found out how to know the truth or otherwise of what they were saying. At least Oldcastle was managing to treat Katy Goldsmith as an individual.

'So,' he said to her, in his best paternal manner, obviously designed to gloss over her indiscretion, 'you had no further contact with Guy Latimer until he rang you after lunch on the day before he was killed?'

'No, I didn't.' She shook her head. 'He rang about two. I could tell from his voice that it was terribly urgent. So, as I said, we agreed to meet here.'

'Right,' Oldcastle drawled. 'Now. You say he came here alone again, but that he said that Hamilton was in the offing, as it were. Is that correct?' She nodded. 'Now, tell me about the second visit. First of all, how was he?'

Katy thought. 'Interesting,' she said at length. 'He was much more excited than usual. You see, usually when you met Guy he'd give you a big smile, a garbled bit of gossip, then leave you to do all the talking, except for the occasional comment or any item of news you could worm out of him. Even when it was something major like his being chucked out of home. And usually he'd sit tight, one expression on his face. But – well, that afternoon he was definitely different. Funny, I hadn't thought about it really. He kept moving all the time. He kept saying things off the top of his head.'

'Sounds as though he was nervous,' Oldcastle suggested.

'Yes, but there was more to it,' she insisted. 'Guy was always nervous. He seemed as though he'd come to some vastly important decision, or was in the process of reaching one. That's it, really. He'd been sort of – galvanised. I think that's the word. I remember it from Science at school.'

'Can you remember any of the things he said "off the top of his head?" '

'A lot of them were very trivial things about films and music, fairly disjointed most of the time. And completely lost on me, I'm afraid. One or two were dreadfully smutty. Half the time he was there I wasn't really listening because I was drawing up the document for him. I asked him if he was sure this time.'

'What did he say to that?'

'He said, "Probably not. But it's quite a laugh, a bit of a giggle. Don't you think?" Those were more or less his exact words.'

'Did you ask him what he meant?'

'No. I wasn't all that interested at the time. I'm not sure he'd have told me anyway. After all he was being decidedly mercurial about the whole thing.' A note of disapproval crept into her voice. 'I mean, he buggered up my afternoon – I had to change a lot of arrangements to accommodate him – then he waltzes in here and calmly announces – well, anything but calmly, but you know what I mean – that all he wants is to make another will. I assumed he was going to put Michael in it, but he just giggled when I said that. When he told me who he wanted put in it, I asked if he and Dominic had made things up between them and he just laughed. I asked him if he was serious and he got almost violent about it: yes, he did, he was certain, he was prepared to pay me. So I just shut up and got on with it. He prattled on, alternating between silly remarks and lugubrious pronouncements, and suddenly he went all serious. He said that if anything did happen to him, he was sure that Dominic needed the money badly and perhaps he hadn't been entirely fair to Dominic, and maybe it would shut up one or two of Dominic's friends, who all really hated him. Then he went giggly again. Then he went serious and silent.'

She stopped. 'Sorry, this isn't very helpful, is it?'

'Well' – Oldcastle pulled a slight face – 'it's a bit baffling, to tell the truth. It sounds as though the lad was up to something to me.'

'Yes, well, I think you could say that. He sort of pulled himself together after that, though. In fact, he went all wistful and sad – but in a rather energetic sort of way, if you see what I mean.'

'Well – ' Oldcastle began.

'Ah. You don't. Never mind.'

'Not entirely, no.' Oldcastle held up his hand. 'There's no need to explain. I think this is all getting a bit too – ah – what word would you use, Sergeant?'

'Me, sir?' Morgan asked. 'I think impressionistic is probably the word I'd use.'

'I am doing my best,' Katy said, equally aggressive and defensive.

'Oh yes, Miss Goldsmith, we're quite aware of that. Actually, to be perfectly honest, the trouble with this bloody case, pardon my French, as I'm rapidly discovering, is that it's all impressions and opinions and no hard evidence. It's very interesting – very interesting indeed – to discover that Guy Latimer was uncharacteristically agitated the day before he was killed, but it's hardly going to convict whoever did it, now is it?' He smiled sweetly.

Morgan felt suddenly embarrassed, and Katy Goldsmith looked as though she shared this feeling. On occasion, Morgan shared his Chief's impulse to divulge things, such as yesterday when telling Marcus Grey about the wills. But there seemed little point in divulging their own feeling of helplessness. Perhaps this was disillusion setting in with a vengeance – and so quickly. But the worst thing of all was that Oldcastle's statement was true. Even now, forty-eight hours after the event, so little seemed to be definite. As they had feared, the lack of concreteness had allowed some strange and juicy speculation in the Press, not least about poor Guy Latimer himself: he had been, according to one paper, 'the toast of London's gay clubs,' although another had placed him 'on the fringes of the notorious vice ring operating out of Victoria Station.' The persecution of the Latimer family had not begun in earnest when Morgan and Oldcastle had paid their visit that morning to conduct the Latimers to Guy's body. As yet the press persecution of the investigators was inchoate: but then, Morgan and Oldcastle had been unavailable for most of the day.

'I wish I could help you,' Katy said to them both, without any evident sign of sincerity. 'What would you like me to do? Produce a dagger or a revolver?'

Oldcastle scowled. Morgan knew he wanted the knife; he suspected that it wasn't going to be found.

'So,' the Chief Inspector went on, 'Latimer didn't stay any longer? He didn't say where he'd been? He didn't say where he was going?'

'Down the road to pick Michael up from the supermarket. That's all.'

'Right.' Oldcastle clambered to his feet. Katy did not look up at him, but examined her fingernails. This rather ruined the effect of superiority which the senior detective was trying to achieve. 'Tell me, Miss Goldsmith, do you know of any reason why anyone might have killed or might have wished to kill Guy Latimer? And is there anything you feel you ought to tell me which you haven't mentioned already?'

And now Katy did look up. 'I'm terribly sorry, Inspector. I've told you all that I know. And I can't imagine anyone killing Guy in cold blood – not even his father, and not even Dominic. I know that Dominic's said he'd like to kill Guy, but – ' She waved her hand, dismissing the notion.

The control and freedom of her gesture contrasted sharply with the almost physically shrivelled female figure they had confronted that morning: Phyllis Latimer tensely, slowly clenching and unclenching her fists. She had hardly presented, on any of the occasions on which Morgan had seen her so far, the traditional picture of maternal grief: tension and anxiety, certainly; and she seemed unquestionably to be, as an Australian would have it, 'three bangers short of a barbie.' If something was weighing heavily on her, in Morgan's view, then that something could be grief only if it were a very bizarre form of grief. For example, she had withstood seeing her son's corpse in a way that was tantamount to offhand negligence, particularly in view of the cuts and mutilation carved on his face. None of the Latimers, he had noted, had touched Guy's body at all.

Morgan rose to his feet now with difficulty: Katy Goldsmith's sofa was evidently designed to trap people and make getting up again impossible.

'Well,' Oldcastle was saying as Morgan struggled up, 'thank you very much, Miss Goldsmith, for your time and what you have told us.'

'That's quite all right,' she said, indicating quite clearly how put upon she felt. 'I take it you won't need to see me again.' This was not a question.

'Well,' Oldcastle disagreed, 'I'm not entirely sure at the moment. When we've got round to seeing everyone else, we may think of something we'd like to talk to you about.'

'I can't think there'd be anything, in fact.'

'That's rather the point, though, isn't it? You can't now. Right. Well – ' he turned to Morgan. 'I think we'd better make our way, Sergeant.'

'I'll see you out,' volunteered Katy. She led the way to the front door, and pointed them down the stairs.

Outside the house, the day had clouded over. Morgan looked up dubiously at the sky.

'Well, sir?' he said tentatively.

'Nice lass. Far too much brass, though. Pff!' Oldcastle blew an exclamation of impatience. 'Bloody psychological insights and not a fact to be gleaned. Let's hope Mr Hamilton can tell us a little more.'

'I dare say he can, sir. But will he? And will what he tells us be the truth?'

'It'd bloody well better be. Christ, what a day. Mind you, Stuart, if we are going to get bloody nowhere extremely slowly, I'd rather it was in Miss Katy's company than chez Latimer.'

This was the first actual private opinion Oldcastle had offered. They got into the waiting car. Morgan was keen to discover if he would hear more.

'They were a bit grim, weren't they, sir?'

'Grim? I should bloody well say so. I can quite believe that PC Latimer beat his son up. I'd be surprised if he doesn't beat his wife up too. That would explain a lot. Jesus, what thugs those dog-shaggers are. It's coppers like him who make the Katy Goldsmiths of this world despise us so much. I particularly liked his touchingly confiding tone.'

Morgan laughed. It had been, to say the least, grotesque when Malcolm Latimer had begun explaining, in a pleading sort of voice, why, all things considered, Guy was no real loss to the world. 'The world' quite clearly in Malcolm Latimer's view failed to extend very far beyond the boundaries of Malcolm Latimer. He had woven a sad and sorry tale of a son who had despised and rejected everything his father had stood for and offered him; who had used the advantages of an education his father had got for him to turn round and insult and humilate that selfless parent. A son who had broken his mother's heart, and who had finally defiantly announced the worst thing a child could ever tell a parent. That he was a pervert; who had walked out of his decent family home to be kept by another man.

Morgan had felt an instinctive distaste for Latimer and his attitudes: but he wondered whether they were actually anything other than his own writ large and graphic. If his own son turned out to be – well, gay (he was getting used to the word), he wouldn't beat him up, would he? But he would still instinctively condemn the whole thing, see it as a failing. And why?

Settling down in the car again, Morgan began to wonder along this line, knowing all the time it was a distraction. But he couldn't concentrate his mind on small, precise, factual details about Guy Latimer's murder; it stayed diverted on large, vague questions as to the inherent merits of finding women sexually attractive or the terrible failing that being attracted to men constitutes.

'You seem lost in thought, Stuart,' Oldcastle remarked, not entirely without satirical intent. 'The burdens of the graduate copper getting you down?'

A rueful, dutiful laugh, acknowledging the pleasantry. 'Not exactly, sir. I was merely considering some of the ramifications of this case.'

'Very grand. Any useful observations to make?'

'Not really, sir. It was more a question of our attitudes. And Latimer's. And so on.'

'I take it you've not known a great number of homosexuals.'

'No, sir. I was just wondering how I'd react if my boy grew up and turned round and told me that he was – one.'

'Well. I don't see you beating him up, at any rate. Or cutting his face to shreds, if it comes to that.'

'One hopes not, sir.'

'Well, Sergeant.' This return to formality returned them to the matter in hand. 'Let's see what Mr Hamilton has to say for himself. Perhaps he can explain his role in this flurry of will-making.'

Yes, and perhaps he can't as well, Morgan thought. But what Michael Hamilton actually told them about his role in it all came as a complete surprise.

Surrounded by his own particular choice of designer lifestyle, carefully casual and discreetly ambitious, Michael sat with his handsome face resolutely set against looking welcoming or pleasant. He toyed with a gin and tonic in an obviously expensive cut glass, and stared at them both blankly.

'I haven't,' he replied, 'the faintest idea what you're talking about.'

'Now come on, lad,' Oldcastle said. This was the first serious question he had asked Hamilton, and he wasn't disposed to be blocked from the word go. 'Miss Goldsmith told us that the will-making binge was your suggestion, that you actually went up there to her flat and waited in the vicinity while Guy Latimer made the wills – '

'I've never been anywhere near Katy Goldsmith's flat. I never discussed wills with Guy. I didn't give a damn about his money or his property. I was, if you care to check, out of the country when he made the first will.'

'Miss Goldsmith says – ' Morgan began, but Hamilton intercepted this.

'Look, I don't give a screw what Miss Goldsmith says.'

He gave an irritated laugh: Morgan sensed a genuine rufflement of the cool Hamilton facade. Examining him more closely, Morgan detected tiredness in the eyes; from the glorious blue centres, thin red lines marched their way to the cheeks and nose. It crossed Morgan's mind that grief had not kept Michael Hamilton at home on a Saturday night.

'I only found out about this macabre little habit of his this morning. I didn't know what the documents were you and your merry men took away. I didn't care much, either.'

'And how did you find out, might I ask?'

'I would have thought that that was fairly obvious,' the young man returned acidly. Oldcastle frowned. 'Marcus Grey told me when I talked to him over the 'phone at lunchtime today.'

'And you claim that that was the first you knew about Guy Latimer's wills?'

'I don't merely claim that: it happens to be a fact. Look, if you don't believe me, just check with my office; they'll tell you that I was in New York for the last three days of July. Until August 2nd, in fact. Now why the hell should I bother to lie about something like that when the lie would so easily be blown to smithereens?'

Oldcastle gave a hum of displeasure. What Hamilton said was true enough. But there was still a possibility which he could pursue.

'Well,' he went on, 'even if you didn't go to Kensington with Latimer, there still remains, I'm afraid, the possibility that you did discuss the matter of legacies with him.'

'I didn't. Why the hell should I have done? I didn't know how much money he had, exactly. I knew he wasn't poor. Anyway, twenty thousand isn't what I'd call money. It's not a sufficiently large sum for me to do the honour of coveting violently. I can fiddle that much on expenses most fiscal years.'

Hamilton was looking a little bemused, a lot amused. He continued his attack. 'Guy and I only ever talked about money in shops, cinemas and restaurants. He never even got round to discussing a contribution to bills and the mortgage for this place, although I fully intended to bring the subject up in the immediate future if he looked like remaining a fixture. It is, therefore, implausible that we should have discussed something as financially intimate as the disposal of his estate, to use an absurdly grandiose term given that it consisted of twenty lousy grand, a knackered stereo and a load of books he shoplifted. And, while we're at it, if I were so keen for him to settle his estate, why would I suggest either his brother or Dominic Palmer as heirs to those riches beyond the dreams of avarice if I were subsequently going to carve him up?'

Hamilton smiled sweetly and insincerely at them, obviously delighted with his verbal fluency. Morgan laughed uneasily.

'You're rather jumping the gun a little, Mr Hamilton, if you don't mind my saying so. Miss Goldsmith actually told us that you suggested to Guy Latimer that he make a will after his parents had thrown him out, so that they wouldn't get his money if anything happened to him.'

'No such conversation ever took place. As I say, I didn't know, until Marcus told me, that Guy had any money worth speaking of. Which in my view he didn't, anyway. And I didn't care.'

Morgan nodded. 'I see. So you weren't privy to his financial arrangements.'

'No.'

'So you can't explain where this twenty thousand came from?'

'Me? Why should I know?'

'Well, Mr Hamilton, it arrived rather suddenly, rather recently. Less than a month ago, in fact.'

Hamilton sat back and gave his questioners a positively insolent glare. 'I'm a great believer in private enterprise. Also in the right of the individual to privacy. Guy's business was Guy's business.'

Oldcastle smiled genially. 'Tell me,' he said casually, 'was the lad badly beaten up when he moved in with you?'

'Fairly. They train you lot quite well.'

'I don't like violence no matter who perpetrates it, Mr Hamilton.'

'Very liberal, I'm sure. No wonder you never made Superintendent.'

'Right.' Despite this jibe at a tender area, Oldcastle seemed nonchalant; but Morgan had seen this technique before. A punch was coming. 'When you left the club briefly on Friday night, where did you go and what did you do before you went back inside?'

'What are you talking about?' The attempt at a note of ignorant protest carried no conviction.

'I don't think the words I chose were particularly obscure, Mr Hamilton. And so far my accent seems to have caused you relatively little difficulty. So I think you're perfectly capable of grasping the meaning of an extremely simple and straightforward question.'

'What makes you think I left the club briefly?'

'I have a witness who will vouch for your having done so.'

Michael Hamilton's expensive cut glass hit his designer carpet, giving it a liberal drenching in gin and tonic. Oldcastle smiled sweetly.

'Oh dear,' he said. 'What a careless slip.'

# 7: Boys Keep Swinging

'So?' Marcus asked. 'Did you actually go out? Or is the doorman wrong?'

'No, he isn't. Yes, I did.' Michael sat back in one of Marcus's comfortable, battered armchairs and momentarily closed his eyes. Then he treated Marcus and Dominic to one of his famous winning smiles which had done such wonders for his sex life over the years. 'Of course I did. There wouldn't be a problem if I hadn't.'

'I'd dispute that actually,' Dominic chipped in irrelevantly. 'It's much harder to deny something you didn't actually do – you don't usually have a defence ready if you didn't do something.'

'Thank you Dominic.' Michael gave him a reproving glance.

'So.' Marcus picked up the threads again. 'You went out and were seen going out.'

Michael nodded. 'Yah. You won't believe me when I tell you why. Bloody silly, actually.'

After a few seconds, Marcus growled with atavistic force. 'Well? Are you going to tell us or are you just going to sit there and look pretty and try and baffle us?'

Michael laughed. 'Well, I thought I might try that for a bit. I mean, the Police didn't take very kindly to it as a tactic, but I thought you two might.' Marcus growled again. 'All right, Marco. I went out to make a 'phone call.'

'Yes, well, that does sound pretty feeble. They do have a 'phone in the club, for one thing.'

'I know, I know. But I wanted to make a very private call. No, not that kind. Well, not entirely anyway. It was primarily a business call.'

'At eleven on a Friday night? Feebler and feebler.'

'Marco, you really should think about joining the Police. You're obviously wasted on that wonderful office of yours. I can just imagine you as the straight man, if you'll forgive the term, of a double act like Newcastle and Gorgon or whatever they're called.'

He adopted a less whimsically reserved tone. 'Of course it sounds feeble. I agree that eleven o'clock on a Friday night is an eccentric time to make a business call. But it wasn't eleven o'clock at night everywhere at that moment. Certainly not where I was calling, where it happened to be six in the evening. In fact, as your lightning brains may have deduced, I was telephoning New York where, earlier that afternoon, someone I met over there a couple of weeks before or whenever it was had performed a rather lucrative transaction on the markets on my behalf. It had to be performed there and not here because of timing, privacy and a certain – well – breach of etiquette which amounted to what some narrow-minded people would term illegality.'

'Insider trading,' said Marcus, who read the newspapers.

'You mean cheating?' said Dominic, rather piously.

'How harsh you idealists are,' Michael said. 'Anyway, the deal had to be done there and not here, otherwise I would have been in a certain amount of – well, without being melodramatic, and using the word only in relation to my professional life, I would go so far as to call it – danger.'

Michael looked, Marcus thought, rather pleased with himself as he recounted all this. If there really had been a 'transaction', then it had obviously been something very impressive financially and something incredibly devious, underhand and clever, in the nastiest sense of the word.

Michael went on: 'You do see, I take it – even two such hard-line anti-capitalists as yourselves – that sensitive financial discussions can't really be yelled down a transatlantic line to the accompaniment of High Energy at 124 beats per minute and the creaking leather of elderly clones. And I hadn't a chance, nor would it have been madly politic for me, to call earlier in the evening. And obviously I couldn't have called from the office. Not now the Fraud Squad are bugging the 'phones, anyway. So I went down to the 'phones at Embankment Station.'

He sat back and smiled. 'Go on, tell me what a feeble story that is. The Inspector did, in terms that could not be called uncertain.'

Marcus got up from the sofa on which he and Dominic were primly perched at opposite ends. 'Hardly very quiet, Embankment,' he commented.

'Quieter than the club. A lot quieter. And marginally quieter than Charing Cross.'

'True enough, I suppose.' Marcus wandered over to the window and stared out into the twilight. 'The lights are coming on all over South London,' he murmured. He turned round again. 'Did you make a lot of money on this deal?'

'Mmm.' Michael smiled happily.

'Well, anyway,' Dominic took up, 'I suppose you just gave the Police the name of the person you rang in New York and there's your alibi.'

Michael practically leapt up in horror. 'What? Of course not. I can't possibly compromise my – um.'

'I take it that this mysterious contact is also some kind of lover,' Marcus said drily, staring out into the evening again.

'Of course. But that's not the point, really. The sexual thing doesn't enter into it. But as far as the business matter goes, I gave my word. And I see no reason to go back on that at the moment.'

'Honour among thieves?' Marcus suggested. 'Doesn't the possibility of a murder charge weigh more heavily than a dubious concept of a very murky form of honour?'

'Look. Marco.' Michael leaned forward. 'If the Police had any damning evidence against me that linked me with Guy's murder, then I might conceivably agree with you. But they don't. They've got nothing. That's why they're clutching at straws and trying to bully me – or anyone – into confessing. Now, I've told them as much as they have to know. If they didn't believe me, they'll probably carry on not believing me, even if I drag out the President of the First National Bank to vouch for me. And I am not jeopardising a lucrative – and sexually rather amusing – contact so that the Police can bully me, him or anyone else they feel in the mood to have a go at.'

'Fair enough,' Dominic said. 'I'm inclined to believe you, actually, although I suppose you could still have done the deed after you made your 'phone call. Just like I could have after –' he stopped suddenly. Michael cocked his head.

'After what, Dominic?'

'Oh – nothing. Marcus knows. I don't really want to talk about it.' Edgily, he too got up and started pacing around sporadically: now still, now restless, he carried on talking. 'Let's just call it an assignation that proved – well – not entirely successful.' He swallowed, as though trying to digest a sofa.

'Now this sounds interesting,' Michael said animatedly. 'Dominic having assignations in clubs. Guy said that you were an habitué of commons and cottages – it must have been someone pretty formidable to drag you into a club. Do tell, please.' He laughed. 'You know, I've always imagined you pining away for Guy. I'm so glad I was wrong.'

'I'm sorry,' Dominic replied with some acerbity, 'I thought you came round here for some sympathy after your terrible ordeal with the Police. I don't really think I'm on the agenda.'

'Oh come on, for Christ's sake,' said Michael with finite good humour. He got up, walked across the room and put his hands firmly on Dominic's shoulders. 'Listen. I think you probably got an appalling deal of shit from Guy. I was prepared when I eventually met you, and I knew I would meet you because Guy had recently started droning on and on about getting in touch with you again – anyway, as I say, I was prepared to feel sorry for you. I was not prepared to be impressed at all. But I am. So please – take it easy. And don't throw Guy's shit at me. But I do think, seriously, that you and I ought to talk about Guy, and about you and me too. There are things we can talk to each other about that we can't possibly tell the Police.'

Dominic didn't reply: he looked back warily, even surlily, at Michael. Michael gave him a gentle shake.

'Look. I think the Police want to believe I did it. Everyone else seems to think you did it. I know there's no evidence, but in cases like this juries don't always give too much of a fuck about evidence. So, to some extent we're both of us in the shit. But, to be honest, I know I can get out of it a bit more easily than you can if the Police decide to go after me rather than you. If they go after you instead, then they just have to troop everyone into court – Derek, Phil, Colin, Terry, Katy, Mummy, Daddy, even me – to convict you on hearsay. So, I think we should try and help each other. You see, I didn't kill Guy. Now, I don't think you did. If I hadn't met you, I might very well have thought you did.'

Michael gave Dominic his most intense and pleading look, and then released him. He looked over to Marcus, who had been watching all this.

'I think he may have a point, Dominic.'

'Thank you,' Michael said.

'And I agree you probably didn't do it, Michael. Not if you stood to gain nothing, anyway. But there's another thing worth saying, Dominic. I think the Police are pretty clueless about the whole thing. Therefore, for the sake of statistics, for the sake of the Press, they'll probably try and pin it on the first person they can build a coherent case against and bugger the evidence. That looks like being one of you two. Anyway, I think they'd rather get another gay person for it. Och – ' he growled again, 'I'm not convinced of their competence to handle anything where gay people are concerned, either. I mean, they were OK to me, but then what's the point of hassling me unduly? I mean, even if I had murdered Guy Latimer in a fit of random psychopathy, there's not a shred of evidence to tie me to it.'

Michael laughed. 'And did you?'

'Not as such.'

'I bet it was his father,' Michael replied decisively. 'Christ, you should have seen what he did to Guy when he threw him out.'

'What?' Dominic said. He looked mystified and concerned at the same time.

'Oh' – Michael gestured airily – 'his father beat him up rather badly. It was a remarkably savage attack. You would say, if you wished to appear naive, that it was the kind of thing no natural father could do to a child. Unfortunately, I suspect it was precisely the paternal instinct that provoked the savagery of the beating. You know, the "how can any son of mine be queer" syndrome.'

Marcus nodded. 'Do the Police know about this?'

'Yes. But not from me. And not, I'll bet, from the Latimers.'

'I bet not. You see, Dominic, there's another problem. You said yourself they'd close ranks and they will, like their lives bloody depend on it. So we have to do the same.'

Dominic was standing very still, looking very uncertain. Marcus now came and made a triangular group. Dominic looked at him with a stare that seemed to be asking for an easy answer, but he also seemed fearful.

'Excuse me if I seem – well – paranoid,' he said. 'But I don't know either of you that well. Sometimes I feel like I'm being set up. I mean, really really set up.'

Marcus reached out a reassuring hand, intending to place it on Dominic's arm, but Dominic flinched visibly and actually stepped backwards. 'I didn't do it, you know,' he said in a voice overcome by terror and panic.

'I know you didn't. Even if you have spent the entire weekend trying to convince me otherwise.'

Michael frowned and returned to the chair he had been occupying. He hadn't reckoned on Dominic's emotional volatility even though he had heard – endlessly – about it from Guy. That kind of thing he could do without. He had found Guy's moods of silence and petulance difficult enough, and they, at least, hadn't been demonstrative, public moods. He watched Marcus lead Dominic back to the sofa.

'I'm sorry.' Dominic stared at a point on the floor between his feet as he sat down. Then he looked up at Michael. 'I was just struck by what the two of you were saying. So. What do you suggest? Are we going to "close ranks" and if so, how? Surely the easiest way out for you, Michael, is to make sure that I carry the can.'

Michael smiled. 'All right. Hamilton comes clean time. Look,' he leaned forward so as to appear more earnest and sincere, 'I admit that a lot of the time I'm a bastard. That's why I'm well off and you two aren't. I admit that, in my personal dealings, I have practically no moral standards or scruples at all. I'm probably incapable of monogamy or fidelity for any serious length of time. I certainly have never ever in my life been "in love", whatever that means. But. Very important but. There are certain points beyond which I just will not pass, and certain points at which even I see predicaments other than my own. This is one of those points. I'm not entirely sure why. Maybe it's just my identity as part of the gay community. Maybe it's just enlightened self-interest. Maybe a bit of both. Maybe I like you two. But I'm not going to be sunk because someone, God knows why, got psychotic over Guy. And neither are you.'

To ensure the personal touch, he laid a hand on Dominic's knee. Dominic looked at him again.

'Jolly good,' he said in a tone surprisingly cool. 'Do you want the Oscar now or shall I gift-wrap it?' He shook his leg, so that Michael's hand was dislodged. 'You can save that for the pretty boys, Michael. What are you up to, anyway? If you didn't love Guy, or didn't care about him at all, as you'd have us believe, why in hell were you giving him furnished, rent-free accommodation? There are a lot of people – well, a few anyway – whom I've fancied greatly, enjoyed sex with, yet not liked very much. Now I must say I didn't feel any great compunction to open up my home to them rent-free. Frankly, a single night was about as much as I could manage of any of them. I know Guy could be quite helpful about the house, but. Well, Michael?'

'His family kicked him out, Dominic. What was I supposed to do? Leave him on the streets?'

'My landlord's kicked me out now because he doesn't want to get tarred by my adverse publicity. Can I come and live with you for nothing?'

'Oh, don't be absurd. Guy had nowhere else to go. That's patently not the case with – '

'He left home for you. He wouldn't have had the guts otherwise.'

Michael shook his head. 'No. He was kicked out, almost literally. Don't be under any romantic delusions, Dominic. Guy and I were not in love with one another. We weren't even very much in lust. I mean, he was awfully pretty, but curiously asexual with it. Well, I thought so anyway. And I like a bit more commitment in bed – and you must know yourself how – well – peculiarly uninvolved he always was with the whole thing.'

'Well,' Dominic said, quietly and savagely, 'how the fuck would I know? Up to the time he and I parted company, he had had sex with one person. Katy Goldsmith.'

'Yes. I know that's the Official Version,' Michael replied

impatiently, 'but quite who you're trying to protect with it, I don't know. I mean, do you think you become more suspicious, more likely a culprit, if you lose your position as the frustrated pursuer of the elusive Adonis? I wouldn't have thought so myself, not unless you – well, no, you split up over the 'phone, didn't you?'

Dominic nodded. His savagery was still there, but now it was tempered by a bizarre amusement. He looked at Michael as though he were an alien species.

'You mean unless we did it and Guy was rude about my performance? Very droll. Listen. I don't know why you should think he and I ever had sex. We didn't. But I'll tell you – one of the reasons I never pushed it too far was that I knew how he'd react if we had done. If he had let me out of pity, or out of his own frustration, I know exactly how he'd have reacted. I could have given the performance of a lifetime, and he'd still have made me feel it was utterly and completely inadequate. Not by saying so. Never anything so crude. But just by comparisons, dropped implications. And for that reason alone I gave up even trying. I sometimes used to think, well, Christ, he's got to give in sooner or later. Once or twice I thought he came close to the point of suggesting it himself. But I was never going to give him the chance for that final humiliation. I kept that much pride, that much self-respect. You know, if I'd simply raped him, screwed his arse off, I think he'd have patronised me. He was brilliant like that. Marcus, I'd like a drink, please.'

Marcus jumped a little, because Dominic was still staring at Michael. One thing also had struck him about Dominic's grand protestation. He laid his hand very gently on Dominic's arm.

'You know,' he said, 'every time you say something like that, you make it more and more obvious.'

Dominic turned in alarm. 'What do you mean?'

'Well – that you couldn't have killed him.'

'Just what I was thinking,' Michael said, 'except that I think you're still keeping that one fib alive. Now look, Dominic, we're all boys of the world, we've all slagged about a bit in safer days – even little Miss Virtue over there who disapproves of casual sex,' he waved at Marcus, 'and we all know that you can tell when it's someone's first time. Whatever they say, whatever they claim, they give it away practically the moment you touch. Well. It wasn't Guy's first time.'

'No, there was Katy –'

'It wasn't Guy's first time with a man, Dombo. Oh, sorry,' he said quickly, 'I know Guy called you that, and I know I shouldn't, but – well, if you're going to be obtuse, I have no sympathy, 'cause you're not stupid.'

'I'd rather you didn't call me that, actually. It wasn't one of Guy's more pleasant little jokes.'

'Sorry,' Marcus said, 'am I being thick?'

'Dombo equals Dumbo, more or less,' Dominic explained, 'a highly witty reference to my build. Guy tried to pass it off as a Rambo joke, but that didn't fool either of us.'

'I'll fetch that drink now,' Marcus said, getting up. He needed to withdraw from the intensity of the past few minutes. He was becoming confused: was Michael giving a performance of some kind, and if so, why? In the kitchen he took his time slowly retrieving bottles – he and Dominic seemed to have worked their way through quite a variety of tastes over the weekend. He had finished making two gins and tonics, one for Dominic and one for Michael, and was about to start on a third for himself when he was joined by Dominic.

'Michael says can he have something with vodka?' Dominic's voice and expression betrayed great strain; as he spoke, he put his hands flat on Marcus's chest.

'Typical. Are you OK?'

'I'll live, I expect. Why's Michael drinking vodka tonight?'

'Because everyone else is drinking gin.'

'You don't really like him very much, do you? Now, anyway.'

'He's too much a part of my history for me to have the luxury of liking or disliking him.'

'Do you believe me? About Guy and me, I mean.'

'Yes. And I also believe you're innocent of his murder. I don't even believe you would have liked to have killed him. No' – Marcus put a finger to Dominic's mouth, which had been about to protest – 'I admit that you think you would. But what you really would have liked would be to have had the choice. Just once. To have had the power over him. Because that was what was so awful for you. The fact that you were powerless. If you'd once been standing over him with a knife, or a gun, or your hands around his neck, you'd just have seen him for what you always knew him to be in your heart of hearts. Insignificant. And you'd have laughed and walked away. That's what I think. But I admit I'm biased.'

Dominic's hands crept up over Marcus's shoulders and met behind his neck. 'Do you know something?' he said with a smile. 'Something really weird's happened.'

'Michael's dropped dead in the other room?'

'No. I've become completely and utterly besotted.'

'What, with Michael?'

'Not exactly, no.' Dominic looked at Marcus very earnestly. 'Oh, I realise I must seem incredibly fickle to you, what with Guy and Dennis and everything. But you must see, Marc, they were different kinds of feelings – different from each other and both different again from this.' A pause, apparently endless, occupied a few seconds. 'Do you believe me?'

'I think so. But I'll believe you better in a month. Or a week.' He leaned forward and they kissed for another few seconds' eternity. 'Now will you do something for me?'

'Anything at all,' Dominic murmured, as his mouth travelled slowly down Marcus's neck and torso.

Marcus pulled on his hair. 'There's time enough for that, later. No, listen. You and Michael have got to talk sensibly about this Guy business, It's the only way forward. Tell him about Dennis, if you can. Look, if nothing else, it'll help you get things sorted out for when you see the Police tomorrow.'

Dominic nodded thoughtfully. 'True. I wish you could be there tomorrow.'

'Look, I'll take the day off. I'll come with you and wait for you, if you like.'

'Have you got any leave left?'

'Weeks. I think we should take Tuesday and Wednesday off as well. If you can manage that.'

'I can always manage that,' Dominic said.

'After all,' Marcus went on, 'you'll have to move your stuff in here. We can't have you roaming the streets.'

'Marc, you don't know me yet. Let's leave all that.'

'For now. We'll talk about it later. Here's your drink. Here's Michael's.' Marcus thrust two glasses at Dominic, one for each hand. 'Now let's go in there and talk this through together.'

'So,' Dominic said, handing Michael his drink, 'you think Guy had, or had had, another man before you.'

'Before and probably during, yes,' Michael replied. His equanimity of tone did nothing to enhance the theory that he had worshipped and loved Guy to the point of jealousy and rage. 'That's why I'm supposed to have done it according to Castlemaine or whatever his name is. A jealous fit. I took the boy in and he repaid me with infidelity. All of this, I should add, is based on his diary.'

'You mean his pocket diary?' Dominic asked puzzled. 'But he only ever kept the most random record in that, as I remember. Appointments here and there, but by no means all. Films, usually.'

'Yes, yes, yes. But: (a) he thought of my place as a sufficiently permanent address to put it in the front, therefore I must have given him to understand it was permanent, therefore I must have loved him to distraction; (b) there were two appointments made with a mysterious person denoted only as "JP", the later of which was at lunchtime the day before he was killed. This must have been another lover. I found out. He told me. I slit him up a treat. Good story, eh, if a trifle obvious?'

'JP?' Dominic stroked his chin. 'Means nothing to me. Apart from being my last two initials. But it does ring some bell or other somewhere apart from that, if I ponder, now I come to.'

'Brilliantly logical,' Marcus commented, to be thumped on the arm for his pains.

'The only P in Guy's address list at the end of the diary is you,' Michael went on. 'In fact, Boscastle and the lad from the valleys seemed to be heading towards the view that you and Guy were really lovers after all, fell out, fell in again, and were about to go off together. Hence the will.'

'But that's utterly absurd. I mean, what evidence is there to suggest that Guy and I ever met on those two occasions? And why should I lie about it? That version leaves me in the clear.'

'Oh yes, it does. If you reckon without the fabulously inventive brains of those two apologies for guardians of law and order. You're protecting me because I'm gay. I mean, they even got round to suggesting a brilliant conspiracy between us to get rid of Guy and inherit his fabulous wealth into the bargain.'

'They can't be serious,' Marcus interpolated.

'You underestimate them,' Michael returned. 'Frankly, I think they watch too much television.'

'JP,' Dominic murmured again. 'Could it have been someone he met through you?'

'It both wasn't and couldn't have been.'

'He'd only seen this person twice, though.'

'Well – there were two meetings recorded in his diary.'

'One the day before he died – and the other when?'

'Two weeks before that. Actually – ' Michael stopped suddenly. 'That's an odd coincidence. Those were the dates of the two wills. You know there were two, I take it.'

'Mmm.' Dominic was so obviously thinking hard it was practically audible. 'Well, it can't be the wills – I mean, Katy Goldsmith is hardly JP – but – well, it's too bizarre to be just a coincidence. Don't you agree?'

'Well – ' Marcus was clearly dubious. 'The cause and effect may be a bit obscure. I mean, if he's meeting a secret lover, why name first his brother and then you as his heirs?'

'JP,' Dominic said again. 'John, Jonathan, Jeffrey – '

'James, Jeremy,' threw in Marcus.

'Jacob, Jocelyn, Jasper, Jolyon,' added Michael whimsically, throwing in 'Judas' for good measure.

'Julian, Joshua,' concluded Dominic. 'I can't think of any more, can you?'

'Only diminutives,' Marcus said. 'Do you want to get the 'phone book and have a few stabs at P?'

'Perhaps it's another Christian name,' Michael suggested. 'John Paul. Hey, that's it. Guy was meeting the Pope. A secret religious streak. No? No.' He giggled. 'I don't really see much point in flicking through the 'phone book, Marco.'

'I agree,' Dominic said. 'Or do I? No, I agree. If we don't know, then we don't know, and we're not going to work it out by some random piece of guesswork. But there is something nagging at the back of my mind if I could only get at it.'

'One of your many passing ships?' Michael offered. 'According to Guy – '

'Guy knew nothing about it,' Dominic cut in, as urbanely as he could manage under the circumstances. 'When I knew him, he lived vicariously off my experience, and so we tended to mythologise my sex life quite a lot.'

Michael nodded. 'I can believe that.' He sipped at his vodka. 'Did you ever detect that Guy might be having some kind of affair?'

'No. Never quite. There were one or two trial runs or near misses – you know, people he almost had relationships with, and then there was Phil Roxby. And, of course, Derek.'

'Well, Derek's hardly a likely candidate.' Michael was conclusively dismissive on this point.

'Derek wouldn't agree with you. I think Derek always felt that Guy would succumb eventually, if only out of frustration.'

'Now there's a thought,' Michael said. 'That scenario I outlined a little while ago – from everything I heard about him, and my mercifully brief glimpse, I'd have thought Derek might fit very well into the part of insulted sexual performer that Guy turned down.'

'Yes, but – ' Dominic pondered. 'Look, if you wanted to kill someone because they insulted your sexual performance, you'd do it at the time of the insult. Well, I would.'

'Derek, on the other hand, is sly, pushy, ambitious and secretive. According to Guy. So he would harbour grudges and take revenge when it interfered with and implicated him least. Like me, really,' Michael added with what was meant to be disarming honesty.

'It strikes me,' Marcus intervened slowly, not willing to give

Michael the reassurance he seemed to want, 'that this whole thing is so full of holes that the minute you offer a solution to fit one presentation of the facts you simply set up a load of inconsistencies.' He frowned. 'I didn't put that terribly well.'

'Not really, no,' Michael agreed.

'What I mean is that any scenario we've invented so far has always had to ignore certain things. Like the major glaring thing – how come Guy went outside? He left his rucksack behind, so he must have been going back in, but why did he go out? Had he arranged to meet someone? Was he called out? If he was called out, wouldn't the door staff remember? I mean, they remember you going out well enough, Michael? So what about Guy?' The pitch of Marcus's voice was rising, as his exasperation grew. 'The whole business is just ludicrously incomplete,' he concluded, banging the arm of the sofa.

'Do you know what I think?' Michael asked. 'I think we should go to the funeral. When is it?'

'Tuesday, Katy told me,' Dominic replied. 'Which reeks of indecent haste on the family's part, if you ask me. But I really don't think I should – '

'Of course you should,' Michael said. 'God damn it, you're his sole heir. You've got nothing to hide.'

'I don't really like funerals.'

'Feeble. All right – we'll go to the family tea afterwards. I assume there will be one.'

'So Katy said.'

'Right, that's settled. All three of us. I can get the time off if you two can.' Michael noticed that, at this, Marcus and Dominic smiled coyly and furtively at each other. Obviously they had been planning time off together in any case. How bizarre, he thought, that Dominic should find that longed-for lover he had always maundered on about to Guy more or less as a direct result of Guy's death. 'Another thing,' he went on, 'Guy still had a lot of stuff in Surrey. There may be something useful there – if his father hasn't burnt it all.'

'Particularly if he killed Guy he might have,' Marcus pointed out. 'Actually, Michael, I would say that whatever there might have been there that could have been useful will almost certainly not be there now. Or not by Tuesday afternoon, anyway. They'd have had four days to seek and destroy.'

'Look – ' Dominic intervened authoritatively. 'I go along with Michael on this. Sudden volte-face. OK. Now, Michael, we are assuming, aren't we, another man involved in all this. Possibly the mysterious JP. So think. How did they meet? Where did they meet?

Where did they go to? Where did they go to bed?'

'If they met two weeks before Guy died – as he and JP did – they could have used my place. I was in New York.'

'But where else?' Dominic went on. 'And they must have gone to films, and maybe clubs, and definitely pubs. Guy was intrigued by the scene, but he hated going out alone.'

'He was alone when I met him,' Michael remarked.

'Yes. I suppose so. Look – a long shot. Was there anywhere he wouldn't go, or specifically didn't want to go?'

Michael thought. 'Not really – nowhere specific, anyway. He used to say we shouldn't go South of the River. Said it wouldn't be fair on you. Actually, that was a damn shame, because I like one or two of those pubs in the South. I mean, I used to tell him that that place in Clapham was madly him, but he was adamant – '

'But you told me that he told you I never went out. It doesn't make sense, Michael. Well, not a lot. And do you think Guy really cared much about being fair on me?'

'Well – since you ask – no, not really. I see what you mean. But what are you driving at?'

'If Guy was regularly seen somewhere with someone else – the same person – he could hardly risk going there with you.' Dominic looked almost triumphant at this thesis. He squeezed Marcus's arm in excitement. 'Michael, did he have any photos at your place? Of any age or whatever – you know, photos he'd taken himself.'

'Quite a few, in fact,' Michael said. 'I can't say I ever paid them much mind. He was quite good at snapshots, I know, but other peoples' photos bore me to tears. I take it you'd like me to dig them out for you? They're yours legally, anyway.' He patted the back of his head, in thoughtful consternation. 'You know – I'm supposed to have accompanied Guy to Katy's and hung around outside while he made his wills. And it was supposed to have been my advice that sparked off this passion for bequeathing.'

'I take it it wasn't,' Marcus said.

'Look,' Michael said, 'if it had been, I'd have made sure he left everything to me. Anyway, I made more on Wall Street last Friday than Guy owned.'

Michael smiled specifically at Dominic. 'Forgive me if I present an appalling picture of myself, Dominic, but I am trying to be honest. For all our sakes. Anyway. I was simply driving at the point that Guy may have been dragging an escort around, palming him off on the world as me.'

Dominic seemed to be getting more excited by the minute. 'Look, look, look,' he said. 'I'm sure we can get somewhere. The real question is, do you want to help me, us, Michael?'

'My dear Dominic, this is all my idea. Whose idea was it to go to the funeral? Whose idea was it – ?'

'Yes, clever Michael,' Marcus said. 'Look Dom, do I get this right? You're going to propose a jaunt around the clubs and pubs of South London? I mean, have you ever been to any?'

'Oh, in my time,' Dominic replied airily. 'When you're as decrepit as I am, you tend to have been here and there, Marc. Actually, you know, both before and after Guy I quite enjoyed the occasional fling around the scene.' He looked from Michael to Marcus and was surprised to see them both open-mouthed. 'Oh, come on, chaps, that's hardly a crime. It can be fun, Marcus, if you treat it like a form of anthropology. Or if you enter into the social spirit of the thing. Right. Do we have a plan, then? I mean, do we agree?'

'I wouldn't miss it for the world,' giggled Michael. 'Not even for a business deal.'

'OK then,' Dominic said, 'let's meet Tuesday lunchtime. Here. If that's all right, Marcus? I mean, even if I weren't a homeless waif and stray, my place would be a bit out of the way. And Michael will bring all the photos Guy had at his place. Right. Now I'm going to make two 'phone calls, if I may.'

He'd sprang to his feet and looked down at Marcus. Marcus, totally baffled, nodded permission. He could hardly refuse anyone beaming quite so ecstatically.

'Well,' Michael said, as they heard Dominic in the hall pressing numbers on the 'phone, 'what an extraordinary transformation. Guy always said that Dominic was changeable, but never once did he lead me to believe it could work quite like this. Has this been a routine kind of – well, alteration – over the weekend?'

'Not really. Actually, a lot of the time he's been hinting that he's really a psychopath.'

'That must be wearing for you, you poor thing.'

'In fact, no. I'd say all in all it was going rather well.'

'Considering he's continually tried to convince you he's a murderer?'

'Oh, I think that's part of his charm.'

'A part it seems you'll have to do without for a while at least.'

'I think I'll survive.'

'Oh, I think you will, too.' Michael rose elegantly to his feet. 'Incidentally, I'm very pleased for you about all this. I hope it works out.' Marcus's expression looked unmoved, so Michael continued. 'Seriously. I know how much a decent long-term relationship means to you. Just because it means relatively little to me doesn't mean I can't appreciate an alternative viewpoint.'

This obviously worked, because Marcus smiled. 'Thanks,' he said. 'Am I to take it that you're off now?'

'Yes. I'll see you on Tuesday, somewhere between twelve and one. Incidentally, if the Police behave at all to Dominic the way they behaved to me, then – well, let's just say he'll be rather fragile tomorrow.' Marcus raised an eyebrow. 'What I mean,' Michael went on, 'is that he may need careful handling. Be patient.'

Marcus nodded. 'Thanks for the advice.' He graciously forbore from adding that this had already occurred to him when he had realised quite how shattered Michael had been by his interrogation, given that Michael's was one of the stablest, most surely constructed egos he had ever encountered, or was likely to encounter. He too got to his feet. 'I'll see you out.'

'No – don't worry. Dominic's on the 'phone, so we don't want to disturb him.' He patted Marcus's arm, and once more Marcus noticed how tired Michael looked.

'Tell me,' he asked, a vague hesitancy hanging around his opening, 'did you go out last night?'

'Marcus,' said Michael reproachfully, 'you know me better than that.'

'You mean you did?'

'Of course.'

They both laughed. 'You like being a bastard, don't you?'

'It has its advantages. For me. But I don't see it as a viable modus operandi for everyone,' Michael said in a voice reserved for spurious pieces of punditry. 'Say a proper goodbye to Dominic for me. And thanks.'

Marcus raised his hand in an all-encompassing gesture. Michael left the room, and, after a moment, Marcus heard the front door of the flat close. He picked up the three glasses and was about to take them to the kitchen, when he heard the 'phone click. Dominic bounded back into the room. He looked, if anything, more jubilant.

'That was quick,' Marcus said, determined not to be too inquisitive.

'What would you think,' Dominic said, coming over and putting his arms around Marcus, 'if I said I was going to talk to the Press?'

'I'd think you'd probably taken leave of your senses.'

Dominic laughed. 'You're probably right. But I'm still going to do it.'

'Why, for Christ's sake?'

'An amusing way of fighting back. An insatiable desire for publicity. A sense of the absurd. Take your pick.'

'Do you actually know what you're doing?'

'Not completely.'

'Are you getting paid?'

'Don't know. Rather a Hamiltonesque question, that. Anyway, it's only the *Standard*, so probably not.'

'And when are you going to give this exclusive?'

'Some time tomorrow. I want it in Tuesday's paper. We can take it to the funeral with us if we pick up a lunchtime edition.' He looked quizzical. 'Or don't you think so?'

'Well, I think the whole idea's mad. Why bother?'

'Look, I have my reasons. I just can't be entirely certain what they are yet.'

He released Marcus. 'Look,' he said, beginning a perambulation, 'we – the three of us – agreed that there were huge information gaps. We agreed that the Police aren't very likely to be able to dig up the information. And we seem to think that the answers may lie out on the scene somewhere. So – we need publicity. Start jogging memories. Then when we start our tour, people will be talking. I mean, there hasn't even been a decent photo of Guy in any paper yet. No-one would recognise his face from that grotty 'bus pass picture. I've got some very flattering photos that might ring a few bells. After all, Guy was fairly memorable as a visual experience.'

'But, Dominic – the *Standard*! I mean, they're so horribly anti-gay. Why not *Capital Gay* or something?'

'Because they don't publish till Thursday night. Look, ideologically it's a gross move, I admit. And I'll quite happily talk to *CG* whenever. And, anyway, do you think I'll give them a chance to be anti-gay? I've got a much more sensational angle for them.'

He smiled. Marcus opened his mouth to protest, but Dominic merely shook his head gleefully. 'Just wait and see.'

Marcus laughed. 'I wish I knew what had come over you. You're a changed man.'

'Oh – yes. In more senses than one. Talking of which,' he went back to Marcus and kissed him. 'I've got a few ideas,' he murmured, 'and there are one or two promises I want to hold you to.'

'Well,' Marcus breathed, 'I'd like to do that. But I don't think you should take the risk.'

'Hey,' Dominic said, stroking his face, 'where's the risk? You said yourself you've been tested. So have I. We're both negative, so – ' He suddenly stopped. 'Christ, of course. Of course. God, how stupid of me.'

'What's the – ? Are you having second thoughts about fame?' Marcus felt marginally catty: he had just been getting rather randy and didn't fancy having to forget it.

'I should have realised.' Dominic slapped himself on the side of the head. 'Guy never used people's initials like that. Never. It was a kind of inverse snob thing – like not referring to people by surnames. Far too public school. JP, Marcus, is not a person. Well, not now.'

'Well then, what? Justice of the Peace? Just Possible?'

'James Pringle.' This drew no reaction. 'The VD Clinic,' Dominic explained, not entirely patiently. Unable to await some kind of appreciation any longer, he gabbled on. 'Oh, I know it's just a guess, but it makes sense. He was having the test, the HIV test. Two appointments two weeks apart: and then, that bizarre conversation I had with him in the club. God, for once he was right, I was being egocentric. He wasn't trying to warn me, he was trying to ask me things – ah.' This exclamation sounded to Marcus almost like a penny audibly dropping. 'Marcus. I think he must have been HIV positive. I really do.'

'You can't know that. You're guessing.'

'Well, the whole thing's a guess.'

'Pretty impressive guess.'

'You think I'm right, then?'

'A fair chance. About JP anyway. Probably.'

'Well, on that ecstatic note of faint praise, let's go to bed.' Dominic smiled. 'After all, I need a good night's sleep if I'm meeting the fabulous Chief Inspector and his dynamic Sergeant tomorrow.'

'Och, you shouldn't pay too much mind to Michael. They're all right. And if you want a good night's sleep, you'll be wanting to use the spare room.'

'Oh – I think the good night's sleep is a few hours off yet.'

'Hours?'

'Wishful thinking,' Dominic replied. 'Or maybe not,' he added, raising his eyebrows hopefully.

By the time they had got round to questioning Dominic in detail, the Police had been able to gather a little more information – as much as was accessible from the various databases to which the Police had access – on the key performers in the drama. Looking down the list of Dominic's academic qualifications, Morgan had been impressed and Oldcastle derisive. Of course, Oldcastle was expecting, whatever Morgan might predict, that Palmer would be quite as arrogant at the outset of the interview as Hamilton had been.

'God, Stuart, I wiped the smile off Hamilton's smarmy face, didn't I?'

He had quite gloried in this, although, as Morgan tactfully

refrained from pointing out, this surprising of Hamilton had hardly cracked the case. Admirable though it had been to witness – an amusing spectator sport, you might say – it had been, from the results viewpoint, not the unqualified success it had initially promised to be. As the arrogant Hamilton had, in any case, pointed out, simply going out of the club hardly constituted concrete evidence of any involvement in Guy's murder. Simply shocking him had not been enough: he hadn't broken down and confessed – well, he wasn't the type to do that in a hurry, even if the evidence were apparently stacked against him – and there just hadn't been anything to follow up the initial shock. Now, if they'd had some evidence about the financial business – well, that might have made a difference. But they hadn't. The Fraud Squad connection had drawn a disappointing blank.

Morgan was getting depressed with this case: all far too elusive. He noticed this morning that Oldcastle's level of interest in it had diminished almost visibly, and he thought he could detect an alcoholic aroma on the Chief's breath. A good start, all in all.

Now the erudite Palmer who had, strangely, elected to come and be questioned on hostile ground, so to speak. Why this should be, they could only speculate: it had very much surprised Morgan who had figured Palmer for a prize neurotic after all that 'I wish I'd killed him' stuff.

But he received a shock: quite simply, this Dominic Palmer was a different person, in all but body, from the one he had met on Friday – and even physically there seemed to be a greater air of togetherness about him. However, from the pleasant acceptance of the offer of coffee, Morgan sensed that at least the change wasn't going to affect Palmer's forthcoming manner of speech. In fact, he had acquired a layer of courtesy which rather put Oldcastle on his guard. And so they all sat down together and the game began.

Palmer rehearsed his relationship with Guy Latimer, and was immediately cross-questioned keenly by Oldcastle. Very good-naturedly he explained that Katy – he was surprised to discover it, though – was under a common misconception. He'd always assumed she knew better. Asked about the will, he admitted now that Guy had, in fact, mentioned it in the club, but in such circumstances as to make it sound like a joke in poor taste. Asked what he was doing between leaving Latimer's company and meeting Grey and Hamilton, he suddenly became rather sheepish. Oldcastle pressed, rather unpleasantly: Morgan followed up, as he hoped, more sympathetically. Palmer looked at him dubiously.

'I am, in fact, trying to protect someone else's reputation,' he said. 'I was with someone – '

'In what sense?' Oldcastle cut in brusquely.

'Oh, any sense you care to take it,' Dominic replied. 'That's hardly the point. The point is that he's a married man and a father in a responsible job, and I'm not prepared to put him in an impossible position.'

'Mr Palmer, I shall have to ask you for his name,' Oldcastle said.

'No you shan't,' Dominic said, 'it's totally irrelevant.'

'Now then, lad, just think. Where did he go after he left you?'

'Home, he said.'

'Out of the club, in other words. At what time?'

'About – oh, I see. The time of the murder. Ah.' Dominic smiled wanly. 'So even apart from giving me an alibi, it isn't irrelevant, is it? Damn. He'll kill me, you see. Probably quite literally.' He covered his mouth. 'Whoops, bad taste. Tact.'

'This is, I take it,' Oldcastle said, 'someone you see regularly.'

'Not exactly. Well, not any more. I arranged to meet him on Friday to try to get him to take me back. He wouldn't.'

'Did you accompany him outside?'

'No.'

'You're sure about that? I mean, did you go outside after him and find him with Latimer – '

'Er, look, Inspector, I don't like to point out flaws in other men's creative works, but your story, the one you're trying to tell anyway, doesn't take account of where Dennis went.'

'Dennis, eh? That's a start. He goes home, and you attack Latimer then.'

'Ingenious. Rubbish, but ingenious.' Dominic positively beamed at the two detectives. 'By the way, I've cracked JP for you. At least I think I have. James Pringle.'

'Well, who's he?' Oldcastle asked imperiously.

'Well, I think he was a skin specialist. James Pringle House, however, more relevantly to the purpose, is the VD Clinic of the Middlesex Hospital, and favoured by sections of the gay community. Such as myself. You see, they're quite sympathetic. They're good, helpful, responsible and truthful. If he was going to go anywhere, Guy would certainly have gone there.'

'But why should he have gone anywhere?' Morgan asked.

'He had a morbid fear of VD generally. I don't imagine that that vanished. And it does put our odd conversation in the club into something like a context.'

'He wasn't promiscuous, though, was he? Everyone seems to be agreed on that.'

'Look,' Dominic said, 'sexually transmitted diseases, including AIDS and the HIV virus, aren't moral organisms, you know.

They're not simply penalties for sleeping with more people than your fair share according to some objective standard.'

'Mr Palmer,' Oldcastle intervened in his grittiest tones, 'if you could just get off the soap box a moment. I take your point, but could you tell me again?' Dominic did so. 'Right, Stuart,' he turned to Morgan, forgetting he was 'in public', 'could you get Ken Bowen to check it out? It sounds like a task fitted for his tact and discretion.'

He laughed sourly. Morgan got up and left, rather nervously, fearing for the interrogation if either Dominic should get too exuberant or Oldcastle too cynically brusque.

When they were left alone, only a silent uniformed constable in attendance, Dominic smiled at the Chief Inspector. 'We'll need this friend of your's name and address,' Oldcastle said wearily.

'Oh, I realise that,' Dominic said cheerfully. 'Still I did try and protect him. I had to make the effort. You could tell him that. And you will be discreet, won't you?'

'If it's at all possible,' Oldcastle said insincerely.

Dominic, recognising the insincerity, laughed. Then he surrendered Dennis Kelly's name and address. Unfortunately, in Oldcastle's eyes, this defeat did nothing to dim his natural exuberance. Dominic beamed at him.

'Right,' he said, 'what shall we talk about now?' At this point Stuart Morgan returned.

'All done?' Morgan nodded. 'Well, Mr Palmer, shall we go over it all again?'

'By all means.'

After two hours, Dominic, still grinning, was surrendered to the patient Marcus. Oldcastle, watching the door close behind Dominic with something like relief, turned to his Sergeant.

'If he's a murderer, I'm the manager of Sheffield Wednesday.'

'Which you aren't to my knowledge, sir.'

'Is that your way of saying you agree with me?'

'In point of fact it is, sir.'

'Right. Where's Ken Bowen? And where are the results of those sodding blood tests? I want them now.'

'Tomorrow, I'm afraid, sir. As for Ken – '

'It's Hamilton, Stuart. I can feel it in my bones. But how can we catch the smarmy bastard out?' Oldcastle sighed, rose ponderously to his feet and left the room.

Morgan followed him and, as he feared, found the trail led back to Oldcastle's office, to the favourite cupboard. The Chief Inspector had just made a more than liberal assault on a brand new bottle of whisky.

# Part Three
# SOMEBODY ELSE'S GUY

# 8: Going Underground

Derek Wilkinson gave a cautious nod and smile to Phil Roxby. Ever since Guy had started talking about Phil – years ago, it seemed like now – Derek had been really rather in awe of him. And usually, if Derek was in awe of someone he tended to dislike them violently.

Guy had a way of talking about Phil that made him seem like the living incarnation of all Guy's ideal and virtuous concepts of style and poise. Actually seeing Phil Roxby for the first time, all those aeons ago, had turned out to be something of a disappointment. To Derek's mind the bloke was weedy, puny and distinctly effete, and as for the famous fashion sense – well. Northern Brideshead on a distinctly off day (and hadn't Brideshead become passé years ago?). That floppy lank hair had been ludicrous, although not as ludicrous as the subsequent attempt at a vaguely more modish style, with shortened sides and pale gingerish wisps gelled into an almost nonsensical upright. And what a stupid nose – like one of those inbred little dogs that has to run around snorting all the time.

Derek, it might be gathered, had not been impressed, and had used his predisposition to be unimpressed to the full. In fact, he and Guy had argued fairly vociferously on the issue of Phil; and it had been during this argument that Derek had first detected the potential for a rift between Guy and Dominic. In an unguarded moment Guy had hurled out, in a condemnatory tone, the accusation: 'You're worse than Dominic.' So for Derek the cloud caused by their argument had had a silver lining.

Dominic, whom he'd met only the once and found thoroughly overbearing and arrogant and truly revolting physically, had been casting a pall over Derek's friendship with Guy by getting completely in the way and overwhelming Guy with his views. Over the few months that Guy had been seeing Dominic (at the same time Derek had first met Phil) his conversation had become more and more littered with 'Well, Dominic says' or 'Dominic told me', just as during university vacations Guy had quoted similar oracular pronouncements from Katy and Simon. But at least Katy and Simon hadn't been gay men; and Derek had offered Guy all the sympathy and true feeling one might have expected over the disastrous night with Katy. Even though Guy insisted there was nothing between Dominic and himself except friendship, Derek found this difficult to accept, at least until he had actually met Dominic.

So he had been very interested to discover that Dominic too found Phil Roxby a threat. First, and worst of all, it bore out Derek's suspicion that, despite Guy's protestation that he wasn't interested, there was something to fear; second, and better, if Dominic were making a possessive nuisance of himself, then Guy would soon give him the chop. That would leave Derek's friendship with Guy unmolested: and then, Derek felt, Guy would have to give in and make the friendship sexual. After all, no-one could hold out in virginity for ever.

Admittedly, Derek's first approaches had passed almost unnoticed, to the point where Derek had begun to wonder whether Guy might not be totally obtuse: and finally a desperately risked outright request had got an outright refusal. Of course, you'd never bring Guy to it that way. He would have to be led, very firmly, and bedded very determinedly. That was the other fortunate thing about Dominic: he was so desperately in love with Guy that he would never ever take that risk, even though Derek suspected the possibility might have drifted closer from time to time than Guy was prepared to concede.

Of course, Derek had always feared that if he ever did succeed with Guy, then the political dimension of their arguments might explode: Guy might have expected a dutiful and positive 'coming out' on Derek's part, and might have become embarrassing on that score. It never ceased to amaze Derek how dense Guy could be on this topic: it was all very well for drifters like Guy himself, or effete, obvious queens like Phil Roxby or fat old has-beens like Dominic, to be open and defiant; but for people like Derek, who had very clear ideas of where they wanted to be within a long-defined Establishment and who didn't espouse a lot of lefty garbage, it would amount to professional suicide. And not even a regular sexual liaison with the very beautiful Guy, his old and close friend, was worth that kind of risk. Nothing was.

Anyway, that was all academic now. Michael Hamilton had made it so. And it was totally meaningless today. The very beautiful

Guy, Derek's old and close friend, was about to be driven from the village church in a brown wooden box.

It occurred to Derek that it might be a good idea to offer Phil Roxby a lift, otherwise he might end up having a carful of Latimers or Diffords forced upon him. By attaching a sexually suspect friend of Guy's to himself, he would ensure that the ride to the cemetery was free of platitudes and banalities. Of course, if Colin hadn't been tied to an official car, then it might have been a different story.

And so Derek nodded to Phil, who was wearing one of his customary truly horrible baggy pseudo-thirties suits. Derek greeted him cautiously, but, he hoped, with apparent warmth; Phil Roxby, however, sensed no warmth whatsoever in this greeting, only more caution than there actually was. Guy had always been pretty scathing about this Walter Mitty-like friend of his, whom he branded in no uncertain terms a fantasist and, worse, a complete political coward. Having met Derek, Phil was not surprised: as he had commented to Neil, his long-standing boyfriend, Derek was 'a bit of a twisted introvert', and quite clearly uncertain as to whether to feel superior to Guy or be jealous of him.

Phil Roxby always knew what he himself felt and always had positive thoughts about what he felt. Of course, Neil helped that. They'd been together for three years, and it all seemed to work terribly well, so well that temptations to do other things never made any serious assault on either of them. Guy, of course, was a case in point. When they had been working together, somebody (one of those 'helpful' friends you tend to find around you in any unit, always keen to tell you what other people have said about you) had gone to great pains to point out to Phil that Guy had 'some kind of crush' on him. Guy was a pretty boy. He was quite amusing in a bitchy way, if you broke through the layers of reserve: but Phil had to ask himself a few, fairly simple, but extremely important, questions. First, fundamentally, was it worth putting everything with Neil at risk for a passing fancy? Second, even if it could be more than a passing fancy, would a 'thing' with Guy ever justify the hard work and heartbreak that starting it would entail? It was pretty obvious to Phil that, even if he were free, Guy would be immensely hard work; and when he'd got to know Guy better, later on, Guy had more or less admitted as much himself.

The admission, in fact, constituted one of the few sympathetic remarks Phil had heard Guy make about Dominic after the great whatever-it-actually-was (and Phil had never quite worked out what it could best be called) had broken up.

'I don't really like getting very close to people,' Guy had

suddenly burst out in confidence, 'it's really a bad idea for anyone to be friends with me. I'm far too reserved and everything. It really upset Dominic, because he isn't. I mean, my moods and everything really hurt his feelings because he always sort of took them personally like they were sort of his fault.'

Guy had rarely, in Phil's experience, made speeches of this length, so he had assumed that something important was being said here: but he had never, in the span of attention he had accorded it, quite fathomed out whether it was meant as a clear warning-off or a veiled come-on, a kind of challenge. Phil knew that had he ever accepted the challenge he would have found himself in a tricky situation: after all, Guy's retention of social contact with him, following the unfortunate dismissal from the bookshop, had been just assiduous enough to arouse the suspicion of more than a fleeting crush which had failed to pass. And, when all was said and done, it came back to the point that Phil's relationship with Neil was not worth swapping for a shot at Guy's moods and pendulum swings.

Really, Phil thought, to have put up with Guy you'd have had to be utterly devoted – like Dominic had been supposed to be. Derek Wilkinson, though, clearly wouldn't have fitted the bill: he lacked the openness necessary for the kind of devotion which would tolerate Guy's less sociable eccentricities – and then, he was hardly good-looking. Guy had even preferred Dominic to Derek physically (just), which, given the way he described Dominic as a physical entity, was certainly saying something. Phil thought he had only ever seen Dominic in photos, unaware that he had frequently seen Dominic in the flesh, in the shop, which Dominic had often visited for an obsessive, jealous stare at him. So he didn't feel he could comment on Guy's judgement. But he found that Derek put him in mind of a balding garden gnome. A balding garden gnome up to no good: Derek had, to Phil's eyes, that typically shifty look peculiar to closet gays.

As he now confronted Derek, he mused on two incongruities: first, the social one, that he ought, for politeness, to pretend not to know that Derek was gay; second, more frivolous, the prospect of a garden gnome in a mourning suit. He returned Derek's greeting with as little warmth as he could muster.

'Would you like a lift to the cemetery?' Derek asked.

'I hadn't really thought about that,' Phil replied, immediately confirming Derek's view of his effeteness. 'I mean, how I was going to get there. Even if I was. I thought maybe the family would want – ' He waved his hand limply to cover the family's wishes.

'I don't think they care much either way. But even if they did,

I'm sure you'd still be welcome. After all, they invited you.'

'Actually, they didn't. I asked that girl Guy used to know when the funeral was.'

'Oh, you mean Katy. Yes. I notice she isn't here.' Derek sniggered. 'Neither of the spurned lovers is.'

'*No?*' Phil returned, putting a very definite inflexion on the negative. Guy had told him everything about Derek's approaches, both direct and indirect.

'Well, I suppose it would be in pretty poor taste if Dominic turned up. But I thought Katy might make the effort.'

'Perhaps she can't get the time off work.'

'Oh, that's what she'd say, I don't doubt. Have you noticed who else can't get time off work?'

'No,' Phil lied. 'Do you think we should make a move then?' He resigned himself to Derek's company for a short while. Clearly at this kind of social event one couldn't go off and mingle and pretend a pressing social interest elsewhere.

'Oh, sure. The car's just up the road.'

They walked along the path of the densely-populated village churchyard. If there'd been a bit of room there still, Phil thought, they could have buried Guy there and he would have been spared a ride with Derek.

'No,' Derek went on, warming to his task, 'what I want to know is where Michael's got to. You'd have thought he'd have made the effort, wouldn't you? After all, they were living together.'

'Well, there could be all kinds of reasons,' Phil offered vaguely, but he had to admit to himself that Derek had a point. 'Anyway, it hadn't been going all that long, had it?'

'A couple of months,' Derek said in that pained tone reserved for disagreeing with contentions. 'Here's the car,' he said, waving grandly at a battered old estate thing as though it were a vintage Rolls. He opened the passenger door from the outside. Phil got in very gingerly, and by the time he had strapped himself in (he always had trouble with seat belts) Derek was turning the key in the ignition.

'Is it far?'

'Couple of miles.' Derek reversed away, without, as far as Phil could tell, looking backwards, forwards or sideways. 'There are so many dead people in Surrey it's difficult to find any space. All those retired colonels who never made it to Eastbourne or Bournemouth, you see.' He drove onto a main road and accelerated wildly. 'So,' he went on, 'have the Police been to see you yet?'

'Yes,' Phil said, 'twice.' If Derek kept driving this fast, the drive would soon be over – one way or another.

'What did you think?'

'Of the Police?' The question seemed odd. 'Do you mean did I fancy them or what?'

'No – just what did you think of them as policemen?'

'They seemed OK. Better than the ones who tried to arrest me and Neil at a garden centre once.'

'Oh yes – Guy told me all about that.'

'Did he?' Phil's surprise was genuine.

'Oh yes. He admired you. And your relationship with Neil. He always held you up as the great example of a gay couple. Total fidelity and all that.' Derek seemed almost scornful. Phil relaxed a little. 'Anyway,' Derek went on, 'I can't say I was madly impressed by these policemen. Particularly the Inspector, or whatever he was. You know, the caricature Yorkshireman. I mean, they didn't seem to have a clue what to ask. They even tried to suggest I might have done it. I ask you,' Derek's voice seemed to get squeaky when he was indignant. 'They kept asking me where I was at such and such a time.'

'They asked me that too. I don't think there was anything personal in it. I think it's just their job.'

Derek snorted. 'If they knew anything about anything and weren't rushing around being regional caricatures or reject P.D. James characters, they'd just hurry up and arrest Dominic Palmer instead of persecuting and pestering the rest of us.'

'Well, I can't say I feel pestered or persecuted. And I know what the Police can be like to out gay people.'

'Oh yes?' Derek had evidently caught the force of Phil's emphasis. 'And doesn't that suggest to you that discretion might be the better part of valour from time to time?'

'Discretion? I think I'm a bit old for that.'

'What did Guy tell you?' Derek suddenly said, slowing the car down with violence.

'I'm sorry, I'm not with you.'

'Oh come on, stop acting dumb. Guy would have betrayed anyone if the gossip was juicy enough. You wouldn't believe the things he told me about Dominic. I didn't believe the things he'd told Dominic about me. All those years we were friends and he just told him practically every private thing I ever said to him.'

'Honestly, he never said all that much – ' Phil was cut off by a violent acceleration. 'Are we nearly there?' he asked, a little feebly.

'I thought we'd go via the scenic route,' Derek said. Phil began to feel nervous. Derek looked at him and laughed. 'What's the matter?

Don't you like my driving?'

'Well, it's – different.'

Derek slowed down to a more conventional speed. 'Yes. I'm sorry. All this has rather upset me. We'd been friends for years, you know. Ever since his family moved to Surrey.'

'I knew you were at school together.' Phil wondered about committing himself to a white lie about Guy's high regard for Derek, but he was too fond of Guy to allow even his corpse to be staked to this untruth.

'I'll say this,' Derek went on, 'you're remarkably discreet, all things considered. Don't feel obliged to be on my behalf. Not here, anyway. I don't imagine for a moment that Guy respected my confidences when he was talking to you.'

'You seem to have a pretty low opinion of him. I can't see why you're quite so upset if you thought he was so disloyal and untrustworthy.'

'Oh, it's not so much that. He was easily influenced, that's all. I mean, he used to say himself he was weak-willed. And if he thought anything of anyone, he'd always try and impress them by telling them things. Things about other people, I mean, not things about himself. That was the difference between him and Dominic.'

'From what Guy told me, it was the difference between everyone and Dominic.'

Derek laughed. 'True enough. Actually, I'm amazed that Dominic had the nerve to do it. I mean, the thing was pretty horrible, and it must have been very messy, if what the papers said was anything to go by.'

'I thought the papers were revolting. I could hardly bear to read them.'

Derek regarded Phil with curiosity. 'Were you and Guy very close by the end?' he asked, adding, as if to cover himself, 'We didn't see an awful lot of each other over the last few months. And he stopped telling me things.'

'Well.' Phil went through the information he had to offer, as if running a censor's check. 'Didn't you see him at all recently?'

'Once a couple of weeks ago. But he didn't say too much, except about his family.'

'Well,' Phil said again, 'we started seeing each other a bit in the New Year. And then, after he came back from holiday, we saw a lot more of one another.'

'You mean after he'd broken with Dominic?'

Phil laughed. 'You make them sound like an affair.'

'Well, they were – in a way.'

119

'That's not exactly what Guy told me.'

'Oh, I know they didn't sleep together. You know what I mean.'

Phil shrugged. 'I suppose I do. But then that must mean that you and Guy were an affair as well, by that logic. An affair – in a way, at any rate.'

'Perhaps so,' Derek said and Phil detected a smile. He wondered whether this was perhaps the notion Derek had somehow been trying to drive at, but had wanted someone else to say it so as to validate it. Derek was obviously, in his own way, fairly possessive, and he had equally obviously regarded himself as having prior rights over Guy Latimer. In any case, Derek was started on a different tack. 'What did you make of Michael?'

'Oh, I never really met him. He once joined Guy and me for a drink when I was about to go home, so we only really said hello. He's very handsome, isn't he?'

'I suppose so. In that boring Australian film star way that appealed to Guy so much.'

Phil looked ahead and spotted with relief the funeral cortège , which was just pulling into the gates of a bleak green expanse covered with those tasteless monuments that people choose to mock their own grief and insult the memory of their loved ones. Derek gestured at one particularly vulgar group of weeping angels.

'Camp tat,' he said. 'Guy would have loved it.' Phil smiled, a tribute to the first genuine acknowledgment Derek had paid to Guy's attractive side. 'I suppose,' Derek went on, 'Michael was late – when you met him that time.'

'Well, yes, but – '

'Oh, he was always late from what I've heard. Worse than Guy. I never really could see, from my meeting, what Guy saw in him. Apart from his body.'

'I thought Guy was quite smitten. He was quite fast to move in.'

'Well, he didn't have much choice, did he? Anyway, I don't think Michael was that smitten.'

'He seemed a fairly cool customer to me,' Phil countered, 'so it would probably be hard to tell.'

Derek guided the car into a convenient space, at what seemed to Phil an unreasonable speed given their surroundings, and then slammed his foot hard on the brake.

'Actually,' Derek said enigmatically, 'I began to wonder whether Guy wasn't putting it all on a bit.'

'How do you mean?' Phil asked, interested despite himself.

'The whole Michael thing,' Derek said. 'I knew Guy quite well. And I know acting when I see it.'

At this point, he shut up, unleashed himself from his safety belt and clambered out of the car. Phil did likewise, pondering. Enigma for the sake of it, or what? If it was, it was in pretty poor taste. Emerging from the car, Phil looked over to where the assorted Latimers, Diffords and Andersons were amassing themselves.

'Macabre and surreal business, isn't it?' Derek said. 'Planting your loved ones.'

He set off towards Guy's final resting place. Phil, still worried about his eligibility to be there, followed cautiously. As they approached the group, everyone present gave them at least a cursory glance. Even the spinster Latimer aunt, oldest surviving family member on either side, scanned the two young men up and down, thinking to herself what poor physical specimens they both were. In her day, men had been strong and big, women graceful and feminine: now it all seemed to be the wrong way round. Only dear Malcolm seemed to fit in with her idea of what a man should be, although his other lad, not this one they were burying now, was a good strapping boy. How that shrivelled shrimp of a woman managed to produce a fine-looking, big boy like Colin was beyond her. Queers were about all you'd expect from her.

That shrivelled shrimp of a woman stood staring at her son's coffin. As she had perpetually done since that Friday night, she felt her fists clench and unclench autonomously. Glancing up, almost with a twitch, she grasped Derek's arrival, almost a source of relief to her; although she'd known how Guy felt about Derek, all the reservations about his tendency to parade cover stories. Why couldn't Guy have done the same? Who was that other boy, though – a friend of Derek's? Perhaps he was some actor, Derek must know a lot of actors, what with all that amateur acting he did himself, and his job at the BBC. Of course, he was effeminate-looking enough to be one of Guy's secret friends. Phyllis Latimer essayed another glance over at Phil Roxby, with some distaste. Then she turned her head slightly, to look at her husband.

What a superb posture of piety. He had declined to speak a word to her since the Saturday morning, outside of dinner table necessities. Of course, he still expected food laid on regularly. Thank God Gillian had been prepared to do more than her fair share. Colin had been absolutely useless, lying in his room moping, as usual. He'd even started talking to his father about the new football season. Phyllis found this hard to credit and harder still to tolerate. Since Saturday she had begun to remember the Guy she'd loved, the Guy she'd got on with so well, the Guy who'd gone with her to the theatre and opera and so on. It was no use expecting

Colin to stand in for any of the roles Guy had played for her: and Terry wasn't her son, however often he'd been their guest. Phyllis gazed with envy at her sister, flanked on either side by a tall son, their long, thin, pale Anderson faces furrowed into suitably grief-stricken expressions. She particularly gazed at Terry: she hoped that he would do for her some at least of what Guy had done for years, but her hold on him was only, after all, tenuous.

At least, anyway, none of the horrible parts of Guy's life had followed him here to his grave. No Dominic. No Michael. She had seen a photograph of Michael which Guy had shown her to try and gain her approval of the whole disgusting escapade, in more or less the same way he'd shown her photos of film stars and tennis players, expecting her to react as though they were just holiday snapshots.

And thank God the Police had had the decency to stop pestering them today, at any rate. She had lived that awful night over and over and over again for their benefit, telling them about the play, leaving the play, the journey home, arriving home, Malcolm arriving home, Gillian arriving home: she had told them all this so often now that it just ran round and round and round her head like an eternal videotape loop. It mingled, almost with the events of the play she and Terry had seen, the intense American squalor and family catastrophe and sense of doom making a suitable inmix. It seemed, at times, to imprint itself on the television permanently turned on in her home at a volume high enough to prevent conversation breaking out. In the middle of a game show, a film or a soap opera, suddenly Phyllis would see herself and Terry arriving to confront Colin lounging as though he'd been there all night.

Not that this eternal loop was unvaried: occasionally it would be relieved by the sight of Guy in the mortuary after they had 'cleaned him up'; sometimes it would be the perennial favourite of her husband's fist smashing unrelievedly into Guy's face, with the bonfire of Guy's discretion and secrecy smouldering away in the background. These two sights tended to lose themselves in each other. In a way, of course, Guy's death mask had been much less horrific than the Police had led her to expect: when you've seen a face pulped once, in front of you, you're more ready to see it a second time, perhaps even a touch disappointed when it doesn't match the first occasion. No oozing blood, no quickly swelling bruises growing as you watch, no closing eyes, not the second time: just a carved trellis where Guy's face should have been, an imaginatively-designed mesh fitting around his eyes.

She stared down at the coffin again, trying to fight down all these repeating visions, but even as she stared and listened to the meaningless garbage the vicar was prating, she saw herself and Terry arriving back again. The Police had been so interested in their trip to the theatre. Far too interested. Whose idea had it been to go? Terry's. It had been a surprise to cheer her up. And were they both there for the entire performance? It had been so sweet of Terry to turn up that morning with the tickets, a sign that someone actually cared. Then there were all the questions about Malcolm's comings and goings. Did he really stay on his allotment until after dark? Did he have another woman? Yes, yes, possibly, probably: who really cared? She wasn't about to explain to two strangers, both in her detested husband's line of work, despicably crawling around the rotten guts and offal of misery, that she and her husband hadn't slept together in years. She didn't care where he took his pleasure as long as it wasn't with her. Oh, she'd keep his secrets if need be. She wouldn't tell them how he smashed Guy to a mess before throwing him out on the street – though they'd probably approve of that, wouldn't they? Anyway, she wasn't quite sure that she didn't. But she wouldn't tell. She couldn't tell, really, could she?

Malcolm Latimer could almost feel his wife's fists clenching and unclenching as he stood beside her. God save us from lunatic women, he prayed gloomily, knowing that he himself had not been saved, and wondering if he ever could be. From time to time he had wondered about the possibility of ending his marriage, but inertia always prevailed. He had always somehow figured that Phyllis would have to be the one to do something. To start with, he had wondered whether Guy's departure, first from home, then from the world, might be the catalyst. But, oddly, his bloody confrontation with his elder son had served only to create a bond between husband and wife: the bonfire of Guy's pervert books had been their first joint action in many a year, and she had not uttered a single reproach about the beating and bruising he had meted out – which had shocked even him. Only since the death had this bond vanished utterly, leaving her a twitching wreck.

He could leave her, of course: but this home had been put together with his money, his effort, his sweat, and he was damned if he was going to let her twitch and froth in it so that his slut of a daughter and her criminal friends could enjoy it all. And then, to start fending for himself again in his fifties, that would be too much like the wrong kind of hard work. If he had had some fairly friendly widow in tow, who would dote on a man (and who wouldn't expect too much in the way of doting, or whatever, in return, least of all a crack at being the second Mrs Latimer) then it might have been different. But at least as things were, Malcolm Latimer had a roof over his head, occupied by people who owed their existence there to his grace and favour, and would do well to remember it. Guy had forgotten it – now look at him.

And just for a moment a sense of regret and lost opportunity settled on Malcolm Latimer, as he looked at the ridiculous wooden box, that bizarre coffin shape just lying in the ground. He had been so proud of Guy once upon a time. Guy had been a golden boy, a lovely child, someone who could have had it all. Or so he'd thought, anyway. Those few recent years of agony as he'd grown more certain every day that his son had turned into a hollow, perverted mockery of his hopes had been heartbreaking in their way. He'd been able to talk to no-one about it, no-one at all; no friends, none of his occasional women, least of all his wife. He had tried broaching the subject with Phyllis. 'Isn't it time our Guy found himself a girlfriend?' he had asked more than once, bracing himself for the reply. But he hadn't been trusted. That hurt most. So he had been forced to justify the lack of trust.

When he had burnt Guy's books and smashed Guy's face, he hadn't really been indulging an intense hatred of homosexuals. God knows, he'd encountered enough of them before without feeling the need to beat them up. It was the years of exclusion, his son's defiant banishing of his own father that he was trying to smash. But it hadn't worked. He'd been in a silent rage ever since the day of the fight – well, you couldn't call it a fight, could you? There you were: Guy hadn't even paid him the compliment of fighting him back. He'd just taken it, without any return of communication or contact.

Now his wife was twitching away, just twitching. If only she'd talk instead of just twitching, for God's sake.

It ought, really, to have been raining. But it wasn't. Obstinately and perversely, the weather had decided on some quite pleasant, unoppressive sunshine. Just the kind of weather Guy used to enjoy most, Derek thought, good tennis playing weather. The incongruity of the climate pointed up the absurdity of the whole funeral rite. Derek wondered whether the inevitable sandwiches and so on planned chez Latimer might not be better avoided: but, on the whole, Derek enjoyed milking events for their entertainment value. And, besides, he wanted a word with Colin. But it would have been nice if some of their schoolfriends had turned up. Still, the fact that they hadn't was Guy's fault really: he'd made such a big deal about telling them all he was gay that he'd managed to put them all off in a fairly major way. Some had been just plain intolerant: others had got irritated by his insistence on treating it as an ordinary subject for conversation, as ordinary as their own heterosexuality. Derek had

124

never ceased to be amazed at Guy's insensitivity on this point. Still, you might have thought that some of them would show up to fling earth on the coffin.

The ceremony was now drawing to a conclusion. Derek assessed the pious, vaguely crumpled, expressions that everyone was adopting. Phil Roxby looked really absurd. It had been amusing, terrorising him in the car. Pity he had been so unforthcoming, but there it was. Perhaps Guy really had said nothing, but Derek doubted that: and, as he doubted, so he also felt he would be wise to stop thinking along these lines for the time being. He would only become angry if he kept on considering Guy's treacheries. And it was quite important at the moment to keep cool.

After all, he had something to ask Colin, something amusing. And so, when the small group around the hole in the ground began to disperse, hesitantly drifting towards cars, Derek made sure that he made his presence formally known to the immediate family whilst rather cleverly managing to engage only Colin in actual conversation.

Colin gave the impression of being as interested in achieving this as he was, and proffered the scowl that tended to pass, with him, for a smile. 'Are you coming back for the party?' he asked. 'Or do you think it'll be too exciting for you?'

'It's all a bit of an ordeal, isn't it?' Derek replied. 'How's everyone?'

'Usual bunch of jokers. Mum and Dad haven't said a word to each other. Gill's incredibly cut up. She's been out or in her room most of the time. We haven't heard from anyone 'cause all the 'phone calls are being diverted. It's all a right laugh.'

'The 'phone's diverted because of the Press?' Colin nodded. 'Have you read any of the coverage?'

'Oh, fucking hell, it's abysmal. Oh, no, I quite liked the one that suggested that Dad might have done it, that was a bit of a laugh. I see they haven't quoted you or anyone yet.'

'No – apparently Katy Goldsmith told them to eff off so they stopped pestering her. They've tried to find Dominic, but he's gone into hiding. His landlord's so paranoid about the publicity that he's told him to get out for good.'

'I half expected him to show up today, actually.'

'Are you serious?'

'Why not? After all, he got all the ackers,' Colin said morosely. 'I thought he might turn up to gloat. You heard anything of him? Or Michael?' Derek shook his head. 'I'm surprised he hasn't turned up. It'd have been a bit of a laugh watching Mum throw a wobbly if he had. Who's that bloke?'

'That's Phil Roxby.'

'Oh, from the shop. Right. Bit of a fairy, isn't he?'

'More than a bit, I think.' Derek paused. 'Are you going back with the family, or do you want a lift with me?'

'Well' – Colin looked towards his parents and sister – 'I suppose I really ought to –'

'I only wanted to ask – did you manage to get hold of Guy after we'd had our little chat?'

'What do you mean? How could I?' Colin asked unconvincingly, blenching.

'Oh, well –' Derek went on innocently, 'I just hoped you had a chance to make up your differences. You seemed quite wound up about it all when you had that drink with me.' He paused. 'Last Friday.'

'Have you told anyone?' Colin asked, not even trying now to be casual. 'I mean, like that guy, what's his name, over there. Or does Michael Thingy know?'

'Of course not,' Derek said soothingly. 'Whatever is the matter, Colin? I was only worried about you, because I know how fond you and Guy were of each other really. And I know you've had to stick up for him a lot recently.'

'I don't quite get what you're driving at,' Colin said without any real conviction. He was looking extremely pale. From a short distance away, his father called him. He looked anxiously at Derek. 'Look, can I talk to you later? Please don't say anything to anyone. I mean, the Police gave me a really hard time, they're so fucking down on me –' His father's voice called again, perhaps more loudly than was decorous. 'I'll talk to you later, OK?' Colin said and dashed off, trying to appear to be moving more slowly than he really was.

Derek watched him go, thinking just what a good time he was having, and how good-looking Colin was these days. He looked back at the grave and realised, suddenly, that Phil Roxby was still in the offing. Phil was standing over the hole, looking down with an almost religious intensity. For a moment Derek felt an irrational pang of jealousy. Perhaps they had slept together. It would have been quite like Guy not to have told him, given that he didn't fancy Phil himself. Whatever the truth of it, Phil very quickly looked up and walked across the green to Derek on the path.

'Just paying my final respects,' Phil said, flippantly almost. 'Was that little brother Colin? Quite pleasant in a boringly butch sort of way.' He paused, as if musing. 'Not many people, really, were there?'

'Not really. I think one or two people could have made the effort. And no surprise or mystery appearances, either.'

'What, JP?' Phil said. 'They asked you about that too?'

'I couldn't help them at all.' Derek took the car keys from his pocket. 'Can I interest you in another lift?'

'Well – '

'Oh, no fancy driving this time. I feel a bit calmer now.' This was a lie, but Derek wanted to keep hold of Phil for the time being. 'Look, at least let me run you to a train or something, even if you don't fancy joining the gruesome tea party. Although I could introduce you to Colin if you play your cards right.'

'Well,' Phil said again. He was in a cemetery miles from anywhere, and any ride seemed better than a long and unknown walk. 'That's very kind of you. Thanks.'

On this journey, the two of them carefully hemmed themselves in with small talk. As both affected a literary turn of mind, this proved relatively easy, to Phil's great relief. The small gathering they joined was every bit as amusing as Colin Latimer had predicted. Phyllis and Malcolm made no attempt to communicate with one another: rather they chose to join little enclaves of their respective families. Gillian and Colin flitted between the two opposed forces, bearing sandwiches and cups of tea – Colin because he had been ordered to, Gillian because she was unable to tolerate any of the relatives on either side for very long. Even Terry wore thin on her pretty quickly. At times like this, she almost wished she'd stayed married: it would have kept her away from the family home, given her somewhere to hide herself away. Then, for thinking this, she cursed her own selfishness: after all, it was poor Guy she ought to be concerned about.

At this point, she spotted the arrival of Derek and the stranger who'd been at the church and the cemetery, the one she assumed to be an old flame of Guy's. She left the room, so as to guide them into the merry throng. When they returned, she spotted Colin look towards Derek – almost anxious, it seemed, nervous. Derek introduced the stranger: the name seemed faintly familiar from Guy's conversation, but she couldn't think, straight off, of a tactful way of finding out whether her initial assumption was at all well-founded. The three of them were joined by her cousin Terry, dressed very carefully for the occasion in a suit that could have come straight out of one of those horrendous designer shops, his pallid features composed into just the right expression of offhand seriousness. He and Derek knew each other, of course. He seemed also to know Phil Roxby.

'Yes, we did meet a couple of times. You came into the shop with Guy a few weeks ago, I remember.'

'Yes, and once before then, I think,' Terry said. 'I wanted a street map of Paris and you didn't know where they were.'

'Oh well,' Phil said dismissively, 'I'm not often in Travel.' He stressed the heading to indicate some distaste, then laughed. Derek looked uncomfortable. Gillian began to wonder whether this Phil person and Derek were connected. But obviously from what Terry and Phil had said, Phil was a friend of Guy's.

'Oh, I'm terribly sorry,' Terry said tetchily. 'You must have a terrible time slumming in the prole sections of the shop, I'm sure.' He turned away as if to leave the little group.

'Sorry,' Phil said sincerely, touching Terry on the arm. Terry flinched. 'I didn't mean anything. Just an in-house joke.'

'OK,' Terry replied. 'I think the strain got to me.'

'Well, you're not under much strain, surely,' Derek said. 'After all, you and Guy's mother were conveniently tucked away in the theatre, weren't you? Now you should hear how the Police have gone on at me because I was on my own.'

'Oh, the Police!' Gillian cut in derisively. 'If you can't say exactly where you were or you say you were on your own, then you must be a murderer. If you can say where you were and who was with you, then you must be a liar as well.'

Derek nodded. 'That does rather seem to be their attitude. What it actually boils down to, of course, is that they simply haven't got a clue. After all, Guy was so secretive about his life that nobody quite knew all his friends or what he was up to half the time. You know, like I only met Dominic the once and none of you ever did at all. Michael was hardly introduced to anyone. None of you knew Phil, except Terry, who met him largely by accident. Guy was like that.'

'Well,' Terry said, 'he was so terrified of large groups and social occasions.'

'That's what he said,' Derek sniffed. 'I always thought all that was – well, I shouldn't say that kind of thing here.' An embarrassed silence descended on them, which was broken by Colin joining himself to the group.

'Enjoying the party?' he asked miserably.

'You do realise,' Terry said, 'that we're bound to be interrupted, now that both the sandwich bearers are here.'

'Derek – ' Colin said edgily ' —can I have a word with you in private? Later or something.' Gill regarded at her brother quizzically. Derek smiled and nodded, looking both gnome-like and gnomic at one and the same time. Terry gave both Derek and Colin an almost disapproving glance.

'Conspiracy?' he said, with a chilling smile. 'That seems rather – ' But he was cut short by his Aunt Phyllis calling across the room. 'Oh dear, I wonder what she wants,' he moaned; but before he could drift over to her, his aunt, still embroiled in nervous reflex movements and seeming more edgy than ever, came across.

'I'm sorry to sort of break in,' she quavered, 'but I need to have a word with Terry about something.'

'Do you, Auntie?' he returned. Gill wondered if there was any connection between the sudden desire for 'words' and Colin's railway ticket, a subject that had lain more or less dormant since she had found it on the Saturday morning.

But then the doorbell rang. Phyllis vividly became struck with panic.

'Who's – I mean, you don't think it's the Police? – Hadn't somebody better – oh dear, I – '

'Shall I go?' Derek asked, and went. Nobody else appeared to have done anything about it. Later, he felt glad that he'd volunteered: it was a suitably dramatic moment, which the amateur actor in him wouldn't have missed for the world. He flung open the door to be confronted by three smart, sombrely suited young men.

'Hello, Derek,' Michael Hamilton said, blue eyes a-twinkle. 'It is Derek, isn't it? Are we too late?'

He tutted at his own bad manners. 'Sorry, this is Marcus Grey.' A tall, well-built young man with short curly reddish hair nodded and said 'Hallo' in an obviously Scots voice. Derek took an instant fancy to him. 'And of course,' Michael said, drawing back a fraction, 'you've met Dominic, haven't you?' Derek's jaw dropped. 'Now,' Michael went on, 'are we too late?'

'Well – there's still some food left – '

'Oh good. That is a relief. Shall we enter?'

'I really don't think you ought to – well, maybe you, but Dominic really shouldn't – '

'Come now, Derek,' Michael replied urbanely, 'are you seriously proposing to exclude Guy's bereaved lover and his sole heir, both of whom have an absolute right to be here?'

'Look here, Derek,' Dominic said, 'I was a very close friend of Guy's until fairly recently. And anyway, I think I have the right to hear for myself all the poison that Guy's family and you, probably, are spreading about me.'

'Well, we haven't said – '

'Oh, come off it,' interrupted the dishy Marcus, 'you wee twister.'

Derek was struck by how much the Jean Brodie cultured accent and the rough manner were at odds. 'Somebody's trying to frame Dominic. We think it's someone here. Oh, hello.' This, Derek realised, was addressed over his shoulder. Turning round he saw Phyllis Latimer behind him in the hall.

'Oh my God,' she said wearily. 'Michael. Well – Dominic. I don't know who you are, but I suppose you're another one. I suppose now you're all here you'd better come in.'

Michael Hamilton almost bowed with mock civility.

'Exactly,' he said. And, psychologically if not physically, he pushed Derek aside and led his party across the threshold.

# 9: Family Man

Oldcastle drummed his fingers moodily on the dashboard, as he and Morgan watched the steady current of besuited men and women pass along the narrow street. It was one of those streets that only a few years ago had been running to seed; but now people like the ones flowing past, returning from their financial and administrative labours, had taken the area by the scruff of the neck and forced it to smarten up. The Chief Inspector hummed a little hum of derision.

Stuart Morgan unobtrusively surveyed his Chief out of the corner of his eye. So, he'd fixed on his culprit, had he? That wasn't good news at all. Morgan himself gravely doubted the theory that put the responsibility at Michael Hamilton's door. It was self-evident that Hamilton was an egocentric bastard; it was quite likely that he'd be prepared, if he thought circumstances warranted it, to commit or at least to connive at murder. But he wouldn't commit a murder from which he stood to gain nothing. Ultimately, in Morgan's eyes, Hamilton's genuinely unlikeable characteristics were, ironically, his strongest moral alibi.

Pure speculation, all this, of course: but, unless Dennis Kelly or someone hitherto unthought of had really seen something, speculation was more and more the order of the day. No fingerprints, no knife, no physical evidence at all: an elusive bloodstain on a washbasin in the club, which might or might not have had a bearing on the matter, was about all they had – and they knew nothing about that yet. Morgan wondered whether they should have been quite so humane and speedy in releasing the body for the hasty funeral which had taken place that day; after all, the inquest had been adjourned until the following week. But the medical boys were sure they'd analysed whatever there was to analyse.

Oldcastle grunted. 'It'd be a help,' he muttered, 'if we knew who the hell we're waiting for.'

'When someone goes in, we'll have a one in four chance of being right.'

'Marvellous. I could have done with his missus being in. I'm terrifically thirsty.'

Morgan squashed the temptation to make a catty remark about alcoholic dehydration. 'I think Palmer said something about her being away last week, sir, when he finally let us have the address.'

'Maybe. But last week was last week, Stuart. Eh up.'

Morgan winced. It was affected Northernism time again. Then he realised that the expression was supposed to attract his attention to a dark-haired, well-built man, probably in his thirties, who was heading towards the door of the house in which the flat of the Kelly family was located. 'I'd lay money on that being him, sir. He fits the description Palmer gave us.'

'Well. Let's go and find out.'

Oldcastle began to struggle out of the car, whilst Morgan leapt out and sprinted across the road. The man was fumbling with keys and, sure enough, he was at the right door. He had just opened it and was stooping to pick up his briefcase again, when Morgan hailed him as discreetly as possible.

'Ah – Mr Kelly?'

The man stood up and swivelled round. He was uncannily, almost devilishly, handsome: something in his deep brown eyes looked intensely wary. He said nothing.

'I'm Detective-Sergeant Morgan, CID, sir.' Morgan produced his identification. 'The gentleman just crossing the road is Detective Chief Inspector Oldcastle.'

'Is anything wrong? Nothing's happened to Anna and Lucy, has it?' The voice had a Northern twang, but not like Oldcastle's; Morgan couldn't exactly place it.

'No, sir,' Morgan replied. 'We're investigating a murder which took place outside a club last Friday night. You may have read about in the newspapers. The victim's name was Latimer, Guy Latimer.'

Kelly looked at him suspiciously. 'You mean the gay boy? I'm afraid I don't see how I – '

'We've been told that you were in fact at that club that night, Mr Kelly, and that you probably left there close to the time the murder was committed.' Oldcastle arrived as Morgan finished this sentence. 'I do think, sir, it would be – well, better, more discreet, perhaps – if you were to invite us in. Not that we can force you to.'

'Mmm.' For a moment Kelly didn't move. Then he turned round and began to enter the flat, first of all stopping to pick up two letters which were lying on the doormat inside. 'Come in,' he said, turning round, but still looking at his post. The policemen moved into the hall. 'Hang on,' Kelly said, disappearing round the corner of a long, dark corridor. 'Sitting room's to your right,' he shouted invisibly, 'go in and I'll be with you.'

Morgan gingerly pushed a door open to his right: and he and the Chief Inspector were straight away confronted with a large white room, lavishly furnished, carefully kept. Oldcastle nodded sardonically.

'Very nice, I'm sure. This responsible job must pay well.'

'Or his wife's well off, sir.'

Oldcastle looked askance at his underling. 'Funny remark to make, Stuart. What prompted it?'

'Just a thought. I mean, it would explain why he stays with her.'

'Well, there is a child involved – '

'Or why he married her in the first place, perhaps?'

Oldcastle coughed at this, presumably to drown Morgan's theory as footsteps softly padded back down the corridor. Dennis Kelly appeared in the doorway. He had changed into impeccably smart casual clothes: a pastel-coloured shirt and well-fitting grey trousers. The man had a compact frame: a tough customer in a brawl, thought Morgan.

'Mr Kelly,' Oldcastle opened, almost musingly, 'it is convenient to talk now, I take it?'

'It's never particularly convenient to talk to the Police, is it?' Kelly said. He stayed where he stood, looking at them with naked hostility. 'I suppose you'd better sit down.' He sighed. 'Thank God my wife's not here, that's all I can say.'

'Your wife is away?' Morgan asked as gently as he could. Neither he nor Oldcastle had yet acted on the gracious invitation to sit.

'She and Lucy – I suppose you know that Lucy's my daughter – are staying with her mother for a fortnight.' A pause. 'She hasn't left me, if that's what you think.'

'No, sir, that's not what we think,' Morgan answered, vaguely reassuringly he hoped. He decided to offer a pleasantry. 'Very nice place you've got, if I might say so.' This didn't seem to go down at all well: Kelly's hostile glare widened.

'I don't suppose either of you want a drink,' he said, 'all that "not while we're on duty" crap and so on. Well, I'm going to get myself one. Look, sit down, for Christ's sake.'

He disappeared again. Oldcastle sat in one of the luxurious armchairs. Morgan stood musing for a moment, trying to place Kelly's accent. Then he sat, almost flopped, down on the sofa.

'We are seeing some nice places, aren't we?' Oldcastle murmured. He looked at his Sergeant and then up again, to see Dennis Kelly advancing on them, clutching a tall wide glass full of brown fizzing liquid clinking with ice. 'Right, Mr Kelly. Do you want to go through all the where-were-you-on-the-night-of-Friday-the-fifteenth stuff, or shall we get straight down to brass tacks?'

'Well, I'd quite like to know why you think I can help you.'

Oldcastle sighed. 'All right, then,' he said. 'You are, I believe, acquainted with a Mr Dominic Palmer. Intimately acquainted, to put not too fine a point on it.'

'I am a married man, Chief Inspector, I'd remind you.'

'Sir.' Oldcastle paused: a bombastic, orchestral pause. 'We are not concerned with your private arrangements. We are not aware of any offence you personally have committed. But last Friday a young man was murdered in a peculiarly vicious assault, and it is just conceivable that, if what we have been told is correct, you were nearby and may have seen something at the time of the murder. Some small irrelevant thing you didn't think about at the time. Some glaringly obvious thing you didn't want to come forward and discuss because of fear of compromising your discretion. But please relax, Mr Kelly. Our interest is in catching a murderer, not in interfering in your private life.'

Kelly laughed. He had a very fine set of teeth, even, white, which were revealed in all their splendour by his laugh. 'It's all very well for you to say that. But if I did see something, I'll have to appear in court, won't I? And then they'll find out at work. My daughter will find out. I can't let that happen, you know. I've got far too much to lose.' He put his glass down on a small coffee table. It was empty already, Morgan noticed. 'So.' And at last he sat down. 'What's Dominic been saying?'

Oldcastle spluttered. 'I think we'd better hear your version first, don't you?'

'Well — Do you mind if I get myself another drink?'

'I think perhaps we ought to suggest you don't,' Oldcastle replied with pomposity, leaving Morgan to marvel at his hypocrisy.

'You think I can't take it? Crap. It's my flat, you know.' He made as if to get up and then suddenly threw himself back in the armchair. 'All right. I agreed to meet Dominic there – at the club – at eleven. He'd been pestering me with letters and I wanted to tell him to stop it.' He laughed humourlessly. 'I mean, he was obsessed with me. I want you to understand, though – there was nothing between us. Nothing at all. But he just wouldn't see that. I mean, there couldn't be anything long-term between us. I told him that all along.'

'How long had you known him?' Morgan asked, wondering as he did so whether this was strictly relevant.

'Well, I met him a couple of months ago, but I hadn't seen him for a month before last Friday.' He sighed. 'He completely misunderstood me. He had this crazy idea I wanted to leave Anna for him. Fucking mad. He thought it was just Anna's money, but I don't care about money.' A pleading tone crept into his voice. Oldcastle was beginning to fidget.

'So. That night. Last Friday,' Morgan prompted.

'I went to the club about five to eleven,' Kelly went on, suddenly concentrating hard on recalling what he had done. 'I stood by the cloakroom place, and pretty soon Dominic turned up.'

'Was he alone?'

'Well, there were quite a few people there – '

'Was he with anyone?' Oldcastle spelt out with irritation.

'Oh. No. No.' An emphatic headshake. 'He looked quite miserable, actually.'

'Did he mention meeting anyone?' Morgan asked.

'He didn't say anything at all really,' Kelly said, 'except a load of crap about him and me being together and how we could make it work if we wanted it to. Usual stupid load of old crap. He just couldn't be practical. And he never thought about how I might feel.'

'So,' Morgan picked up the thread, 'he didn't mention anyone else at all?' Kelly shook his head. 'You're sure? He didn't say anything about Guy Latimer?'

'No, nothing. I mean, he talked about him the first time I met him – what a vicious little cu – boy he was, things like that. But he didn't mention him on Friday. I don't think he did, anyway. No. He just whined on about being in love with me. I reckon he's either a bit mad or a bit obsessed with melodramas about love. He ought to be on the stage.'

There was another pause. Morgan wondered if these reflections were really getting them anywhere at all. They certainly underlined Palmer's doubtful status as a murderer: it was likely that he was with Kelly right up to the time of the actual deed, and extremely improbable that he would have been capable, after a scene of the kind Kelly was hinting at, of committing a murder and then covering up his tracks with a ruthless efficiency. To lose the murder weapons and clean himself up as well, Palmer would have had to have been calm and capable, not in a highly emotional state. Motive too receded if he was obsessed with Kelly and not with Latimer; he seemed to have no interest in the money. But Palmer was not currently the main suspect, anyway: so it was to be hoped that Kelly had managed to notice something as he left. Morgan felt it incumbent upon himself to give a push in this direction.

'Can you remember what time you left the club?' he asked, perhaps more abrasively than he had wished.

'Actually, I can. I looked at my watch just as I went out. It was 11.17, more or less exactly.'

'Did you come straight home, sir?' Oldcastle asked.

'Yes – I got the Northern Line from Embankment.'

'Now, Mr Kelly,' Morgan said deferentially, 'I want you to try and think very hard, try and remember. Did you see anything unusual or untoward going on in the alley outside the club? And above all, did you see anyone who looked like this?'

He took from his jacket pocket the travelcard that had been in Guy Latimer's rucksack and handed it over. Kelly scanned it critically.

'I've seen better pictures of him than this,' he replied with a laugh, 'although I'd forgotten that till now. He's quite a pretty boy, isn't he? Oh, sorry, I don't suppose you've given it much thought, have you? No, I remember, Dominic showed me some photos of the two of them in Italy. Anyway, that's hardly relevant, is it? I must say, though, the picture didn't come out very well in the papers.'

He went back into concentration mode. 'Obviously there were people outside the club – I mean people had scarcely started arriving at that time – but, come to think of it, there was a couple standing together a little way away who didn't seem to be going anywhere particularly. They were having quite an intense conversation. I remember thinking that one of them might have given Dominic a run for his money.' He laughed. 'The other one was blond. I know he was blond because I always notice blonds.'

Morgan noticed the odd intrusion of overt defiance into an otherwise closeted manner, and began wondering about the Kelly marriage and its internal working. His wife, it had been said, knew about it all: how did she feel, though?

'But I couldn't really see the blond boy's face,' Kelly went on, looking down at the photograph again, 'so I can't really say – the hair's certainly right, though: the style of it, I mean. Yes, definitely. Come to think, I remember something about the blond boy rang a faint bell. I would say it was him, actually.'

The two detectives looked at each other, almost with a sense of relief. Both began questions, and stopped immediately. Never before in the career of either man had such an objectively negligible and indefinite piece of information proved such a catalyst of hope. Morgan, made benevolent by a sense of progress, deferred to his senior.

'Sorry, Stuart,' Oldcastle began, almost sincerely. 'Right, Mr Kelly, what did you notice about the other person? The not blond one, that is. You said they were having quite an intense conversation. Did you hear any of it? Would you go so far as to call it a quarrel?'

Kelly sat in thought. Then he stood up. 'Before I answer any more questions, I'm going to have another drink,' he announced, obviously having sensed that a festival atmosphere was sweeping over the gathering. And without waiting for a response, he left the room, carrying his glass with him.

'Well, Stuart,' Oldcastle beamed. 'I think we may be onto something at last.'

'Possibly, sir,' Morgan replied, suddenly overwhelmed by a sense of caution, 'if he can actually remember anything.'

'Oh, he's got to,' Oldcastle said, 'he's got to. I mean you'd agree that he saw Latimer?'

'The balance of probability tends to suggest – '

'Oh, for Christ's sake, Stuart, you sound like a bloody lawyer. Of course it was Latimer. Two blond boys outside having arguments at the same time? Are you asking me to accept that kind of coincidence? We both know that it probably happened around then – ' Oldcastle gestured emphatically.

'Well, if he can come up with anything – ' Morgan paused. 'You don't think he's done a bunk, do you, sir?'

'Now, why in God's name should he want to do a bunk?' Oldcastle laughed. 'He just likes a drop or two. It's not unknown.' Morgan repressed instinctive comment here. 'It might even help. Loosen his tongue. Who knows?'

Morgan vaguely cleared his throat: but, as if to allay his doubts, Kelly returned, clutching another fizzing glass. Morgan tried to catch its scent. Whisky and Coke, he suspected on reflection, a thoroughly unpleasant mixture.

Sitting down, the subject of their interrogation gave them a totally insincere smile, revealing again his fine, carefully groomed teeth.

'Well,' he said. 'As one of the two was blond, I didn't give the not blond one much attention. But I did get a sort of look at him. Actually, he wasn't that far off blond himself – quite fair. Well, not dark, anyway. A kind of light brown.' The detectives both nodded, indicating that he should carry on if he possibly could. 'Let me think. They were both about the same height, I think – possibly the not blond one was slightly taller. Yes, he was, definitely.'

'Ah – ' Oldcastle paused melodramatically ' – did you see his face at all? The slightest thing you can remember would be extremely helpful, I mean, the smallest detail...'

Dennis Kelly took a long drink, closed his eyes and considered. 'I didn't really see – well, I got a glimpse, sort of. You've got to remember, I wasn't really looking. I mean, the business with Dominic had been a bit upsetting – he'd said some nasty things to me, you see. But let me think. He wasn't what I'd call handsome or pretty: but not horrible or ugly, or anything. I'm sorry, that's not very helpful, really.'

'Oh, I wouldn't say that,' Oldcastle replied airily. 'But – sorry to push you – was this chap – well, how old would you say he was? Twenties, thirties, teens, what?'

'I'm not very good at guessing ages,' Kelly said speciously, 'but I'd say twenties. Not more than twenty-five, probably less. I can never tell these things. Actually,' he relaxed back into the chair, 'and I hope you won't mind my saying this, but it is the truth as it happens, I lost interest in them, because a very handsome boy came by. He must have been exceptionally handsome, actually, because he wasn't blond and I still looked at him.'

Oldcastle sat bolt upright. 'A good-looking, dark-haired young man,' he said slowly.

Kelly nodded. 'Oh yes. I can see him quite clearly. Actually, for a minute I thought he was looking back at me. But he wasn't. I suppose he must have been looking at the other two. I didn't stop to find out, though. I just wanted to get home, really.'

Morgan sat forward on the sofa and gave Kelly a careful appraising look. 'The two you saw – the blond one and the not blond one. You said that it was an intense conversation. Do you mean they were arguing?'

'Well – ' Kelly paused for another swig. 'The not blond one was doing most of the talking. I wouldn't say they were arguing. It was just – well – intense. Oh, I don't know. Private. Close. Not the kind of conversation that more than two people can have.' He smiled a little more convincingly than on the previous occasion. 'I'm sorry, I'm not being very helpful.'

'Oh, far from it, Mr Kelly,' Oldcastle replied generously. 'I must say that you've been most helpful. And – er – well – under the circumstances, most – well – forthcoming.'

'Oh. I suppose you mean my marriage and so on by the circumstances.'

'Well, I – '

'I can assure you,' Morgan cut in, 'that if you should need to appear in court, we'll do everything we possibly can to make sure there's no problems arising from unwanted publicity. Won't we, sir?' He turned emphatically to his Chief.

'Oh, aye, yes, absolutely.'

'Don't get me wrong,' Kelly said expansively, 'I'm not ashamed. I'm not ashamed of what I am at all. But there is my job to think of. And Lucy. I mean,' he went on, obviously determined, after two drinks, to get extremely involved in self-justification, 'my wife knows about them all. All the boys. Dominic and all the other little Dominics. The more important Dominics than Dominic. But she knows that I never really get serious about any of them. Dominic couldn't – or wouldn't – ever appreciate that.' He laughed. 'I don't know why I'm telling you all this. I mean,' he stopped again for a high-pitched giggle, 'it's totally ridiculous to think that I'm sitting here telling two policemen all this crap. Would either of you like a drink now?' he asked vehemently. 'I'm going to have another one.' He got up again.

Morgan was about to refuse, but he reckoned without his Chief.

'That's extremely kind of you. I'll join you, if I may. If you have any Scotch.'

'Certainly. And for you?'

'Oh – er – just some orange juice, if I may.'

Kelly laughed. 'I'm not sure if there's any in. Anna deals with that side of things. I'll have a look.'

He left the room again. Oldcastle beamed seraphically at his sergeant.

'Well, Stuart,' he said, 'that's more or less cracked that.'

'Has it, sir?' Morgan feared this sudden optimism might be hard to handle if it provoked extremes of certainty.

'Of course it bloody has. Don't be thick, lad. Latimer goes outside with this long-standing mystery man – '

'How do we know he's long-standing, sir?'

'Oh, just a guess. An educated guess. Anyway, Latimer and he go outside, presumably so that Hamilton won't catch them inside.

Only they don't know that Hamilton's gone off to make his secretive cloak and dagger 'phone call. Hamilton comes back, sees them, waits for the other man to go and then kills Latimer. Jealousy. The insult to his arrogance, to his stupendous ego, whatever you like to call it. It has to be something like that.'

Morgan nodded, but not in agreement. For him it didn't ring true as a scenario. 'One thing, sir – who's the mystery man? Why hasn't he come forward?'

'Frightened of getting the blame. Hmm. Hang on. Sort of fair. Quite tall. Not conventionally handsome. At a guess, I'd say that it could be that Roxby lad. Wasn't Latimer supposed to have been quite keen on him? Didn't that other friend of his – that what's his name, Wilkinson – say so?'

Morgan nodded again. That explanation had plausibility – but was it anything more than that? He covered his eyes with his hand, a visual sign of thought, but couldn't really see beyond what Oldcastle had suggested, if only because of its novelty value. He took his hand away and looked up, to see Dennis Kelly bearing drinks.

'You're in luck, Sergeant,' he said, proffering a glass, a wine glass, filled with orange juice. Oldcastle was sitting savouring a generous helping of neat whisky. It struck Morgan again that Dennis Kelly was a somewhat mercurial character.

Kelly reseated himself and picked up his bubbling brown concoction. 'Well,' he said, 'what shall we talk about now? I seem to be in a talkative mood suddenly. You'd better take advantage of it.'

Oldcastle grunted pleasantly. Morgan winced: the Chief had obviously decided that everything was over now bar the proving. But one or two things still wandered around Morgan's mind. He decided to take Kelly up on his offer.

'It's a very nice flat,' he said, playing for time, 'your job must pay well.'

'That's a laugh,' Kelly replied. 'Pays next to nothing, actually.' Morgan looked askance at this. 'Oh, Anna's family are terribly well-off, you see. And they're very generous to her, always have been. Generous to me, too. You see, they never thought she'd ever get married.'

'Oh really, why was that?' Morgan's curiosity was roused, and suddenly he pictured a hideous and deformed crone. This didn't quite match up with Dennis Kelly somehow, or, perhaps more significantly, the wedding photograph decorating one of the room's two bookcases.

'Oh,' Kelly laughed, 'she only likes poofs. She's never fancied a straight man in her life. I'm the nearest she ever got, you see.' He paused. 'It's not the money, you know.' Morgan sensed a certain pugnacity returning to his tone. 'I hope you don't think that.'

'I'm sure, sir,' Morgan lied in return. He remembered one thing that had been in his memory, slightly nagging. 'When we talked to Dominic Palmer, he suggested, well – he implied, anyway – that when you met him that night there might have been some sort of – ' He stopped dead in embarrassment: no matter how far into this case he got, the idea didn't cease to worry him, the idea of men together for sex, the idea of actually suggesting to other men that they might have been doing things with other men. He tried again. 'Some sort of, well,' was as far as he got this time. Just having been talking about Kelly's wife didn't make it any easier.

'You're talking about sex?' Kelly asked good-naturedly. He gave another high-pitched giggle. 'Is that what Dominic said? Oh, he's exaggerating, like he always does.'

'It doesn't really matter, Mr Kelly,' Oldcastle intervened, 'so long as we know that Palmer didn't go out of the club with you.'

'No.' Kelly shook his head. 'I just left him standing. I was a bit disappointed in a way – I thought he might chase after me. But he definitely didn't. When I told him I was going, he just stood there, actually. Didn't look like he'd move again all night. He just watched me go – didn't even throw one of his crying fits. They're very good, his crying fits.'

'He sounds a bit unstable from what you say,' Oldcastle remarked dubiously.

'Moody,' Kelly replied. 'A lot of the time he's fine, you see, but – well, I'm talking about when I've seen him.'

'He seemed all right yesterday,' Morgan replied.

'I hope so,' Kelly said, in a quite kindly tone. 'He needs someone to straighten him out, so to speak. Someone a bit practical who can actually do things and not just talk about doing things.'

Morgan nodded. It explained the recent transformation in Dominic Palmer. As for Kelly, he was obviously, whatever he might tell his young men (and Morgan suspected that he told them quite a lot) deeply rooted in his marriage. And how could you expect him to turn his back on all this luxury, all this comfort?

'Well, Stuart, when you're ready,' Oldcastle murmured, rising ponderously to his feet. 'Well, thank you very much Mr Kelly, we appreciate your time and trouble. You've been most helpful.'

'Did I have much choice?' Kelly smiled as he stood up. 'Still, it's nice to be helpful once in a while.' He opened the sitting room door. 'I'll see you out.'

'Thanks,' both policemen replied, following him. He opened the front door: an almost severe look descended over his face as he did so.

'I won't say do get in touch again,' he said, 'because after Saturday it won't be very convenient for you to call again.'

'Oh, I'm sure that won't be necessary,' Oldcastle said breezily. 'And, anyway, as Sergeant Morgan said, we are capable of discretion. Contrary to popular opinion.' He smiled directly at Kelly as he passed him, and left the flat. Morgan followed, nodding pleasantly at their host. He heard the door shut behind him.

Outside the house Oldcastle was waiting. 'Well, Stuart,' he said, leaving Morgan to supply any further comment. Morgan decided to play dumb.

'Well, sir?'

'I get the impression that you're not entirely happy about what Mr Kelly saw. About the scenario – bloody awful word, that – I outlined earlier.'

'Well, sir – ' How to phrase this tactfully? 'I don't think it's enough to get a conviction on, sir. Not a single positive identification – '

'Well, not yet, Stuart.'

'Even if we can get one, sir, a clever defence brief could rip it to shreds in a moment in court.'

'Now look, lad,' Oldcastle replied belligerently, 'you know as well as I do that the next move is to get the culprit to own up. Crack him. It's the only sure way in a case like this. A nice, neat, signed, truthful confession. Then the courts can argue about whether or not he was a loony when he did it. As long as we've got him to admit he did it. That's all I care about. Cracking the bastard.'

'Him being Hamilton in this case?'

'Too bloody right,' Oldcastle replied. He had arrived at the car slightly ahead of Morgan. 'Come on, Stuart. They must have got those effing blood tests back by now. I want to radio on. Pity that sodding clap clinic insisted on maintaining its bloody discretion. Bloody doctors. They look at a few willies and suddenly they think they're on a par with priests in the confessional.'

Morgan unlocked both doors. Oldcastle heaved himself in and started a radio dialogue. The radio operator seemed to be suffering from terminal obtuseness. 'No, I just want to talk to DC Bowen. Bowen. Bo. Wen.' Crackle, crackle, she replied. After an exercise in rank-pulling, Oldcastle prevailed. 'Well come on, boy, out with it.' A masculine crackle emanated. 'Oh, have it your own way. Over and out.' He put the radio down.

'The results are through, Stuart, but Ken Bowen thinks he can't discuss such matters over the radio. I mean, he's right, but bloody hell. Well, Sergeant, start the car. Let's get back. For God's sake,' he fumed, 'hasn't this thing got a siren or anything? Because if it has, I want it going at full blast. There's some real evidence waiting for us. And when we've got it, then I'm going to find Mr Hamilton and crack him like a walnut at Christmas.'

He squeezed his right hand into a fist.

# 10: House of Fun

After Dominic, Marcus and Michael arrived, the funeral party limped from bad to worse. It was particularly affected as a social function by Dominic's innocent production of the lunchtime edition of the *Standard*.

'IT'S A COVER UP' screamed the banner headline, supported by an explanation in only slightly smaller lettering: 'Gay Club Murder Suspect Accuses Police.' Next to the story was a picture of Guy, dressed in tee-shirt and shorts and standing in front of an unidentified panoramic view, laughing at the camera. It had actually come out in print rather well and it was, he claimed, in order to make this point that Dominic had pulled the paper from his pocket.

'I'm not a very good photographer,' he said, 'not as a general rule, but I do think that this was one of the best I ever managed. Don't you think it catches Guy well?' He was now addressing all members of both families, with a loud breeziness completely out of keeping with the occasion. 'I don't know whether anyone would like a copy. I mean, I'd be only too delighted to get some done.' He smiled around the room.

Michael turned to Marcus and gave an ecstatic grin. This was glorious. He turned his attention next to surveying Guy's cousin. Wet piece of lettuce, that young man was – like most of Guy's friends. After a few seconds Terry seemed to register the surveillance; for a while he returned it steadily; and after a few seconds more, he detached himself from talking to the animated garden gnome whom Michael recalled with no fondness whatsoever. Michael permitted himself a private smile as this process with Terry took place: it had been uncannily like cruising, really – the last sort of thing you expected at a funeral tea. Not that he would, given a choice, have cruised Terry, but then he wasn't exactly spoilt for choice in these surroundings.

He turned and smiled politely at Marcus, who drifted understandingly to Dominic's side, as Dominic explained at great length to some ghastly aunt or other about the photograph, simultaneously waving the newspaper under Guy's mother's nose. Michael smiled coyly – my God it *was* like cruising – at Terry, as he slowly presented himself. He stood in front of Michael and demurely returned the smile. Michael raised his eyes to get a proper look at Terry's pallid physiognomy. 'So,' he said, 'we meet at last.'

'Ah.' Terry gulped a bit. 'Are you absolutely sure we haven't met before?'

'Absolutely. Unless of course I have suddenly become a prey to premature senility or amnesia or any like affliction. Which I haven't.' Michael smiled humourlessly.

'Ah.' Terry gulped again. 'I suppose I'd better explain. You see, I told everyone – all the immediate family – that I'd met you once.'

Michael shrugged. 'Was that merely for the social cachet of laying claim to my acquaintance? An understandable enough reason, Terence. Or was there what we might euphemistically call an ulterior motive?'

'Well – ' Terry paused. Michael noticed that his general level of fluster was not great, which was odd given the implications behind the subject under discussion. He ought, this young – well, boy, but he seemed less boyish at close quarters than he gave the impression of being from a distance – he ought to have been somewhat more agitated than he seemed. His hesitation now, for example, was as redolent of calculation as of self-collection.

'Well,' Terry began again, 'a couple of weeks or so ago, I stayed in town. Everyone here knows that. They gossip quite a lot, my mother and all the aunts – Guy's mother's one, obviously – actually, that's why they were quite fond of Guy, because he was such a superb gossip. Well, you know that.'

'I'm sorry,' Michael said, 'it wasn't a quality in him I was ever in a position to appreciate fully. We had no mutual friends to gossip about.' He hoped that the second statement, a fact, compensated for the first, an outright lie. Michael didn't like being considered a gossip in any form, either participant or listener: if people thought you were a gossip, they would tell you little and believe less.

'Well,' Terry went on, 'I told them all that I stayed at your flat.'

'My house,' Michael corrected. 'First rule of lying: get your facts

143

right.' He smiled viciously. 'And did you?'

'Well, obviously I didn't, or we'd have met.'

Michael was struck by this. So ingenuous: or was it totally disingenuous? Interesting. 'This was about the end of July?' Terry nodded. Michael smiled, pityingly. 'I was out of the country. So, you see, you rushed in rather pointlessly with your alibi. I couldn't corroborate your story even if – hey,' and just for a moment his cool was perceptibly jolted. 'What the hell am I supposed to have been an alibi for, anyway?'

'Well, you see. There's this woman I've been seeing. But I didn't really want anyone to know. Guy knew. But he wouldn't tell the family. I could rely on him not to.'

'That's not entirely consistent, you know. "Guy" – and I quote – "was such a superb gossip." How could he resist a little item like that?'

'Well, there was also the fact that he wasn't seeing anyone in the family apart from me by then.'

'A more cogent reason to rely on him. But it wasn't true, was it? He saw his brother and sister. I know that for a fact. Indeed, I had to take great pains in order to forego the dubious honour of meeting his brother the hooligan.'

'Oh, Colin's all right.'

'Colin's a thug and we both know it. Quite attractive, but a thug.' Michael looked across the room: tall, dark, handsome Colin Latimer stood in a corner engaged in what seemed to be a fairly serious conversation with the garden gnome. Michael permitted himself a private laugh: perhaps Wilkinson harboured thoughts of transferring his thwarted passion from the dead Latimer brother to the living one. Whether or no, his success would remain at the same level. Michael was a dreadful snob when it came to looks. He returned his full attention to Terry, even though the conversation was beginning to pall. 'So you'd say that Guy never gossiped with his brother or sister, would you?'

'Well, no, but – '

'Right. So your story, Mr – what's your name? Difford, thank you – your story's pretty feeble really.' Michael laughed, but out of malice pure and simple. 'Don't look all offended. I didn't say I didn't believe you. Just that the story was pretty bloody useless. As stories go.'

'Look – ' Terry Difford drawled, and there was no other word to describe it – 'I'm not asking for a critical opinion. If I wanted a literary assessment I'd probably go to Dominic. I believe that's his department. I'm just telling you as a matter of politeness. Actually,

Michael, I'd have thought it was in your interests to play ball, so to speak.' He concluded with a smile every bit as insincere as Michael's had been.

'Well, well. The cat shows its claws. You begin to interest me, Terence. But how would you say that it's in my interests exactly to cover up some grubby little sexual escapade of yours?'

'Guy and I were very close.' Terry took full advantage of his edge in height over Michael to place a threat behind these words. 'It is only to be expected that he told me a lot of things about his private life. For example, how things really stood between you and him. How possessive you were. How violent. How easily prone to jealousy. And so on.' The last three words were delivered with a breathtaking slowness which made Michael marvel. Terry continued. 'He also explained a few things to me about his recent financial arrangements, and what a help you'd been to him.' The colour drained from Michael's face. 'I imagine this is particularly close to your heart. You see, Guy mentioned you'd had some peculiarly fraught discussions on that subject very recently. Very heated little chats. I suppose that faulty memory of yours stopped you from telling the Police all this.'

'What a bizarre little discussion this is,' Michael said at length, offering one of those looks commonly regarded as a potential killer. 'Do you know, I would have thought that your exploits with women would have been paraded as openly as possible in front of the family, if only to prove your so-called virility. There must be something eminently unsuitable or sordid about this little liaison of yours. A tart? No. Ah, I know. A married woman with kids. Yes. Do you wish to confirm or deny?'

'You're very perceptive,' Terry said crisply. 'Let's just leave it at that.'

'Now flattery may get you anywhere. Ah, hello, it's Phil, isn't it?' The willowy figure of Phil Roxby was wandering towards the two of them. 'We met in a pub, didn't we?' Michael said, offering his hand and feeling a brief limp response. 'Good. I was beginning to think that my memory was going. I mean – how could I have forgotten meeting Terry?'

'Oh, you have met then?' Phil asked. 'It seemed to be quite a topic of conversation over there, whether you had or not.'

'Yes, it was a very brief meeting,' Michael lied glibly. 'I was rushed off my feet the time he stayed at the house, very preoccupied with work, which is my only excuse. I suppose I'll have to rush round and set the record straight before I go. Otherwise tongues will wag.' He smiled at them both. Terry smiled back.

'Oh – understandable lapse,' he chaffed affably, 'that you should forget me.'

'Well,' Michael addressed Phil again, 'what else, if anything is everyone talking about?'

'Oh, er, well,' Phil almost giggled. 'Dominic's raising a few eyebrows. He's got guts, hasn't he? I mean, coming here at all was fairly brave. But what he's doing now – '

'Yes, what the hell does he think he's doing?' Terry asked.

'Oh, I think that's pretty obvious,' Phil replied in a blandly dismissive manner. 'He's forcing them to face facts. He's making them remember Guy as he really was, not Guy as they were trying to pretend he ought to have been. If you ask me, he's doing what Guy would have wanted, for what that's worth.'

Michael nodded. 'I hadn't thought of it that way. But you're right.' He turned to Phil so as to exclude Terry. 'Guy often spoke of you. God, that sounds formal, and vaguely rude. But he used to talk about you a lot in the highest terms.'

'Er – so I gather,' Phil replied as modestly as he could. 'That's what Derek told me – '

'The gnome? Ha!' Michael snorted.

'The gnome?' Phil asked. 'You know, that's just what I was thinking earlier – '

'Give him a long white beard, a pointed hat and a fishing rod...' They all laughed and tried to stop when it became obvious that Derek had realised they were laughing at him.

'I suppose we shouldn't laugh,' Phil said, 'at a funeral.'

'I think we can take some comfort in the thought that the corpse would have,' Michael said. Terry nodded.

'He hated things like this. Formal occasions. Weddings and so on. Giggled all through them. Phil's right, thinking about it.' Terry was trying hard to be ingratiating.

'Have you read the story in the paper?' Michael asked Phil. 'It's tabloid journalism at its most glorious.'

'Guy would have loved that too,' Terry said wistfully, still trying to draw attention to himself. 'Oh God,' he said suddenly, 'look.' This was more than a ploy. They looked. 'Dominic's pestering Uncle Malcolm. Oh God, he's reading it to him. Michael, what does it actually say?' The poise of the blackmailer with whom Michael had been dealing but minutes before had vanished completely. A kind of hysteria seemed to have overcome him.

'It was all Dominic's idea,' Michael replied, as if in warning. 'I can't honestly claim that I knew what he was up to.'

But Michael's explanation did not get a chance to develop.

Across the room, Dominic had gone into public address mode.

'I can't see why you should complain at all, Mr Latimer. You can't say I've said anything unjustifiable or untrue. If I have, you're at liberty to prove it and put your case. But otherwise – ' He wagged his finger twice, an obvious public speaking gesture. Although stocky, next to Malcolm Latimer's imposing, bulky figure he looked minimal, small and insignificant. Latimer looked down at him, his once handsome features contorted with fury.

'Look, you piece of filth. How dare you come here? How dare you upset us? You've got a bloody nerve. I should have done what I wanted to do when Guy started knocking around with you. I should have had you locked up. You ruined my son, you and your perverted filth.' He took hold of Dominic's lapels. Dominic remained calm – astonishingly so.

'You're disgusting,' Malcolm Latimer went on, 'you took Guy away from his family, perverted him and turned him against us – '

'You're incredible,' Dominic said, 'I didn't know that people like you still existed. Look, I didn't throw him out of his home. I didn't beat him up so his face was a pulp of blood and bruises...'

'No, you queer bastard. But you bloody murdered him.'

Malcolm Latimer had let go of the left lapel and was already drawing back his right arm, hand clenched in a fist. He began to swing the punch, but suddenly stopped – and then he let go of Dominic totally, creating an effect of throwing him away, although actually Dominic scarcely moved at all. He didn't even brush himself down; paying no attention to the state of his jacket, he gave an amazed smile.

'Would you care to repeat that?'

'As often as you like. You killed him.'

'Thank you.' A nod of satisfaction, almost, was the reply to this. Dominic turned to face Michael and Marcus, a couple of yards to Michael's left, where he'd been talking to Gillian Latimer. 'I take it you heard that?' They were too astonished to reply. 'Witnesses, Mr Latimer. I shall be consulting with some solicitors about this. Well – ' he shrugged, as if helpless, 'I can't do anything else, can I? You've accused me of a criminal act which I did not commit. I cannot stand idly by and – '

'And what about you in that bloody paper? You bloody accused me.'

'No. No.' Dominic turned to the assembly again. 'Let me read what I actually said.' He picked up the paper from a table, smoothed it out, and read aloud.

' "It seems clear to me," said Palmer, 32, a leading suspect in this inquiry, "that the Police are worried by the fact that Guy's father is a policeman. They'd much rather pin it on another gay." Palmer went on to relate how Latimer, 24, had been savagely beaten by his father before being thrown out of his family home. "Guy was all blood and bruises. He was too ill to go to work or anywhere." '

Dominic broke off. 'Now I agree that's an exaggeration, but it's theirs, not mine. I just said he was a mess.' He resumed the reading.

'Palmer, a close friend of the murder victim, feels sure that the Police are deliberately ignoring the grim possibility that Latimer's father may have been embarrassed by having a son who was a self-confessed homosexual. And he feels sure that somewhere in London's large gay community there may be witnesses who are too frightened to come forward after reading that Guy's father is a Police Constable. "But I would urge them to come forward," he said, "if the Police are looking after their own, then so must we." '

Dominic looked up again. 'End of piece. I don't think,' he went on, 'that it could be said that I at any point accuse anyone of murdering Guy. All I say is that the Police don't want to face certain possibilities. That's all.' He smiled sweetly and simply: Malcolm Latimer snarled and stalked out of the room.

Dominic, surrounded by an air of triumph, took the initiative and went on: 'Now, if you don't mind I'd like to see Guy's room. After all, the things in it will be mine soon enough.' In case of any shock at this, he looked down demurely. 'It's not that I really want any of it, but – after all, Guy and I were very close friends for a while...' His voice trailed off, and one of the Anderson branch of the family murmured sympathetically. Derek Wilkinson made a mock vomiting gesture at Colin Latimer.

'My God,' he said, 'he's taken them in. It's disgusting.'

'What do you mean?' Colin asked. 'I thought he was pretty cool, actually.'

'Oh – ' Derek gestured, 'he's got a nerve, that's all.'

'You mean, you think he killed Guy?'

Derek shrugged. 'I still think he's the most likely candidate from the Police point of view. Or he ought to be. At the moment.'

'Well, that doesn't make much sense, does it?' Colin said viciously. 'Not going by what you were just saying to me.'

Derek smiled sourly. 'Let me explain. I don't necessarily mean that he killed Guy. But I think that, as things stand, he'd the most likely person to go to prison for it.'

'You want him to, don't you?'

Derek closed his eyes. When he opened them again, he resumed his smile. 'I can't say it worries me unduly. There's no advantage for me in Dominic not going to jail. Whereas – ' He broke off and looked up pointedly at Colin.

'My God,' Colin whispered. 'You expect me to pay you, don't you? You really think I'll just keep shelling out and shelling out – '

'Well,' Derek said, 'I don't see you've got much choice, Colin.'

'Fuck that,' Colin snorted. 'I'd rather tell the Police the truth.'

'What? That charming Inspector? You were telling me that he's convinced you'd carve anybody up as soon as look at them. Would you tell him about your row with Guy? How you knew that Guy had made a will in your favour, but not that he'd changed it? And would you really tell him that you were up in town on Friday, in the early part of the evening?'

'I only came up to see you. To ask you to talk to Guy for me.'

'And you expect the Inspector to believe that? Particularly after you've told him something else up to now? And even if he did, your alibi is wrecked and you're inconveniently close to the scene of the crime. Think about it, Colin – surely it's worth the hassle and the grief you'd get from him. You couldn't handle it and you know you couldn't.'

'Christ, you slimy little – I should have realised.'

'You should have stood up to that other slimy little – whatever you were going to call me – in the first place,' Derek replied without apparent concern. 'If you hadn't been so terrified of all your mates down at the Bridge finding out that big brother was a woofter – if you hadn't started paying him – oh, what's that wonderful phrase? – hush money, that's it – if you hadn't had that almighty row with Guy because you asked Guy to keep supplying you with money to pay him – well, you do see, don't you, Colin? It looks like a motive to me.'

'I didn't want Guy's money. Christ, I didn't know he'd got that much. And I didn't want any of it for myself.'

'No. But your mate wanted lots for himself, didn't he? It must be very macho, this little mob of yours.' Derek laughed unpleasantly. 'It's all a bit out in the open, now, though, isn't it? Unless the lads at the Bridge can't read, of course, and one of them must be able to, if only by the law of averages. You might as well not have wasted your money,' he said as if in conclusion, and then suddenly adding as a nasty afterthought, 'or your effort.'

'Fuck off,' Colin snarled and turned, without any attempt at being discreet. Derek caught his arm.

'But you won't forget, will you, Colin?' he asked sweetly. 'I'll meet you on Friday.' Colin shook Derek's hand away. 'Just think, that's all. I'm sure even you will see reason.'

Colin turned his head and gave Derek a stare of contemptuous hatred. Then he turned away again and went over to his mother, who was jabbering away to her sisters. But as he joined his mother from one side of the room, so from the other a hand descended on her shoulder – Dominic's hand. She turned in fright. Dominic gave her what was obviously meant to be a reassuring smile, which transformed itself into a slightly more knowing one as he looked above her head up towards Colin. Colin felt totally confused. What the hell could he say to Dominic? They'd never actually met face to face before, but they'd been part of each other's life for what seemed like a long time now. It didn't make it any easier that he was fairly sure, from something Guy had said once, that Dominic fancied him from a photo Guy had shown him. In the face of all this, he did the only thing to be reasonably expected of him: he blushed furiously, said nothing and looked down. Dominic turned his full attention back to Phyllis Latimer.

'I do apologise for that appalling scene,' he said, exuding apologetic charm at every pore. 'I fully accept that I went too far, but my only excuse is that this is a genuinely upsetting occasion for me as well.' Guy's mother looked up at him, trembling.

'You – you want to see – want to see – Guy's things,' she stammered. Dominic nodded.

'If it's not too much trouble.' He laughed nervously. 'It's ridiculous. I never ever saw Guy's room.'

'I know, I – I once told him to invite you, but he – he – '

'We fell out very suddenly,' Dominic said, as if in explanation. 'One minute in each other's pockets, the next – nothing.' Phyllis looked up again, and for the first time allowed herself to look, simply to look, at Dominic as he actually was.

'I'll show you – show you. It's upstairs – just excuse me – a minute, I'll – ' She took one of her sisters aside. Dominic turned and made a very slight gesture towards Marcus. Marcus saw it: so did Colin. So did Phil and Michael.

'Is that an affair?' Phil asked.

'It may well be. Marcus is an ex of mine,' Michael explained proprietorily, 'but he's far too serious and steady for me. I'm not the marrying kind, I fear. Oh, I know you are. Guy was very proud of your relationship. But Dominic and Marcus, well, it's new, it's interesting, and it may well work. The great thing going for it is that both of them want to make it work – Marcus probably more than Dominic, I suspect.'

Meanwhile, Dominic introduced Marcus to Colin. 'Marcus used to know Michael quite well, didn't you?' Marcus nodded. 'Look,

Marc,' he went on, turning his back on Colin and leaning very close to the sturdy redhead. Colin stood dumbfounded: Dominic was actually whispering into this man's ear. Marcus suddenly laughed: his light blue eyes went wild with amusement. His left hand squeezed Dominic's arm gently, Colin noticed with a kind of fascinated horror. Dominic pulled back. 'OK?' he queried gently.

'Yes, that's fine.' Phyllis Latimer, still trembling, came back to Dominic and Dominic introduced Marcus to her. She twisted her mouth into a ghastly parody of a smile directed towards the young Scot. 'Well, I'll see you in a few minutes, Dominic,' he said quietly, as Dominic more or less physically steered the mother of the corpse out of the large sitting room. Colin wondered if he should go with them; and in the split second he wondered, he found himself suddenly facing his cousin Terry.

'Where's Auntie Phyllis going?' he asked with some agitation. 'Are you just letting her go?'

Colin looked at him, baffled. 'What's worrying you?' he countered abrasively.

'Well, for God's sake, Dominic could well be a murderer – ' He broke off as he observed at first amusement, then scorn, gallop across Colin's face.

'Even if he did kill Guy, and I bet he didn't, he's hardly going to put a meat cleaver through Mum's head here, is he? Fucking hell, Terry, I though you were supposed to be intelligent.'

'God, you're so dumb sometimes,' Terry hissed, lowering his voice. 'Does it occur to you that your mother isn't completely in control of herself? For example, she might start talking about railway tickets...'

Colin stopped laughing. 'What are you on about?' This tea party was turning into a nightmare.

'The railway ticket in your kagoule pocket. Gillian found it. She showed it to me and your mother. I mean, it doesn't prove you were in town in the evening, but it certainly proves you weren't here all day like you said you were.'

'Look, I – you don't think I – do you? I just went up town to talk to Derek. I wanted him to ask Guy something for me. That's all.'

Colin was trying to keep his voice under control and not to look too conspicuous. Uncertain what to say to this, Terry turned to see Marcus Grey frowning: he had obviously heard parts of their exchange. Colin too looked round anxiously. But their conference was cut short by Gillian. She approached first Marcus, then Colin and Terry, and drew them all together into a conversational quartet.

151

'This is Marcus,' she said. Colin explained that he was already aware of this: Terry nodded politely but distractedly. 'I've been explaining to Marcus who everybody is – all our gruesome family.' Evidently, Marcus deduced, cousin Terry was sufficiently intimate with the immediate Latimer circle to be a party to such anti-family jokes. 'I offered to introduce him to them all, but he didn't seem too keen. Then Dad started his little party piece.'

'Oh – I'm here under false pretences, anyway. I never even met Guy. I'm just here for the fun – the wit, the glamour, the beer.' Marcus made a not very sincere gesture of self-reproach. 'Sorry, bad taste.'

'It's better than all this pretend grief,' Gillian said. 'That really makes me sick. They don't care. All this is just a big show to prove that everything was respectable really, that Guy died a nice, clean, middle-class death, even if he was only twenty-four, and he'd have had a lovely life and wife and lots and lots of children. In a way, it's nice for them all that Guy's dead, because they can pretend whatever load of shit they like. Thank God you and Michael and Dominic and – oh, what's his face – Phil turned up to remind them.'

Terry coughed with embarrassment; Colin merely nodded. 'Look,' Terry said, 'I really think that someone might go and see if Auntie's OK.'

'Yes,' Colin said. 'I think you ought to, Terry.'

'I don't see what you're so worried about,' Marcus asserted pugnaciously. 'But if you're that worried, why don't you come up with me? Dominic asked me to go up after a discreet interval had passed. So unless you think I'm his partner in blood, I don't see that you need to be too alarmed about Guy's mother lying in a pool of gore.' He gave Terry a smile, while Gillian hid her own.

Upstairs, in Guy's quite spacious bedroom, unnaturally tidy through lack of use, Dominic Palmer and Phyllis Latimer were at the large window which looked out over the back of the house. In the garden the dogs were wandering on long tethers.

'My God, they look terrifying,' Dominic murmured. He sighed. 'I'm sorry that it had to take this to bring me here at last.'

Phyllis twitched nervously. She wished she knew what to say. She was now thoroughly confused about Dominic. He'd been very easy to cast as the Devil Incarnate as long as he hadn't been physically present: but he so patently didn't look the part. He had a kind, weak face that sagged a bit, not the face of Irresistible Temptation. And Guy's more spiteful remarks seemed somehow misplaced, flattened by the barrage of Dominic's niceness and his determination to stand up to her husband's bullying. Oh yes, there he was, she noticed as she looked out into the garden. She looked up at Dominic again: he seemed lost in reverie.

'I'm – glad you came,' she said, not sure if this were true or not. 'I should have asked you anyway.'

'Oh – there's no need to say that. You don't owe me it. But I am sorry, now, that Guy and I fell out.'

He walked away from the window and sat down untidily on the single bed. 'It's only now that I begin to realise how bloody stupid I was being. You know, I can't say any of this to anyone else. Guy was so important to me, for so long – ' He broke off and sniffed.

Phyllis suddenly realised that he was crying. Crying. Of course, Guy had said that Dominic was 'in love' with him, but she'd thought she'd known what that meant. Guy was a pretty boy. Dominic was older and not so pretty: physical infatuation. She'd felt it for Malcolm. But that didn't make you cry. And she realised that she was crying too, for the first time since Guy had been killed. She walked over to the bed and stood directly in front of Dominic and looked down at his dark brown hair.

'Dominic.' He looked up, evidently surprised by the direct address. Two jagged streams, one from the corner of each eye, trickled down, evaporating somewhere on his cheek; but there was also a query in his eye, visible through the saline. 'Dominic, listen.'

'Is this going to be something I don't want to hear? Something Guy said?'

'No, please listen. It's about last Friday.'

'What, you mean – ?' Visibly, his attention was grabbed. 'Do you know something?'

'We've not been telling the truth. I've got to talk to someone about it. I never thought I'd tell you.'

Blimey, Dominic thought in his mock-Londoner pose, something's shocked her into lucidity. This would make the whole enterprise worthwhile. 'I promise,' he said gently, 'I won't tell anyone else.'

She gulped and nodded. 'You'll probably have to. No...What the Police were told, it's not – ' But a noise outside the room shut her up.

'Auntie Phyllis!' Terry came through the doorway, followed, at a decent distance, by Marcus. 'Oh,there you are.'

'Yes,' Dominic said pointedly, 'here we both are.' Phyllis Latimer had turned and dashed – there was no other way to describe it – back to the window.

'There, you see,' Marcus said darkly to Terry, 'no blood.'

Dominic looked quizzically at his lover. 'Terence here thought his aunt might be in danger. Alone with the mad fiend and all that.' Dominic laughed.

'For God's sake,' Terry burst out, 'that's not what I thought.'

'Well, perhaps not,' Dominic said equably. 'I do wonder, Terence.' It was in its small way a historic moment. At one time, only a few months ago, the two men, about twelve years apart in age, had been close enough to Guy Latimer to holiday with him. And now they met for the first time, their eyes full of hostility and suspicion.

But then, Phyllis drew their attention away from each other. Suddenly the strain of the day told and her legs buckled beneath her. She didn't pass out. She remained distressingly conscious and resumed the recently-suspended clenching and unclenching of her fists. She half-lay, half-sat, her back against the wall; and, uncannily, a smile seemed to pass over her face.

'Oh no,' she murmured – and something like a laugh escaped her.

'For God's sake – ' Dominic hissed.

'Terry, go and get – oh – your uncle, anyone. Get Gillian.' Marcus assumed command. Dominic now sprang to his feet.

'I can't leave her here with him,' Terry said, trying to keep his voice to an undertone.

'And what the fuck are you so terrified of?' Dominic jeered.

'I'm sure Guy would tell us if he could.'

'You little bastard – '

'Dominic!' Marcus grabbed hold of him. 'Don't rise to this rubbish. Terry, if you won't trust Dominic, trust me.'

'Well – '

'Look. I'll come down with you,' Dominic articulated through clenched teeth, as best he could. 'Then I'll come back with Colin and Gillian. Does that suit you?' He walked out of the room.

'Look – ' Terry began, but Marcus cut him short.

'Go and get help,' he said. He knelt down next to Phyllis. 'Mrs Latimer,' he said, 'just hang on and we'll get you to a bed and get you a doctor.'

'I don't think a doctor's going to – going to be much use.' She tried to focus on Marcus. 'You're the other one, aren't you?' she said. 'You came with Dominic and that boy Guy – Guy – lived with.'

'I'm Marcus.'

'You're Scottish aren't you? We love Scotland. Guy always loved the mountains in the Highlands. The further North we got, the happier he was. Are you from the Highlands?'

'No.' Marcus shook his head. 'I'm from a small town near Edinburgh. Though I've been to the Highlands quite often.' But he abandoned any thoughts of launching into autobiography when a hubbub gathered on the stairs and then burst into the room. Looking over his shoulder he saw Colin and Gillian, who dashed forward and knelt down next to their mother.

'Oh, mum,' she wailed. She looked at Marcus and sniffed. 'Can you and Colin carry her to her bedroom?'

Marcus nodded. He raised his eyebrows at Colin. 'You go round that side,' he directed. 'Now – ' Between them they lifted Phyllis Latimer, who was no great weight, and carried her in a more or less sitting position. Dominic appeared in the doorway and backed out again immediately. Marcus looked towards Gillian as they reached the doorway, looking for direction.

'Across there,' Gillian replied, although obviously Colin knew the way and he kicked open a door across the landing, revealing another large bedroom occupied by dressing tables and a small double-bed. Marcus grasped instinctively that it was a purely feminine bedroom: nowhere at all was there a trace of anything male. Colin and Marcus, intruders in this domain, lowered Phyllis so that she was sitting on the edge of her bed. Then they lifted her legs round, turning her through ninety degrees. Phyllis looked up at her son and the stranger. This was ridiculous. She wanted to laugh again. She looked round, to see her daughter enter the room.

'Gillian,' she said, quite crisply, 'the white pills.' Gillian went to the dressing table and started picking up bottles, examining them critically. As she did so, Dominic came in, followed by Terry Difford.

'Are you OK?' Dominic asked, approaching the bed, 'can I get you anything?'

'Some water,' Gillian cut across, 'to take these pills with.' She pointed to the dressing table. 'There's a glass here.'

Dominic retreated and joined Gillian at the table. Just as he placed his hand on the glass, the door was thrust completely open, and Malcolm Latimer's bulk loomed in the doorway.

'What the hell is this, a bloody circus?' he asked. He scrutinised his wife: she returned the look, but said nothing. Everyone stared at Latimer. 'For God's sake,' he went on, addressing his wife, 'you've got guests downstairs.'

'Dad, for Christ's sake,' hissed Gillian.

'Ah – excuse me,' Dominic said meekly, 'I've been asked to get some water.'

'You.' Malcolm Latimer snorted.

'Ah – me, yes.'

'Dad, Mum needs some water.'

'Your mother needs nothing from him. God knows what she'd catch.'

Dominic rolled his eyes in disbelief. 'I wasn't proposing to manufacture it personally. Anyway, I've had a test – '

'I don't want to hear.' Malcolm Latimer snatched the glass from Dominic and turned and offered it to his nephew who had appeared behind him. 'Terry, get your aunt some water.'

Dominic smiled humourlessly as Terry failed to grasp the glass properly. It spun in the air and hit the door-frame. Splinters hit the floor. Terry gave a sigh and squatted down to pick up the pieces. This was becoming a farce. Even more so when he misjudged the edge of one of the larger fragments; suddenly blood was gushing from the fleshy part of his palm. He cursed.

'Terry!' Gillian almost shrieked. Dominic moved towards him and tried to take his hand, but Terry snatched it away.

'For God's sake,' he cried, 'just leave it, won't you!' He calmed slightly. 'It's only a cut. Just let me see to it. OK?' He headed away from the doorway.

'Some water too, please,' Gillian called after him. Dominic also left the room, muttering an insincere apology as he passed Malcolm Latimer. Gillian handed her mother two white pills. Phyllis, careless for water, placed one on her tongue. Marcus, careful for Dominic, backed slowly and apologetically out of the room. On the landing he stood and paused; looking one way he could see Terry washing his cut; looking back the other way, there was Dominic in Guy's room. He was standing at a chest of drawers, examining the contents of one layer. Marcus padded up behind him, lunged and grabbed him round the waist. Dominic jumped; he turned round slowly.

'Ah. Thank God.' He kissed Marcus on the mouth. 'I was just looking.'

'Anything?'

Dominic pointed to several packets of photographs which he had arranged there. 'I think they may be useful. There's some goodies here, judging from my brief flick through.' He smiled thoughtfully. 'I've had some ideas. I'll be interested to hear what you think.'

'Can we go soon? This is gruesome.'

'Gruesome? Where's your sense of fun? Give it a few minutes yet. Now,' Dominic went on primly, 'let me go. This is the most inauspicious place for us to fondle each other, although the idea of

156

consummating our passion on Guy's bed has a certain ironic appeal above and beyond the purely physical. Right.' They separated. 'Let's go and see if Terry's hand is better.' He pocketed the photos, making his suit jacket seem rather bulky, and they left the room.

'You know,' Dominic said, 'it's a funny thing, but I'd almost charmed Mama into making some amazing confession just now when you and – ' He broke off; they were standing face to face with Terry Difford. 'Ah. Terence.'

Terry attempted a smile. 'This is all getting a bit fraught, isn't it?'

'As Guy would have said, a grand faff.' The three of them had come to a halt outside Phyllis Latimer's bedroom. Dominic smiled. 'I'd like to say my farewells, if you don't mind. Did you get some water, Terry?'

'Oh, Christ.' He returned to the bathroom.

Dominic looked towards the bedroom. 'I wonder if the Incredible Hulk's still in there.'

'Well, he's not blocking the doorway. That's something.'

Marcus entered the room first and saw Malcolm Latimer towering over his wife. Gillian had returned to the dressing table. Dominic sidled in and stood next to her, mouthing a silent greeting. She raised her eyebrows at him in return. He picked up some of the pill bottles on display.

'My parents had a lot of these,' he whispered, noiselessly waving one bottle. Malcolm Latimer turned round and glared at him. Marcus stepped forward, prepared to be pugnacious, but, as if to prevent any dispute, Terry arrived with a glass full of water. He reached around his uncle and passed it to his aunt.

'Is your hand OK now?' Gillian asked. Terry held it up, revealing a liberal helping of sticking plaster swathing the injured area. She smiled. Dominic caught Terry's eye again and smiled, not at all pleasantly. He was still toying with the pills: he stopped, put them down again and nudged Marcus.

'Time we were going. We have places to go tonight.'

'Do we?'

'Places in the South,' he replied significantly. 'North of here, but South to us. South of the River.'

'Ah yes,' Marcus said. Sometimes Dominic's drift was obscure, to say the least.

'Well,' Dominic went on, 'thanks for the hospitality, and if there's anything at all I can do – '

Malcolm Latimer moved towards him meaningfully. Colin and Gillian offered a mutual 'goodbye.' Terry said nothing. Phyllis Latimer turned her head to look at the doorway.

'Do come again, Dominic,' she said quite clearly. 'I do want to talk to you properly, if I'm allowed to.'

Suddenly everyone went dead quiet. If Marcus had had a pin about him, he would have dropped it just for the effect. Phyllis was evidently unnerved by the effect she'd managed. 'These bloody pills,' she said. 'They make me talk too much. Load of rubbish.'

'Well then,' Dominic said, waving and drifting out. Marcus followed, thoughtfully pulling the door closed behind him. Before he had done this, Dominic had darted into another bedroom.

'What are you doing?'

'Being nosey. Looking for clues, as the Famous Five always used to say. This must be Colin's, judging from the paraphernalia.' Dominic waved an arm at football scarves, team photos and programmes. 'I used to fancy him like mad, you know.'

'Colin? Christ, he's only a bairn.'

'Thank heaven for little bairns. Well, well, what an interesting day, and there's lots of it left yet. Let's go and pick Michael up, if he's finished trying to pick Phil Roxby up. Hang about.'

Wandering out of Colin's room and in through another door, half-open, the two young men were confronted by a serious looking collection of foreign language texts in an otherwise sparse room. 'The spare room,' Dominic said, as if this were a brilliant deduction. 'And in it are the accoutrements of cousin Terry.'

'If they're as fascinating as he is you'll be in a coma in thirty seconds.'

'Oh, don't underestimate young Terence. He's terribly bright.' Dominic sat down on the bed. 'It's affected me very strangely, you know. Coming here, I mean. I've started remembering all sorts of things.'

'What, things about Guy?' Marcus came over, sat down next to him, and placed an arm lovingly around his shoulder. But there was no real physical response. Still, he left the arm where it was, just in case. 'Do you want to talk about it?'

'I'm not sure that I can, really. It's just – well, I was trying my hardest to be courageous, charming and discreet by turns, because I thought someone might be provoked into letting something slip. And it sort of worked. But – well, maybe I just conned myself. But you've got to remember, Marc, I was in love with him for quite a long time. And you never lose it completely, do you? A little piece of me, somewhere, will always love Guy Latimer, just like another little piece of me will always love Dennis Kelly. You understand?'

'Yes.' Marcus tightened his arm, in the hope of provoking a reaction himself. 'If that wasn't true, you'd be like Michael.'

158

'Would that be such a terrible thing?' Dominic suddenly got up and walked away, out of the room. Marcus sat for a moment, then followed: as his intuition had predicted, Dominic had gone back to Guy's room. He was back at the chest of drawers, searching randomly through the second drawer down.

'Any clues?'

'Not a thing. I suppose – ' But what Dominic supposed was lost at the ring of the doorbell. 'I wonder if these gatecrashers will get a better reception than we did.'

Turning round and looking back out of the room, he and Marcus saw Malcolm Latimer, followed by Colin, cross the landing and head down the stairs. Marcus wandered to the door of Guy's room: listening down, he recognised the voices of Chief Inspector Oldcastle and Sergeant Morgan.

'It's the Police,' he reported. 'A nice party surprise.'

Dominic gulped. 'Oh. I hope to God they've not come to arrest me.'

Marcus laughed. 'Are you still paranoid about that?'

'I'm still the hot favourite to take the rap, I'll bet.'

'Hardly – the odds on you have lengthened dramatically. Come on,' he said, suddenly bounding up and out of the room. Dominic followed him down the stairs at a slightly more dignified and sedate pace.

In the sitting room they found Michael eyeball to eyeball with Oldcastle.

'Look,' Michael said, coldly and reasonably, 'I fail to see what you're implying or why. I'm afraid your heavy irony is lost on me.'

'And your little display of acid isn't going to help you any,' the Chief Inspector replied. 'But if you want me to put it bluntly, I will. There are,' he cleared his throat, 'certain matters in connection with the death of Guy Latimer which we would like to discuss further with you.'

Michael gasped – almost laughed. 'Are you arresting me?'

'No – unless we have to.'

'Oh, for God's sake – ' Michael began, but Phil Roxby cut in. It was clear that he knew how to handle himself with the Police.

'Are you prepared to substantiate your suspicions?' he asked very formally, in a nasal Northern voice which rather charmed Marcus. 'I mean, this is all a bit peremptory, you have to admit.'

'Right.' Oldcastle breathed in. Morgan discreetly looked away. He'd tried to talk the Chief out of this immediate blundering in, which he considered definitely tasteless in this setting and certainly far too public. But to no avail. In fact, the Chief had wanted to charge Hamilton there and then, but had finally faced the fact that there wasn't quite enough to warrant that yet.

'I don't know,' Oldcastle began, 'how much you actually know, Mr Roxby, and I have reason to believe that you know a good deal more than you have admitted hitherto, but setting all that aside, I have a positive identification of Michael Hamilton at the scene of the murder at or around the time of the event.'

Morgan winced. This wasn't after all strictly true; Oldcastle, though, was going into overdrive.

'I would remind you, Mr Roxby, not that it's any business of yours, that I don't have to offer any justifications if I want to talk to someone.' Oldcastle slowly, confidently, looked around everyone gathered in the room. 'I think you could all do well to bear this in mind. Of course,' he said, glaring at Dominic, 'some of us prefer to talk to the newspapers. Mind you, I'll be talking to them myself, very soon now. Certain facts have come to light which I feel the public have a right to know.'

Only Morgan was conscious of the irony here: there had been a blazing row for most of the morning between Oldcastle and his boss about the Chief's reluctance to inform the Press of anything. The Superintendent, on the other hand, was very conscious of media profile.

'I'm afraid, Mr Hamilton,' Oldcastle went on, wheeling back to give Michael his undivided attention once more, 'that you won't like the facts that I'm about to reveal. You see, they don't reflect very well on you. In fact, we think you did your best, stopping at nothing, to prevent them coming to light. You didn't like the truth and you probably still don't.'

Michael had turned completely white. 'What truth?'

'The truth that your boyfriend had AIDS.'

Morgan intervened. 'He had the virus, sir, the H thing.'

'HIV,' Phil Roxby said.

Dominic and Marcus had been prepared for this, but it still came as a visible shock to them both. Phil too was clearly stunned, his correction of Morgan having been an instinctive political reflex. Derek Wilkinson stood up in surprise. Michael, however, regained his colour and some of his composure.

'Well,' Oldcastle said at length, 'just think, Mr Hamilton, if this had got out, of the effect on your neatly-ordered career and life. Not just that you were living with someone who'd got it, but that he must have got it from you.'

'Well, that's not true for a start.' It was Phil, not Michael, who said this.

160

'Yes, Mr Roxby? And how can you be so certain?'

'Simple medical facts. Michael, how long is it since you and Guy first slept together?'

'Nine weeks at the most. It took him a week to overcome his nerves and get round to it.'

'Less than three months?'

'Certainly.'

'Three months ago, Guy and I had only just stopped seeing each other,' cut in Dominic.

'Well, there you are,' Phil said. 'It takes at least three months for the antibodies to show up in the bloodstream. At least three. So Michael's not the carrier Guy got it from.'

Oldcastle frowned. 'Eh, but if he knew – ' he began, clutching at any straw to save his theory.

This was too much for Michael. 'I hadn't got a fucking clue. Guy was the last person I would ever have thought – '

'The evidence still doesn't favour you, Mr Hamilton. There were blood traces inside the club lavatory which have been identified as Guy Latimer's blood. So whoever killed him came in from outside after killing him. We know you went back in.'

'And how many other people arrived from outside after eleven thirty that night?' Marcus threw in sardonically.

'Look,' Michael said, seizing the initiative, 'I'll quite happily talk to you tomorrow. But not now. Not tonight.' He glanced at Marcus and Dominic.

'Boys' night out?' sniped Derek Wilkinson under his breath. Michael and Phil subjected him to a glare reserved for vermin.

'Well.' Oldcastle hovered uncomfortably. He'd lost the initiative and he knew it. The best thing was to withdraw and take Hamilton up on his offer. Time enough to crack him tomorrow. He couldn't get far, if he tried to do a bunk. 'Tomorrow morning then, Mr Hamilton. At ten, if you please. Our place, not yours.' He turned and left. Morgan smiled apologetically and followed.

'God!' screamed Michael. 'Thank you, Phil.'

'Oh, I don't mind educating straights,' Phil said affably, 'not even straight policemen.'

'Very generous,' sneered Malcolm Latimer.

'So,' Derek said, 'who'd have thought that Guy was a slag all along?'

Dominic looked at Phil. 'Does your education programme extend to closet queens?' he asked, a play for a cheap laugh which all present were too tactful or too ignorant to provide. Phil instead put a question to Michael.

'Are you three off out tonight?'

'Yes, we thought we might ask around – ' Michael began, but Marcus started coughing very loudly, so he shut up.

'Shall we be going now, Michael?' Marcus asked pointedly.

'Ah yes. Yes. Well – ' He smiled around the room. 'Goodbye.'

'The Three Musketeers are going, then?' Derek sniped again.

'Yes,' Michael said. Phil Roxby stared at him, baffled to see him dither so much about a simple act of departure: Michael didn't strike him as a ditherer. Then he grasped its point: Michael had manoeuvred himself into a position where his back was turned on Marcus and Dominic. He mouthed something at Phil – the same word twice. Phil looked and deliberated.

'Clapham,' he said to himself. 'So they're going to Clapham, are they?'

# Part Four
# THIS GUY'S IN LOVE

# 11: Going to a Go-Go

Marcus knew of old that Michael took hours to get ready if he was going out. He had tried to suggest that this was one occasion Michael didn't really need to dress to kill: it was, primarily, an investigative mission. But Michael was – well, just Michael: it was completely alien to his nature to go out on the scene without having prepared himself properly. Even the argument that it was only Tuesday didn't seem to weigh very heavily. 'An old woman breathed a spell on me in my cradle that Tuesday would be my lucky night,' he had replied.

His conversation on the way back had been full of such flippancies, and neither Marcus nor Dominic needed to be particularly intuitive to realise why. He had been very badly shaken at the funeral tea and was trying to cover the fact. They both assumed that the shock had come from the Police, but then Michael had let slip, as casually as he possibly could, most – but not all – of his conversation with Terry. Listening to his account, Marcus and Dominic found themselves distinctly unsatisfied.

'You swallow all this, do you?' Dominic asked.

'I've heard less convincing stories. Mine about my 'phone call, for example.'

'Are you going to play along with him?' Marcus asked.

'Do I have a choice? Of course, it would fuck up my alibi about the wills a bit, so I don't really want to have to pretend to the Police that I met Terry in London at a time I've told them I was in New York. Which I was. I mean, they already think I'm a liar. In fact, they're so sure of it, I'm beginning to think I must be.'

'All the more reason to take tonight seriously.'

'Maybe. Or maybe I should just grab my quota of fun while I still can.'

Marcus marvelled at the way in which Michael and Dominic had reversed roles: Michael was casting himself in the role of Fate's victim, the scapegoat, whilst Dominic was visibly gaining in self-confidence.

'So anyway,' Michael went on, 'we're going to Clapham, are we?'

'Yes. As you kept trying to tell everyone,' Marcus said severely. 'Quite why you did that, I can't imagine.'

'Or perhaps you can,' Dominic laughed. 'I should warn you, Michael, Phil is a happily married man.'

'So Guy tediously informed me on three hundred separate occasions. Speaking personally, I'm a great believer in adultery. At least, I'm prepared to argue the case with young Philip. Incidentally, it was very mean of you to drag me off and not let me offer him a lift. You do realise he had a nightmare journey from the church and the cemetery with the Laughing Gnome? He was saying that he's sure the Gnome's psychotic.'

'I think they all are,' Marcus said. 'They're all mad in some way or other.'

'What do you think Derek's hold on Colin is?' Dominic asked suddenly.

'What makes you think he's got one?' Marcus asked.

'The conversation they were having. I was keeping a close eye on it.'

'In that case,' Marcus said drily, 'given your interest in Colin, I'm surprised you missed that intense little discussion the two cousins were having. Mind you, I think you were chatting Mummy up at that point. But does it occur to you that, however much you may fancy him, Colin might have something quite serious to hide?'

'Colin?' Dominic practically curled up with laughter. 'Sweet hunky little Colin?'

'As far as I could gather, he was in town on Friday evening.'

'Well – so were we all. Look, Marc, you can't think it was Colin. I'm sure there's an innocent explanation for him. I mean, Colin doesn't fit into the scenario, does he? And it's proved right so far, hasn't it?'

'Dominic's right,' Michael said. 'Colin just doesn't fit. Unless you believe there was some wild incest going on. I think contact with the Latimers is beginning to turn your brain, Marco. I mean, look at Mummy and Daddy. Crazed. A couple of fruitcakes.'

'Not much fruity about Malcolm Latimer,' Dominic observed.

'That's not what Guy used to say. He once told me that Daddy was always staring at young men in the street.'

'Purely professional, I imagine,' Marcus said. 'He strikes me as being the type who thinks everyone under thirty is up to no good.

Not, in my opinion, a closet case.'

'Guy was rather obsessed with the idea that everyone was a closet case, actually,' Dominic said authoritatively.

'I'm beginning to think,' Marcus said, 'that a closet case got obsessed with Guy. Obsessed enough to kill him, in fact.'

'Or closet enough to be frightened of the truth getting out,' Dominic took up. 'It was a shocker about the HIV, wasn't it? I mean, even though I'd already guessed, actually hearing about it knocked me for six.'

'I suppose I'd better go for a few check-ups before I go to prison,' Michael commented.

'It would be sensible,' Marcus said, adding encouragingly, 'and there'll be ages before the trial.' By this time they were back in town. 'Right, Michael, you'll meet us in Clapham – when?'

'Well – it's gone seven now. Say ten? That'll give me just about enough time if I hurry and skimp a bit.'

Marcus groaned. However, when the two of them were safely returned to his flat, he found that Dominic was taking a tolerant view of Michael's attitude. 'Give us a bit of time to pay a couple of other calls first,' he said. 'Anyway, I've got an idea.' He put his arms around Marcus and began to kiss his face, licking it gently.

Marcus laughed responsively. 'That seems to be one of your favourite ideas, as far as I can tell.' Dominic's hands were covering vast areas of his body, busy and sensual. He squirmed with pleasure as Dominic stuck his tongue right inside his left ear. His hands ran inside Marcus's shirt, tweaking his nipples gently and then slowly travelled down his back. Marcus let out an involuntary gasp. Dominic grinned. And then the 'phone rang.

'Shit,' Dominic muttered, not loudly but with great expression. Marcus stood still for a moment, then realised that he ought to answer it. He wandered out of the sitting room into the hall, where the hideously trendy thing he had inherited from the flat's previous owner fluted piercingly. Bemusedly, he picked it up, his mind still running on erotica. He barked down it.

'Er – is it possible to speak to Dominic?' The voice was slightly older and – Marcus thought – North-Eastern in origin. Presumably it was the landlord, wanting to deliver another ultimatum.

'Hang on,' Marcus said gruffly. 'Dominic!' Dominic ambled out, taking the receiver from Marcus with his left hand and fondling Marcus's backside with his right. Marcus was about to make himself discreetly scarce, but Dominic stuck his fingers into the waistband of his trousers, thus keeping him there.

'Hello,' he said inquiringly. Marcus tried to listen to the other voice, but the line wasn't wonderful. Besides, Dominic's right hand had delved a little further down and was now gently fondling his cock. It responded to the stroking, stiffening, and as it did, Dominic's grasp grew firmer. Through all this, he kept his 'phone conversation going.

'Oh, hi.' Pause. 'Yes, well, obviously you did.' Pause. 'No. Impossible. Sorry.' He seemed a bit crestfallen at this, but squeezed the head of Marcus's now full erection. 'No, I'm not being awkward, only – ' Pause, and his eyebrows went up. 'That was Marcus.' He smiled at Marcus and tickled his balls. Marcus shuddered. 'Yes, I should think so. Yes, I suppose that's OK.' But the eyebrows went up again: obviously he didn't mean what he said. 'OK, then I'll see you. No, not really. Right. Take care. Bye.' He took the receiver from his ear, gave it a concentrated stare, then put it down again. He pulled Marcus closer to him and began to unfasten his trousers with his left hand, keeping his right hand exactly where it was. 'Sorry about that.' Pulling down both trousers and boxer shorts, he let Marcus's cock stand free and began licking it gently.

'Was that your landlord?' Dominic didn't answer immediately; he stopped licking and started to unbutton Marcus's shirt and feel his chest inside.

'Mmm,' he said, 'creating problems. Wanted me to go back tonight. I'll have to nip off tomorrow late afternoon, when he's going to be there. I think he wants to fix my moving out date.'

'I thought everything was all right when you went back yesterday morning. He didn't sound too aggressive just then.'

'Well – when I went back yesterday, I deliberately chose a time I knew he'd be out. Best way of avoiding a lecture. And he has his own peculiar way of being tetchy over the 'phone.'

'I thought, though,' Marcus said, returning the compliment of the unbuttoning, 'we might go out to dinner tomorrow night. Splash out a bit.'

'How madly unScottish.'

'Racist.'

'Such a heartless brute, aren't I?' Dominic suddenly grabbed Marcus by the shoulders and pulled them both to the floor.

'There is a bedroom, you know. Or a sitting room with a sofa.'

'Bet you've never done it in the hall before, have you? I like to be original.' And with this, Dominic stuck his mouth onto Marcus's and filled it with his tongue.

Later, after they had dressed to go out, Dominic spread out the photographs he had brought away from the Latimers' home. A lot were of Phyllis and her sisters on various family holidays, usually somewhere rocky. Quite a few featured Colin. There was a whole series of Terry and Guy in France, although only two or three with both of them in the picture together, and several of Guy and Terry's family looking around their mutual university town. There were none of Michael: those featuring him had been provided by Michael himself earlier that day. The pictures of Guy and Dominic in Italy were also in this batch. Both sets, from Surrey and from Michael, featured Derek Wilkinson, usually at the seaside. There were also a lot of old, childhood pictures. Marcus surveyed these cheerfully, with the usual derision reserved for such exhibits.

'Well,' he said, 'he may have been a pretty boy, but he was an ugly child.'

'Oh, I don't know. If one likes children – I think they're all loathsome personally.'

'His father was quite good-looking, wasn't he? Unfortunately.'

'Yes – quite hunky,' Dominic replied, giving the subject his professional attention. 'My God,' he exclaimed, 'why did the silly boy take quite so many pictures of bald, boring landscapes?'

'Have you seen these ones of the awful Terry?' Marcus threw Dominic a picture of Terry in a greatcoat with his trousers tucked into his boots, looking soulful under grey Montmartre skies as ordinary Parisians walked past staring at him as though he'd escaped from somewhere. 'Aha!' This cry was provoked by a picture of Terry being sketched by a street artist. For this he had adopted a concentratedly serious expression and was clearly a subject of amusement for several of the Gallic characters in the crowd surrounding him.

Dominic in turn offered his prizes to Marcus. 'Derek Wilkinson in a swimming costume playing Spot the Muscle. Actually, the only muscles on view are in shells and spelt differently. Derek and Guy together pretending to like each other. Derek Wilkinson's impression of Terry Difford staring soulfully out to sea.' He handed these over. 'Mmm,' he said salaciously, pawing at the next one. 'Hunky Colin doing sporty hunky Colin-type things.'

'Like knifing his brother?' Marcus asked. Dominic pulled a face at him and kissed the photo exaggeratedly. 'Oh, for God's sake, take it off somewhere and have a wank if that's what you want.'

'Only if you promise to come with me,' Dominic replied, using emphasis to create a double entendre. He changed mental gear and became serious again. 'Right. I'm going to choose four or five of these to take with us.' He sighed. 'I'm afraid I'm including a couple of these rare snaps of Michael's new heart-throb. I can't myself entirely rule Philip out of the frame.'

'He seems fairly straightforward. Quite sweet, I thought.'

'Too cool by half,' Dominic said, darting a suspicious look at Marcus.

'Anyway, I think I managed to stop Michael telling him what we were up to tonight.'

'Do you? I wouldn't be so sure. Anyway, perhaps it might be a useful idea to have him along.'

'Was I wrong then, to try and stop Michael?'

'God knows. We seem to have entered a Nietzchean realm beyond such concepts as Right and Wrong.'

'That wouldn't be an entirely inaccurate description of the gay scene.'

But the first pub they found themselves in, around nine o'clock, was so deserted that it seemed like a place where misconduct was unheard of. This was, to say the least, ironic: it had a reputation for being a bit 'heavy' and was also famous as a drag venue. And so Marcus was surprised to see that Dominic was obviously not unknown to the bar staff. Not that he was on pally first-name terms, but a glimmer of recognition and a more than formal 'good evening' passed between him and the moustachioed Irishman of early middle age who turned on the lager taps at their request.

It was years since Marcus had been here. Well, not many in the literal sense, but metaphorically it felt like a century. Belting around them was an extended, interminable remix of a new, upbeaten version of a ten year old soul song, featuring lots of swooping vocals and screeching from a man who sang falsetto and a woman who sang like a man. One of Marcus's problems with the scene had always been a total inability to tolerate the music around which it spun. Dominic seemed to be singing along with it, however.

Marcus looked at his surroundings. It was fairly dark, except at the edges and behind the bar. The seats and tables were all on a raised platform to one side of the door: the side of the bar opposite this was entirely taken up by a stage. Beside the stage a board told of entertainment treats in store: Marcus had little interest in the drag scene, and wondered whether Mitzi Lambretta, Lovely Rita and Suzette were really all the same person. A reasonably-sized standing area had two pillars and two fruit machines to break up the monotony: each of the pillars had a ledge around it, on which were exhibited various free gay papers. Reflected particles of light, given off from a silver globe and broken up at various points, swept the floor like a neurotic and failed searchlight. It all seemed rather tawdry when empty as now.

Apart from Dominic and Marcus, two couples were hidden at opposite corners of the raised platform. Marcus noticed that each couple had surveyed them with suspicion as they had ordered their drinks. Two single men leaned against the bar, each one feverishly attempting to look as though he were interested only in the free paper he wasn't really reading. Typical clones, thought Marcus.

He waited for Dominic to pull the photographs out of the pocket of the brown, near military top he had donned for the evening to match a pair of carefully faded jeans. An outfit which had surprised Marcus, who had thrown on his usual kind of clothes: and one which indicated that Dominic wasn't really as unused to this kind of jaunt as everyone had been supposing. Still, even if it was a bit of a pose, Marcus had to admit that the effect was rather pleasing.

But Dominic didn't get out his photos. Instead he walked over to one of the machines and dropped a pound coin into its slot. Looking at the machine properly, Marcus registered that it wasn't a fruit machine, but one of the quiz machines that he'd heard about that had appeared recently and were now all the rage.

Dominic took a mouthful of lager, pressed a button. 'Right.' Marcus started to read the screen, but Dominic made an instantaneous thump on a button and the screen changed.

'Do you come here – ' Marcus began, but was immediately interrupted by Dominic slamming two buttons in quick succession.

'Occasionally. Largely for' – slam, thunk – 'this.'

'I've never actually seen' – bang, crash – 'one of these before.' Thunk, wallop. The machine gave a camp little electronic rendition of the first line of *Congratulations*, only just audible beneath the voice of a woman singer informing anyone who might want to know that her man had to have a J-O-B if he wanted to be considered a serious proposition in her life.

'Right, Marc, watch and wonder,' Dominic said arrogantly.

Marcus tried to follow this advice, but usually before he had even read a question, Dominic would have slammed a button and be onto the next. A little clock in one corner of the screen seemed to get faster with each question.

'The time – ' he began, then stopped, wondering whether Dominic could bear distraction.

'Yes, it does get faster,' Dominic said equably, slamming a button again. 'You get more points the quicker it gets. Now, Marc, fingers crossed it's not horse racing or boxing. Shit, fucking horses – hang on, I know this. Red Rum.' Slam. 'Easy. Hang on,' he said to the machine, 'I've had this one before. 1523 miles. Phew. Oh, simplex.' He slammed the buttons twice more and when the next question appeared, made no effort to answer it.

'I know that,' Marcus yelled. 'It's B. Turin. Go on. What were you doing?' The machine informed Dominic that he had run out of time.

'I'd already hit maximum winnings,' Dominic said, as the machine played another camp electronic rendition, forming a bizarre counterpoint to a man with constipation moaning from the pub sound system that love couldn't turn around, a sentiment whose precise meaning eluded Marcus. 'If I get any more questions right, the number of points I'll need to win money in the next game will go up to something impossible.' The machine started to make a metallic vomiting sound. Dominic stood unconcerned, and made no attempt to gather his winnings. He simply pressed the start button again. 'I tell you what,' he said, 'why don't you get the photos out of my pocket and ask around at the bar while I finance our evening?'

'Do you want me to ask around the rest of the immense crowd? You only really wanted to come here for this thing, didn't you?'

'Ah – possibly.' Dominic stared at the screen, banging buttons in a manner which he obviously hoped was nonchalant.

'You're being greedy, trying to win more.'

'Only way to be. Top left hand pocket.' Marcus unbuttoned the pocket and reached in. 'Give us a kiss while you're there.' Marcus pecked him chastely on the cheek, restraining anything more affectionate as a punishment for his obsession. 'You're not like this when we're playing House together,' Dominic said, banging buttons. 'Next time I want to be Mummy.'

'You said yourself you hate children.' Marcus took the photos in one hand, his pint of lager in the other, and stepped over to the bar.

He signalled with his eyes at the barman who had served them: of the three lolling behind the bar, he looked the most friendly and authoritative. Thinking about it, and being fair to Dominic, it was more sensible to visit places like this early: at least they had audibility, ease of communication and ease of movement. However, they could lose breadth of research if they wanted to question clientele as well as staff. The barman approached and suddenly a new problem presented itself. What exactly was Marcus going to say?

'Er – excuse me,' he began, 'I was wondering – did you read about that boy who was killed up in town last week?'

The barman looked suspiciously at him. 'You're not a policeman, are you? I know I've seen your mate in here before, but I don't recall you.'

'No, no, nothing like that, nothing at all. It's just that he – the boy, that is – was a friend of – ours.' Marcus lied a little for the sake of simplicity. 'So is the bloke the Police are trying to nail for it, and we're just trying – '

'Private investigations?' The barman laughed, not unkindly. 'That's not a game for amateurs, young man. Sure, you want to be careful. I read in the paper today that the Police are protecting someone. Now if you and your friend go poking your noses into that little lot – ' He drew an extravagant gesture across his throat.

'Well – I just wondered if anyone in these photos was at all familiar.' He put the pictures down on the bar. The barman picked them up.

'Now, don't look so sad. By the way, your friend's milking that machine dry. I think we'll have to ban him from it.'

Marcus turned round to see Dominic drinking casually while the machine spewed forth its cash innards. He turned and raised his glass at Marcus.

'Now listen,' the barman went on, waving the pictures amiably, 'I'm quite happy to look at your pretty holiday snaps and show them to the lads if you like. What I'm saying to you is, be careful. You know what those bastards can be like. And if you don't, you shouldn't be playing this kind of game.'

He smiled again and wandered along the bar to where his two younger colleagues, both with closely-cropped hair, stood gossiping. Marcus ambled back to the machine, where Dominic let out an almighty curse. He sighed and bent down to start clearing his winnings out. He looked up and smiled, a little absently, as he fumbled for the coins.

'Twenty-eight fifty,' he said. 'God, you look so good I could give you a blow job here and now. Here, hang on to this.' He dropped a handful of silver into Marcus's opened hands. 'Any joy?'

'A friendly warning about the dangers of private investigations. He's having a look and showing them to the other barmen.'

'Good. Good.' Dominic stood up, his hands wrapped around his booty. 'Are you impressed?'

'Not excessively. By the way, you're banned from playing any more.'

'By you? Cheeky cow.'

'No, by him.' Marcus waved his hand at the barman. 'I think it constitutes our bribe to him.'

They returned to the bar. Dominic piled his coins there, and went back to the machine for his drink. Marcus took a long draught, more or less draining his glass. 'Do you think,' he asked, 'we ought to come back here later or on another night? Maybe when the show's on?'

'I did wonder myself,' Dominic said, 'but I tend to think that if the bar staff don't remember people, then nobody will. After all, between them they do see everyone who comes into a pub, more or less. And we are assuming that Guy and whoever were regulars, aren't we?'

'Yes, I suppose that's true. Ah,' he greeted the barman coming back.

'Very nice pictures,' he said, putting them down on the bar. He winced at Dominic's pile of coins. 'I suppose you want me to change all that.'

Dominic nodded with an ingenuous smile. 'Don't want me jeans sagging at the pockets, do I?'

The barman picked up the coins, counted them, pushed one pound back at Dominic and went over to the till. He returned with two ten-pound notes and a fiver: the tenners he handed over, but the fiver he held onto. 'You might, might you not, wish to buy a round of drinks.'

'Conceivably. Just conceivably. Whatever you like. Marc?' Marcus shook his head. 'Then not for me personally either. But for the hard-working bar staff, their very pleasure. And?' he concluded, pointing to the photos.

'Now,' the barman said, 'we're not sure. We don't recognise the boy, except from the pictures in the paper, to be honest, but maybe this chap's shown his face in here. Usually later on in the evening, though. Showtime.' He threw a picture from the pile across the bar.

It was of Derek Wilkinson, although this time fully-clothed. Marcus raised his eyebrows. Dominic nodded slowly. 'We're not sure, mind,' the barman averred.

'You've never seen him – if you have seen him – with Guy – the boy who was killed?' Dominic asked.

The barman shook his head. 'We're fairly definite we didn't see the poor boy in here. One of us would have noticed him. After all, he's – he was – terribly pretty, isn't he?'

'Not my type,' Marcus rejoined decisively. He felt Dominic's hand touch his and give it an affectionate squeeze.

''Right,' Dominic said. 'Thanks a lot. I – er – gather I'm banned from the machine?' He picked up the rest of the photos and put them back in his pocket.

'You most certainly are, my boy.'

'For good or just for tonight?'

'Oh, I think we might let you have another go another day.'

Dominic saluted and moved away from the bar, taking Marcus gently by the arm. The barman saluted back.

Outside, they stood still for a moment, watching the evening traffic pass through the lights. Marcus looked at Dominic and signalled a question with his eyes. Dominic gave a mock scowl.

'Did that help us at all?'

'What, you mean discovering that Derek Wilkinson goes to a well-known drag pub? Hardly. He's into theatrical things. He does Tina Turner impressions, so Guy told me. If he'd been there with Guy – Still. You see, Guy had a slight weakness for drag, which is why I thought he might have shown his face there. Never mind. Maybe we can help someone along the way with what we have found.' Dominic gave a salacious giggle.

'Oh my God,' Marcus struck his forehead, 'your obsession with Colin Latimer really worries me. I mean, I take it you're referring to Derek Wilkinson's hold on poor wee Colin.' Dominic nodded mischievously. 'I don't see how it would help if poor wee Colin was the murderer, though.' Dominic glared. 'So,' Marcus went on, 'where are we going now? Clapham? It's getting on for ten now.'

'Yes. No. We're going two stops down the line. Then we'll go to Clapham. Don't worry. You know Michael will be late.'

'Of course Michael will be late. But I'm not sure that's any excuse.'

'Oh, you Scottish boys are so proper. Come on.'

Dominic punched Marcus playfully and ran round the traffic barrier, across the road and onto the traffic island. Marcus scurried after him. They raced each other to the Tube station, using the ticket machine as a finishing line. Marcus won easily, as Dominic was horribly out of condition: in fact, Marcus was able to run at half-speed and stay in front, once he'd established his lead. Dominic scowled breathlessly. It struck Marcus that Dominic didn't like losing, even when he deserved to.

Accompanied by the sound of Dominic's panting, they made their way down onto the trains. One arrived surprisingly quickly: they got into a relatively empty carriage and sat down side by side. An elderly black man was falling asleep three seats to their right on the opposite side of the carriage; no-one else was sitting at that end. Marcus surveyed the adverts for temp agencies, assuring efficiency, high standards and smartness.

'Guy was a temp for a while, wasn't he?'

'Yes,' Dominic laughed. 'I don't think he did a single clerical thing all the time he temped while I knew him. It was all office furniture moving and messengerial duties.'

Marcus nodded. The train roared on. 'You were pretty sure about Derek not being involved in all this. The actual murder anyway.'

'Oh, I'm not entirely sure. I just don't think that the fact he goes there condemns him.'

'But you don't think he did it, do you?'

'Well, no. Actually, I don't.'

'So who do you think did? I mean, Dominic, I think you've made your mind up.' Marcus turned his head: the two men looked each other in the eye. They both smiled.

'Ah, how well you know me already,' Domonic sighed. 'Yes, I have made my mind up. I made my mind up this afternoon, in fact.'

'Well, come on, who are you blathering about?' Marcus practically climbed onto the seat-arm dividing the two of them. 'If you don't tell me there'll be another murder committed.'

'Look, I can't say anything now. I mean – I may be wrong. I just need proof, that's all. And until I've got it – ' Dominic raised a finger, leaving Marcus to deduce what he could.

'You can't bear the idea of being wrong, can you?'

Dominic gave a weary shrug. 'Not madly, I'm afraid. It's not a wonderfully attractive trait, I fully accept that.' He leaned back in the seat and closed his eyes. 'I'm sure there's some deeply-rooted psychological explanation,' he murmured, just audible over the noise of the train.

The steps at the station where they made their exit were dotted with various people trying hard to look outlandish. A thin spotty young man with greasy spiked hair asked Marcus, almost unassumingly, for money. Marcus smiled and shook his head; he was now inured to such appeals, and yet couldn't refuse one without a slight pang of conscience somewhere along the line. Dominic, he noticed, had steered a wide, eccentric course up the stairs so as to avoid the mendicants in the first place. People milled about in the street outside, some drifting into the station, some drifting out, some waiting at bus stops, some waiting to cross the road. Dominic turned left and led Marcus through the human obstacle course. The road seemed to have a never-ending succession of bus stops, each with an enormous throng vaguely masquerading as a queue. These finally yielded to a junction with another road: a large pub rounded the corner on the same side. Marcus, recognising the name, realised that this was their destination.

He touched Dominic lightly on the arm, to attract his attention, something he seemed largely to have lost since the quiz machine's intervention. 'Is there any particular reason for coming here?' he asked. 'Or are you just being thorough?'

'I used to live round here,' Dominic said, without really looking at Marcus, 'and Guy and I came here a couple of times. He said that he quite liked the place, so I thought it might be worth checking out.'

He stepped into a doorway, pushed open a door, and immediately Marcus's heart and soul groaned. The typical music came blaring out: glossy, vulgar and anonymous vocals drowned by production noises that threw in not just the kitchen sink but the cooker and the fridge to boot.

The pub seemed to shape itself around a huge semi-circular bar. Just to the right of the entrance, a partition created a section with tables arranged as on a train – there the music didn't seem to be quite as loud. Evidently this was for sitting and talking. On the other side of the partition, near the entrance, was the main floor space, with tables and chairs bunched up towards the outer wall: most of this area was demarcated for dancing, and above it swooped and hovered a knobbly black sphere, throwing lights, colours and confusions onto the empty space in time to the frantic excesses of the music. Beyond this, shrouded in darkness, lay a stage.

Marcus and Dominic went up to the bar; here the staff were younger, cleaner-cut and trendier than before. A rather presentable blond boy came forward and smiled. Marcus began to order, but Dominic cut him off.

'My treat,' he said, 'just to show I'm not hopelessly greedy. Two pints of lager, please.'

'We'll be pissed before we get much further.'

'Does that matter?' Dominic surveyed the clientele: there were more people than in the last pub, but the larger area made the place seem even more sparsely populated. Its size also served to underline its drabness: as before, there was nothing that couldn't be found in the most underdecorated pub in a back street, even in the area devoted to sitting and chatting. This had given the first pub a certain tacky charm: the compactness of the place and its lack of pretensions had served to create an atmosphere of homely warmth, even when it was empty. Here the lack of decor, the size and the emptiness created together a shabbiness which Marcus found merely depressing.

'Did Guy really like this place? I suppose there were more people when you came here before, though.'

'Not that many. Guy never liked being out too late at night, you know. He was always terrified of what might happen to him.'

Marcus began to laugh and then apologised. 'He was right,

177

wasn't he?' He looked round nervously. 'There aren't any of those bloody machines in here, are there?'

Dominic laughed. 'Can't your nerves take the strain?'

'I never saw you as a gambler. Do you play fruit machines as well?'

'No. As you correctly observed, I can't stand losing. But I do have a gambler's streak, I think. So I try and restrict myself to calculated gambles, if you see what I mean.'

'Yes, I do. I suppose if you play those things often enough, the questions start coming round again, as well.'

'That doesn't always help. I can't always remember my previous guesses, even if they're right.'

Marcus picked up his drink and took a long, thoughtful draught. He noticed that Dominic was surveying him with extraordinary intensity. He put down his lager and smiled. 'Some burning thought is practically eating you up.'

'I was thinking about you. Well – about us.'

'Does that need a lot of thought? I was under the impression that "us" was going quite nicely.' Marcus picked up his drink again. 'You know, I think there's an awful lot of crap talked about relationships generally. Most of them are a matter of taking what comes, trusting it, and not thinking everything into knots and complications.'

'You may be right, but – well, I always think. A perennial and nasty habit of mine, I'm afraid. I mean, Marc, let's be honest – we don't really know each other. The last hour's proved that.'

'You never really know anyone,' Marcus pointed out. He stroked the back of Dominic's hand, which was idly trailing on the top of the bar. 'Relax, Dominic. We've enjoyed ourselves so far. Once we get all this business out of the way – ' He gestured. 'I think you're just a bit confused by events. You're bound to be.'

'Oh, I'm confused all right. I go to a club to meet the man I love, get ditched by him, picked up by someone else, find the body of a man I used to love, fall in love with the person who picked me up, who seems to be interested in me, get accused of murder – yes, I think we can safely say I'm confused.'

He stood up straight and fished in the relevant pocket for the photographs. He smiled coyly at the blond barman.

While Dominic tried a tactful questioning of the barman, Marcus wandered around the pub a little. The clientele so far was younger than at the other place. Marcus caught sight of a young man with short brown hair, wearing only jeans and a vest, looking intently at him from a corner. He permitted himself a brief smile, but turned away immediately. The young man too looked in another direction. Then, as he began to wander back to Dominic, Marcus found his way suddenly blocked – no mean feat, given the expanse of space – by a small, scruffy youth with greasy blond hair and pimples. His eyes were the eyes of an old man. He nodded at Marcus with the speed of a blink.

''Ere,' he said suddenly, 'that bloke at the bar. 'E a mate of yours? 'E is, in 'e?' He pressed up against Marcus. 'Are you the law?' Marcus laughed and shook his head. 'I reckon you must be the law. Only the law asks things.'

'That's an interesting theory.'

''Cause if you're not the law and you're asking things, you want to watch out.' He reached into his pocket and pulled out a knife. 'There's a lot of these round 'ere, you know,' he explained, almost casually.

'I'll bear that in mind.' Marcus tried to pass by. The youth prodded the knife into him, not so as to cut him, but to make him realise that he could if he felt like it.

'I think you'll do a bit more than that. I reckon you and your mate'll piss off now.' He smiled. 'Don't you?'

Marcus looked round. Dominic was thanking the barman. He waved, pointing to the unfinished drinks on the bar. Marcus signalled him over with his head. Dominic brought the two pint glasses across. He smiled. 'Who's your friend?'

'He reckons we're going to piss off now.'

'What, before we've finished our drinks?' Marcus pointed downwards to the youth's knife. 'Ahh. Hmm. One thing I should point out that you don't know about me is that I am absolutely fucking useless in a situation like this.'

'I don' s'pose you've got any money you don't want before you naff off, 'ave you?' their new friend asked. Marcus smiled at Dominic and took the two glasses from him.

'Dominic's got plenty,' he said affably. Dominic looked at him furiously, horror-struck. The youth moved slightly, pressing the knife into Dominic's jacket. As he did this, Marcus speedily up-ended both pint glasses over his head.

'Run, for fuck's sake,' he yelled at Dominic, pushing him, and dropping both glasses. They dashed out into the street: Marcus was about to run for the Tube station, but Dominic pushed him across the main road, dodging traffic. Looking back they saw the boy with the knife emerge wet and spluttering from the pub.

Dominic suddenly put on an unexpected spurt in a dangerously diagonal direction. They arrived on a traffic island as a bus went past in front of them. Dominic pointed at the bus as it stopped and Marcus sprinted ahead of him, managing to leap onto the platform just before the conductor rang the bell. Panting heavily he pointed at Dominic. The conductor, a friendly Jamaican, laughed and slapped Marcus on the back as Dominic heaved himself onto the platform. The conductor laughed again and rang the bell. The two made their way inside the bus and took the lefthand front seat.

'Where's this bus go, anyway?' asked Marcus.

Dominic wheezed: 'Clapham Common. There is – method – in my madness.'

Marcus laughed hysterically. 'That was great. I haven't had fun like that for years.'

Dominic squinted at him. 'Fun? Fun? I suppose you Scots love all that. See you Jimmy and headbutting. Sorry we couldn't have made it a real Glasgow fight.' He squeezed Marcus's hand. 'Mind you, you were pretty impressive back there. Had me pretty worried, though. I didn't guess what you were up to. I thought you were selling me out. What did he want anyway?'

'Oh, nothing really. Just your run-of-the-mill paranoid psychotic wanting to show off his knife. Did you have any luck?'

'No, not really. They only employ two full-time barmen, and they didn't recognise anyone in the pictures. Not even Guy after his photo's been in all the papers. In fact, they hadn't really heard of the whole business.'

'Aware folk who keep in touch with the world.'

'They'll read about it in *Capital Gay* and be vaguely shocked.'

The bus trundled along, without many people seeming to want to get on or off. It passed through some traffic lights and they saw the familiar dome of Clapham Common Station heaving into sight, their signal to disembark. Clapham, as ever, was full of people: the long-standing inhabitants wandered idly around and the newer, plusher yuppy element strode purposefully about their business in groups of two and three, all easily identifiable by their clothes and their accents as they addressed each other loudly. Marcus parodied one group and Dominic shuddered with mock horror.

'It's a purely personal view,' he said, 'but people like that have ruined the place we're going to. Have you ever been there?'

'A couple of times, but well over a year ago.'

'Ah, that would have been the old regime. It's now been tarted up in an effort to keep pace with the area.'

'Michael quite likes this place, doesn't he?'

'Michael would. He's a piss-elegant yuppy.'

Marcus stopped dead for a moment. He looked at Dominic. They resumed walking. 'That was pretty devastating. Do you realise, by the way, that it's probably the first definite opinion of Michael you've ever expressed?'

'I'm quite prepared to say it to his face, if that's what's worrying you. I mean, it's only the truth, isn't it?'

'It's one way of putting it. Pungent, concise, perhaps a little unfair...'

'Oh, I quite admire the man. But he is a piss-elegant yuppy.'

They walked a little way along Clapham High Street. The entrance to this pub was in a side street. A dark corridor gave way to a cloakroom and lavatories on the left, a large, long and fairly dark bar on the right, and a small, slightly better lit bar straight ahead. Both bars were blaring out more of the same music. Marcus and Dominic entered to the full blast of someone insisting that they didn't have to take their clothes off to have a good time.

Marcus looked around. It was a distinct contrast to the other two places: carpets, plants, art deco baubles, lightly coloured decor, plush seats. In one corner was a stage, but this stage actually had curtains of crushed velvet. In the centre of the bar was a long leaning-post, decorated with beer mats and more free papers. Propped against the bar stood the piss-elegant yuppy himself. Michael pointedly looked at his watch.

'I naturally assumed I'd find you here waiting. I can't imagine what you found to do to make you late.'

'Oh, Dominic's been winning money – '

'And Marcus has been getting us into fights.'

'You don't look any the worse for it. Drinks?' Michael smiled at a barman. He ordered in compliance to their requests. 'Now. Where have you been?'

Together they explained the events of the evening so far. Michael laughed at the recognition of Derek Wilkinson. 'Guy always said he was a drag queen manqué.'

'Guy didn't know what manqué meant until I told him.'

'Oh I dare say that's true.' Michael had clearly recovered a great deal of his poise in his extensive preparations for going out. His clothes had the usual mixture of elegance, trendiness and sex appeal, and his hair had been gelled into place strand by strand. 'Well,' he went on, 'shall we get our business done, so that we can get on with our pleasure?'

'Your pleasure, you mean,' Marcus said. This bar was perceptibly fuller than the other two: and Marcus's greatest wish was to get it all over and done with and get home. He felt, in any case, that the answer was most likely to lie here: why else would Guy have refused so adamantly, as Michael had described, to go to this particular pub?

'You still don't like it any better, do you Marco? Dominic, the pictures, if you please.'

'Ooh – little Miss Masterful,' Dominic quipped. Nonetheless, he handed the photographs over. Marcus suspected that Dominic's love of asking questions of total strangers was no greater than his own. Michael looked through the photos, smiling and wincing; suddenly he stopped short.

'Why is this one of me here?' he demanded, looking at Dominic with no great friendship in his face.

'Oh – to eliminate you from our enquiries. I mean if the barmen recognised you as Guy's companion, then – '

'Bullshit. You couldn't trust me. Let's not forget, Dominic, that you have always been the most likely candidate for this.'

'Look,' Dominic replied in the tone of voice reserved for troublesome children, 'you tried to win my confidence by telling me you're an untrustworthy bastard. Brilliant rhetorical ploy, that speech. But look at yourself, Michael. You're an ambitious yuppy banker who likes doing dodgy deals. Now I agree that you wouldn't have killed Guy for any silly emotional reasons. But there are one or two questions we've all skirted round. Such as where did Guy suddenly get twenty thousand pounds? It seems a bit unlikely you didn't know anything about that, doesn't it?' Keeping his eyes steadily on Michael, Dominic took a mouthful of his drink.

'Just what are you saying?' Michael asked in a voice dangerously low. 'Marcus, can you credit this?'

Marcus shrugged. 'I don't know. It's a fair question, Michael.'

'All right. I did Guy a favour. He asked me if I could help him make some money quickly. It took him a lot of beating around the bush to ask – well, you know what he was like, Dominic – a lot of swallowing his designer-socialist ideological style.'

Dominic laughed. 'I bet you enjoyed that.'

'Naturally. It's rather good for the ego to have managed a successful conversion to the cut-throat capitalist ethos. You could tell Guy felt terribly guilty about falling into the tentacles of the City. He got fearfully petulant after the cash came through. Quite boringly so.'

'I take it that you made Guy's money for him illegally,' Dominic said drily.

'One reason, Dominic, that you'll never have any significant financial reserve is your belief in a scrupulous adherence to petty technicalities.'

'In other words, it was a dodgy deal,' Dominic pressed.

'You can hardly expect me to incriminate myself.'

'And because it was dodgy, Guy started pushing you. Getting boring, in your words.'

'He did seem to think that he had some form of advantage over me, yes.'

'Hang on,' Marcus intervened. 'Do you mean Guy was blackmailing you?'

'Well – he made a threat. At the time of his death I hadn't issued any formal response.'

'You have to admit,' Dominic said, 'his murder was awfully convenient for you.'

'I didn't do it,' Michael said quietly and savagely.

'Oh, I know. At least I think I do. Well, I believe you, anyway. But I can't be sure.'

'You really are paranoid, aren't you? Guy always said you were – '

'Yes, perhaps. Not that that's too relevant in this context.' Dominic turned to Marcus. 'But be warned – '

He stopped as a familiar figure entered the bar, smiled in recognition and ambled up and presented himself. 'Well,' Dominic said, 'this isn't a surprise.'

'You got my message, then?' Michael asked.

'Of course,' Phil Roxby replied. 'So what are you all doing here?'

'Oh, just finding out how little we trust one another,' Dominic replied with a cheerful edge to his voice.

'We're conducting an investigation by means of these photographs.' Marcus pointed to the offending items, still in Michael's hands.

'Ooh, let's see.' Michael handed them over. 'That's a nice one of you, Michael. Oh no, dreadful Derek. Oh worse, tedious Terry. No, that's not fair. I prefer Terry to Derek. Why is there one of Colin?'

'A little whim of Dominic's.'

'He's a bit young, isn't he?'

'Dead hunky, though,' Dominic said pugnaciously. 'OK, Miguel, if we're still speaking, do the business. Then we can boogie on down.' Phil handed the pictures back to Michael. Dominic smiled insincerely at the young Lancastrian. 'Well, this is an honour, Philip, to have the chance of buying you a drink, if I may.'

'I'll have a lager, thanks.'

Dominic handed Marcus some cash. 'Do you mind, Marc? Only it's the first chance I've ever had to talk to Phil.' Marcus gave Dominic an odd look and then turned to the bar. Dominic gave Phil a kind of Edith Evans double take. 'I feel I know so much about you.'

'Yes. I know a lot about you, too.'

'Ah. The difference is that everything I've heard has been exuberantly complimentary. I don't think Guy ever said anything nice about me behind my back. In fact, he wasn't fulsomely complimentary to my face. Still – ' he smiled again. 'So where's Neil tonight? It is Neil, isn't it, your other half?'

'Yes, Neil. He's at night school, learning German.'

'Gosh, how self-enhancing. You already speak German, do you?'

'Languages don't interest me particularly.'

Dominic was trying to think of something peculiarly snide to say to this when Michael gave out a yell. The others crowded around him, Marcus pushing a pint of lager at Phil. Michael contemplated the young, small, moustachioed barman. 'Say it again,' he said, 'so my friends can hear.'

'Well,' the barman said with an embarrassed smile, 'I just thought that this photo was really sweet of the two of them together. I never read papers though, meself. A friend of mine said something awful had happened, but I didn't know...The blond one you said? Oh, what a shame. And to think they were in here together last Thursday, the night before, well...'

He put the photograph down on the bar and Dominic let out a long sigh of relief. Marcus grinned.

'You were right, then?'

Dominic nodded. 'I was right. For what that's worth.'

'You'd probably say you were anyway, if you hate being wrong that much.'

'I hope, Marc, that you don't believe that.'

'In fact, I don't.' Marcus gave him an affectionate fondle. 'Will you do me a favour?' Dominic nodded. 'Apologise to Michael, and stop bitching at Philip.'

Dominic nodded again and turned to Michael. 'I'm sorry I was tactless and paranoid.' Michael nodded ruefully, and then shook his head. He seemed to be terribly upset. Dominic touched his arm. 'Are you OK?'

'No. I'm badly hurt, actually.'

'What, you?' Marcus said, laughing. 'What – by Dominic?' Michael shook his head vehemently. 'Well – not by Guy's infidelity, surely?'

'Well, yes, actually.' Michael took a drink. 'It's not the infidelity that hurts. Not the principle of it. It's the thought of the other person I can't take. I mean, of all the tasteless, unjustified – and

Guy was using me as a cover to see him. I shall never recover from this, never.'

Phil surveyed him disdainfully. 'Is that really how you feel?'

'How else should I feel?'

'Well, you could think about everyone else's safety and call the Police.'

'Oh, I'm seeing them tomorrow,' Michael said dismissively. 'Now I'm going into the other bar for a bop.' He stalked off.

Marcus watched him depart. 'Well, well, well. I've never seen Michael take anything quite so badly.' Turning to Phil he smiled. 'So, how did you escape the Latimers?'

'I slipped away to the station on foot. Look, don't you think we should call the Police?'

'Ah – ' Marcus pondered ' – yes.'

'No,' Dominic asserted. 'I think he'll be here tonight. Soon.'

'Well then,' Phil said, 'we can have the Police here waiting for him.'

'I quite agree. You're not the ideal candidate for confronting danger, Dominic, if your display earlier is anything to go by.'

'Look, look,' Dominic said, waving both his hands, 'let's leave it a second, go in the other bar, find Michael – '

'Leave it a second?' echoed Marcus incredulously. 'Don't you know what we've just found out? We've just blown this whole business wide open, and you want to leave it a second – '

'Yes. Now. Follow me,' Dominic commanded, walking away from them and out of the bar.

Phil looked at Marcus. 'Are you and he – ?' he asked, gesticulating.

'I think so, the last time I looked.'

'Oh. Well, I won't say what I was thinking then.'

'Dominic is certainly volatile. Shall we follow?'

They entered the second, larger room. Once their eyes had become used to the darkness, they surveyed it. There was a large raised seating area near the door, and more seats beyond the dance floor. Michael was dancing in his calculatedly abandoned style to a song about a woman who claimed to believe in dreams. There were several couples circling him, and two or three people on their own, eyeing him and each other. Michael seemed to be ignoring them all. Dominic was standing at the edge of the dance floor: he saw them and gestured frantically.

He moved to the bar and ordered three drinks as they joined him. Although the bar area wasn't crowded, oddly enough the dance floor was: for this reason, presumably, the person in charge of the disco lights had decided to give the stroboscope an early run. The glaring ultra-violet flashes froze the dancers in their various positions, then catapulted them into darkness, to freeze them again in marginally different poses, like a film with every other frame missing. The powerful glare cast light way beyond the floor itself, catching some of the tables on the far side, right into the corner furthest away from the entrance. It was there that Dominic was pointing.

'I told you so,' he said.

Their eyes followed his finger. At first it was difficult, however long the flashes, to focus properly, but soon both Marcus and Phil could see the lone figure sitting in the corner, captured in poses of drinking. He had obviously seen them too, for suddenly he sprang, in jerks and flashes, to his feet.

There, in the corner of a gay pub in Clapham, stood tall, pale-faced, light brown-haired Terry Difford: the very person who had featured in that 'really sweet' photo of himself and his cousin Guy looking around Paris together.

# 12: The Boy With the Thorn in His Side

Terence Anderson Difford had his first sexual experience at the age of fourteen, almost by accident.

Escaping one empty Saturday afternoon from the family home in Kent, he had squandered every penny in his pocket on a day return to Charing Cross and an Underground ticket. At this stage of his life, London had been a place which he knew only through his parents: so he had ridden around a bit on the Underground, changing lines and generally getting what he felt to be his money's worth until, after doubling back on himself, he had decided to get out and above ground at Piccadilly Circus.

But it had been raining, a heavy summer rain against which he had no protection: so instead he'd retraced his steps into the station, back along the curving tunnel into the circular concourse. Desultorily he'd studied the map of the Tube lines, the map of the world that explained what time it was everywhere else; he'd tried to read the magazines without being noticed, had even attempted to summon up the courage to shoplift a bar of chocolate. People were still coming in dripping wet when he'd exhausted these delights, so he leaned back against the outer wall of the concourse, digging his hands deep into the pockets of his shabby old jeans, and idly dragging one heel up and down the wall.

It was crowded with people, of course: Terry watched them idly, resenting the ones who had enough money to do what they wanted. Then he realised that a fairly insignificant-looking, but nevertheless quite pleasant middle-aged man with greyish hair was staring back and smiling. Terry stared harder. The man, who by the expensive cut of his grey suit obviously wasn't poor, approached steadily but not quite directly, and stood next to him. Terry was a somewhat naive boy, so he wasn't really sure what was going on. But when the man said 'Hello' it seemed impolite not to say 'Hello' back. And what followed seemed to Terry a logical enough progression, and not a particularly unpleasant one.

As far as sexual feelings went, he was a late starter: he'd been told about what was supposed to go on, but found it strangely uninspiring, as if it didn't really apply to him in any obvious way. But when he and this man stood huddled together nervously – the man much more nervous than Terry – in a locked cubicle in the station's public lavatory, it all seemed perfectly reasonable, if dramatically brief. Terry stood fascinated as the man took his prick out – long, thick, a bit floppy, set in a bed of greying hair – and realised, when the man started unzipping his jeans for him and feeling inside, that his own was hard – really hard. The man gasped almost like someone in pain; and it was only then that Terry began to sense his own power.

Later he justified it to himself that a bargain had been struck. 'Give us the twenty quid first,' he said in his not too unconvincing London street boy voice, 'or I'll start yelling.'

The man, bright scarlet, reached inside his jacket, extracted two ten-pound notes from his wallet and handed them over. Terry deftly tucked them into his back pocket. Then, being not without humour, he put his hand on the man's cock and pulled it, quite hard. Almost immediately, the bloke started coming. Terry pulled his hand away, wiping it on the bloke's jacket, and then, with an arrogance which he would later look back on as ludicrously dangerous, unlocked the door and slid out. He heard it bang back, to be relocked in a series of panic-stricken clangs. He laughed. and through his jeans squeezed his prick, which was still hard. By the time he went back to Kent later that afternoon, Terry Difford was forty-five pounds better off.

You couldn't say that he subsequently 'became' a rent boy. It was only a weekend job, a Saturday job at the meat counter, so to speak. He never realised at the time how much luck was with him: for the three years or so he supplemented his pocket money in this way, he never once met a maniac or a potential murderer and never once attracted the attention of the Police. Nor was he around often enough for any of the pimps to take an interest in him; and the other boys didn't find him intrusive.

And he never caught anything – or so he believed, anyway, until the day came, some six years or so after the start of his adventures, when his cousin Guy came out of the doctor's little room at James Pringle House. Yet Terry was just as likely to have caught the virus from one of his more 'respectable' liaisons – even, it had to be admitted, from one of his two or three women. From whatever source, at some point it had invaded him. And if Guy hadn't been madly paranoid, he might never have found out.

Arguments about sexual responsibility had never had much effect on Terry and, oddly, it had never occurred to any of his 'respectable' partners that he was anything other than shy, virginal and naive: Terry Diffident, as one lover from his nineteenth year had called him. Perhaps his ability, away from the meat-racks of Central London, to inspire a belief in his innocence lay in his profound capacity for deluding himself, for denying himself any sense whatsoever of his own sexuality. The business with the man in the grey suit (his first punter, as Terry contemptuously thought of him) had been natural enough: but Terry knew definitely that he was never going to identify himself as gay. Not even to himself. Not because he wanted women: although when women offered themselves to his virginal seemliness he took them casually, aroused by their flattery and interest. Not because he was ashamed in any way: although by the time he was eighteen he realised that, whatever liberalism might supposedly prevail, there wasn't much fun or kudos of a public kind to be got out of being openly gay in a straight world. He certainly wouldn't want other people to think of him, worse to treat him, as 'one of those'. And when AIDS hit the headlines, insofar as he thought of it at all, it was as merely an agent which proved the accuracy of his belief that any supposed liberalism had been only superficial.

But ultimately his refusal to acknowledge himself as possessing any kind of sexual identity derived from a kind of perverse sexual existentialism. Every sexual experience he had was separate, in a void, existing only in itself, not anticipated as a future, not contemplated as a past. Even when he was spending his clients' money, Terry never thought back to how he'd earned it. Spiritually, his maidenhead repaired itself within an hour of each new defloration. And so, you might say, people believed in Terry's virginity because he did so himself.

His cousin Guy had certainly believed in it. What happened to Guy as he discovered his own sexual identity, of course, only reinforced Terry's prejudices about being 'identified.' It was, when it happened, probably the most ironic sexual partnership you could hope to encounter: strident, neurotic Guy who forced his sexuality on every passing stranger, every workmate and even his own family, yet who was, apart from a catastrophe with a woman, completely inexperienced; and shy, unforthcoming Terry Diffident, in reality a part-time hustler with a trail of sexual partners to stretch from London to Brighton.

When Guy, in a cafe in Paris, had finally admitted to Terry without evasion that he was actually uninterested, sexually, in women, Terry did allow himself a rare indiscretion, informing Guy that he had 'wondered' himself if he didn't 'like boys at times.' He left it at that, though.

'I can't say,' he said, referring to Guy's announcement, sipping his coffee thoughtfully, 'that I'm very surprised.'

'Well, no,' Guy replied, blue eyes a-twinkle. 'Actually, everyone I know outside the family knows.'

'I think everyone you know inside the family knows. Even if they won't face up to the fact. My mum's suspected it for a long time, actually. Ever since Dominic appeared on the scene, she's been certain.'

'Dominic?!' Guy choked on a mouthful of croissant. 'I don't sleep with Dominic. I don't fancy Dominic at all.'

'No, perhaps not,' Terry said hurriedly, 'but what about Derek?'

'Derek??!' Guy looked for a moment as though he were about to empty his demi-tasse in Terry's face.

'Oh. Well. Do you – er – have a – er?'

'Actually, to be honest, actually,' Guy replied turning bright red, 'I've remained totally celibate. Well, time and place. And I'm very frightened of all this AIDS thing. And living at home, it's – ' He broke off and started to gabble again, saying nothing.

It was at this precise moment that Terry had been seized by the fatal desire. He had to have his cousin. He had always tried to avoid thinking of Guy in a sexual context (or Colin, if it came to that), but suddenly the blond hair, the blue eyes, the sharp and lively face, the quite hunky torso, the superb bum, even the pathetically spindly legs – they just cried out to be had. Terry Difford's sexual nature broke its own rules: he anticipated pleasure when he couldn't be sure of achieving it within minutes.

He tried to deal with it playfully. 'Saving yourself for Mr Right?'

'Something like that,' Guy said gloomily. 'Although I don't think I'll ever find him.' He stirred his coffee moodily.

'She's nice,' Terry said, acting enthusiastic over a girl whom he actually didn't fancy at all.

'Oh, I prefer him,' Guy said, pointing at a greasy, dark-haired youth with a square jaw. 'You've – you've never slept with – well, have you, actually?' he gabbled suddenly. 'I mean, I've always assumed you haven't, but – '

'Oh, I haven't, no.' Terry replaced his cup in its saucer. 'Shall we get the shopping back to the flat? I'd quite like to go to the Pompidou Centre again before lunch,' he lied.

Guy nodded and hurriedly finished his coffee. They had, through a contact of one of Terry's old teachers, been loaned a flat in a not too outlying arondissement: a comfortable, if traditionally small apartment, with TV and all mod cons. They returned there quickly and took the shopping into the small kitchen.

As they were putting things away Terry bumped heavily into Guy, as if by accident, and then stood quite still. So did Guy. They stared at each other, Guy looking up slightly as Terry was the taller of the two. Guy laughed self-consciously and said 'Blimey,' softly.

Terry put down the item of shopping he was holding. And within seconds he came to understand just how sexually frustrated Guy was: he was being embraced by a dervish, a tornado. A clumsy tornado, admittedly, but an excited and eminently involved one. Terry guessed – correctly – that Guy was beyond noticing or caring that Terry wasn't quite as inexperienced a performer as he ought to be. They spent the rest of the morning and the whole afternoon in bed.

What Terry hadn't anticipated, though, was what Guy would expect of the whole business: he was soon to realise that Guy was keen on more than just a holiday romp. Guy expected it all to go on back home: and he expected it to go on more or less in public.

It must be said now that Terry was severely tempted. There was something about cousin Guy that fascinated him as no other person ever had: but that fascination was not, in itself, quite enough. And so, when they returned, Terry played for time.

It was absolutely imperative that Guy didn't tell anyone anything: and all the time he was away in Italy with Dominic, Terry was on tenterhooks, fearful of what Guy might confess ecstatically under a foreign sun. Alternatively, of course, Guy might just change his mind about it all, which would, on balance, be a welcome let-out. But he didn't. Although there was one bonus out of the trip from Terry's point of view: Dominic had clearly gone beyond the pale as a confidant and friend. That was a great comfort: there was no-one else to whom Guy was as close, and no-one else to whom he was so likely to confess anything or by whom he was as likely to be eased into glowing confidences. Terry didn't bother to listen to Guy's endless bitches and complaints about his erstwhile best friend: he just sat, nodding sympathetically, staring into the middle distance, breathing deep (and hopefully inaudible) sighs of relief. Terry felt now that he had bought himself time: and maybe Guy would have second thoughts about their relationship.

They were, in any case, totally unprovided with anywhere to have sex. Terry still, infuriatingly, wanted Guy's body, wanted quite simply to fuck him senseless over and over again. It was odd, something he'd never felt before, to want the same person again and again, to actually see his sexual experiences as related in a temporal continuum. He would wake at nights, obsessed in his dreams by the thought of coming and coming and coming in Guy's tight arse. Yet against this extreme concupiscence he was beginning more and more to feel trapped – trapped by Guy's astonishing infatuation for him.

And then came Michael Hamilton. When Guy made his excited, guilty confession, tearful and tender, Terry too had felt guilty: guilty that he was overtaken by a sense of relief. This surely would bring the whole thing to an end and let him off the hook. Guy would live his open relationship with this handsome, rich, slightly older man, and only the two of them would remember their fling privately. But it became clear, abundantly clear, that Guy still wanted Terry.

'I only do anything with Michael because – well – you know – I'm not as strong-willed as you about being celibate. I didn't go with him first time – or even second or third time. And I don't enjoy it with him. Well, not much.' He gulped and giggled. 'And we're pretty careful.'

And then, on top of it all, came the expulsion from home. Terry was by now a captive of events: when Guy got in touch to announce that Michael was going away for most of a week, Terry simply made his excuses at home and seized the sexual opportunity. He let his cock think for him. But it was during these few days that Guy sprang on him the surprise that shattered the sexual existentialist's poise and brought his six years of sexual activity to a crisis point.

'Oh God!' Guy had exploded as they walked past a newsagent.

'I – I really hate those awful papers.'

Terry looked and saw a headline: 'GAY ROCK GAVE ME AIDS KISS – TV STAR'S FEAR'.

'Well,' Terry replied non-committally, because he hardly thought about the subject at all, 'everyone is pretty frightened by it. You said yourself that you were.'

'Oh. Oh, yes, I am. Actually, I don't know why, really, but I've decided to go for a test tomorrow. I mean, I made the appointment last week.'

Terry stopped dead in the street. 'What for?'

'Oh I – well, I suppose it's got something to do with being kicked out of home. I don't know, I just feel I ought to. Anyway, they run a Hepatitis B check and give you all the vaccinations against that, so I suppose it's worth doing for that,' Guy sighed. 'Actually, Terry, you know I get morbid. I mean, supposing I've – well, I know I couldn't have, but – and supposing I get beaten up or killed or something – '

'What's got into you?'

'I want to make a will.'

'Guy – ' Terry laughed.

'Look, I've got quite a bit saved up. If anything happened to me now, the pig would get it.'

'Your father? What about your mother?'

'Oh – oh – I can't even think about her. I'll never understand why she – anyway, I'm going to make a will. I'm going to see Katy Goldsmith tomorrow afternoon. Well, I haven't told her yet, but I know she'll see me. Will you come with me?'

'Guy, I can't really meet any of your friends yet. Not like that.' Guy looked at him dubiously. 'Supposing Michael found out. He'd throw you out. And I haven't got anywhere for you to go.'

'Yes,' Guy agreed, but was clearly disappointed. 'Shall we go to Clapham tonight?' Over the months since Paris they had frequented only the one gay pub: this was largely at Terry's insistence, once he had assessed the safety of this particular bar, as a precaution against ghosts from the past turning up.

'That sounds like a good idea.'

'It's really good that we're together again.' Guy clutched at Terry's arm. A warning shone in Terry's eyes. 'Well, you can come down to Katy's with me, can't you? I mean, not go into her flat, but wait for me. Actually, Terry, I want to leave it all to you.'

Terry stopped dead again. 'No. No. No, you can't do that, Guy. Why not Michael?'

'Michael's a bourgeois middle-class capitalist who's already stinking rich.'

'Well, then – Gillian. Or Colin. But not me. That would be a little dangerous.' An understatement: Terry didn't know if he could count on this Katy Goldsmith's total discretion. And what if Michael found the will and put two and two together? The implications of Guy's suggestion threatened his sense of independence.

'Are you ashamed of our relationship?'

'It's not that. But the time just isn't right yet, is it? Not to go public. I mean, we've got nowhere to go, and I'm sure you can't have saved enough to buy, or even to rent, a decent flat – well, not for long. I'm at university half the year – shall I go on?'

Guy smiled. 'No, look. I've got lots.'

'How much? Two thousand? Three?'

'Twenty.'

'Twenty thousand?'

'Twenty thousand. I gave some money to Michael to invest for me. He did some crooked dealing and brought back twenty thousand. And I could always ask him to get me more.'

Terry marvelled at Guy's complete ability to ignore the principles he gave as ruling Michael out as his heir when it came to acquiring wealth himself.

'You see,' Guy went on, 'I've been thinking about the future. About us.'

'Yes, but – Guy, we have to go slowly. Even twenty thousand won't last for ever. If we go too fast, well – we may ruin everything. And if we keep things dark – and if you stay with Michael a bit longer – well, you can get more, can't you?'

'Maybe. But it's risky for him to do too many dodgy deals.'

'Something you could always point out to him, actually.'

'What, you mean – ?' Guy looked up at his cousin.

'Your silence and co-operation have a market value now. For Michael. Think about it. And if he found out about you and me just now, he'd have something on us. So it may just be worthwhile being discreet for a bit.'

Guy sighed again. 'You're right, I suppose. Not that there's any need for Michael to ever know. But – oh, I'll put Colin's name in for the time being, if you think that's best.'

It had once been said by a woman he had met through one of his temporary jobs that Guy Latimer had a clairvoyant streak in him. It was only two weeks and two days later that Terry Difford recalled this, thinking back on Guy's sudden penchant for will-making as he stood in the Latimers' kitchen making coffee for the family the morning after the murder, attempting to cohere them into a united front against the world, in the sure knowledge that they all had something to hide. It was then that he realised that his suggestion for the heir named in Guy's second will had been brilliantly inspired.

Of course, Guy had asked Terry again if he could name him this second time, despite the results of the HIV test which seemed to implicate Terry as the source of the virus. He had seemed to feel that this strengthened their relationship, made it socially necessary, a thing it was now their moral duty to parade before the world.

'Look, I don't care how you might have got it. Well, we don't know for certain that you have yet. I could have got it some other way,' Guy said as they sat in the small smelly cafe near the clinic, drinking unpleasant coffee immediately after the stunning news had been broken.

'But you do think it's me, don't you?'

'Well – ' Guy sniffed tearfully and then clutched at Terry's hand across the table. 'That doesn't matter. We'll just have to live together with it now, won't we?' Terry retracted his hand to the side of his chair. 'Look, we owe it to everyone else – to other gay people, anyway, even if we didn't want to do it right away.'

Terry nodded. The past and the present were conspiring to deprive him of the future he wanted. That future was not one to be lived under the shadow of a virus the world considered gay. Terry was socially ambitious. Damn this, Guy seemed almost to be enjoying it all in some macabre way. Now he'd started prattling on about wills again.

'You see, Colin was really nasty to me. He asked me for money and when I wouldn't give him any he was really horrid. So I don't want that greedy boy ever to have a chance of getting any of it. So I'll go to Katy's and make a new one and leave it all to you. Because I love you.'

Terry looked round uneasily in case anyone had heard this. 'Guy – you know full well that's still impossible. Has Michael said anything yet – about the money, I mean?'

'Oh, no, well, actually, he sort of got quite stroppy. Almost violent. It was quite frightening. He said he'd let me know after tomorrow.'

'After tomorrow? Oh, I suppose that'll have to – oh, I don't know.' Terry laughed. 'Well, why don't you leave everything to Dominic for the time being?' Suddenly he began to calculate the chances of making everything look like Dominic's fault.

'Silly boy.'

'No, seriously. Why not put Dominic in? After all, it's not going to be for long, is it? I mean, he's never going to get the money. But you can't say he's a bourgeois rich capitalist, from what you've told me, anyway.'

Guy pondered. 'Actually,' he said. 'I've been thinking. Maybe I'd like to see Dominic again some time.'

This made Terry both wince and feel relief. On the one hand Guy might get over-voluble. But the return of Dominic was fairly helpful to his plan. So he simply nodded and smiled.

'Well, you were very close friends, weren't you? It seems a bit silly that you don't see each other any more.'

'You'll still come with me to Kensington, though, won't you?' Guy asked anxiously. Terry patted his hand circumspectly.

Sometimes, a lot of the time, you would have been forgiven for thinking that Guy was the younger of the two.

'I'll just have to pick up some theatre tickets, though,' Terry said thoughtfully. 'I promised your mum I'd get them for her.' He examined his adoring cousin carefully. 'Guy, what are you doing tomorrow night?'

'Oh, I think Michael said something about a film. You know, the dykey one.'

'And afterwards?'

'Well, he's quite keen to go out to a club or something. I'm not sure about that, actually.'

'Why not go? I'll meet you there. We could maybe go off for a drink.' Terry steeled himself for a monumental, but vital, lie. 'And maybe I could – well – come back. Maybe we could even talk to Michael. But I do think you should think about seeing Dominic again. This thing isn't exactly the recipe for guaranteed social success and acceptability and you're – we're – going to need all the friends we can get.'

Guy listened and nodded avidly. The dire news seemed, so far as Terry could tell, to have affected Guy strangely: he was obviously upset, but it was almost as though he felt he'd paid a price which entitled him to have whatever he wanted. Terry was simply numbed by the whole thing. To think that he must have that awful thing – how long for? How? Was it going to turn into – well – It? And here Terry was sitting, trying to be calm, planning, trying to get rid of Guy. It couldn't go on like this. It had to be finished sooner rather than later: Guy was getting increasingly out of hand.

Guy cut through his fearful contemplation. 'What time tomorrow? Elevenish?'

Terry nodded. 'That'll be fine. You're going to the club near Embankment? I'll meet you outside there. It'll save me going in and paying.'

But now Terry Difford stood face to face with Dominic Palmer, Marcus Grey and Phil Roxby, in the corner of the Clapham pub which he and Guy had always regarded as their 'safe house'.

His first thought on seeing them all had been to run away again – but why? After all, he'd known all along they were bound to be there: Dominic had pointed it out to him at the funeral tea party.

'Was it my deliberate hint you picked up, or Michael's feeble attempt at a discreet message to Philip here?' Dominic asked when they had all sat down at the table in the corner.

Terry smiled sadly. 'I never saw Michael's hint to Phil. Is he here too? Oh, I see.' Dominic was waving his hand towards the dance floor, where Michael was still keeping himself company.

'Well.' Terry looked around the assembled company. 'Isn't this fun, all of us meeting again so soon? About as much fun as the jolly party we all abandoned earlier.'

'How's your aunt?' Dominic asked pointedly. 'I hope you've not tried anything foolish, Terence.'

'She's fast asleep. Very fast asleep. I must admit, it was massively tempting to shove all those pills down her to shut her up, but – '

'It would have been moronically obvious.'

'Can you explain what you're on about?' Phil Roxby intervened.

'Shall I, or will you?' Dominic asked.

'Oh, I wouldn't deprive you of the pleasure. Guy always said you saw your life in terms of books. I bet you're wetting yourself with all this – the suspect solving the case.' Terry laughed.

Dominic smiled. 'It is a bit of a cliché, but there we are. Anyway – what you don't know, Philip, because you didn't see it happen, is that this afternoon, before she passed out – and while she was passing out – Guy's mother tried to confide in me. I don't know why: I think she was so surprised that I was actually upset by what had happened that her opinion of me swung from one extreme to the other in two seconds. Anyway, Terry and Marcus stumbled in on her about to tell me something – and she later expressed as strong an interest as a fainted person can in seeing the confidence through. Well, it would have been obvious even to a cretin that she wanted to say something, wouldn't it, Marcus?'

'Well, I suppose you could put some of it down to having her son murdered – but I would agree with you.'

Phil Roxby demurred. 'Mind you, she is known to be a bit of – well, a loony.'

Dominic nodded. 'True. But once she'd said there was something she had to say, that she had to tell the truth – well, part of her strangeness this afternoon was explicable. And as soon as she hinted she'd been lying, I started to think, well, whom could she have been covering up for? There were only two people for whom she provided anything like an alibi – Terry and Colin. And of those two, the only one she really effectively covered was Terry. Never out of each other's sight the whole night – but if it was a load of garbage? Terry might have left the play before the end, and nipped out to keep a rendezvous with Guy, and met up again with Auntie later. And that makes sense, doesn't it? After all, Terry, you and Guy were lovers, weren't you? We all know that now, because you're here, and the barman recognised your picture. Said what a nice couple you and Guy made. But things – one incident this afternoon particularly – told me that if Guy had a secret lover, then it had to be you.'

Marcus clicked his fingers. 'The broken glass.' He raised a finger. 'The blood. If Guy was HIV positive – '

'Which he was,' Dominic went on. 'Yes, Terry, that was a bit of a giveaway, keeping us all so determinedly at bay when you were bleeding copiously. The normal reaction is to solicit sympathy and attention.' He smiled at Terry. Terry scowled back. 'So – you had to be Guy's secret man. When did it all start? In Paris or before? Never mind, I'm sure the drunken Inspector will charm it out of you. Yes, there was something he said as well that pointed to you. You remember, Phil, when he was trying to drag Michael off and you intervened, that he said he'd want to talk to you again.'

Phil nodded. 'I didn't know what that was supposed to be about.'

'No. He was merely jumping to a false conclusion from one true premise, one false premise and a statement from a witness, if my guess is correct. Somebody positively identified Michael at the scene of the crime. Well, who that somebody was – and whether he did or not – is open to question. But it struck me that a casual description of either of you two' – he waved at Phil and Terry in one gesture – 'wouldn't be madly dissimilar. I hope that doesn't insult either of you. Presumably the witness in question gave a general description and the Police, knowing that Phil is gay and assuming that Terry isn't – '

'That's ridiculous,' Terry hissed. 'He can't possibly have seen anything.'

'Terry, Terry,' Dominic said, shaking his head, 'it's no good pretending any more. I mean, you don't deny that you and Guy were having an affair?'

'Yes, we were, but – '

'And you knew he was HIV positive, didn't you?'

'Yes, I did – '

'And you knew he must have got it from you. God knows what

you've been up to – '

'Nothing worse than you in the public loos of South London.'

'And you went with him to Katy's, didn't you? You went to the clinic with him on Thursday. You arranged to meet him on the Friday night, didn't you? You sneaked out of the play – when, the second interval? What did you tell your aunt? I mean, you can't have told her you were meeting the Prodigal Son.'

'No. No.' Terry scowled absently. 'I said I was going to meet a girl I had to finish with. Which is sort of true. Look, look, look. What you've said is true. But you can't say I killed Guy. I mean, what proof have you got?'

'Terry, Terry...Terence. You went to meet Guy with an overwhelming need to get rid of him...That's enough. I don't – no-one has – such a low opinion of your intellect to assume that you'd leave clues and proof littered all over the shop...'

Terry laughed bitterly. 'God, it's such a joke. That you of all people should be sitting here talking about all of this. Oh, God. I don't suppose you'd believe me if I tried to tell you I didn't do it? That I only found his body and ran away?'

'I can't say I'm wildly convinced,' Phil Roxby said drily. 'I mean, if that was all that happened, you'd have called the Police.'

'Yes,' Marcus added, 'I mean, you could have explained it away to the family easily enough without mentioning that you were sleeping together.'

'I mean,' Phil went on, 'if you just found the body, what did you do?'

Terry laughed, more loudly. He was getting towards hysteria. 'Oh, what do you expect? I went into the club for a drink, of course, to try and calm myself. And to wash my hands. Naturally. All that blood. Guy's blood on my hands, you see.'

Marcus, Phil and Dominic eyed each other carefully: supposing Terry got out of hand? And even as their fears began to mount and communicate themselves through eye contact, a further turn of the screw was effected.

'Jolly little party this.' Michael swayed uncertainly at the end of the table. Obviously he had managed to get a lot of drinks down very quickly after dancing. 'Well, well,' he went on affably, 'if it isn't my late boyfriend's secret lover. What price blackmail now, Terence?' He sat down. 'You know, I swallowed all that guff about the married woman.'

'Well, it was mostly your own guff. I just didn't deny any of it. You were so pleased with your little story that it seemed a shame to jolt you out of your self-satisfaction. You're not the only bloody con artist in the world, no matter how many yuppy deals you may cheat your way through.'

Michael bowed from where he sat. 'I thank you. The one thing this business has managed to bring home to me is just how self-satisfied I seem to be. I never sussed you out, Terence – you take whatever comfort you can from that. Not even when you were making it clear how close you and Guy really were this afternoon. You fooled me. Any use? No, probably not. Well, there we all are. Terence gets life, Dominic gets Marcus, Phil gets to go home to wifey and I get drunk. I'm only sorry it wasn't his father who did it. Anyway, there we are. End of story.'

Terry rose to his feet, fuming hysterically. 'You think that's it, do you? It's all nicely wrapped up, and the Police will come, and I'll confess like a good little boy. Oh no. Oh no, no.'

'Terry, Terry. In the real world we accept our responsibilities.'

Marcus looked at Dominic. 'I applaud that typically English understatement. But could I, as an uncouth Scot, suggest that you sit down, Terry, or I'll teach you some tricks I learnt in Scotland as a boy.'

'I learnt some tricks too,' Terry said. Reaching into his jacket pocket, he pulled out a small, but vicious-looking knife. 'Now I'm going. And I suggest you let me, if you know what's best for you.'

'You're being bloody stupid,' Phil said. 'Where are you going to go? We've all heard you here, and – what is it?'

Something had seized Terry's attention. He was staring across the bar, right through the sizeable crowd, a look of panic in his eyes. One by one the four at the table turned to see, struggling across the bar, the burly, suited figure of Chief Inspector Oldcastle, followed by the equally incongruous-looking Morgan.

'Who called them?' Terry shouted.

His shout drew the attention of other people at other tables, who had hitherto been quite gamely ignoring the eccentric events in the corner, in the hope that they would sort themselves out peaceably by the end of the evening without needing anyone else's involvement. Marcus heard someone say, 'Oh my God, he's got a knife' at precisely the moment he felt Terry Difford jerk him up and place the knife at his throat. Behind him Terry snarled.

'Right, Scottish boy. Let's see your tricks. And then *you* can have a blood test.'

Through his back, Marcus thought he could feel Terry's heart beating fast enough to generate enough power for a fair-sized city. Or was that his own heart?

'Right, Scottish boy,' Terry said, 'let's say goodnight to the nice policemen and your nice boyfriend and all the other nice people.'

'Terry,' Marcus piped up, trying hard not to move too suddenly or surprisingly, 'do you think this is such a wildly brilliant idea?'

'Oh dear,' Michael volunteered from somewhere else, 'perhaps it wasn't a desperately clever idea of mine to call the Police after all.'

'It was you, was it?' That was Dominic. Looking out, Marcus could see Oldcastle and Morgan standing at the other side of the table.

'Sorry, Inspector,' Terry said, 'we were just going.'

'Oh, for Christ's sake,' Oldcastle said wearily, 'bloody TV stuff again. Come on, Difford, lad, stop being a clot. This isn't going to achieve anything.'

'I don't know about that. It might just get me out of here, which'll do nicely for starters. Now, let me out of here, Dombo, and move that fucking table.'

As Terry said this, Marcus was calculating his chances of pulling a street fighting trick. Could he somehow give Terry a hard blow in the balls without forcing either a voluntary or involuntary stab from the knife? Maybe a knee in the groin and a quick jerk of his head to one side would do the trick. But in the split second he was calculating, the most unexpected thing happened. The arm with the knife was wrenched from his throat: Marcus seized his chance, shoved his knee into Terry's balls and then gave his hardest punch to the chin. Terry Difford sat back down rather hard. The knife lay on the floor. Marcus turned again, to see Dominic standing looking amazed.

'Did you do that?' Marcus asked.

'Apparently so, Mr Grey,' Morgan said.

Marcus laughed, his laughter exaggerated by relief. 'I thought you were absolutely fucking useless in a situation like that.'

'He shouldn't have called me Dombo.' Dominic tried to look casual. Marcus, heedless of Police presence, kissed him lingeringly on the mouth. Then he stooped down and picked up the knife. He put it on the table for the detectives to examine.

'Well, wasn't that thrilling?' Oldcastle said. 'Now, Mr Difford, you're still with us, are you?' Terry looked up, rubbing his chin miserably. 'Terence Anderson Difford.' The Chief Inspector cleared his throat. 'I am now going to place you under arrest. I should therefore advise you that you are not obliged to say anything, but anything you do say may be taken down and used in evidence against you. Now, I'm going to take you to headquarters, where we'll discuss your statement, and you will then be charged with the murder of your cousin Guy Malcolm Latimer.' Marcus noticed that Morgan had produced a notebook suddenly.

Terry stood up again. 'All right, Dominic,' he said, 'I accept my responsibilities. But remember this – he despised you. And he loved me.'

He moved gingerly around the table as Morgan noted these words. Terry confronted the policemen. Then, quite suddenly, he pushed past them and dashed off through the crowd.

'Stop him!' Morgan yelled. But by the time the yell registered itself at the far side of the bar, Terry was through and into the corridor. The policemen followed.

'Did you put the uniformed men on the door, Stuart?' Oldcastle asked as they pushed and shoved.

'Well, not exactly, sir,' Morgan replied. 'I didn't think it was entirely tactful. They're out on the High Street, but – '

'Oh, bloody wonderful. Excuse me, excuse me. Oh, thank Christ.' They were out of the bar: they headed for the street door. Behind them, Dominic, Marcus, Michael and Phil were following.

Marcus led the way out and up towards the High Street. But before they got there, they heard screams, the squeal of brakes: and when they got there, they saw Oldcastle and Morgan waving back a small crowd of people from the middle of the main road, with uniformed policemen stopping the traffic heading towards the Common. The traffic heading away towards town was being held up by a stationary bus. It had stopped after running into Terry Difford, who was now lying still in the road, sprawled out where the bus had thrown him.

The quartet tried to follow, but another uniformed policeman came and told them to remain on the pavement. They stood in silence as a police car arrived, weaving its way through the traffic jam, its siren blaring. Radio messages began crackling into the night as Morgan walked back to the pavement and joined them. He waved them around him, in a confidential manner, like a captain gathering his team for a brief tactics talk during a match of some kind.

'Look,' he said quietly but crisply, 'Difford is dead. It looks as though he just ran out into the road – the driver didn't stand a chance. We're going to have to ask you to hang around, I'm afraid: we'll need to know everything that happened in there. But we'll do our best to let you go as soon as possible.' He was thinking, but didn't say aloud, that most of the paperwork here could be left to the traffic boys.

Morgan returned to Oldcastle. 'Well, sir,' he said, 'this looks like it, doesn't it?'

Oldcastle nodded. 'Aye. It certainly does.' He mused. 'It was a messy way to wrap it all up, though.'

Later that night, after the four young men had given their statements, they were offered lifts to their respective homes, but by common consent they agreed to go back, in the first instance, to Marcus's flat. At first, while Marcus and Dominic made coffee, not a lot was said. Phil rang his Neil to reassure him. Michael wandered around the sitting room, picking up objects, failing to examine them, and putting them down again. When they all sat down with coffee, it was Michael who eventually broke the silence.

'I still think it should have been Daddy.'

Phil looked askance at him. 'I sometimes don't follow your sense of humour.'

'The politically correct ending. I'd have thought that you three would have preferred that.'

'I'd have preferred it not to happen,' Phil replied. Marcus half-nodded.

'It's sad, isn't it?' Dominic asserted suddenly. 'He found the love of his life. I really think Terry must have been that. I mean, I wonder if he thought that having the virus, being HIV positive, was the price he had to pay.' He shook his head in wonder. Marcus reached over and put his hand on Dominic's.

'Well,' he said, 'there it is. But let's be brutal. We can start putting things back in order now.'

Dominic looked up and smiled. 'Can we? It's going to be very hard not to be forever feeling guilty.'

'Oh, that gets no-one anywhere,' Phil Roxby said positively. To reinforce the point, he gave each person present an individual smile. Michael laughed uproariously. Marcus stood up.

'Do you know what I want?' he said. 'For once in my life I want to hear some of that revolting raucous rubbish they play in all those ghastly clubs and pubs. The more vulgar, the better.'

He went over to his stereo and record collection. 'This record, Michael, belongs to you. You left it with me when we went our separate ways.' He fished out a single and slipped it on the turntable, pressed a few buttons, and put the needle to the record. 'Let the neighbours complain,' he said, as a very deep voice urged them to 'Keep that, keep that body strong' at a remarkable pace.

'There are times,' Marcus went on, shouting, 'when vulgarity is the only answer.' He leaned over and kissed Dominic. Then, crouching down, he laid both his hands on his lover's left knee. 'It's really over, Dom. Really.'

Their eyes met: Dominic smiled sadly.

'Yes,' he said, 'I suppose it must be.'

# 13: Dolce Vita

Dominic Palmer lolled on the sofa. In his right hand was a drink, brown and slightly fizzing, with a lot of ice swimming around in it: in his left hand was a copy of an afternoon edition of the evening paper.

'Well, there we are,' he announced proudly. 'Listen to this.' He cleared his throat and read aloud: 'At a press conference this morning, Detective Chief Inspector Oldcastle, who has been in charge of the murder inquiry, revealed last night's tragic accident. He said that it would probably result in the closure of the inquiry into Guy Latimer's murder. The body of Latimer, 24, was found outside a well-known gay night club last Friday. The Chief Inspector also confirmed that the victim of the accident was Terry Difford, aged 20, a cousin of Latimer's, who was under arrest at the time of the accident. His arrest was, it was confirmed, directly connected with his cousin's murder.'

Dominic lowered the paper. 'There. Do you believe me now?' He patted one of the knees which was more or less in his lap, and ran his hand along the bare leg to the crotch.

Dennis Kelly, to whom knee, leg and crotch belonged, adjusted his position a little: the arm of the sofa was digging uncomfortably into the small of his back. 'It only says they'll probably close the inquiry,' he said. 'They might change their minds.'

'Why should they?' Dominic asked. 'They're only too delighted to get the whole thing wrapped up and out of the way. And Terry can hardly deny it, can he? I mean, what's he going to do, send messages from beyond the grave? Face it, Den, we've got away with it. In a couple of months or so, I'll get the cash – *we'll* get the cash. And then – ' Despite the fact he was still holding a quite full glass, he hurled his head down into Dennis's midriff and started undoing the sports shorts the older man was wearing.

'God, you can't get enough of it, can you? I bet you've done all this with that Scottish boy, haven't you? It's all just cock to you, isn't it?'

'How can you say that?' Dominic looked up. 'You know it's not the same for me with anyone else. I only did anything at all with Marcus because I had to. You know that.'

'Oh, you're perfectly entitled to do what you want. After all, we don't own each other, do we?'

'You own me, you know. But you know that whatever I did with Marcus was part of the plan, so it was for us. I mean, once it was obvious that he didn't want to believe I was guilty, then I had to hang onto him till it was over. It would have been bloody stupid not to.'

'But did you enjoy it, though? I bet you did? Did you let him fuck you? I bet you did. After all, he had a cock. That's all you care about.' Dennis's voice as he said all this was soft and gentle, his Geordie accent lilting; he even ruffled Dominic's hair.

'Of course I didn't let him,' Dominic lied. 'I just thought of you all the time I was with him.' This was slightly more true, but only slightly. 'I love you, you know.' This was unvarnished truth.

Dennis smiled broadly and ruffled Dominic's hair again. Dominic stared back at him with a demonic intensity that told its own story.

'Yes,' Dennis said, 'I know you do. You're a good boy. Give us a kiss.' Afterwards, Dennis drew his head back and looked at Dominic with amusement. 'But I do wish you hadn't given my name to the Police. That was a bit risky. Specially as I had to read that note you sent me, with them actually here in the flat.'

'You obviously managed it rather well. It didn't seem to alert them. Actually, I reckon it would take a fucking nuclear missile to alert them.'

'Oh, I don't know. The younger one's quite sharp, I think.'

'For a policeman he is. No, I'm sorry I had to drag you in, Den, but there were some good reasons. To start with, I let something slip to Marcus – '

'You see, pillow talk is dangerous. That's what they warned me when I started my job.'

'Actually, this was before I'd ever been in bed with him. Something just slipped out.' Dennis gave an obscene chuckle as Dominic said this. 'And anyway, it was possible that someone had seen us together, in the club or when we went out together. I mean, I'm still amazed that no-one noticed us leaving at more or less the same time as Guy.'

'Just as well you decided to pay to get back in, too.'

'Smarmy Mike nearly cut his own throat by being mean, you

know. Still, he was quite useful in the end. Anyway, dragging you into it helped to cover me – and you as well. I mean, like I said to you last Friday, if they tried to pin it on me, they were always going to try from the revenge angle, the obsessive maniac bit. With you around upsetting me and me totally obsessed with you, there's no way I'd be interested in taking revenge on Guy, is there? And everyone knows, as you told them, that I have no interest in money. Not enough to kill for it, anyway. The great thing about our Police Force is their total lack of imagination, particularly when it comes to character analysis and motivation. Anyway, I never told the Police that I knew how much money there was. And I never told them that money was the problem with us.'

'I don't see why you have to say something like that, Dominic. You make it sound as though money's all I care about.' He looked and sounded quite hurt at this notion. Dominic wanted to avoid conflict on an occasion which was, after all, a celebration. He put his hand on Dennis's.

'That's not what I mean.'

'I'm not greedy, you know. I think you think I'm a mercenary bastard.'

'I don't. It's just that you're financially practical and I'm not. You've got responsibilities and duties, I know that – '

'I couldn't just walk off and leave Anna to cope with everything. I mean, the flat and all of Lucy's things.'

'No, of course not, I understand that. Lucy's your daughter and Anna's her mother. I understand.' This was old ground: and once again Dominic was tempted to suggest that actually Dennis could just walk off.

'I mean, I don't want you or anyone thinking that it's just money.'

'Look, Denny, money is no problem now. As soon as it comes through – ' Dominic waved his arms to signify boundless possibilities. 'Anyway, shall we go out for a drink?'

'I'm very tired,' Dennis said peevishly. 'Oh, all right then. Give me your drink and give us a suck.' He took Dominic's drink, put it carefully down on the carpet and opened his shorts. 'Good boy.' He laid his head back and closed his eyes. This, to his mind, was where Dominic's real use and talents lay. 'Now the balls. That's good. Right. That's enough for now.' He yanked Dominic's head back up again, pulling him by the hair, gave him an affectionate swipe on the back of the head. 'You're a silly boy,' he said, not unkindly.

'Well, at least I've managed to get hold of some money,' Dominic replied proudly. 'You never thought I'd manage that, did you?'

'You needed me to help you, though, didn't you? You couldn't have done it alone, could you?'

'It would have been more difficult, I admit. But I could still have achieved it somehow, I suspect.'

Dennis laughed and shook his head. 'You're proud of it, aren't you? You're really proud of yourself. That poor little boy. He was very pretty, wasn't he? I could have thought of better things to do with him than keep hold of him while you cut his face to bits. You know, the expression on your face was horrifying. If I ever see you looking like that, I'll run.'

'Oh, don't worry, I'm not naturally violent. Anyway, we both know you're a sadist – you enjoyed it, didn't you? And I could never do anything to hurt you, you know that.'

'I bet you said that to Guy once,' Dennis said pointedly. 'Come on, I'd better get dressed.'

He and Dominic disentangled themselves. Standing up, Dennis reached down and handed Dominic's drink back to him. 'You're quite sure,' he said, looking down thoughtfully, 'the Police haven't got anything at all to link it to you and me?'

'Well, how could they have? I mean, what is there? The gloves we wore and the knife – you got rid of those yourself. I mean, I hope you did. You said you would.'

'Of course I did. I burnt the gloves and chucked the knife in the river miles away, somewhere they'd never think of looking for it. But what did you do with the bag, Dominic? Little Guy's rucksack.'

'Oh, I took it back into the club and deposited it in the cloakroom. After checking it was clean, of course, no bloodstains. Good job he'd been carrying it in his hand, not wearing it over his shoulder when I knifed him.' Dominic smiled with pleasure at his own stratagem: Dennis adopted an expression near to fury.

'Well, that was bloody stupid, wasn't it? I mean, to start with, what did you do with the ticket for the bag?'

'Stuck it in his pocket when I discovered the body. Nobody saw me.'

'Yes, but it's still bloody stupid. I mean, was the ticket traceable? Could they tell at what time it was given out? There's that to consider.'

'Don't worry, I thought of all that. They stopped changing cloakroom ticket colours at various points of the evening ages ago, so there's no way they know when anything was left there.'

'But it might occur to someone that if he was going off with his boyfriend he'd hardly be likely to leave his bag behind.' Dominic's mouth opened slightly. 'Oh, you're too bloody clever by half, you are.'

'Well – I don't think it has occurred to anyone. I think everyone's assumed he was taking Terry back into the club with him. I don't know. But it was the best I could think of. I mean, supposing I'd met Michael and Marcus and still had the bag? It added an element of confusion, too – made his movements less obvious. No, it wasn't that daft an idea. Almost as good as my discovering the body in front of witnesses.' Dominic was talking himself back round to self-congratulation now. 'Nice touch that, Den: it meant I knew all the relevant details of the investigation. And I really don't think there's a person in the world suspects me now – let alone having any idea that you were involved in any way.' He laughed. 'I think I deserve an Oscar.'

Dennis shook his head. Then he gave one of his high-pitched laughs. 'I think you're mad. Still, you do a first class blow job. Really first class.' He stepped over ansd stood in front of Dominic and pulled him by the hair towards another demonstration of his talent. 'Did you tell the Police you did this on Friday?' Dominic gave an indistinct gurgle. 'That was naughty of you, you know. You should have warned me you'd told them that. And it was pretty risky bringing that letter round yourself.'

Dominic pulled his mouth away. 'Calculated risk. Had to. Anyway, nobody saw me. People never notice other people in London unless they fancy them.'

'Typical clever-clever Palmer remark. Just thank Christ that for once you were lucky. No, stop that now, I'm going to get changed. Finish your drink and go and clean your teeth.'

Dominic sat back. Despite Dennis's fears, he really felt, for the first time ever that he could recall, that he was the master of his destiny. Luck was actually running with him. He was like a poker player who has managed to bluff his way to a jackpot on a pair of threes: after all, he had, on the face of it, been playing from an incredibly weak hand. But everything had conspired to help him, to keep him ahead of the game. He had had this mystical certainty right from the moment he had conceived his brilliant plan.

Of course, when Guy had telephoned on the Thursday, he had been annoyed (to say the least) to hear Guy's voice again after such a break in communication.

'I need to talk to you quite urgently,' Guy had said almost straight away.

'I can't say the feeling's mutual, to be frank.'

'Please, Dominic, I can understand, but – ' Guy began to gabble. 'Look, can you meet me for a quick drink after work? Say about six?'

'It may be feasible,' Dominic said, intrigued despite himself. He named a pub near his office which he had originally frequented because he fancied one of the barmen. At the appointed hour he and Guy met. On seeing him again, Dominic instantly felt an instinctive spasm of sexual desire and loathing. He attempted to disguise this by greeting Guy in an offhand manner, looking ostentatiously at his watch.

'Hi,' Guy said, offering the automatic smile of greeting which Dominic knew so well. 'What're you having?'

Dominic sniffed and requested a lager. Guy fetched it for him and suggested sitting at a nearby vacant table. Dominic shook his head. 'I'd rather not. So. What is it?'

'You know I got kicked out of home?'

Ah, that's it, Dominic thought, he needs somewhere to live. 'No, I didn't. Probably for the best in the long run, isn't it? So you're searching madly? Poor you. I wish I were in a position to help...'

'No, I've got somewhere. I'm' – the pause for effect was perceptible – 'living with someone.'

'Good for you,' Dominic replied coolly, without any evident enthusiasm. 'Is that why you had to see me urgently?'

Guy waved a hand effetely in the air. 'No, no, actually. Actually, I don't quite know how to say it.' Dominic looked at his watch again, extravagantly and pointedly. 'It's nice of you to come and meet me, actually.'

'Yes, I thought so too.'

'I'm HIV positive,' Guy gabbled very quickly – so quickly that Dominic almost missed it.

'You're... You?' His heart leapt in a weird combination of pity, horror and triumph. He reached out and touched Guy's hand surreptitiously, an instinctive gesture of sympathy; Guy, with equal instinct, drew his hand back. Perhaps if he hadn't done that, Dominic said to himself days later, I wouldn't have remembered quite how much he used to humiliate me, quite how much he fucked me up. Dominic, who in his melodramatic way was a great believer in moments of irrevocable decision, liked to see that as the moment at which Guy Latimer's fate was sealed.

But it wasn't: that moment had come later, when Dennis Kelly suddenly, almost out of weariness, agreed with Dominic's scheme. And if he hadn't known that he had a chance of considerable material gain, as Guy had gone on to reveal to him, Dominic wouldn't have dreamt of depriving Guy of the prospect of a long, wasting disease, even if it was only a one in ten or whatever chance. Nor would he ever have put himself at the risk of arrest, had not Guy revealed that his naturally secretive behaviour was once again getting the better of him.

'So you've just come back from Katy's with Terry?' Dominic asked as the saga was unfolded to him. 'So Katy knows about you and Terry?'

'No – Katy thinks I went off to meet Michael. No-one knows about me and Terry. Except you, now.'

'And you're sure it was Terry you got the – thing – from? Well – where did he get it from?'

'Well, that's one thing I wanted to ask you – could he have got it apart from through sex?'

'I'm not a doctor, Guy.'

'No, but you're quite well-informed. I wasn't listening to what they said at the clinic, actually.'

'Well – does he inject drugs?'

'Terry? Hardly.'

'Well – ' Dominic shrugged. 'So whose idea was it that you should get in touch with me again?'

'Oh – well – actually Terry doesn't know I'm meeting you now. He thinks I'm with Michael, sorting something out about tomorrow night.'

'Hang on. Katy thinks you're with Michael, Terry thinks you're with Michael. Where does Michael think you are?'

'Fuck knows. He doesn't really take much interest in what I do when he isn't there. He's awfully selfish, actually.'

'So am I, I thought.'

'Oh, not like Michael. I mean, Michael will boot me out the minute he finds out – '

'About Terry?'

'No, about...Actually, that was why I wanted to see you. I'd like us to start being friends again. That is, if you want to, I mean, I know it might be a bit painful if you still, well...Is there anyone around at the moment?'

'Yes, there is. But it's fairly complicated. He's fantastically handsome and wonderful, and we love each other very much.' This gross over-simplification was near enough to the truth for Guy Latimer, he reckoned. 'So. You want us to be friends again.'

'Yes. Terry thinks it's a good idea, too.'

'So Terry knows you're meeting me?'

'No, I've not told him yet. I shan't tell him quite yet. Actually, he's taken it all worse than me.'

'You seem to have taken it remarkably – unbelievably, if I may say so.'

'I expect it hasn't quite sunk in yet.'

'Guy,' Dominic began in a tone so casual that it really should have alerted Guy, who knew Dominic well enough to know that he was never casual about anything, 'Guy. Don't you think it would be better if perhaps I arrived back in your life by accident?'

'How do you mean exactly?'

'Well, if Terry's rather upset – and of course he must be – he might feel a bit paranoid if he finds out that you rushed straight to me – he might feel that you don't trust him enough. After all, you've got to be able to rely on each other totally now. And then, this Michael. He might start wondering why you suddenly got in touch with me. However selfish he is.'

'Mmm. He does like gossip, actually. I know – why don't you bump into us at the club tomorrow night?'

'You mean, like a complete surprise? I'll have to act a bit when we meet, you know. I mean, as if I wasn't very keen to see you. It would be more in character, more convincing. After all, we didn't part on the best of terms.'

'Yes, well, actually, I'm sorry about that, I mean, I was a bit – '

'Forget it,' Dominic said, savouring every moment of the memory of the petulant telephone argument which had ended their friendship.

'Well. Actually, Dominic, you're being very nice about all this. I'm glad you came here to meet me. I'm glad I put you in my will.'

'Oh, don't be morbid, Guy. I'm not anticipating inheriting, you know.'

But he was already counting on the twenty thousand pounds entering his bank account. Not an inestimable fortune, by any means, but quite enough to impress the bank and get them to trust him with some kind of loan for a mortgage: enough to impress Dennis too. If he could buy his own place, that would make things so much easier for him and Dennis. All that was needed was to get rid of Guy, preferably with Dennis's help.

Dominic's motives for wanting Dennis's involvement were a bizarre mixture of the intensely practical and the absurdly symbolic. An accomplice, with whom he couldn't be linked except on his own admission, could get rid of incriminating evidence, could help create a confusing picture. Dominic was no fool: he knew that all eyes of Guy Latimer's acquaintance, family and friends would turn immediately on him when searching for a culprit. But Dominic had the advantage over everyone else: he knew everything. Guy's secretive nature was Dominic's greatest ally. The only problem would be not appearing to know anything. Be that as it may, having Dennis along would help, both in the act and in ridding the scene of debris. And then, of course, to enlist the aid of the man he now loved in the destruction of the one he had loved with such intensity, who had maimed him so badly, had a certain grim justice.

'I always thought you were crazy,' Dennis said with a high-pitched giggle when Dominic raised his proposal later that Thursday evening. 'Come here, little poofy boy, and give me a blow job.'

'I'm serious. It's twenty thousand pounds. We could use that, couldn't we?'

'Well, that goes without saying. Particularly you could, with that fucking juggling act you do with your money. But you can't kill this little boy just because he upset you once.'

'But he's got AIDS. He's dying anyway.' Dominic had decided that exaggeration would help here.

'Oh, the poor little sod. If I got it, I'd kill myself. I've already got the sleeping pills, you know.'

'Yes, I do know. Look, what's the best thing for Guy? Quick and easy now or slow and horrible?'

It was a preposterous argument and Dominic knew it; but he also knew his audience and the sentiments that would weigh heaviest. Dennis had never quite understood how people who were diagnosed antibody positive could bear to remain alive, largely because he had always failed to distinguish between this diagnosis and a diagnosis of AIDS. Dennis's wasn't a view to which Dominic subscribed – besides, he did know the difference – but he was quite happy to use it to get his own way. So he argued, cajoled and used other skills (those which Dennis considered his best), until eventually Dennis wearied of the whole topic and more or less caved in.

'All right. Well, I'll go with you tomorrow night. I'll meet you there. I'm not promising anything. I bet you wouldn't have the fucking guts to do it, you nancy boy. You couldn't kill a fly without fainting.'

'So you'll be by the cloakroom at eleven?'

'I've said I will. If I say I will, I'll be there. You know that.'

And so all the arrangements were made. After Guy and Dominic had their 'accidental' meeting, Guy reminded Dominic that he was due to meet Terry, and Dominic explained that he was meeting Dennis: perhaps they could all go to Clapham? Guy nodded enthusiastically and together he and Dominic made their way towards the cloakroom, Guy prattling maliciously about Michael. When they found Dennis, Guy sneaked Dominic an approving smile. Guy and Dominic had always had quite similar taste. Dominic smiled and made the introductions.

'I thought you'd like to meet Guy,' he said to Dennis, 'because I know how you feel about blonds. Right, shall we go?' Dennis started a pre-arranged complaint that he had only just paid to get in. 'Oh, don't be so crabby. It's dead boring tonight, anyway.' Dominic turned to Guy and handed him a cloakroom ticket. 'Could you get my bag for me while you're getting yours?' he asked. Guy obliged, and Dominic conferred with Dennis. 'OK?'

'I still say you haven't got the guts.'

'Are you prepared to bet on that?'

'Any money you like.'

'Twenty pounds. Right? OK, in my bag are two pairs of kitchen gloves. I'll give you a pair when he isn't looking: put them on outside – then, when I give the word, grab him by the neck.' Dennis laughed. 'I'm serious. Then I'll put everything in the bag again and give it to you. Take it with you and get rid of it as far away from here as possible. And let's make sure no-one realises we're leaving with him. We won't have long, 'cause his cousin's about to turn up. When it's over I'll come back in here and probably try and get picked up.'

'You really are crazy.' But Dennis was completely spellbound. He had let himself leave the realms of reality and enter Dominic's fabulous construct. After all, if the worst came to the worst, it would be funny to see Dominic make a spectacular fool of himself.

Dominic suggested to Guy that he precede them outside, just in case Terry was already waiting; he did so, and when they were out of anyone's sight, Dominic took out the gloves and slipped Dennis his pair. Dennis, giggling, put them on: Dominic frowned at him. They caught Guy up, keeping their hands hidden in the half-light, and walked up the alleyway until they were level with the dustbin and the garbage. Dennis noticed an eerie lull in people and then heard Dominic say, 'OK, Den.'

Dennis really rather fancied Guy: he took hold of the blond boy's shoulders quite gently. Guy looked at him almost with a smile: had Dominic promised him some sexual excitement, Dennis wondered? But Dominic pushed both of them, quite forcefully, into the shadows, looking like Vengeance personified. He produced a vicious knife and, before anyone could react, struck deep into Guy's face. Guy whimpered. Dennis murmured, 'Dominic,' very quietly, but it was too late to back out now . Dominic struck again and again, with surprising speed and fury: Dennis was amazed at Guy's lack of voice. Then he realised that he had instinctively put his hands around Guy's throat and begun to throttle. Very quickly indeed, he had choked the life out of Guy Latimer.

'Out of pity,' he explained as he let Guy slide to the floor. 'Hey,' he said, suddenly struck by something anomalous. 'Feel my cock. It's hard.' He felt Dominic's hand rub him.

'So's mine.' Dominic giggled.

'We're a right couple of psychopaths.' Dennis suddenly panicked. 'Come on, let's get out of here. Give that stuff to me.' But Dominic was doing so with a calm that amazed and frightened him. 'Oh Christ, his rucksack. Shall we leave it here where he dropped it?'

'No. I'll see to that.' Dominic sounded very positive. But for a moment he stood still, staring down. Guy Latimer was dead. Good. The next thing was to get away with it, which meant pinning the blame on someone else. The hard part was just starting.

'Come on, don't just stand there. Look, you've done it now.'

'We've done it.'

'Do you want to come back with me?'

'No. That would be fatal.' Dominic picked up the rucksack. 'He'll be safe there for a while before anyone finds him.'

'People'll think it's just another tramp. God, you've really made a mess of him. He's hardly got a face left.'

'Payment in kind. Look, you go. I'll 'phone you as soon as I can. Don't worry, there's nothing to link you with this.'

'If you bring my name into it, I'll kill you. You know I could.'

'Never mind that. Go.'

He watched Dennis bustle off towards Embankment Station. He stared at the rucksack, and then crossed the alleyway. No, the body wasn't really visible, not unless you were looking for it. Dominic stood amazed. Was that all it took? And his luck had held. No people.

But here were people now. Dominic hid in the shadows as they walked past: they didn't seem to notice Guy or himself or anything much. He watched them go into the club. Then some others came out of a pub further up the passage: they too walked past oblivious and disappeared into the street. He was about to move out and retrace his steps, but froze suddenly.

Coming towards him was the handsome dark-haired boy he'd met with Guy earlier: Michael. He shrank back against the wall: he mustn't be seen by Michael. Of course, ordinarily the handsome yummy Michaels of the world didn't notice him anyway; unfortunately this one already knew him. Dominic's passionate loathing of the very handsome took over and he wondered how it would be possible to throw the blame onto Michael for what he had just done. After all, Michael had been out of the club at the time, hadn't he?

And someone as handsome as that was bound to be noticed, was bound to have used his charm to get out of paying for readmission. Slowly, cautiously, Dominic made his way back into the club, and paid for a second entrance. No-one realised, of course: why should they? He wasn't anything memorable to look at. But at that moment it was better to be an unmemorable Dominic than a beautiful Michael.

Dominic slowly circulated the club, first of all depositing the rucksack in the cloakroom and being careful to pick up the ticket in his handkerchief by feigning a sneezy sniff as he did so. What he intended to do with the ticket was, as yet, hazy, but he was beginning to become fascinated by the idea of 'discovering' the body himself. That would need witnesses, of course, the more the merrier. But if he could do that himself, it would, he felt, remove an element of uncertainty from the business: he'd know what questions he was going to get asked. What he wouldn't have admitted, of course, is that the idea of involvement attracted him like an itch, like a sore he just had to rub.

He looked round, wondering where Michael was; perhaps he would make a convenient witness, if it could be managed. He spotted him chatting to a rather cute-looking number. Dominic took up a position, adopting his best little-boy-lost look. And then came the real stroke of luck. Inexplicably, Marcus Grey took a fancy to him.

From that devolved all that followed: 'discovering' the body (and how easy it proved to plant the ticket in Guy's pocket right under their noses) and everything else. Dominic found himself having the time of his life. An actor manqué, he used a combination of actual fears and inspired performance to appeal to Marcus's better nature – and the Sergeant's too. Dominic loved performing for Marcus: all through the weekend he kept working on, honing and refining his character. It was a pity, really, that he hadn't met Marcus a year or so ago: they might have made a go of it. Marcus's determination to believe in his innocence was a godsend.

But then, like everyone else involved, Marcus had a pet obsession which blinded him to alternative readings of the signs: Marcus persisted in searching for Mr Right and was determined to believe that Dominic was he. The Sergeant was clearly obsessed with not seeming too obvious and not victimising the main candidate. The Inspector had been obsessed with hating Michael: very usefully, as it turned out. Michael's obsession with his own cool and his secret fraudulent deals had been of invaluable assistance too.

Perhaps he shouldn't have enjoyed the sex with Marcus so much (and there had been rather a lot of it) but then, who would tell Dennis about that? It had been rather a bonus of the excellent performance Dominic had given. Thank God Marc's priggishness didn't extend to bed; still, he was a bit of a prig, and not the kind of person Dominic could ever have told too much about the seamier side of his life – of which there had been a fair bit. But anyway, it had taken the murder to bring Dominic and Marcus together – and the point of the murder was to bring Dominic and Dennis together. Of course, he'd now have to bring Den to the point of leaving his wife. That moment would have to be chosen with care. More pressingly, Dominic had to find somewhere else to live: he had qualms about using Marcus any further. He might lie to Marcus about loving him, but he wouldn't use him any more than was strictly necessary.

After all, Dominic did have some principles: in the end he hadn't tried to pin the murder onto Michael, although he had asked Dennis, in the hasty note he'd written warning him of the imminent visit by the Police, to keep that option open. That had been mainly principle: although it had been obvious from the word go that really the strongest case could be made against Terry Difford. However much Michael had to hide, he couldn't be panicked into guilty behaviour, but Terry – well, at the first sign of trouble he had gone overboard. Producing a knife – a knife, for God's sake – in front of the Police – well, that had been suicidal and a gift to Dominic. If Dominic had gone up to Terry and said, 'Excuse me, do you think you could have a go at convincing these nice policemen that you are the murderer', he couldn't have got a more co-operative response.

Anyway, in a way Terry really was Guy's murderer: he'd infected him and set events in motion. Still, that bus had been awfully convenient: if Terry had denied his guilt strenuously for long enough, even those policemen might have begun to start thinking that he might be telling at least a half-truth. In a way, though, Dominic was sorry that he hadn't had the means to build a case against Guy's father – or the appalling Derek. No, Terry had been the best available, looking at it objectively.

Considering all this whilst waiting for Dennis to get changed, Dominic turned his mind to his two most immediate problems: where he was going to live for the time being and how to get rid of Marcus charitably. He was supposed to be meeting him later that evening: Dominic had had half a mind to cut the date, but felt that such a tactless deed might well rebound on him. The simplest thing, he felt sure, was tearful volatility and selfish sprightliness, such as he'd given a dummy run of the previous evening. Old Marc wasn't really the kind to put up with that sort of thing: and once exposed to it, he'd soon agree that they ought to call it a day. A shame, Dominic felt, that he couldn't keep both Marcus and Dennis: but he couldn't. But what a luxury. He chuckled to himself: he was in the position Guy had thought he was in when he died. But Guy was dead and Dominic was alive. Well, thought Dominic, I have my revenge on you, Guy Latimer, and what was yours is now mine.

'Are you ready to go?' Dennis re-entered the room, in green shirt, pale blue cardigan and grey trousers, and light-coloured shoes. 'God, you're looking scruffy. A good job we're not going out to dinner anywhere: I couldn't be seen out with a messy cunt like you. Where is it you're running off to? Is it that Scottish boy? I bet it is.'

'I can't quite abandon him just yet. It would look a bit odd. I'll get him to chuck me, though, that's the kindest thing to do.'

'Very considerate – for a murderer.'

'Actually Dennis, you're the murderer. I'm just the accomplice. You're the danger to society.'

'Crap. Your mind is extraordinary, do you know that? The things that pass for logic up there. Go and clean your teeth, now, boy.'

Dominic went obediently to the bathroom. 'Use the green toothbrush,' Dennis shouted after him. Spitefully, Dominic picked out a red one and used that. He returned to the sitting room. 'You used the green one?' Dominic nodded. 'Good boy.' Dominic debated with himself whether or not he ought to feel guilty, and decided by an overwhelming majority that he shouldn't. 'Right.' Dennis led the way out.

Outside in the street it was perceptibly evening, although still quite early in terms of the hour: it was funny how suddenly towards the latter part of August the end of summer became a fait accompli. They went up to town to a relatively new and stylish bar. For some reason the place – which, to tell the truth, he didn't greatly care for – always reminded Dominic of an ocean liner. This wasn't the impression it was trying to create: its style was more Art Deco Revisited, with tubular steel fittings, odd lightshades, strange-shaped ashtrays, ornaments and vases. The bar staff were young and beautiful and extremely aware of the fact. It was the kind of environment Dominic had always hated visiting on his own, or with Guy: but he hoped that with Dennis it might be tolerable, even enjoyable. Being in public with Dennis – a rare enough event, as yet – gave Dominic a great glow of pride and joy in any case: he couldn't walk along a street or sit on a Tube with him without turning again and again just to look at him. So perhaps being in this ultra-trendy bar with him would give the place a new magic by bestowing on Dominic a new self-confidence. After all, there was a lot to be self-confident about now.

Dennis handed Dominic a pint of lager, sipping carefully from his own. He pointed over to a space in the crowd in a darkish recess. 'We'll go over there,' he said, 'where we can see what's going on.'

He led Dominic through the considerable throng, until they reached their objective. They stood under a curved ledge decorated by some rather wan potted plants which draped and drooped their lower leaves into inaccessible ashtrays. Dominic's head flitted through a perpetual ninety degrees back and forth, staring at Dennis then out into the bar, then back to Dennis again. Dennis was, as ever, wonderful: the clientele, on the other hand, was an oddly mixed bag of City suited types and young trendies – and quite a few older men, who drifted about, if anyone could be said to drift in a crowd like that, staring wistfully at the younger ones. Some were not being entirely unsuccessful. Clearly a lot of people had dropped in after work.

'I sometimes come here from the office,' Dennis said, as if reading Dominic's thoughts. A fair-haired, fresh-faced youth of sturdy build and a curvaceous bottom went by, very close to them. Dennis smiled lasciviously. 'He's nice.'

'Yes, isn't he?' Dominic said, attempting to appear liberal and unpossessive whilst fuming with jealousy.

'You wouldn't know what to do with a bum like that.'

'I have my moments.'

Dennis feigned astonishment. He let slip some obscure north-eastern expression which Dominic didn't quite catch, so, playing it safe, he smiled as if at a witticism. Dennis's gaze went elsewhere: Dominic followed it greedily. It was fixed upon a youngish man (younger than either of them, anyway) of medium height. He had, as far as Dominic could see, a rather bad complexion which would otherwise have been pale: it looked like the ashen dust surface of the moon. His hair was unconvincingly blond: he had allowed it to grow too long, and everywhere roots betrayed the truth, as it spread untidily, untrendily, forwards on top of his head. His was, in Dominic's view, a weak face, despite the sharp nose and long chin. His clothes hung relatively loose on his slight frame. He smiled. Dennis smiled back. 'I've got an admirer,' he said.

'That makes two,' Dominic said. He paused: but he had to ask the question. 'Do you fancy him then?'

'Of course not.'

'He's not very wonderful, is he?' Dominic concurred, relieved. 'Another drink?'

He took Dennis's empty glass and began to fight his way to the bar. Suddenly he felt insecure: perhaps they could go somewhere else. He was desperate for the evening to succeed, desperate for them to celebrate properly. Nervously he pushed himself forward and attempted to attract the attention of a barman; at least two of them were doing absolutely nothing. Eventually one, with a yawn, took his order and pushed a glass under a slow hydraulic trickle of pale brown. Dominic moved back from the bar a little way, so as to have freer access to the change in his pockets. He cast a longing glance in Dennis's direction: to find he had been joined in the alcove by the young man who had been smiling at him. Dennis was obviously enjoying himself, chatting and laughing. Dominic bit his lip. Self-control was the thing: after all, what he and Dennis had done together bound them properly, almost like a marriage.

He paid for the drinks, and began the perilous journey back. A little liquid slopped out of one glass: he kept that for himself and gave the unspoilt pint to Dennis, who nodded a curt thank you. Dominic waited for a word, but none was forthcoming.

'Excuse me,' he said, 'I must go to the loo.'

Dennis pulled a face at the young man. The youth laughed. Dominic put his drink on a ledge and ran off down the stairs leading to the lavatories.

Once in, he spotted an elderly man hanging around rather obviously, and locked himself in the cubicle. Idly he read the graffiti, mainly consisting of messages to the bar staff written by customers eager to advertise their personal details. He couldn't quite make sense of these messages: he couldn't quite concentrate. No, he would not cry. For good measure, he attempted to piss, then, swallowing back the lump in his throat, he walked out again and up the stairs. At the top, back in the bar, his nerve momentarily failed him and he almost fled back down again. Dennis and the youth were still keeping each other company. Dominic pulled himself together, imagined he was Bette Davis and pushed his way through to rejoin the man he loved.

'Hello,' Dennis said, 'this is Geoff.'

'Jan,' the boy said in an indistinguishable accent.

'Very nice to meet you. Enjoying yourself?'

'Yes thank you.' Dennis raised his eyebrows in mockery. 'What about you? He's nice, isn't he?'

'Are you nice?' Dominic asked the youth. He smiled awkwardly. 'What have you two lovers been doing today?'

'Oh, hasn't Dennis told you? We've come into some money, so we've been celebrating, you see.'

'That's very nice for you.'

'Isn't it just?' Dominic turned and smiled wanly at Dennis. 'Shall I go?'

'Not unless you want to.'

'Do you want me to?'

'No. Of course not.'

'Looks like it. What would you do if I did this to you?'

'Walk out. But you couldn't. Stop being such a rude cunt. How do you think he feels?'

'How do you think I feel?'

'Typical of you, always thinking of yourself.'

'Er – ' the boy intervened ' – I think maybe I'd better go now. I think I see someone I know.' He edged uncertainly away, still smiling at Dennis. Dennis waved back at him. Then he turned on Dominic.

'God, that was pathetic. Who do you think you are, trying to stop me enjoying myself? We were only talking, you know. Do you really think you're going to stop me fancying blond boys? Do you think you're going to stop them fancying me? I'm a good-looking bloke, you know. You don't own me. We're not an affair. If you've told anyone we're an affair – '

Dominic tried to interrupt. He could feel the tears starting to roll now. 'But I thought that once we had the money, we could – '

'God, what makes you think I want to give up my nice home and live with you in some squalid little pit? Do you really think I've gone mad or something? I know you're crazy and sick, but I'm not.'

'I see,' Dominic sobbed quietly. 'So after everything I've wanted and tried to do for us both, you humiliate me like this. After everything we've done together – '

'We aren't an affair and I've never said we were. I am married, after all, and I love my wife and daughter.'

'Yes. And your wife's money. I suppose twenty thousand isn't enough, is it, on reflection? Not for long. You're used to living off much more than that.'

Dennis's face became a frozen embodiment of rage. Dominic clapped his hand over his mouth, but far too late. Dennis glared at him. 'I could hit you. I can't believe you really said what you just said.'

'I didn't mean it, really, I didn't mean it.'

'I'm very tempted to go and get that boy back. I could, you know. Anyway, I want you to go, please.' Dominic stood still, too scared to move. 'Now!' Dennis thundered. People stared at them. Dominic leapt back in fright. 'Look,' Dennis said, quiet again, 'go before I hit you. Don't try saying anything. I'll call you. Probably. But just go.'

Dominic drained his glass. A strange instinct took hold: he turned tail and ran.

Outside, in the dark narrow street which ran parallel with a main West End thoroughfare, a sudden August rain was falling. Dominic stood for a while under the awning outside the bar, watching the lights reflected in the puddles. He wasn't quite sure whether to be relieved or annoyed at this excuse for having a wet face: after all, there is something to be said for attracting attention to one's grief. He moved forward into the rain and was almost instantaneously drenched; his bright sweater, worn specially for this celebration, was sodden and dripping long beads of rain, his hair flattened against his head. He could hear a loud howling noise and he realised suddenly that he was making it himself. Passers-by weren't stopping to stare, it was far too wet for that. He walked along slowly, screaming: then, with supreme effort, he managed to reduce himself to something like silence.

Looking to his right, he could just see a corner of Charing Cross sticking out, way across the road from the end of a paved street sloping down towards the Embankment. The pale brown paving stones glistened as they were pummelled by the heavy downpour. It was raining even faster now. Dominic let out another wail. Well, there was a lot to cry about. What had he done? Whatever it was, that bizarre, horrible act, he'd done it above all for Dennis. And what use was that? The humiliation he had just endured – well, even Guy wouldn't have done that. Oh, what had he done? The fact that he'd got away with it, the fact that he'd made himself richer by it – well, what did that matter now? Revenge and love – his prime motivations, and in the end he hadn't achieved either.

Suddenly every fair-haired man he passed was Guy, every dark-haired man Dennis. He wandered along the pedestrian street. Suddenly he decided to run. Maybe if he ran he'd hold himself together. Maybe. But it didn't seem to work. He was running fast and furious, faster than he normally could, his breathing operating of its own accord, not impinging on him, not running out inconsiderately. He arrived at the road – he couldn't stop now, could he? He ran out – perhaps that would solve everything. But, typically, the lights changed as he jumped off the pavement: and a little green figure with open legs mocked his feeble attempt at suicide. Running between the taxis, he sprinted into Charing Cross Station. What now? He wanted to cry out loud again. What could he do?

Well, there was one possibility. He could 'phone Marcus. Trapped between madness, misery and anger, Dominic realised a need to talk – but why? If he told Marcus one true thing, then he'd end up telling him a few more true things into the bargain. Or he could offer a bizarre silence instead. Either way, it was all beyond logic now. Dominic picked up a 'phone. '999 CALLS ONLY' it flashed at him. There wasn't another vacant.

Another impulse seized him and he ran into the Tube station, down the stairs and through the barrier. This attracted a yell from ticket collector: Dominic stopped dead and waved his travelcard. Then he was running again, down an empty escalator. Which line? Any. A fluke led him onto the Northern Line. Standing at the edge of the Southbound platform, Dominic began to cry loudly again. Two women standing nearby stared at him oddly and he wondered why. He looked down at the tracks to avoid their eyes.

'Excuse me, are you all right?' a voice at his elbow asked. He looked round and saw one of the women right next to him. For a moment he was almost touched by the concern, but then he examined her properly: pink plastic briefcase, yuppy clothes, probably on her way back to Clapham South after working late. She wasn't worried about him as a person: she just didn't want anything holding up her journey, like someone throwing himself under her train. Dominic gave her as good an attempt at a cynical glare as he could manage in the circumstances and said, 'Oh yes, I'm terrific, thanks a lot.' And then fortunately a train came. He didn't throw himself under it, so the woman went back to her friend and they all got on board.

At Kennington, he hurled himself onto another train, which, miraculously, left almost immediately. But after the train had stopped once, Dominic couldn't bear it any more: he felt as though he were trapped in a silver coffin. He got out and was running again, up and up until he hit the barrier. Taking stock of where he was, it occurred to him that there was a quite notorious cottage just outside: perhaps he should go there and lose himself in some anonymous, childish sex which wouldn't involve anything more than cocks, hands, maybe mouths, possibly even bums – but nothing dangerous like names or love or real emotions.

But once through the barrier, his nerve failed him and he threw himself at the telephones, shoved in some money and pressed some numbers. After a few rings he heard the reassuring Scots voice, the voice of the boy he had been so brilliantly fooling all weekend. Hearing the voice, he gulped and snivelled.

'Dominic, is that you? Dom, are you OK?'

'Marcus,' he said with another sniff and a gulp. For days he had been acting various emotions, at best exaggerating: now for the first time Marcus was getting the benefit of the full force of Dominic's real feelings.

'Look, where are you?' Dominic gulped a reply. 'OK, stay there and I'll be with you in five minutes.'

Dominic gulped again and stared at the receiver as it started whirring at him. He replaced it and wandered around the station forecourt, avoiding the eyes of the people standing there. He blinked and cried a bit; then he set his stare at a pillar, large, thick and affording good protection, for what seemed like an eternity. He felt a hand on his shoulder and he jumped: and turned round to see Marcus.

Marcus reached out and grasped his arm: Dominic shuddered, not because he didn't like Marcus's touch, but because he knew how incredibly little he deserved it. Marcus looked shocked – yet how Dominic could shock him if he really wanted to. Dominic stared back, almost returning the pity evident in those clear grey eyes, as he done so often over the past few days. But now Dominic's pity was mixed with the full horror of what his achievement had been: the horrific way he'd done the horrific deed; the horrifically low valuation he'd placed on this amazing man standing in front of him now; and the horrifically high price he'd set on Dennis.

Marcus squeezed his arm. 'Dominic,' he said, 'what's happened? Was it your landlord?'

And immediately Dominic was offered a lie. Another lie. At that moment it seemed to Dominic that his entire fate hinged on whether or not he accepted this offer. Take it and he could bluff through, safe and sound, move in with Marcus and live happily ever after on Guy's money. Refuse it and – well, where the hell would that lead?

Dominic blinked, sniffed, looked up at Marcus and nodded. Marcus, uncaring of public opinion, took Dominic in his arms.

'Come back with me,' he said.

Dominic nodded tearfully, appalled at his terrible duplicity, but full of admiration for his talent as an actor.

## Also by Jeremy Beadle
## DOING BUSINESS

No one seems to believe Gordon's claim to have witnessed a murder in a seedy Soho pub. After all, he's been through a lot of strain lately and the mind can play strange tricks. He's nearly persuaded to forget it ever happened — until an attempt is made on his own life and there's a second killing. Soon it becomes obvious that the person behind the murders is one of Gordon's own group of friends and out to silence him.

Set among the dangerous world of West End rent boys and City sharks, *Doing Business* is not only an absorbing mystery thriller but also a provocative comment on the values of Britain today.

"Beadle has a lightness of touch and marries it to acute observation to produce a thriller that is never less than grippingly entertaining"
— *Gay Times*

ISBN 0 85449 110 4 (pbk)     160 pages
UK £5.95 / US $10.95 / AUS $14.95 / DM 22.00

GMP books can be ordered from any bookshop in the UK, and from specialised bookshops overseas. If you prefer to order by mail, please send full retail price plus £1.50 for postage and packing to:
GMP Publishers Ltd (GB),
P O Box 247, London N17 9QR.

*For payment by Access/Eurocard/Mastercard/American Express/Visa, please give number and signature.*
A comprehensive mail-order catalogue is also available.

In North America order from Alyson Publications Inc.,
40 Plympton St, Boston, MA 02118, USA.
In Australia order from Bulldog Books,
P O Box 155, Broadway, NSW 2007, Australia.

Name and Address in block letters please:

Name _____

Address _____

_____

_____